HONOUR
&
HERESY

HONOUR & HERESY

MAX FRANCIS

HARPER
Voyager

Harper*Voyager*
An imprint of HarperCollins*Publishers* Ltd
1 London Bridge Street
London SE1 9GF

www.harpercollins.co.uk

HarperCollins*Publishers*
Macken House,
39/40 Mayor Street Upper,
Dublin 1, D01 C9W8
Ireland

First published by HarperCollins*Publishers* Ltd 2026

1

Copyright © Max Francis 2026

Designed by Alison Bloomer
Book and ink illustration: Shutterstock.com
Background illustration © Jorge Jacinto
Orphic Basilica illustration by Virginia Allyn

Max Francis asserts the moral right to
be identified as the author of this work.

A catalogue record for this book is available from the British Library.

ISBN: 978-0-00-881027-6 (HB)
ISBN: 978-0-00-881028-3 (TPB)

This novel is entirely a work of fiction.
The names, characters and incidents portrayed in it are
the work of the author's imagination. Any resemblance to
actual persons, living or dead, events or localities is
entirely coincidental.

Printed and bound in the UK using 100% Renewable Electricity
by CPI Group (UK) Ltd

All rights reserved. No part of this publication may be
reproduced, stored in a retrieval system, or transmitted,
in any form or by any means, electronic, mechanical,
photocopying, recording or otherwise, without the prior
written permission of the publishers.

Without limiting the exclusive rights of any author, contributor or the publisher
of this publication, any unauthorized use of this publication to train generative artificial
intelligence (AI) technologies is expressly prohibited. HarperCollins also exercise their
rights under Article 4(3) of the Digital Single Market Directive 2019/790 and expressly
reserve this publication from the text and data mining exception.

For Chloe, who's been by my side since the start

CONTENT WARNINGS

This book explores some dark and potentially triggering topics. A list of content warnings can be found pinned on the author's Instagram (@maxfrancisauthor).

Tenants of Dawnseve Manor,

I regret to inform you that your brother and son, Gabriel Dawnseve of the 27th Platoon, has been reported absent from his post. As such, we are obligated to presume his death.

I understand that this will prove to be a difficult and emotionally taxing time, and I am amenable to any suggested adjustments that may alleviate your situation, but immediate preparations must also be made for the following heir of the family. My colleagues and I have reviewed the matter at hand and, after much deliberation, have decided upon a solution that will both adhere to our laws of primogeniture and clear the confusion brought on by recent developments—namely Roy Dawnseve's fondness for old-world literature.

While I am loath to admit this, I will no longer stir rumors of false hope: Northgard is on the precipice of defeat. We have held our own for three years, thrust into battle against an unassailable enemy, but to no avail. We must thwart the Old Ones' advance—and now. In all fairness, we are in a state of relative safety, protected by our Radiant Droves and their batons and muskets. But once, if ever, this storm dies down, there will be nothing to impede these soldiers from instigating full-scale invasion and subsequent annihilation. Northgard will be laid bare by winter's end and laid to waste by spring.

Despite our labor, particularly the hundreds of aborted military campaigns launched to rout the Old Ones, there has been close to no word on their identity, their reason of attack, nor their objective. Evidently, the details my informants have procured, scarce as they may be, have done little to dispel the pall of fear cast over Northgard. Even the Edict of Containment, once believed to be a surefire method of limiting contact with neighboring islands, has been rendered futile by the Old Ones.

Usually, I am not one to resort to desperate measures, especially those in which old-world literature are concerned, but as you can see, I am at a loss. I write to you, Dawnseves, not only as the leader of this society but as a man bedeviled by his plight. I entreat you to consider the following proposition.

I am offering Roy an opportunity to resume his studies, but rather than for his own gain, he would be working personally for me, investigating the Old Ones. If you approve my proposal, he will promptly be sent to the Orphic Basilica to conduct research over the course of six months. Supplies—food, beverages, notebooks, and any other necessities—will be provided upon arrival, then every month thereafter. Alternatively, if you decide that my proposition does not bode well for you, Roy will follow in the footsteps of his brother and be sent to the barracks at the Iron Citadel, where he will be inducted into the Radiant Droves.

This is not a matter of business I take lightly. This mission is of utmost importance. If any individual whose involvement I have not sanctioned were to become aware of this assignment—including the maids and butlers in your employ, who are not to spread word of Roy's task—or interfere with it, it would be considered a breach of the Law of Intervention. At that point I would have no choice but to ascribe an appropriate punishment to their, and thus Roy's, crime.

Again, I implore you to take this proposition into consideration, and I expect a response within the following week. The fate of our city depends upon it.

Signed,
The Governor

THE ORPHIC BASILICA

Part One

1

ROY DAWNSEVE COULDN'T REMEMBER HOW MANY times he'd read the Governor's letter, but when the horse-drawn sled came to escort him to the Orphic Basilica, the paper was covered with thumbprints, coffee stain rings, and tears.

He was in the sitting room, stoking the coals in the fireplace with an iron poker, when he made out the clopping of horseshoes approaching from outside: soft, rhythmic, and subdued by snow. Dread clamped down on his heart, then passed in nauseating waves over his body. His hands trembled, his knees buckled, and his black-silver curls were plastered with sweat to the nape of his neck.

I never sent a reply; I never said a damn word, he thought. Three days had gone by since the letter had been delivered, and while he'd felt stuck in a fever dream during them all, now cold clarity washed over him—along with an unsettling epiphany. *It was Mother.* She *must have answered.* She *must have approved the proposition without bothering to ask me.*

But as Roy slid the poker back into its holder, the screech of metal grating against metal dampened by the pounding in his head, hope flickered in him. He wondered how likely it might be that he could stay here, safe and sound in the same space as his sister, how logical it might be to isolate himself from the war by simply ignoring its existence and maintaining his peace. He stared into the flames and saw himself, in the dancing shadows, poring over outlawed books of philosophy and history by candlelight—naive, ignorant, and aware of the screams ripping through the city streets... but too scared to do anything about them.

Roy shook his head at this impossible prospect, swallowing the bile that had risen to the back of his throat. There was nothing that could be done or reversed; he couldn't stay cooped up in his room forever. The decision had already been made for him.

On the heels of this thought came another, far more daunting in its implications. *I've been exposed... but by whom?* For years he had been startled awake by the same nightmare: one of the Governor's agents, someone Roy had once believed to be a fellow scholar in hiding—a *friend*—was turning him in, dragging him in shackles to the Governor's manor to be flogged, beaten, and burnt at the stake.

Roy's fears weren't unfounded. He had heard on the grapevine that fifteen scholars had once held a theoretical discussion regarding the works of Edelrin, an old-world historian, in the charred basement of a demolished bookshop. They'd all been executed promptly upon discovery.

These weren't the only stories he'd heard of modern scholars throughout his twenty-five years, though, and he supposed that comforted him to some degree—that despite the flame of wisdom and learning having mostly been extinguished, an underground network of academics was still determined to keep alive the knowledge of the old world. There were even intimations of a scholar-led revolution, but none of the rebels reportedly participating in the uprising had ever gotten past the planning stage of a riot before they were discovered and then executed for the Governor's sick satisfaction.

But, as the Governor had explicitly spelled out in his letter, Roy *wasn't* to be executed. He'd been given an opportunity. It did not escape him, however, that if he failed, he would be blamed for the fallout.

Panicked, he drew away from the fireplace, crossed the sitting room to its entrance, and then rested his hand on the doorframe. Thoughts streaked down his mind like raindrops down a windowpane.

For the three years since the Iron Citadel had sounded its battle cry against the Old Ones, Roy had been thankful for, even dependent upon, the privileges that his aristocratic title—the second heir of Dawnseve Manor—bestowed upon him. He had a family. He had a home. He had stability, for the most part, and though he had always known that these precious luxuries would have to be taken from him eventually, Roy had allowed himself to indulge in the writings of old-world academics, to study the fields of research of which Northgard had been deprived. He had never considered that his studies could amount to something of value, and he supposed he could hold his brother accountable for that feeling of worthlessness.

Roy shook his head, ridding himself of his darkening thoughts. He strode out of the sitting room, the insoles of his slippers stuck to his feet with sweat, and made his way across the hallway beyond, which would lead him directly out to the forked staircase at the back of the foyer. Uncertain what to do with his hands, he unclasped the pins from his hair, and his curls tumbled down to just above his shoulders, brushing the back of his nightgown.

Desperate to ground himself, Roy tucked the hairpins just above his ear, nearly drawing blood as he did so, then looked out through the frosted window spanning the left wall. He immediately wished he hadn't. While blanketed in a fresh layer of snow, the city of Northgard—the greatest and last-standing city on the continent—could not conceal its misery. A gale blew through the streets, rattling the spears of ice dangling from the chimneys of white-stoned commune shelters and manors. Another gust came roaring past the throng of citizens clustered along the thoroughfare, and they screamed in earnest, frantically looking up and down as though uncertain to whom they should pray. Even from afar, it sounded like the residents of Hell pleading for redemption.

But there was no redemption, not that Roy could see. Winter had fallen hard upon Northgard three years ago and had shown no signs of easing up since. If anything, the snowstorm had intensified during the war, stirring up rumors regarding its implications. Some believed it might deter the Old Ones, or at least stall them; the Governor had even drawn especial attention to this in his missive, along with the Edict of Containment—the iron-constructed wall he'd ordered after rumblings of a black-armored army had spread across the city—which sealed Northgard's coastlines from neighboring islands. Others assumed that the seemingly perpetual winter was an ill omen, a premonition of calamity. Considering the way his day was unfolding, Roy wondered whether these superstitious allegations might not be correct, for he could not fathom what scientific phenomenon might explain the weather.

Roy pressed his hand against the windowpane. The chill seeped through the glass and spread across his palm. A stuttering exhale escaped his lips, blooming out before him in frosty white clouds. Through the fog he saw, faintly, the slope of the hill upon which his family estate sat, shrouded in acres of thick snow. Leading down to the city's first square of buildings was a narrow pathway furrowed by a winding trail of sled tracks.

He braced himself, then started at the creak of an opening door.

Briar stood at the threshold to her chambers, staring at him, a look of stupefied denial in her wide brown eyes. A crimson-and-gold woolen nightgown was draped about her shoulders, which were slumped with either defeat or resignation. By the desolation on her angular face and the disarrayed condition of her black ringlets, Roy thought it was probably the former. In her hands was a wooden carving of a two-faced woman, the left half of the figurine in golden battle armor, her mouth contorted into a sneer, the right garbed in a scarlet dress and wearing a serene smile.

It occurred to Roy that Briar might never have connected the carving's appearance to its symbolism. Their mother had once whispered to him, moments after she had given birth to Briar, the aphorism associated with the carving:

What was once war may bring peace. Or war again.

Had their mother not shared this with Briar? Roy supposed not. Years ago, if the Reaper had ever come knocking on Dawnseve Manor's doors, she might have been the first to answer, defending her young, but Roy couldn't now align the woman she'd once been, a doting if somewhat pedantic mother, with the hard-faced demoness known to most—even her children, the majority of the time—as Matron Dimestra, who now ruled in her stead. Once those locks had clicked into place, Roy had almost forgotten he had a mother at all.

"You heard it, too," Roy muttered, returning Briar's stare. "The sled."

Briar gulped, her hands tightening around the carving. "I couldn't dare to sleep, Roy, not when I haven't had the chance to see you go, to . . . to say . . ." She closed her eyes, took a deep, uneven breath, then burst into tears, which slithered in glimmering tracks down the sneering half of the carving. She rushed over to Roy and threw her arms around his waist.

Roy stiffened at the contact at first, then gradually rested his chin upon her head, the two-faced figurine—still clenched in Briar's grasp—jutting into his ribs. "What was once war may bring peace," he murmured.

Briar withdrew from Roy's embrace and looked up at him, her cheeks wet with tears. "Or war again." *So Dimestra did tell her,* he thought.

Agony cut through Roy, cold and sharp as frozen glass. He regarded his sister, waiting for her to confess and let free every fear, every worry, every horror trapped behind her tear-laced eyes. But she said nothing. Roy was hardly surprised; they had performed this tragic spectacle too many times to count. He tried to recall the exact moments when their open lines of communication had receded to tacit discomfort, but he could only think of their sideways glances, of shattered glass, of their brother Gabriel's white-knuckled fists, scarred, calloused, and red with Roy's blood.

This is what you're leaving her with, Roy scolded himself. *These memories of pain and hate. This is all she will ever know.*

He had never outright discussed the matter with Briar, mainly to preserve what they had left of their bond. Still, she would ask him, after returning from her classes at Rasileus Academy, why there were broken plates and blood on the floor or, after staggering into the kitchens in the middle of the night for a glass of warm milk, why there were bruises on Roy's face. But despite her attempts to broach the subject, he had kept his silence. It was better this way, cleaner, than disclosing that Gabriel had been the cause of this abuse, even if she had known all along. Not to mention that if he admitted to Briar the scars Gabriel had inflicted on him, it was inevitable that an interrogation with Dimestra, who was also oblivious to Gabriel's torment, would be in order.

By the Scribes, he couldn't bear the thought of facing the Matron after this, nor could he envision her reaction if or when she stumbled upon the truth. Roy could hardly process that it had happened to him, and yet the memory of that night four years ago rushed back to him with undeniable, perfect lucidity. Gabriel had straddled him, a knife gripped in his fist, his lips stretched wide into a maniacal smile. Time had congealed, and then frozen, suspending the two of them in a bright shaft of silver moonlight. Roy had been too numb to move, to shift his muscles and retaliate.

He always had been.

Gabriel, he'd pleaded. *I've never judged you for what you do, for who you are.* The knife came closer. *Why can't you accept that this world needs scholars like me? Why can't you accept that I must rewrite history?*

A look of morbid curiosity overtook Gabriel's features. *You'll be history, little brother. And everyone will forget the weak, weeping pig you are. When you're lying cold and alone on the battlefield, you will forget who you truly are. Besides, it's better, and more satisfying, to beat sense into you than see you burn.* His grin widened. *So let me remind you. Let this be the one word you can run back to.*

Then the knife descended, and Gabriel scrawled the word into Roy's chest—H-I-S-T-O-R-Y. Blood poured down his chest. Black stars flickered across his vision. Gabriel had pressed his hand over Roy's mouth—

Pulling himself out of the memory, Roy studied Briar, but he couldn't parse the thoughts no doubt cycling through her head. *What do you know?* Roy wanted desperately to ask her, but there was no use, nor time. Instead, he placed a hand on Briar's back and guided her along the hallway.

As if sensing his proximity, a rapid succession of three booming knocks sounded from the front door, briefly drowning out the wailing of storm winds. A heavy silence descended, and as it settled, Roy and Briar halted at the top of the forked staircase. She let go of her carving with one hand and gripped his forearm with the other. Then they went down, silent, together.

The foyer was a small room, the smallest of Dawnseve Manor. Gilt-framed portraits of the Matron's predecessors, her long-departed husband—and Roy's father, whom neither Roy nor his siblings could recall meeting—among them, were hung from the walls on either side at the foot of the staircase. A chandelier was suspended from the domed ceiling, casting a dim golden glow upon the plush crimson carpet and the entryway towering before Roy now. The iron-studded rosewood door was engraved with the centuries-old emblem of the Dawnseves: a bloodshot eye, glaring with scathing accusation, set inside a rising sun.

There was also, haphazardly stacked beside the door, a pile of bookbags and satchels. One of the butlers, an overweight, doughy-faced man whose name eluded Roy's memory, added one last satchel and then stood aside, his hands clasped behind his back.

Unease coiled around Roy's gut, tightening with every breath he took.

Perhaps it was the sight of the bags, which he presumed contained his clothes and other necessities, but suddenly his circumstances became all too real. He knew that he had little to provide to Northgard's warmongering population beyond half-hearted prayers; this emblem, with its evocation of austerity, condemnation, and vigilance, was a testament to that. He couldn't conceivably fool himself into thinking otherwise. The intellectual contributions of a scholar meant nothing in a city engineered by military power.

Meanwhile, Gabriel had brought *worth* to the city. After

being recruited into the Radiant Droves—the soldiers sworn to protect Northgard—three years ago, his interest in battlecraft and guerrilla warfare no doubt bolstered the city's reputation. He'd ranked far beyond the standards the Droves demanded of its soldiers; his mind had been a powerhouse attuned to, and filled with, the principles of historic generals and commanders; and his passion for denouncing and punishing old-world enthusiasts had been equal to that of the Governor. He'd been perfect, exemplary.

Now he was gone. And while the letter had noted Gabriel's disappearance, Roy couldn't fathom his brother running away from the battlefront, so he was most likely dead.

Roy wasn't as comforted by this as he imagined he ought to be. After all, if Gabriel hadn't been enough to ward off the Old Ones, how was Roy, a measly scholar, supposed to uphold the Governor's expectations?

Briar sniffled, swiped the heel of her palm across the tear-wetted bags under her eyes, then wrapped her arms around Roy again. She squeezed tight. "Goodbye, Roy," she said. He almost went into hysterics at the hitch in her voice, the trembling of her chin. How could he just *leave* her like this, lost and wandering through this big, old, rambling house, with nothing but shadows and memories—and no one but the occasionally present maid or butler—to keep her company? He was worse than Dimestra and no better than Gabriel.

They had a choice, though, Roy rationalized.

It was enough, at least, for him to lean down and kiss her forehead without being plagued with guilt.

"I'll miss you," Briar whispered.

"And I you, Briar." He brushed back a stray strand of her hair, his fingers quivering across her face. "You . . ." He winced, then tried again. "You mustn't let her get to you. Don't allow it, Briar. Not for one second. Once she has you, there is little you can do to get yourself out."

A shadow crossed Briar's face. "I won't."

Roy shook his head, his eyes on hers as he grasped her shoulders. "Promise me, Briar. *Please.* Swear to me you won't bend to her will. I don't know what's going to happen in these coming days, but with Gabriel . . ." He sighed, lowered his voice. "With Gabriel missing, and me gone, I need to know you won't—"

"I won't," Briar said, straightening her posture. He marveled at the swiftness with which she gathered her composure. "I won't give in. Besides, Mother spends most of her days at the Citadel. I'm on my own here."

These words did little to assure him.

Seeming to sense this, Briar squeezed him for what Roy knew would be the last time in a long while, then pulled away.

Roy inhaled deeply, turned toward the large brass knob affixed to the door, and tugged it open.

On the left, directly in front of him, stood a tall, burly man, his upper lip obscured by a thick gray moustache and his hair covered by a slanted green felt cap. He was dressed in a neat, stark white military-style coat, his eyes a startlingly deep shade of blue. The lapels of his coat were decorated with an impressive, if inordinate, number of silver and gold badges.

But it was clearly the woman on the right, standing rigidly in front of Briar, who wielded the upper hand here. She wore a pair of black gloves and had pulled back her raven-black hair into a tight chignon. Her gunmetal-gray eyes were cold and unfeeling. Her hands were clasped at her waist. Time had dug deep grooves into her skin, though she wore them, and her white coat, with pride.

"Mother," Briar whispered.

Dimestra ignored her daughter. Hard-faced, she pinned Roy with a sharp, disapproving glare, then thrust the spare coat and pair of boots she was carrying, identical to her own, into his arms. "Put these on."

Roy glanced down at the stark white clothes he was holding, grimacing, then pushed them back at Dimestra. "I would much rather wear my own."

Sneering, Dimestra shoved the coat and boots against his chest. "Put them on."

Roy set his jaw but gave in, begrudgingly accepting the clothing. He took a few steps back into the manor to avoid the snow blowing in through the open door. He donned the coat, on top of his nightgown, then shucked off his slippers and put on the boots. As he laced them up, he had the sudden and inexplicable impulse to bite back at Matron Dimestra with some retort or accusation. *Why let this happen?* he would say. *Why let the Governor take me away, Matron? Why the change of heart? Why stop at risking the life of one son on the battlefield when you can dispense of them both? After all, what use am I to you?* But as much as he tried, he could not find it in himself to summon the words.

"Are you ready?" Dimestra asked.

"Yes," Roy said, his voice shaking, once he finished buttoning up his coat. He strode toward the door. The wind whipped around him, dragging the hem of his coat out into the snow, and it was then that Roy knew it was time to go. He'd delayed the inevitable long enough. "I'm ready."

Behind Dimestra and her companion—a Citadel emissary, if Roy had to guess—was the horse-drawn sled Roy had spotted earlier. The driver, a sour-faced man swaddled in a scarf, heaved Roy's bags onto the rack in the rear of the sled and then secured the cargo with a long length of rope. The horses shook their heads and nickered impatiently, bristling in the cold. Roy hung his head, bracing himself against the chill, and then stepped up into the sled, accepting the driver's proffered hand.

Scowling, Dimestra sat down in the seat opposite Roy, next to the emissary. She leaned over and rapped on the door of the sled with her knuckles. "Let's be quick about it, shall we?" She looked at Roy. "It's best we don't keep the Governor waiting."

Roy looked away, licking his cold, chapped lips, and aggressively scratched his wrist until he felt satisfied and grounded. He attempted to sneak a glimpse of his sister and her small carving, but it was too late. Dawnseve Manor had already faded far behind them, and Briar with it.

His sister was lost in the snow.

2

IN FAIRER CLIMES, THE RIDE TO THE ORPHIC BASILICA—which rested in an isolated clearing far beyond the northwestern outskirts of Rasileus, the largest town in Northgard—would've taken no longer than twenty minutes. However, the road was layered thick with snow, and even in a sled, it forced the driver to stop every so often and shovel it out of the way. This happened a few times, eliciting grumbles of disapproving impatience from the Matron, but it allowed Roy a closer look of the vista he'd seen from Dawnseve Manor. A breeze lashed across his cheek, sweeping toward him from the right, and it was there that he looked.

In the distance, through the building haze of the snow, he saw the bulky outline of a commune shelter, made of cobblestone and weather-worn pieces of wood, all covered with a sheet of brown canvas that served as the walls and ceiling. Around the structure were snaking lines of citizens, as Roy had seen before. He was close enough now to make out a group of people clustered together. A family, perhaps? A Drove was trudging toward them with seeming purpose, all her features obscured by a strip of woolen cloth but for her downcast eyes, which Roy could just barely see.

The sled driver, who'd cleared the majority of the snow blocking the road, hopped up onto the sled. It gave a sudden jolt, and the Drove whom Roy had been observing looked up, her gaze snapping to his with frightening alertness. Her eyes looked foggy, though that was probably an effect of the snow, and vividly bloodshot.

Then she turned back to her business, disregarding Roy and his companions as though she'd never noticed them. She raised a black baton, which Roy hadn't seen before. The family shrank back, their mouths drawn into horrified grimaces, though the Drove continued her advance. One member of the family—a young boy—tried to run, but the baton whipped down in a blur and cracked open his skull. The boy was dead before he, and a pink splatter of his brains, hit the snowy ground.

As the sled glided onward, Roy, terrified, said to the Matron out of the corner of his mouth, "Did you see that?"

"See what?" she said, then looked where he was pointing. "Oh—yes."

"You stand for this?" Roy asked. "This is part of the alliance you've forged with the Governor?"

"I do," the Matron said, her gaze set forward. "It is. He was in dire need of some additional soldiers, so I contributed, and I . . ." She shook her head.

"What? What could you *possibly* be getting out of this?"

The Matron sniffed contemptuously, as though she'd smelt something foul. "Well, the aristocracy deserve *some* sort of safety for all their—*our*—labor."

Roy went rigid with sheer disbelief. "You're preserving the lives of the entire aristocracy at the expense of one aristocrat?" *At the expense of your own son?*

She did not reply.

A little while after, they passed around two dozen scholars skewered on the finials of a gate to an abandoned manor, like a row of scarecrows. A book covered each of their faces, some at angles that concealed their features and others positioned so that their grim rictuses or dim, glazed eyes were visible. Driven into the spines of these books were massive iron nails, each one encircled by a pool of frozen blood.

They've been bookmarked, Roy thought. He'd heard of the penalty and its apt, cruel name before but had never seen it with his own eyes. The macabre sight calcified his distanced dread into irrepressible horror.

As the sled moved on, Roy inspected the impaled corpses, searching for a familiar face among those whose features were partially revealed, but immediately realized there was no point. He hadn't met another scholar before, so none of these corpses stood out to him. He still watched them, though, until they gained the ethereal aspect of phantoms and then disappeared entirely.

A shiver had coursed through Roy during the entire journey and now made his muscles tremble and lock together. He huddled deeper into his coat, his teeth chattering, his hands wedged into his armpits. He didn't particularly mind the cold; this was his ideal element for a late-night bout of reading, a warm glass of cider in his hands, his feet propped up on a stool before the fireplace.

As soon as the thought formed, though, a seed of guilt sprouted in his stomach. Had he taken these forbidden literary pleasures for granted? Or was it because these pleasures were forbidden that he hadn't deserved them in the first place?

"You ought to be more grateful for his assistance," Dimestra said to Roy, breaking the silence. "He's given you garments, he's giving you food—"

Roy gave up fussing with his coat and pressed his hands into his lap. "I'd argue it's my assistance that takes precedence here. Aren't I the one helping him?"

Distaste passed over Dimestra's features. "I understand that there has been little reason for you to visit the city, so I'll forgive your confusion, although I will not forgive your complacency. You should consider yourself lucky you weren't spirited off to the Iron Citadel, Roy. At least now, you're getting what you wanted."

That was the problem, though. Roy wasn't sure this *was* what he wanted. He had been satisfied, maybe even content, learning the lost and fragmented history of the old world—the Age of Scribes—from the works of the authors, poets, and playwrights who had come from that time . . . but exploiting these invaluable resources for a man who would gladly exile or kill Roy's fellow academics felt like betrayal. He didn't know if it was worth it. Even if this *did* win Northgard the war, he recoiled at the prospect of living with the shame of divorcing himself from his peers, for he had no doubt that his place as a scholar would be finished no matter the results he produced.

Roy narrowed his eyes at Dimestra. "I'm a member of the aristocracy, a son of the matriarch of a noble house. I should be carrying on your legacy, not doing housework for your superior." He was contradicting himself, he knew—desperate to uphold Dimestra's values, to belong somewhere, *anywhere*, despite his antipathy toward what she stood for. Maybe once, before he had discovered the strength of the written word, Roy had been as much a part of Dawnseve Manor as its other tenants, but those days were long behind him. Now he had no clue what he wanted, nor how he might go about obtaining something of value for *himself*. He was adrift, untethered.

"You're indifferent," Dimestra snapped, a trace of anger cracking through her glacial expression. "*That* is your true weakness, Roy. You want to live in a cocoon, safe and protected by those who provide that safety. And now that you're being given the chance to prove your worth, there stands yet another issue: I don't believe you *have* any."

"You don't understand."

"Nor do I care to," Dimestra retorted. "You read the letter. You know the facts. And since that doesn't seem to be enough to enlighten you, let me do the honors: Our soldiers are dying by the dozens, and in some quadrants of the city, the *hundreds*. The Edict of Containment was our sole source of hope, and the Old Ones shattered part of that iron wall like it was paper. Five units of their soldiers, hammering through Northgard from the southern coast. All of this, and yet somehow you *refuse* to put down those damn books." She sneered, her cheeks reddening. For a second, just a fleeting moment, Roy was convinced she would strike him or punch him, bloody his nose. She watched him for a long while, then asked, "Do you know what your apathy could do to the Governor's reputation?"

An ugly kind of resentment swelled within Roy. But even though he did not sympathize with her concern, he at least understood it. If he failed this assignment, it would not look good on the Governor's end. He would not take well to knowing that he had placed all his bets on a dithering, disobedient scholar—the son of his most loyal war commander and, if the rumors were true, his strongest political ally—just for Northgard to be defeated by the Old Ones. There was no doubt that the Governor would somehow find a way to pin the blame for his own faults on Roy.

None of this had stopped Roy from consuming old-world literature. He only had a small, secret collection of texts, which he'd salvaged from the rubble of a destroyed bookshop near Dawnseve Manor. On multiple occasions, Briar had tried to cover for Roy, but on the morning after one of these escapades, Gabriel had beaten him over the head with a book he'd pilfered on the grounds that he was "succumbing to temptation." Whether Briar had received some similar form of punishment for her role, Roy did not know.

If anything, *that* was his weakness—his inability to see beyond his own narrow desires. So maybe Dimestra was right . . .

"What could I possibly offer to the cause?" he asked Dimestra now. "Why does he need *me* when any other scholar—or, Hell, even one of his soldiers—could do?"

"Because, unless I'm mistaken, there aren't any other scholars who were *stupid* enough to get caught!" Dimestra snapped, startling Roy. She looked out the window; something had caught her attention. Roy was about to follow where her gaze had strayed when she gave him an accusing glare and said, "The Governor will tell you the details of your assignment once we arrive, but I assure you, Roy, he does not trust you or your . . ." But she didn't finish the sentence.

Your kind. That was what she'd been about to say. Because though Roy was a scholar as much as any of the others hiding in secrecy were, he was still an aristocrat. Perhaps that didn't mean the Governor could place his trust in him, but he at least knew that Roy would get the job done.

Dimestra continued, "We're cornered, Roy. We have no means, no external assistance, with which to inform the rest of the Hasdan Isles of our plight. This is our only option."

Roy shook his head, exasperated. "The Basilica has no place in our predicament. Perhaps the library could function as a sanctuary, an infirmary for wounded soldiers."

Derision slashed across Dimestra's face. "I assure you, the Droves would rather *die* in the Basilica than be healed in it. No, the Governor has more useful intentions for the library."

"I'm sure he does," Roy muttered, his vitriol for the Governor—a man whom he had never met; a man who, up until now, had been mistreating and puppeteering scholars' lives (if not outright destroying them) from the shadows—only intensifying. The feeling struck deep enough that he felt compelled to ask, "Where has he been this whole time? Sequestered in his manor? Why has he suddenly decided *now* is the time to come out of the woodwork? I've never met this man before, never even seen his face, and yet he's taken it upon himself to dictate—"

"The Governor has been . . . *absent* since his wife passed some few years ago," Dimestra interjected with curt impatience. Roy was more taken aback by the swiftness of her response than by the fact that she'd given him an answer. "Her death has taken a mercilessly heavy toll on his health." Her lips twitched, though apart from that, her expression was as implacable as before. "Like I said, Roy, be thankful. His wisdom is plentiful."

Roy rolled his eyes, then stilled. The sled had come to a jostling halt. He stumbled to his feet, a little unsteady from the ride, and then followed the Matron and the emissary out of the sled.

The banshee shriek of wind filled the space around him, and as it passed by, its echoes sounded to Roy like the dwindling cries of a spirit. Unnerved, he trudged forward, his boots sinking deep into snow. A vicious chill, much colder than anything he'd ever experienced throughout this endless winter, accosted him, creeping inch by inch across his skin and into his bones. Then he noticed the pointed shadow only a hundred paces away from him, rearing up over his head like some incorporeal black blade, and the cold, the world, and all his mounting fears felt inconsequential in comparison. He'd been so distracted by arguing with the Matron he hadn't even taken stock of his surroundings.

Roy had made it to the Orphic Basilica.

3

THE LIBRARY WAS BY FAR THE LARGEST, TALLEST building Roy had ever seen. He had only read three books on architecture, and so he didn't have the best frame of reference, but it crossed his mind that if an artist ever tried to depict the sheer scope of the Orphic Basilica, they would never quite be capable of putting into comprehensible scale its majesty, its impossible vastness.

Constructed of obsidian-black stone, the Orphic Basilica was seven stories high. Its great steeple stretched toward the soot-gray sky like a banner proclaiming safety, and its ridged roof pierced the lowest-hanging clouds, disappearing into the congregated thunderheads. A large staircase, made from huge slabs of glistening, snow-sprinkled limestone, led to five white pillars, which supported the black-wooded double doors of the front vestibule. Two clay bird baths, brimming with murky, algae-spattered water—now long frozen—flanked the entryway. Roy made out several windows on each of the library's stories, but the thick ebony-colored curtains hung over them provided him with nothing to stir his imagination.

Then a flutter of movement on the fifth floor caught his attention. A curtain parted, revealing the orange light of a lamp, which shone out like a big golden eye. Behind it stood a figure, but their features were entirely cloaked in shadow.

The sound of Dimestra's muffled footsteps startled Roy into motion. He followed her up the stairs, then stepped aside as the Citadel emissary hauled open the left of the double doors, grunting through his gritted teeth.

As soon as Roy stepped across the threshold and into the Orphic Basilica, the very moment that his boots struck the crimson carpet runner before him, he took in a deep, even breath and closed his eyes. A trancelike sense of calm and comfort came over him. He had gotten so tangled up in Northgard's cynicism and lies that he'd completely forgotten where he was being taken. This building, he knew now, was not like those few he had read about because it *wasn't* like any other. This library was a relic of the ancients, and though they no longer held the keys, and nor were they around to prevent Northgard from possessing them, Roy let himself believe they could see him now. He hoped he would not disappoint them.

Then he opened his eyes, and the fear of failure and of what might happen should he not succeed crashed down upon him with horrible force. Maybe he would become as forgotten as the library itself.

But he thought otherwise. A scholar—their identity, their purpose, their drive—was not to be underestimated. Razkamun, a highly renowned philosopher during the Age of Scribes, had once written on this: *The drawn sword is to the warrior what the written word is to the scholar.* There was a reason for academics and their deviations, no matter how contemptible those deviations might seem to Northgard.

This damn city is trying to steal these thoughts from your conscience, Roy told himself. *Your beliefs, your education; all of this will lose meaning if you give in, if you join the war.*

Something awoke within Roy then, tenebrous and beckoning, as though a secret, watching pair of eyes had heard his affirmations. The doors slammed shut behind him, a resounding thud that echoed through the Basilica's hallowed halls. Flames roared to life in fireplaces, dispersing the cold that had wound its way around Roy's muscles. A brilliant assortment of candles, lamps, and torches illuminated the space, revealing redwood floors, which were now bathed in a vermilion glow. Firelight and shadow shivered across the hundreds of thousands of books that lined the walls and stretched far back into corners, seen and unseen, and around alcoves and nooks discarded by scholars long deceased. The gilt-lettered titles on the spines of countless volumes shimmered a beautiful, enchanting shade of gold. Roy looked upon it all, enraptured. The works of a million authors, neglected, left to rot and decay.

And now, possibly, his . . . for six months, at least.

He marched past the threshold with haste, determined and enthused, then slowed to a stride, giving himself a chance to marvel at the shelves upon shelves of books. He felt somewhat like a thief, stealing glimpses of a world that was not his own. There were immaculately sculpted busts of literary visionaries on either side of the carpet runner: Tahaluth, who had penned twenty-seven expositional essays on the symbiotic relationship between the lecturer and the listener; the aforementioned Razkamun, one of Roy's heroes, the creator of the Warfare-Philosophy Principle; Polisworth, who had dedicated his life to helping other scholars by researching suitable processes for achieving mental durability during intense academic projects; and Atticus Walestone, admired by few, scorned by most, yet crucial for his investigation of other realities and other worlds.

Some figures Roy couldn't identify, some names eluded him, but this filled him with excitement. He found himself grinning at the idea of absorbing new information, of linking the ideologies he'd learned from his idol philosophers to historical events he had previously not heard of. He only stopped smiling when he remembered his mother would not take kindly to such a display.

Overhead, small portholes surrounded a large skylight covered thickly in snow, wrapped around which was a panorama illuminated by dreary gray light. Curved bas-reliefs depicted a series of foregone affairs: a queen sitting within a palanquin, carried by six knights whose helmets were capped with plumages of blue-gold feathers; the sails of a ship set aflame, drifting across a dark sea toward a distant shore; and an ambushed army, pristine silver shields raised, encircled by the cavalry cantering over the hills around them. Roy could almost hear the drumming of their horseshoes, the battle cries of soldiers carrying over the wind.

He turned his attention to the balcony railings at the edges of the upper six levels. Each ascended higher and higher, black as pitch, peaking at the seventh story like a pyramid. He couldn't see much of the fifth, sixth, or seventh stories from his vantage point, despite the dim illumination offered by the skylight, but he imagined bookshelves lurked there in the dark, filled to the brim with novels and poems, treatises and theses. He was suddenly seized by the compulsion to dash off into the shelves and explore, and he might have done just that, but the responsibility that had been heaped upon his shoulders was too heavy, the price of failure too steep.

By the Scribes, the Orphic Basilica had to be as large as three countryside villas. Dawnseve Manor was considered by other noble families to be one of the most ambitious domiciles in history, but the Basilica dwarfed even that. Moreover, the library seemed alive despite having been half forgotten. There was still a heart here, in these seven floors of sagas and fables, and Roy fancied that if he closed his eyes and strained his ears, he might've heard it.

He trailed Dimestra and the emissary up the spiraling staircase resting in the middle of the first floor, the black wrought-iron railing adorned with grinning, sharp-fanged basilisks. The carpet runner had ended before the first step, and so the percussion of three pairs of boots rang through the library, creating an eerie symphony of overlapping echoes.

Roy looked up at the remaining stairs they had left to climb—he figured the fifth floor, from which the lamp he'd seen outside had glowed, was their destination—and then felt a wave of vertigo. The skylight seemed darker, subdued. He cast his gaze down and saw much of the same: a fine layer of shadow lay upon the carpet runner and spread outward, encasing the surrounding bookshelves in gloom.

He was so distracted by the illusory sensation that he lost all sense of where he was going and stumbled into the Citadel emissary. The tall, burly man had stopped in his tracks, his eyes wide with shock, and was twisting on his heels and whipping his head around as if someone from his past, a bully he thought he had long outrun, had called out his name. He clasped the felt cap lying askew on his head, his hand shaking.

Dimestra looked over her shoulder, annoyed but also a little discomfited. "Evan? What is it?"

Evan shook his head, then wiped away the sweat that had gathered on his brow. "Thought I saw someone, Matron. Never mind me." He continued up the stairs, darting quick glances over his shoulder, and added in a mutter, "But I can't say I much like this place."

Roy disagreed, mainly on account of what it contained and represented, but he could see why Evan was frightened by his surroundings. Though the Orphic Basilica had seemingly sat in neglect for thousands of years, lain untouched—and this was immediately evident in its appearance—it did not *feel* abandoned or unused. Had someone been here, maintaining it, dusting the books, tidying what had been disorganized? He had no reason for thinking this; everything he knew about the city made this a ridiculous notion. The anti-intellectuals of Northgard had no love for academia and so would undoubtedly bear even less love for a librarian, let alone the building itself, which had inexplicably withstood years of attempted acts of arson.

And yet the question wouldn't leave Roy alone.

Is there someone here? he thought. *Someone whom I cannot see?*

Anxious, Roy could barely keep himself from stumbling; the snow on the soles of his boots had melted, making the stairs slick and glossy. They were on the second floor now, the deep and heavy silence irregularly broken by Evan's rasping breaths and Dimestra's grunts of discontentment. If there was ever a time to run, Roy realized, it was now; they were losing their focus, they were disoriented. But he couldn't deny the truth. He was intrigued. He could not leave now. He had barely made his foray into the academic community; how could he simply abandon it after being handed an opportunity such as this?

That is your true weakness, Roy. You want to live in a cocoon, safe and protected by those who provide that safety.

Again, he couldn't help but think that Dimestra had been right. But what was so wrong about wanting to survive? Or had survival in Northgard become something so impossible to imagine that the very act of imagining it was selfish?

Roy staggered into something hard and tall. He stumbled back, rubbing his forehead with the heel of his palm, and realized he had once again stumbled into Evan, who was murmuring to himself, almost spinning in circles with horror.

Strangely disinterested in whatever Evan was experiencing, Roy felt drawn to the balcony. Once there, he leaned over and saw shadows and hazy sunlight slashing stripes across the red carpet. Small reading alcoves, in which tables were cluttered with stacks of documents, were scattered throughout the library, and rolling ladders were intermittently placed between the bookshelves. Then his eye caught on the four balcony railings jutting out like bookmarks. They had made it. They were here.

We're on the fifth floor.

"Roy," ordered the Matron, somehow shaping the three letters into a cruel demand. She clenched her jaw, agitated, like she was restraining herself from scratching at an itch, though she eventually relented and raised a hand to her temples, massaging them. Between the rapid decline of Evan's senses and what looked like the Matron's developing headache, Roy was baffled. He felt fine, perhaps even saner than before entering the Basilica. What affliction had so debilitated his companions but had done nothing whatsoever to him? "Present yourself to the Governor with utmost respect," she told Roy. "Remember your station, if only to remember his. A higher power most will not behold."

Roy took advantage of Dimestra's confusion, as he didn't think her capable of violence in her current state, and said, "Likely because he's too busy shoving children into uniforms and calling them soldiers."

"Did you hear me?" the Matron hissed. "Are you listening to me?"

"As ever."

Dimestra gave him a displeased once-over, then turned on her heel, dismissing his dry remark.

They kept walking. To Roy's left was a glass cabinet occupied by books on wooden stands, and five paces ahead it curved into a small, dark room. There was a heavy, though remarkably pleasant, scent of spilled ink and parchment pages hanging thick in the air. Study spaces, fully equipped with lanterns, quills, inkwells, and long-backed armchairs, had been set up about the area.

There came a brief shuffle of movement from the study space tucked into the far-left corner, where sat a hunchbacked elderly man, his white hair pressed back slick across his scalp like a cap. He wore a pristine cream coat, the lapels covered in a menagerie of swan feathers, and long white trousers that complemented his thick gray boots. An onyx necklace hung about his throat, glittering dimly where the lamplight struck it. His eyes, an unnerving shade of bottle green, initially seemed lifeless to Roy ... but the longer he looked, the more aware he became of their hidden depths.

"Is this the boy?" the man asked, squinting. There was a feeble smile on his pale, spotted lips. "Come, Roy. Take a seat."

Roy had expected this man—*The Governor*, he forced himself to acknowledge—to lunge at him as a predator would do to its prey. He'd expected to be beaten, to leave this room with a mouth full of blood. But he was shocked to find the Governor, who appeared well into his eighth decade, looked as powerless and hopeless as Roy himself.

Dimestra crossed over to Roy and grasped his forearm, fingernails biting into his flesh. Her features were cool, inscrutable.

The Governor held up a hand, stopping her. "Release him, Matron Dimestra. This message is for the boy and the boy alone. Of all people, you should know this. I have given ample thought to the proceedings that shall take place here. Would it not be appropriate that I see these through myself?" He nodded to her, then to Evan. "Neither of you are required here on this day. You may vacate the premises."

Dimestra's grip slackened on Roy's arm, and he twisted,

freeing himself from her clutch. He looked askance at her, surprised to see a flicker of disbelief cross her face as she regarded the Governor, cocking her head. "I must confess, Governor, I did not anticipate this turn of events. I considered it my responsibility to administer all aspects of my rule as both a Matron and a commander of Drove squadrons and, as such, would have thought my presence for this discussion necessary."

While the Governor oversaw the administrative duties of Northgard from his manor, the Radiant Droves operated separately from him. Some war commanders chose to form alliances with the Governor to win promotions or other privileges, caring more for power and influence rather than directly dissenting scholarship, while others opposed academia *and* wanted to curry favor with the Governor. But Matron Dimestra had only ever remained in league with her soldiers, not with Northgard's ruler, which, to Roy, raised the question of why she wanted so badly to sit in on his meeting with the Governor. Maybe she believed that she ought to be further compensated for expanding the Governor's military force.

But why? He had already guaranteed the safety of the aristocracy.

"He is safe in my hands, Matron," the Governor assured her, an edge creeping into his voice, like a blade under silk. "Besides, this business is well beyond your area of expertise. I'm as upset about the scholastic nature of Roy's involvement in the war as you are. However, what I have planned for your son"—*your son*; the words so casual, as though Roy and Dimestra weren't on separate planes of existence—"will push the Old Ones back. Of that, I have no doubt. So, yes, Roy's safety is guaranteed."

Roy didn't think that his safety was where Dimestra's concerns lay, though. Regardless, with nary a thought, Roy's silent hope—that the Governor might not be of the same mold as the figures he had tried his hardest to avoid—had been extinguished. Generals, soldiers, Matrons, and Masters; they beat the world black and red and then pitted one against another until loyalties became unclear, impossible to tell apart. And yet the Governor had the audacity to place a sure bet on Roy's survival.

Dimestra's cheeks went red. "Yes, Governor." She left the alcove, the echo of her muffled bootsteps like a phantom's fist thudding on a door. Evan followed behind her at a jog, digging his fingers into the side of his head. Roy was still not sure what was wrong with the man.

"Now, then," the Governor said to Roy, gesturing to the armchair opposite him, "why don't you take a seat?"

4

UPON FURTHER INSPECTION, ROY COULDN'T HELP but notice the Governor had a most peculiar face, his features conspicuous, giving Roy the same feeling one might get from staring into a pitch-dark room: It took some time to find the eccentricities, but once you did, they were almost impossible to forget. The moment Dimestra and Evan left the room, the Governor's thin smile broadened, and his expression shifted into one of keen readiness . . . and avarice. Roy didn't like that look; it reminded him of his brother.

"Well, Roy," the Governor said, "does it live up to your standards? Is your imagination sated?"

Roy considered the question. If he were in a mood for honesty, he would tell the Governor that his imagination had never ventured farther than the doors of Dawnseve Manor, that the few books lining the shelves in his home, rescued from the wreckage of immolated bookshops, were just enough to escape the clouds of gunpowder and the cries of children. But admittedly, Roy was still so awestruck by the magnitude of the Orphic Basilica and its surreal possessions that he confessed, "It's outstanding. I've never seen, nor even thought to imagine that there could be, so many books contained in one space."

"The prospect isn't quite as plausible as it might have been in the Age of Scribes," the Governor agreed, a slight tinge of amusement to his voice. He pursed his lips, musing. "You must have quite the collection, given the intensity of your... enthusiasm."

Roy shifted in his seat, discomforted by the reminder of the Governor's awareness of his crime. "I've read them all six times or so," he said. "There wasn't anything of much import except a few anthologies and journals. Some were... bland, though."

"Oh?" the Governor said. He steepled his fingers together beneath his chin, then insisted, "Tell me more."

Frowning, Roy scratched his wrist, nonplussed by the Governor's inquiry. "Why? What could you gain from that information?"

The Governor straightened, giving Roy a puzzled look. "Ah well, I'm not exactly an adept reader, you see. I thought it might help me better sympathize with your situation if you could impart upon me the good and the bad of philosophy, its workings and its flaws."

Roy was assaulted by a thousand thoughts, none of them particularly reassuring. *It's impossible to teach within minutes what scholars have been trying to discover for millennia. In fact, if you could teach me, Governor, that would be wonderful, because sometimes I haven't the slightest clue what I'm doing.* But it was this that baffled Roy: *Why are you, someone who has single-mindedly fought for decades to erase knowledge, suddenly interested in it? What sort of trap is this?*

What do you truly want from me? From all this?

These thoughts continued to revolve through Roy's mind until he stumbled upon a goal. If the Governor's interests were somehow entangled with his own, then maybe by expressing his exclusive devotion to philosophy, Roy could persuade the Governor to withdraw his proposition, thereby preventing Roy from being embroiled in the war.

After a silent moment, during which he hoped his convictions were strong enough to coax the Governor, Roy said, "Think of philosophy as a quest, an exploration for suitability. A philosopher tests their limits, guides their mind into subjects both daring and trivial. One way of thinking may enable one scholar to access a plethora of information, while on the other hand, their colleague might find the same work drab and uninspiring. You aren't asking the wrong question, as it is undeniable there are good and bad *approaches* to philosophy, but as far as choosing what is most appropriate for oneself, the question becomes a matter of the senses, of human instincts."

"And what have your instincts told you over the course of your studies?" the Governor asked.

"Many things," Roy said, "though I doubt these have all been correct. I would hope they weren't, anyway. A great amount of exploration is involved, is *necessary*, before a revelation can be yielded. Some philosophers have gone their entire lives without such a revelation. Of course, that isn't to suggest their efforts should go unmentioned by future scholars. After all, unlike most circles of influence, the academic community has a unique, indomitable sense of universal acceptance." He belatedly added, "The community as it once was, of course," and hoped that the Governor didn't notice his slipup.

The Governor, however, simply smiled.

By the Scribes, he knows about the scholars in hiding, Roy thought, adopting an impassive expression. *But of course he knows. How else could those scholars I saw on the way here have been bookmarked? How else could I have been exposed? Neither the Matron nor Gabriel would have said anything; harboring a criminal is as much a crime as anything I've done.* He wondered who among his few correspondents had been colluding with the Governor all along, who had decided that Roy's fascination with literature had gone too far, that enough was enough, and turned him in.

"And where among this *community* do your interests lie?" the Governor asked, still smiling. "Surely not all philosophers fight the same battles."

"Sometimes, we may come to similar conclusions," Roy said. "And sometimes, our findings may intersect with one another, like threads overlapping, becoming a string and, if you're fortunate, a pattern of congruencies and theories. But usually, the exploratory process of philosophical discovery is a personal affair. I've made it my own goal to understand the psychological framework of human existence, behavior, and thought within a philosophical context."

He stopped himself there. The explanation was broad, but it was also as detailed as he would allow. He could not afford to go on, to articulate the true depth of his love for philosophy, how its abstract concepts had imbued his life with purpose, if only momentarily, before the reality of his torment and sorrow crept back in. He could not expose his deepest wounds to the Governor, who was already capitalizing on Roy's bibliomania to drive out the Old Ones and turn them from Northgard's shores. All, no doubt, to further his own ambitions, which had nothing to do with Roy's . . . let alone the city's.

And so Roy hated himself when the words came pouring out of his mouth, but he could not hold them back. "Some philosophers may even go so far as to demonstrate their theories on a colleague. I haven't conducted such experiments yet, though."

The Governor leaned forward, raising a brow. "If given the chance to collaborate with a partner, would you prefer them to have a similar mindset?"

"Oh yes, certainly," Roy said, nodding. He blamed the promptness of his replies on his excitement; discussing the possibility of a collaborative research project was gratifying beyond measure. Such a thing would mean he wasn't alone. Somewhere in this city, in the streets he'd looked out over in Dawnseve Manor only hours before, there were still people like him, their heads bent over stolen books, their hands stained with ink. "It would be useful for my exploration of human thought, too, to work with a colleague."

The Governor nodded, then pressed a hand against his brow with a wince that drew lines across his forehead. "Do you think you would benefit more from having a partner, as opposed to working alone?"

Another silence passed between them, one weighted with meaning that Roy could not decipher. The Governor didn't appear to possess any vindictive qualities, nothing that stood out to Roy. But then again, deceit was not always immediately visible to the naked eye, and he would be naive to think the Governor had gotten where he was through pure honesty.

Roy swallowed, frustrated. He cursed his struggle with interpreting the emotions of people he wasn't familiar with, because while he plainly understood Briar's and the Matron's feelings through their facial expressions, the Governor was a virtual stranger to Roy. He felt lost, uncertain how to proceed.

"'Silence is the maker of small reminders: your breath, your heart, your reason to be,'" Roy said after a moment. "That was Polisworth, a famed philosopher. In his thesis, *Ambrosia for Curses*, he explored remedies for times of mental duress, silence being an utmost priority. I entered philosophy through Polisworth's findings and subscribed to his Silent Song Theory, which encouraged me to work in solitude. The practice is blissful, for the most part." He shrugged. "I'm not able to conduct discussions, though, which I *would* prefer, but there are downsides to every principle."

"Which, I presume, comes back to the question of educational suitability. An approach to philosophy might not apply to *all* philosophers, but there *is* an approach available for all philosophers."

Roy begrudgingly agreed with the Governor. "Not every style of research, nor every subject of discussion, should cater toward one individual."

"But if philosophy is considered among the academic community to be a place of universal acceptance, why stop there? Why not evolve into a place of universal understanding while you're at it? Why help one person when you can help them all?"

"Philosophy heals the consciousness through mental expansion, which is anything but selective, this is true. It *is* a collective process. Excepting his thesis, even Polisworth worked with other philosophers."

"And you?"

Roy hesitated, a thought hitting him hard just then. If the Governor did know of the others, then it came back to the idea of *Why me? Surely there are others more accomplished?*

He wasn't sure, though. He was proud of his thought work, and because he'd had correspondence with others, as well as seen their responses to his scholarship, he was now confident that they did not hold a candle to him, even more so than when he'd asked Dimestra in the sled, *What could I possibly offer to the cause? Why does he need me when any other scholar—or, Hell, even one of his soldiers—could do?*

So Roy said now, finally, "I am very much interested in collaboration, if the other scholar is able to both understand and push me. I believe philosophy can bind us together until we are inextricably unified, and only then can we showcase our genius. Only then do we become history itself." He hadn't realized until he finished speaking that he was furiously scratching the back of his hand. It was now covered in a red patch of crisscrossing marks.

His eyes flicking briefly to Roy's hand, the Governor said, "This world tends to disregard those undeserving of success. I trust you understand this."

It was the only thing Roy knew. "I do."

"There was a time when scholars were rational," the Governor said, "when they held the same views as the aristocrats of the Iron Citadel and were thus trusted by my predecessors. My grandfather, long may he lie undisturbed, once told me and my siblings tales of ancient battles fought not just with blades and bows, but with battlecraft strategies handpicked from dusty tomes. 'Those war books of old,' he would call them." The Governor shook his head, clicked his tongue. "In my experience, though, I've discovered that such tomes do little but create false hope and ultimately fail us." He said the last with just enough of a touch of bitterness—and *heat*—that Roy found himself shrinking slightly in his chair. The Governor regarded Roy with unsettling scrutiny, a wily half smile now on his mouth. "And yet, I am in desperate need of some hope and therefore of someone of your intellect, Roy, as I trust I made clear in my letter."

It *was* clear, though Roy couldn't tell whether the Governor had any inkling about the enormity—the damn near impossibility—of the task he was asking. The fact that nobody knew the motivations of the Old Ones, nor why they'd besieged Northgard, was potentially the study of a lifetime, not six months.

Upon receiving the letter, Roy had already started to go through his limited knowledge of the enemy soldiers, and he realized now it was more hearsay and conjecture than solid scholarship. Some claimed they'd come to rescue the scholars, though *that* theory had been discarded when the Old Ones began indiscriminately assailing academics and Droves alike. Some believed they'd invaded to steal the Governor's plans for Northgard's future. But after three years the Old Ones hadn't yet stormed his manor, which was based close to the Iron Citadel, the Radiant Droves' stronghold.

They had still made horrifically efficient progress in their decimation of the city, though. Roy had overheard from several military reports discussed between Matron Dimestra and her soldiers, who held infrequent meetings in Dawnseve Manor to save her traveling to the Iron Citadel, that the Old Ones were gaining close to the family estate. It hadn't been until two months ago, when the Old Ones had raided a village he'd once visited with Briar, that Roy had begun to fear every book he read would be his last.

All this, and so much was still unknown, including something that niggled at his mind now . . . something Dimestra had said to Roy on the ride to the library.

"The Matron told me that you would elaborate on the details of my assignment," Roy said, absentmindedly itching his hand again. "Did you intentionally omit these details from your letter?"

"Not without good reason," the Governor explained. "Truthfully, I anticipated that you wouldn't be as amenable to my conditions if I addressed them in my letter in their entirety. I simply couldn't risk your absence here today, and while this city *is* in dire straits, I'm a man of my word. Had you declined my offer, had you known what I am now about to tell you, I would have had you brought to the Citadel, no questions asked. But seeing as you've accepted my proposal, as I planned, now seems the right time to enlighten you.

"This task, as my earlier inquiry about partners may have implied, will not be laid on your shoulders alone. Although you may prefer your studies to be independent, I'm glad to hear you're not completely averse to collaboration. Besides, I think we can both agree this library is large, excessively so. It would take *years* to explore the Basilica on your own—conceivably decades if you felt emboldened to range over all its nooks and crannies—so my associates and I have recruited another scholar to work alongside you. This will hopefully lighten your workload and expediate the process. If all goes to plan, your allotted six months may be three. It may even be two."

Roy didn't realize how much of a relief this news brought him, and he found he could have cried at this development, for as beautiful as the Orphic Basilica had appeared upon arrival, he was continually intimidated by the breadth of the Elder Scribes' collection. Yet that relief was soon tempered by his earlier thought of the scope of what the Governor was asking them. If he was lucky, if he put his head down and sacrificed as much sleep as he could possibly go without, Roy fancied he could get through two hundred or so books in six months. So even with a partner by his side, doubling their productivity, the number of books they consumed would hardly come close to a fraction of the number he'd seen on the first floor alone. But he had to admit success was much more feasible with two than by himself. He would just have to hope his partner, and Roy himself, could bring their available materials down to a manageable selection.

They chose me out of all the scholars in the city, Roy thought, and from this he deduced: *Surely their selection for the other was just as thorough.*

A small tremor of excitement coursed through him. *Finally, a peer to talk to, to share ideas with and to work together to* grow those ideas into more than just trivial fancies and suppositions.

Maybe he'd only be a true scholar for six months, but it would be six months more than he'd ever had before.

"Who will I be working with?" Roy asked, trying to keep the eagerness out of his voice.

"You haven't heard of Percival Atherton, have you?"

"No," Roy said, "I can't say that I have." Not that he would acknowledge it either way—he owed the other scholars that much anonymity if they still had it.

"Well, there you are," the Governor said. "I should expect that the investigation moves a little quicker with Percival accompanying you. He arrived a few hours ago, actually. It took a rather lengthy conversation to convince him, but he came around to the idea once I presented him with the alternative."

Oh, I'm sure, Roy thought. *I'm sure that the threat of being thrown as fodder against the Old Ones versus six months of barely interrupted reading was a hard choice.*

Tamping down his frustration at the Governor's austerity, Roy said, "This does lift some of the weight off my shoulders. Although . . ." He hated that he had to admit this, knowing the Governor might see it as testament that he wasn't up to the task, but he added, "There has been close to no word discovered on the Old Ones. I'm sure that you need as many Droves at hand as possible, but would it inconvenience you to assign some of your soldiers, or the Matron's, to the task as well? I won't speak on behalf of Atherton and his reading fluency, but there must be a million books stored here. Even I could only dream of getting through a fraction of these."

What Roy really wanted was to request the aid of more scholars, of whom the Governor was certainly aware. But that he hadn't recruited more than just the two had given Roy pause.

Had the Governor asked the same of others? Had they declined? Were these the scholars Roy had seen bookmarked?

No, Roy wouldn't do anything to contribute to another scholar's danger. It had been his lifelong dream to come to the Basilica, to study among like-minded academics, to produce writings that revolutionized the world.

He resolved, then, to be content with one other man ... and the soldiers the Governor would hopefully provide.

However, the Governor only gave a deep sigh. It sounded rehearsed, like he'd prepared for this, and all of Roy's other questions. "I've led numerous investigations of this building over the past fifteen years, since I ordered for the immolation of all bookshops, libraries, and old-world research institutions." Roy had been only ten then, but he remembered it well. All of those priceless archives, all within reach, suddenly gone up in flames. If the Governor saw even a glint of the pain those memories induced in Roy, he didn't let on; he only continued, "Every time, the guards who accompanied me swore to have heard voices and seen faces long gone. And some ... some did not fare nearly as well with their hallucinations. Twenty-seven Droves, if my count is correct, have taken their own lives by firearm. The last to do so—a young fellow, mind, not much older than you—claimed to have seen his deceased mother in the Basilica. On the carriage ride back to the Citadel, he took out a chunk of his skull with his musket. His sister, also a Drove, could not cope with the grief of losing her last living relative, and so she ripped out her own throat with her bare hands."

Roy sucked in a sharp breath.

He considered the Citadel emissary's skittishness and the Matron's headache. How could all these seemingly superficial anxieties, which the Droves had apparently experienced themselves, have resulted in such hysteria and madness? How hadn't the Governor yet succumbed? Wasn't his downward spiral into insanity inevitable, too?

The Governor leaned back in his armchair. "So, no, aside from yourself and Percival, I have not given my offer to another member of nobility. Most nobles are forced into armor, but you and Percival have the potential to bring an end to this war. Hell, you can restore hope in Northgard."

Percival hails from a noble house, then, Roy thought, his eagerness bubbling back in his chest. He folded his hands in his lap, no longer overcome with the urge to scratch them. He would be meeting not only another academic, but another *noble-born* academic. He couldn't believe his luck, nor how quickly his emotions seemed to vary with each new piece of information the Governor was presenting. *He was* just *talking about Droves killing themselves, and now I'm excited that my new playmate is also a noble? What is wrong with me?*

Roy tried to keep his voice even. "That's good to know. Yet I can't help but notice that you kept those deaths out of your letter too?"

The Governor scowled. "Of course I did." He spoke brusquely, as if incensed by the idea that he owed Roy anything. "This isn't information I share with *you* lightly. I am only doing so just so you see the extent of what you're dealing with. And now that that's done, I'll tell you this is no longer a matter of agreement, Roy. You *will* do this."

It annoyed Roy that he was surprised, both by this obfuscation and by the implication that this assignment had ever been something he had the ability to agree to or not.

He knew there had never been a choice.

Again, the Governor appeared unmoved by the vexation almost certainly plain on Roy's face. Then he lowered his brows and shocked Roy by saying, all ferocity gone from his voice, "I must ask ... You haven't heard any voices since you arrived, have you? Anything that might have steered your mind toward violence? Or even suicide?"

Roy recoiled at the Governor's chilling forthrightness, but he shook his head. He *had* detected some voices, and he *had* been scratching his hand incessantly while in the Governor's company, but neither of these were so disconcerting as what the Governor was describing.

"I see," the Governor replied, a tinge of curiosity to his voice. "Neither did Percival. Listen, Roy, I want to be very clear: I was opposed to calling on the help of any scholars, but this library clearly shuns those who have no interest in academia, confirming something I've long suspected—"

He cut himself off, his lips pinched, and before Roy could parse what that meant, the Governor went on, "You and Percival will use this building to ferret out the Old Ones' origins and, more importantly, their objectives. Prior to my arrival, my guards deposited a portion of rations—bread, cheese, and waterskins—on the sixth floor. The first chamber on the left. These shall last you through the next month, at which point I shall return every three or four weeks, both to deliver your additional supplies and to observe your progress ... provided the Old Ones haven't made a charnel house of Northgard by then. It's clear this task won't be simple, but I'm beyond caring. Our city is poised on a knife's edge. If it falls into ruin, that is on you two."

Red curled in at the corners of Roy's vision. His heart pounded erratically. His earlier feeling of uncertainty, of being perched on the crumbling border of a cliff, returned.

Six months, he thought. *Six months to find answers on an enemy whose identity has eluded Northgard for three years.* It had already sunk in how little time they had, but coupled with the check-ins every four weeks or so, he realized just how ludicrously short that was. And for once, the idea of being surrounded by books inspired no enthusiasm within him.

Roy could not deny how daunting his prospects were. At the same time, though, he couldn't deny that there *was* a chance here. If nothing else, the chance of the outcome the Governor wanted was simply too alluring. He saw that well and clear enough: A final chance to halt the war before it spanned across Northgard and cast surrounding islands in its pall. A chance to save lives before the Old Ones could reach foreign shores and their great obsidian boots could darken more snow-glazed earth.

A chance to make sure Briar was safe.

Questions still took up space in the back of Roy's mind, though. For starters, how could he and Percival use their specific educations to identify the enemy? But the longer that he contemplated it, the clearer the answer became. Philosophy subscribed to the arcane, the subtle, the forgotten fragments of the world's secret past. Roy didn't believe in magic, but there was an unmistakable mysticism in ancient transcripts and ciphered messages. For thousands of years, scholars had undertaken projects to solve conspiracies. What was this task but another such project? What was the difference between the Elder Scribes' scholastic expeditions and what Roy was tempted to undergo?

A conquered island, Roy thought. *That's the difference.*

He hadn't seen the Old Ones, nor did he wish to, and he couldn't fathom what atrocities they were capable of, but the thought of the Orphic Basilica, a mystical sanctum, shattered to ruins; of shelves of literary relics destroyed . . . it almost broke him. It almost shattered his soul. Because maybe the Old Ones would accomplish what the Radiant Droves had not.

"I'll do it," Roy said. "I . . . I'll do it."

"Of course you will," the Governor said. "But it's wonderful to hear you say it anyway." And then, with a magnanimous smile that didn't quite reach his eyes, the Governor spread his hands out before him. "Who could ever say no to a good book?"

NCE THEIR DISCUSSION HAD COME TO ITS END, THE Governor informed Roy that he could choose one of the rooms on the sixth floor as his personal chamber, then left the reading room and, soon after, the Orphic Basilica. The door boomed shut on his way out.

Roy wrung his hands, overwhelmed by the sheer amount of information that had been brought before him in the past hour. Though it had been the Governor who had imposed this monumental task upon him, all Roy could think of was the Matron—her stoic expression, her complete disregard of his interest in the old world.

Dimestra had always hated him, though. She had always criticized his lifestyle and ambitions, so abnormal had they seemed to her, and this assignment was just adding fuel to the fire. For as much as it was a punishment for Roy, he imagined the Matron must've been infuriated by the abrupt loss of the control she wielded over her son. But Roy cared little for her opinion; he was much too entangled in what it might mean for him if he and Percival failed. Their lives would be forfeit, forgotten only months after they'd been given a purpose, and they would be—

You'll be history, little brother, Gabriel whispered in his mind. *And everyone will forget the weak, weeping pig you are.*

Because these were the consequences of failure that the Governor had presented to Roy. And the only thing he wasn't sure of, on that front, was whether it would be at the hands of the Old Ones or of the Governor himself.

He was just sure of the inevitability.

Roy pressed the heels of his palms into his eyes and dragged his hands down his face. When he opened his eyes, he looked up. Bookshelves towered above him, dimly illuminated by lantern light. The scent of spilled ink hung heavy in the air, thickening, urging him to rest.

"Get up," he told himself, shaking his head. "You have to get up. You have work to do." He attempted again to concentrate, but exhaustion had long set into his muscles, making him slouch in the armchair and pulling him into a thin, broken sleep.

He jerked awake with a sharp, indrawn breath, unsure how long he'd been passed out. He rose from his seat, overcome with defeat and fatigue, then sighed, doused the lanterns, and left the room.

Night had fallen since his meeting with the Governor. The Orphic Basilica lay entrenched in deep shadow, lightened only by the fireplaces and lanterns that had lit upon his arrival. To his right were multiple reading rooms and study nooks, each overlooked by ancient busts of poets, authors, historians, and philosophers. At first, he could not place them, but two of the names engraved into the plinths Roy knew intimately. He'd read their works countless times before. One was Eran Grusmoor, the author of six epics about a family of sailors voyaging the fabled Never Sea. The other was Charles Patiny, a writer of more than fifty romance novels and twice as many poems, all inspired by an unreciprocated love.

Roy remembered a fragment of *Hearts Unsung*, Patiny's last

novel: *By all accounts, it was not Love—that fatal heathen—which killed him but Memory, that thief of spirits.*

Unnerved, Roy started to continue up to the sixth floor when a chill passed through him, snaked beneath his coat, and left his skin covered in gooseflesh. Wind stirred through the reading room he'd stopped beside, and for a moment, Roy was convinced that Charles Patiny was watching him, *leering* at him, with his cold stone eyes.

Roy strode past the reading room, quickening his pace. While he didn't think that he was being followed, that didn't alleviate his dread over the impression that someone, Percival perhaps, was taunting him from the shadows. His heart thundering in his throat, he darted around a corner, where he found a black iron staircase.

As he mounted the last step, the Orphic Basilica's sixth floor sprawled out around him. Overhead, a sparkling glass orrery spanned the ceiling. It was a dazzling display of twelve worlds, only one of which he knew—Kalthis, his home world. Spinning about the worlds were moons and suns, sculpted from silver and gold glass respectively and attached to the overall exhibition by near-invisible cords of string. Beneath the orrery were writing desks, armchairs, and divans, arranged in a star.

As with the lower floors, the sixth was adorned with an inordinate number of teak and mahogany bookshelves, so many that Roy envisioned hundreds, thousands, of aspiring poets, playwrights, and authors loading books into their arms, intent on mastering the craft taught to them by their tutors. Between the aisles were moth-eaten cushions and threadbare gray quilts, next to which sat silver trays laden with the dust of long decomposed meals. By the light of the lanterns suspended from rusted iron hooks, Roy made out a tin plate scattered with dead maggots. It didn't elude him that this was the first true sign of the library's age he'd seen thus far.

Despite the need to select a room to retire to and sleep off his troubles, Roy couldn't resist the temptation. He'd spent years holed up in his bedchamber, rifling through outlawed texts, but as he'd pointed out to the Governor, his collection was limited. When was he ever going to get another chance like this, a library stocked with more books than he knew what to do with?

I'll fuss about the Old Ones tomorrow, Roy resolved, *when my mind is clear for conjecture. But tonight is for me.*

Grinning, he wandered over to the long stretch of shelves behind the orrery. Two tall glass cabinets stood in front of them, filled with relics: a dust-coated tablet; an abacus; a steel letter opener; a sheet of parchment, all black except for a large eldritch white symbol of some sort that dominated the page; a corroded metal device designed to decrypt coded messages; and a journal, opened to an entry written in looped cursive penmanship.

> *I am beset with grief, my love, for the life we might have had, the children we might have raised, the legacy we might have made. Are our hopes naught but fleeting dreams? Are we forever cursed with the agony of longing?*
>
> *Were I not of the common folk, I wonder if our circumstances would be the same. Or if, in every alteration of events, however slight, we are forever doomed.*
>
> *Stretch out your hand once you reach the Above, my dear. There, and there only, shall I find you. And perhaps then we shall begin life anew.*

Roy wiped away the tears that had welled up in his eyes. He could *see* the strength of the author's love, preserved upon the page. He understood their personal strife, their rage and hope and frustration, through the power of their message: If they recorded their doom, would it undo what had been set in stone?

Again, a small part of him wanted to go to the room he'd been promised, but as his exhaustion burned away, determination—and curiosity—seized him. He turned, his coat billowing behind him, and made his way toward the bookshelves.

His choices, he soon discovered, were boundless. There were books on literary theory and philosophy, etymology and linguistics. There were books written in unfamiliar alphabets, some of whose characters vaguely resembled the common language most Northgardians were taught in their classes at Rasileus Academy, where the professors eschewed expounding the more spiritually enlightening subjects in favor of educating students on military campaigns and the tenets of Governorship. On one shelf, Roy found an ancient clothbound volume bursting with densely packed lists of birth and death dates. By its length, he determined there to be hundreds of thousands of names, all scrawled in intricate symbols. Though the Orphic Basilica housed books from both the Age of Scribes and before, there was simply no telling from which age this book originated. For all he knew, this might be a record of anti-Scribe citizens declaring their involvement in a violent uprising, or even an inventory of rural farmers and their allegiances of trade.

The next aisle was no less versatile in its selection of literature, and random in its arrangement, than the last. He found a romance novel about two women oblivious to their ordained love. He found a horror book about the disturbing consequences of defying fate. He found an atlas of the known world, but all the illustrations had faded, leaving behind murky outlines of oceans and islands.

After a while, Roy looked about him, a little perplexed.

Was there no cataloging system here? Perhaps he hadn't done a thorough enough search of the library, but he was intimidated by the thought of navigating these shelves without some written guidance and directions. But he would address these worries again tomorrow, when he officially began his research on the Old Ones.

He pictured himself huddled in one of those study nooks he'd passed, piles of books teetering around him. Yes, his exploration of the Orphic Basilica might be restricted by the Governor's requirements, and he would thus have to stay on task, but maybe when his duties were done for the day, Roy could continue to seek solace here, as he was doing now. He would soar to distant worlds and fall in love with brave princes and cursed warriors.

But as much as he loved fiction, Roy was utterly enamored with philosophy. Even though he had read only a few texts in his years, those few had begun his lifelong search for scholastic self-realization, a complete understanding of what it was, *who* it was, he wanted to be.

However, he did not find many books upon the shelves that belonged to this category. He moved to the next aisle, hopeful, and was surprised to find three: *The Maxims of Altruism*, *A Canticle of Being*, and *Which Life to Critique?* He was about to continue his investigation when a breeze skittered up the shell of his ear and swirled into the shelf. There, shoved behind the philosophy texts he'd discarded, was a decrepit, dog-eared red text entitled *Crisis Inverted: An Examination of the Nonexistent*.

Roy blinked, mystified. He reached forward, intrigued by the otherworldliness of the book's title, the wind that he'd sensed moments ago fluttering around his fingers.

Then a shadow swept past the other side of the bookshelf.

He stiffened, his heart climbing inch by inch up his throat, and waited for the owner of the shadow to follow. He stood for long moments like this, his outstretched fingers just near *Crisis Inverted*, tears trembling in his wide, unblinking eyes. He felt another shift in the air, the wind passing through and over him, and then he shuffled slowly back. After a moment, he glanced to the right, where the shadow had gone, and fear spread through his chest, coiling and twisting like black roots.

There was a monster at the end of the aisle. It wore the shape of a human, but all its contours and edges were made of shadow. Jagged chunks of burning scarlet light shone where its eyes should have been, like rubies excavated from the darkest trenches of Hell. It was hovering above the redwood floorboards, its unnaturally long hands splayed at its sides. As its gaze passed over Roy, scrutinizing him, the curve of its cheeks and the slope of its shoulders grew clear.

Somewhere in the back of his petrified, screaming mind, it occurred to Roy that this creature could be a mirage, a hallucination, as the Governor had described. And yet, the longer he stared at the shadow, the harder it was to confirm this suspicion. The anthropoid quality of its features was undeniable, even more terrifying for its familiarity. Was it possible, then, that this creature was of the same breed as those that had compelled the Radiant Droves to take their own lives? Or were they one and the same?

And does that mean there's a third fate awaiting me? Roy wondered, recalling his earlier rumination about how these apparent hallucinations and supernatural sightings would inevitably conclude. *Is that to be my end, too? Suicide?*

For one paralyzing moment, he forgot why he was where he was, in this artifact of the old world, why he had left Dawnseve Manor at all. He could not move, nor could he shift his gaze from the shadow's. His skin was clammy, his hands slathered in sweat. It tilted its head toward him, but the implication was lost on Roy. All he could see were those piercing scarlet eyes, ogling him. An unearthly interrogation. The shadow glided forward, a single daring movement, and then Roy turned and ran down through the bookshelves.

He stumbled forward, disoriented, his hair tumbling across his face and the laces of his right boot coming undone. Then the boot itself slid off his foot. The ground came up to meet him, and by instinct his body braced for impact, but as his sock-clad foot hit the floorboards, relief punched through his chest. He resumed his sprint, racing around the corner.

His breathing ragged and dry, Roy lurched forward step by aching step, his enervation and disorientation turning his vision into a blur of parchment pages and foggy moonlight. But he ran on, his foot striking the floor and producing intervals of resonant *thwacks* through the library. He gasped, sweat plastering his tailcoat to his flushed, feverish skin, and miraculously found the courage to glance over his shoulder.

Somehow the shadow had almost caught up to him, and its dark, transparent hand reached out toward him in a hooked claw. Its eyes blazed in the night like cavernous wells of magma, throwing hectic red shadows across the books. He was not sure how he hadn't heard it before, but Roy could now distinctly make out a low, ululating cry.

He dashed around another corner and into the next shelf passageway. He was nearing the last dregs of his energy, though, and he realized only then he had nothing with which to defend himself—nor, if he was being honest, the ability. Another quick look over his shoulder revealed the shadow—the ghost?—to be unarmed, but that did nothing to quell his anxiety. Maybe he could confuse it, make it lose its way. But he was becoming quickly delirious himself, and the pressure and tiredness that had been piled upon him were doing little to help matters.

A feral, shrill scream exploded through the library, echoing about the bookshelves and rattling the glass cabinets Roy had observed earlier. He started, then staggered back, trying to find his balance, before the wind whipped past him and released a hysterical shriek. He shot out a hand and clutched the shelf nearest him but was interrupted by another blast of wind, which pummeled him in the gut. He keeled over, breathless, let out a wheezing gasp, and then fell to his knees, holding the shelf all the while. But he could not keep up his weight a moment longer.

Roy crumpled to the ground, burying his hands in his hair. He squeezed his eyes shut and clenched his teeth, a bolt of hot pain shooting through his muscles. He uttered a raw, broken scream, but it sounded so quiet beneath the bellowing wind. Pressure built behind his eyes, and tears leaked out, streaking down his face.

Ahead of him, the breeze quieted, as if a door had been shut in the face of a storm. He looked up, hesitant. The shadow was still staring at him, but it only stood there now, its finger pointed at him in silent accusation. He grimaced, waiting for its killing blow, for some black, infectious mist to spiral out of its finger, seep into his chest and quiet the pounding drum that was his heart, but the shadow performed no such move. Instead, it swung its finger back and forth, swaying from Roy to the shelves, the shelves to Roy. A pendulum determining his fate. He was so absorbed by the cryptic gesture that he didn't even notice the shadow advancing toward him until it was bearing down upon him, its blank, murky face a hairbreadth from his own.

Panic overtook his body. His hands shook; his skin tingled; his vision fragmented and blurred like he was looking through a smudged kaleidoscope. He thrashed on the floor and flung out a weak fist at the shadow, but it flew through the creature with frightening ease. As skin and shadow connected, a sound materialized in his head, pitching higher and higher until it clarified into a crazed cacophony. He heard distorted screams and guttural howls, akin to those of a wolf, and earth-rumbling roars rebounding as though from the bottom of a deep, deep well.

And for a split second, flashing before his eyes like a flare of light, Gabriel was looming over him, rising up from Roy's memories, his deranged grin stretching wider and wider across his lips, pulling at the skin of his mouth, *ripping* it—

Roy shrieked, his eyes rolling in his skull. He scratched the sides of his head, trying to burrow into his temples, tear flesh from bone and rip the voices out of his mind. "*Stop!*" he screamed. "Please, Gabriel, not tonight! *Stop!* Please, just stop—"

Then a hand closed around his arm and hauled Roy to his feet.

"Look at me. *Look* at me, damn you! Are you hurt? Are you all right?"

Roy froze, his hair strewn in knots across his face, and laid his hands upon the chest of the shadow. But it wasn't the shadow, he saw as he opened his eyes.

It was a blond, hazel-eyed, and strikingly beautiful man.

"I'm . . ." Roy whispered. "I'm fine."

The man released Roy, glowering. "Wonderful. Then give me one decent reason why I climbed three staircases to find you screaming and sprawled on the ground."

R OY REGARDED THE STRANGER CAREFULLY.
He looked close to Roy's own age, twenty-four or twenty-five. He was dressed in a loose-collared tunic, brown trousers, and tattered black boots, the half-done laces sagging across the floorboards. A pair of square-rimmed spectacles sat upon the bridge of his long nose, and his hazel eyes were as bright with beauty as they were shining with suspicion. A stray thread of moonlight flickered across his short blond hair. His defined features possessed an imperious cruelty: brows sharply furrowed, cheeks sharp as a snake's fangs, his full lips crooked with unconscious judgment. If men were weapons, this young man was carved from the steel that had been cast aside: too sharp to lay in a warrior's hands.

"One reason," he repeated, his cheeks scarlet. He nodded to his left hand, which was gripping a thick leatherbound book. "I have quite a lot of work to do—unlike you, it seems—and I do not take kindly to interruptions." He showed no strain, no sign of exertion, but Roy wasn't surprised. He had likely heard Roy screaming, rolled his eyes, and then wandered up from his burrow at a leisurely stroll.

Roy stepped to the side, looking at the space behind the man, but there was no trace of the shadow that had accosted him.

"Time is a precious commodity," said the man, "so I suggest you stop looking around for the answer and start using your words."

"It's not there," Roy babbled. "It's... It's not *there*."

The man glanced behind him, then turned back to Roy, his nostrils flaring. "Come off it, would you? I haven't a clue what you're talking about. Now tell me why I came up here."

Roy parted his lips to sputter the truth, but doing so would only give the man, a decidedly irritable fellow, incentive to use Roy's illusions as bait. No, perhaps he didn't need to confess what he'd seen. He could reshape the narrative, distort the truth to improve his image, but when he closed his mouth, then opened it again, what came out was far beyond what he'd planned.

"I fell over," Roy said.

The man studied him for a long moment, as if he'd heard wrong, then sighed. "You fell over."

"Yes."

"And it was then that you chose to scream like demons were tearing through your chest and break my concentration? Do I have that right?"

Roy refrained from telling him he hadn't been conscious of the man's whereabouts, and therefore unaware that he'd been absorbed in his research. He had an inkling he wouldn't believe Roy. "Is it so hard to imagine that people scream when they're in pain?" he asked, kneading the muscles in his legs, a sore attempt to follow along with his ridiculous story. He debated the merits of telling the truth, but he knew he was too deep into his contrived narrative to raise his hands in defeat now.

"*No*," the man said. "But it *stuns* me that I walked up three staircases to watch you flail on the ground."

Roy was taken aback. How long had the man been standing there? He shook the question off. "I appreciate your efforts, but I didn't need to be saved."

"And *I* appreciate not being interrupted." The man sighed. "We're going in circles here. Look, would you care to exchange more pleasantries, or can I return to my book and, Above willing, some quiet?"

"Listen," Roy said with a tone of quiet command. At this, the man raised his eyebrows. "I apologize if I disturbed your studies. Trust me, I understand the frustration; I'm not so fond of interruptions myself. Perhaps we ought to reattempt this encounter." He lifted his lips into a small smile and extended his hand. "Roy Dawnseve. Pleased to make your acquaintance."

The man blinked, either startled or impressed, then rearranged his expression to its previous frustration. "Ah, *you're* Roy, are you?" he said with theatrical amusement, as if there was supposed to be anyone else in the library. "Well, it appears that old bastard has a wicked sense of humor." He clenched his fist around Roy's fingers, tightened his hold until it felt like iron. "Percival Atherton. Now"—he let go of Roy's hand—"are we done here? I have a long night ahead of me."

Before Roy could think of how to answer, Percival chuckled under his breath, turned to leave, and opened his book.

But something caught Roy's attention. He stood on his toes and peered over Percival's shoulder, scarcely making out a black-and-white sketch accompanied by dense lines of text. The words looked written in a short, hasty hand, as though the author had hurried to jot down the budding spark of an idea before it winked out in their mind. In some places, the ink had faded into stained parchment, lost to the reader's imagination. But despite its state of decay, Roy recognized the book; he had researched this philosopher's oeuvre for years.

"You're reading Razkamun," Roy blurted out.

Percival snapped the book shut and twisted on his feet,

facing Roy. "And you're invading my privacy. For the second time now, too."

"No, you don't understand. I've been working through his bibliography since I first read his thesis, in which he introduces his Warfare-Philosophy Principle. Well, I haven't found *all* his projects, published and otherwise, but I'm certain the Basilica will help with that."

Percival laughed, waving a hand in dismissal. "Have a wander about the library, then. You would learn as much from reading the door signs as you would from Razkamun."

Indignation simmered in Roy's chest, but he refused to let it get the better of him. "I know I disturbed you, but beyond that, I haven't a *clue* what I've done to hurt your feelings. You're being annoyingly excessive."

"Is that so?" Percival smiled. "A spell of reading might ease your agitation. I hear Razkamun is a delightful source of entertainment. *Chaos over Nature* will do. A real jester's handbook, that one."

Roy sneered. He couldn't remember the last time he'd done that. "You're only jealous," he spat.

"Jealous of you?" Percival said, then nodded to the book he was carrying. *Upon Attrition*, Roy guessed by the moss-green binding. "Or jealous of Razkamun for writing a subject that a chipped spoon could understand?"

Roy spluttered. "I would hardly say *that*."

"Yes, *you* might not," Percival agreed, "but anyone with at least a morsel of aptitude and self-respect, such as myself, would've read up enough on Razkamun to know of his madness and of his desperate dependance on philosophy to preserve his sanity. Have you even read his last three projects?" He scoffed. "His brain was so addled with hallucinations, it's undeniable he had the voices in his head write his texts."

"You have no clue what you're saying," Roy repeated.

"No, darling, you're confusing yourself," Percival said. *Darling.* Roy didn't consider himself a violent man, but regardless, he found himself resisting the urge to punch Percival in the mouth. "*Razkamun* hadn't a clue what he was saying. Face the facts, Dawnseve: The man was delusional. A philosopher should never compare war to his own studies. It's unforgivable, it's vile. It's a gross violation of the entire field of study, and despite knowing this, Razkamun was unrepentant in his teachings."

A possessive sense of defensiveness seized Roy. He felt his cheeks heat up, as if he'd struck a match too close to his face. "Your conclusions are baseless. I've read an analysis of his publications. Razkamun was a genius who instituted an entire avenue of philosophical research. Authors in his following generation praised his name."

Percival stiffened for a moment, and Roy thought he'd won the argument, only Percival threw up his hands with exasperation. "For *money*. For fame. For all benefits save for true recognition of academic theory. Those authors wanted nothing more than to rise into glory, to have their own theories eulogized, because *they* once respected a scholar of their previous generation."

"Ah, I see. Did you ask Razkamun personally?"

Percival glared, his right eye twitching. "Well, *no*, but that's irrelevant—"

"His influence spanned generations, Percival," Roy cut in. "That cannot be denied. He quite literally *coerced armies* to perceive war as its own philosophy. 'The drawn sword is to the warrior what the written word is to the scholar.'"

Percival hardened his jaw. "Here's another quote for you. 'The sword is an extension of the warrior's bloodlust. The written word is encouragement to the scholar.'"

Roy combed through his memory but came up empty.

Other than Razkamun, he couldn't think of any philosophers infamous for analyzing the complexities of war. "Who said that?" he asked.

"Me, you *idiot!*" Percival boomed. "War serves no place of honor—damn, no place at *all*—in philosophy. Talk to a scholar who believes otherwise and you've wasted your chance at success."

Under other circumstances, Roy would've felt scolded by this slight, but he was more intrigued than anything else, especially by one nagging detail. "Why are you reading his work, then? If you believe he was a madman."

"There's no *theory* regarding his lunacy," Percival countered. "I read the old-world journal of an administrator at the asylum where he died. He leapt from his balcony; his body shattered on impact."

Roy shook his head, revolted. "That's absurd. He died on his deathbed, surrounded by loved ones." Then again, the critical analysis Roy had read, late at night when the moon was bright and his chest was bleeding after he'd stumbled into Gabriel, was, in retrospect, flimsy, unreliable. The story could've been pulled from the grief-distorted memories of Razkamun's family, then reinterpreted throughout time. History was not always a reflection on a still lake. Sometimes the water rippled.

"So go the rumors—or, rather, the revisionist histories—but the truth is hard, darling," Percival said. He winked. "It looks like you might need to find a new hero."

"Yet I ask again: Why do you continue to read Razkamun?"

Percival ran his fingers through his hair. "I'm never going to escape this hell, am I? Fine. Let me explain. My brain could use a bit of softening." Roy elected to ignore this. "Why have I been slogging my way through Razkamun's work? That's rather simple, frankly: I thought it would hold the answers I'm looking for."

"You're already making headway with the investigation?" Roy asked. "You're studying Razkamun to research the Old Ones?"

Percival slanted his hand from side to side. "Indirectly, yes, I suppose so. I figured that, since the subject matter is well beyond my purview as a philosopher, it may be easier to start with what I know best. I initially avoided Razkamun's work—I've heard the most *baffling* things about the man—but I decided this morning I should probably cover all my bases."

Roy frowned. "That's ... understandable, I guess, but it concerns me that you're more concentrated on your disregard for his fame than what he was famous *for*."

Percival rolled his eyes. "I am *quite* aware of his prolific work ethic and profound success, thank you kindly. But there is a difference between *deserved* success and working diligently solely for the approval of the academic community. The creatives who have endured years of assiduous research, who have isolated themselves for the sheer purpose of developing their projects, are often undermined by those whose projects are meager and weak in comparison. I suppose we might never fully understand their biases, though." A dark melancholy rippled across Percival's face. "Anyway, I've clarified my motive, as you requested. I just wanted to see if he had anything interesting, and worthwhile, to offer. But alas ..."

"There's nothing in there regarding the Old Ones?" Roy nodded to *Upon Attrition*. He couldn't recall any mention of them in Razkamun's work.

Percival glowered. "The Governor might have chained us together, Dawnseve, but you're deeply mistaken if you think I'll show you any of my notations. I work *alone*."

Roy suppressed the anger building in his chest. "The Governor assigned us this task for that very reason: To exchange ideas, to share theories, to understand why the Old Ones came here.

What they want with—or *from*, I should say—Northgard. Did he not stress that to you?"

Percival tilted his head back, displaying the prominent jut of his chin, the shadowed hollow at the base of his throat. The moonlight behind him shifted, dragging a quilt of gloom across his face. He looked at Roy with his tired, dark gold eyes. Time slowed around them, pulling at the space between them, yet neither he nor Roy made a single move.

"You're remarkably brave, darling," Percival said. "Our first encounter, and you've already gotten on my nerves." He sighed, then, once again, turned to leave.

Indecision tore through Roy like a wildfire. Here was his chance, a rare occasion, to conduct research with a fellow scholar, and a passionate one at that. Clearly, Percival was not the most restful soul, but perhaps this might be attributable to his exhaustion. Roy himself had snapped at Briar multiple times on the delirious, sleepless nights he'd devoted to his studies. Once the morning came, and winter's cold sunlight with it, he had no doubt that Percival would be content, if not acquiescent, to study alongside him. Besides, didn't he realize the stakes?

Galvanized by this line of reasoning, Roy called out, "Percival."

Percival stopped, *Upon Attrition* still clutched in his grip. He offered Roy a sharp, impatient nod.

"I *just* spoke to the Governor," Roy said. This caused not the merest flicker of recognition or surprise across Percival's face, though Roy forged on. "He told me about the war, why Northgard and the other islands have been so ruthlessly beaten by the Old Ones. The Edict is growing frail, the Droves' strength is flagging, and . . . Well, leaving a long story short, there's little stopping these soldiers from slaughtering the city. If we don't make a stand, we could be swimming in blood within the next year."

Percival remained silent, but he cocked his head.

Roy continued, "But that's why the Governor summoned us here—to help push back the tide. There must be some way to retaliate. I'm not sure if the Governor thinks it can be done explicitly through research, but if nobody tries, if nobody steps up, the Old Ones will make a wasteland of Northgard. And if there's a chance to prevent that, then we should take it. Then *I* should take it." *Because I've been proven wrong so many times before. Because, if I can do this, then I can prove my worth.*

"Yes, that's wonderful, Roy. I heard the old man say all that to me, too."

They stood there for a moment in silence. The bookshelves stretched tall around them like sleeping wooden sentinels. No sound broke the quiet but for the hushed, ghostly wailing of the wind.

Then a soft whisper came from Percival's lips. "Come closer." He crooked his finger to Roy, who stepped toward him, though he couldn't guess at Percival's intent.

Nevertheless, Roy obeyed. He came closer to Percival, and when Percival kept making that beckoning gesture, closer still. Eventually, he was standing near enough to Percival that his breath danced across Roy's brow, down the curve of his cheek and across his upturned throat like a noose made of softest silk.

Then Percival gripped Roy by the back of his neck, holding him firmly in place, and squeezed. "You will listen to me very carefully, darling. If you approach me again—even to ask where to find a fucking *book*—"

"What will you do?" Roy spat back. "Kill me?"

Percival glared, and to Roy's immense surprise, there shone in his eyes the finest patina of tears. He blinked them away, though he looked more angry than sad. Yet he couldn't force the crack out of his voice when he said, "Leave me be. We're better off on our own."

Roy nodded, and finally, Percival let go. Roy stood there for some time, the echo of Percival's hold lingering like a scar. He hadn't a shadow of a doubt that, come morning, there would be a strain in his neck, something to remember this disastrous, strange encounter by. Already, he could feel the imprints of Percival's fingers and the insistence of his counsel—*Leave me be*—sinking in.

Percival uttered a grunt of resignation. "Go. Just go."

Roy didn't require any further incentive. He left the reading room and, not long after, discovered a hall not far from the bookshelves where he'd been chased by the shadow and found—*saved*, he supposed—by Percival. He wanted to look around more, but he was too tired, his mind too scattered to take in his surroundings.

Instead, Roy opened the door of the first chamber he came across, a heavy weariness pressing into his bones, and trudged toward a four-poster bed. He slipped beneath the soft satin sheets and immediately fell asleep.

A face appeared in his dreams that night. It was blurry but distinctly familiar: short gold hair, a firm mouth, and a pair of stunning hazel eyes. Stunning, yes, but deeply sad, too. Roy tried to unveil the tragedy lurking behind those eyes, like a stagehand pulling back the curtains, and yet every time he stretched out his fingers, it was always just out of his reach.

7

ROY'S SPIRITS HAD LIFTED CONSIDERABLY SINCE the night before.

In his chamber, which contained a chest of drawers sprawling with clothing ensembles—silk button-downs, suit vests, tweed and wool coats, blazers and overcoats—Roy decided on a long tailcoat suit adorned with floral black and scarlet embellishments, strangely tailored to his exact size. He didn't much like the design, but the fabric was far softer than the others he'd browsed and tried on, most of which had scraped against his skin and caused him severe discomfort. It had taken him nearly a half hour of sitting on the side of his bed, his head in his hands, before his unease had worn off. Now he put back on his boots—having retrieved the one he'd left behind during his encounter with the creature—and left his chambers, ravenous for the bread, cheese, and water that the Governor's guards had provided. The rations wouldn't nearly fill Roy's stomach, and studying with a hunger headache didn't sound like a promising start to his investigation.

But when he opened the door to his chamber, there rested at his feet a silver platter covered with a glass cloche—a tiered platter of exotic fruits, dried meats, roasted almonds, fresh strips of lettuce, and a perfectly brewed cup of black tea. He consumed the meal within minutes, curious as to who'd set out the spread.

It certainly couldn't have been Percival; last night's encounter didn't strike Roy as a reason for Percival to gift him food. He would have asked, but Roy's desire to explore the Orphic Basilica won out over his curiosity.

He strode out of his room and roamed about the shelves. He was shuffling from alcove to alcove, hallway to hallway, when he heard the ruffling of paper.

Roy halted. With a hand pressed to his chest, he looked around, intent on tracing the source of the noise. Perhaps it hadn't been paper but wings. Had a bird flown in through an open window? *Were* there any open windows in the Basilica?

A labyrinth of enormous bookshelves sprawled before him. Low-lying tables sat in the middle of each aisle, a lit lamp atop each of their surfaces. Every aisle seemed to tunnel farther into darkness, like the maw of a deep crypt. On the left was a black-wooded archway, which gave out onto a dimly lit reading den. Armchairs rested against the walls, similar to the alcove where Roy had spoken with the Governor, though whereas that chamber had appeared to be designed for casual reading, the den was a high-ceilinged, extensive hall, something a lecturer or professor might have used to address their students. There were two long tables in the middle of the room, overlooked high above by tall arched windows, beyond which somber gray clouds churned and rumbled.

Roy started forward, resting a shaking hand upon the archway, then immediately paused.

Percival was sitting at the end of the table on the right, close to the desktop, his back bent like a question mark. A thick tome lay open before him, along with a brown leather notebook, in which he was recording his thoughts with his left hand. The index finger of his right hand trailed across the reference book, his eyes darting back and forth with intense focus and heightening rapidity.

Roy was spellbound, ensnared by a voyeuristic compulsion to watch Percival, to bear witness as he poised on the brink of discovery and sat back, satisfied, complete. Roy had felt this rush of fulfillment many times before, but for him, there was no reprieve, no breaks or lapse, no bursts of motivation. His brain operated on clockwork consistency, attuned to his constant need for self-approval. There was no one else, after all, from whom he could receive support, no one else to whom he could recite his findings. Maybe Percival shared this same sentiment. It would have made sense, then, why he'd refused Roy's cooperation. Maybe he'd assumed Roy couldn't match his stride and had opted, as Roy had for many years, to work in solitude, the Governor's directives notwithstanding.

Percival bit into his lower lip. He dipped his quill into the half-empty inkwell sitting beside his notebook. With a frustrated sigh, he resumed his studies, a glaze of concentration forming over his eyes.

Roy knew their first meeting hadn't gone spectacularly—far from it—but his circumstances were too good to resist. He could make a connection in his field of study, a link stronger than the correspondents he'd kept in contact with over the years. Perhaps the world would always live in shameless ignorance; he couldn't change that. But he was positive two like-minded scholars were better than one, especially with a task as enormous as this.

Nodding to himself, Roy straightened his spine and knocked on the archway.

Percival didn't lift his head. He didn't even blink, so engrossed was he in his work.

Roy crossed the threshold and wandered over to Percival's side. Once he was standing a few armchairs away, he asked, "Are you still reading Razkamun?"

Percival jolted. His hand lurched to the side, scrawling a jagged line of ink across the page of his notebook and knocking the side of his inkwell. A blot of midnight liquid splashed onto the tabletop, then spread out like crawling rivulets of black blood. The reference book lay unharmed. Percival sat upright, his finger quivering on the opened page.

"You fucking *imbecile*," he spat. His voice was pronounced and full of inflection. He quickly set the inkwell upright before he could lose any more of its contents. "Damn lunatic."

Roy stared, frozen, his cheeks warming from the unswerving weight of Percival's scrutiny. He shook himself from his reverie, then leaned forward and wiped away the spilled ink with the corner of his suit. He moved closer to reach a puddle that had gathered near Percival's notebook, but Percival clasped his wrist, digging the pads of his fingers into Roy's bones.

Clenching his jaw, Roy tried to wrench his wrist out of Percival's hold, but Percival tightened his grip with a warning shake of his head, as if to ensure that Roy didn't misinterpret the gesture. "Don't," he said. "You've gone far enough." There was a rugged edge to his voice, and now that Roy was looking at him directly, he saw why. Deep mauve shadows encircled Percival's foggy eyes, his irises were surrounded by thin veins of blood, and his fair skin was sallow beneath the weak sunlight. Had he even slept since their chance encounter the night before?

"I didn't mean to startle you," Roy said. He cleared his throat. "I was only looking around, but then I heard a noise—"

"If I wanted to hear about your morose, banal life, Dawnseve, I would've asked you to write it down so I could read it at my leisure. Now stop your prattling and leave before I spill this ink over your empty head."

Roy gaped. He searched Percival's expression for a shred of amusement, to no avail. Other than Roy interrupting Percival last night—and it still felt like a stretch that his horror was truly an interruption—there seemed no reason for his mood. And yet that was all moot to the larger issue: that they were meant to work together. Had the Governor planned for this clash of opinions? Pitted them head-to-head in a battle of wills? It would be a swift waste of six months, though, and Roy couldn't see why the Governor would hinge this task on the shoulders of two men possessing opposite comportments. Roy was certain he would not risk his city on a lark.

"I told you," Roy said to Percival, "I didn't mean to startle you."

"And I told *you* to leave me be. You must be experiencing either a bout of idiocy or incomprehension, though judging by how I found you yesterday, I'd guess the former. Shall I show you the door?"

Roy massaged his temples, then blew out an irritated breath. "I know where the door is, I am not an idiot, and I am *quite* capable of listening to instructions—"

"By the love and mercy of—"

"But I appreciate your concern. I just wanted to find where the noise came from." Roy made his voice stern. "That was all."

Percival grinned and spread his arms wide, careful not to rattle the inkwell once again. "Well, lo and behold, you've found it! A study hall, prepared for any scholar's keen attention. Are you quite pleased?"

A sudden flare of agitation came over Roy. His right hand flexed unconsciously. A muscle in his brow twitched. Why was he simply allowing Percival to aggravate him? He needed to defuse Percival's arrogance, but Roy liked to think he had a wise soul, and there was nothing wise about confrontation—a point of counsel he had read in many philosophical texts.

Roy nodded to Percival's book. "Razkamun?"

"I'm fully equipped with the mental capacity to read a book in less than a day. No, thankfully I'm *not* filling my head with that deluded jargon anymore. Although the fact that I'm speaking to you suggests otherwise."

Roy snorted. "Yes, you've made your opinion on my idiocy quite clear. I do appreciate the reminder, though."

Percival gawked, as though he hadn't expected Roy to bite back. He shook his head, then cleared the bewilderment from his face. "No, I'm not reading Razkamun. It's this collection of essays on political manipulation. I'm quite certain it was written by a circle of tittering old nursemaids, as is the case with most of these blasted books, but it holds some fairly decent information."

"I wouldn't be surprised. Nursemaids are fond of gossip."

"It appears so," Percival mused. He inclined his head to the recorded binding of essays. "Arngard's obsession with writing on external affairs, as opposed to the social unrest brewing in the Western Ranges, his homeland, alarms me. Politics is a useful discourse to navigate, so long as you've researched and thus comprehended the harm your stance might pose to your own country. Prioritize the virtues of one's own nation before all others and all that."

"Who is to say Arngard didn't do precisely that?" Roy inquired. He hadn't read Arngard, which, unless he was too in over his head to notice, Percival would infer from Roy's question.

Percival said, "For one, his prose showcases creative talent, I suppose, but the content of his writing itself exhibits a glaring shortage of research, opting for flowery reports over hard, cold logic and evidence, thereby abusing the notion of the importance of opinions in politics. I feel as though I'm reading a fantastical tale, not the history of governing powers."

"Why would you continue reading it, then?"

"Why do I need to explain myself?" Percival shot back . . . only to proceed to do exactly that. "If a scholar leaves a book incomplete, there remains a good chance the answers they seek are within what is left of the text. Hence, if a scholar reads the *entire* book . . ."

"Does that rule not apply to essentially all books in existence? To mirror the structure of your theory: If a scholar leaves *all* books incomplete, there remains a good chance that the answers they seek are within the books they *haven't* read."

Percival scowled. "I have no desire to read *all* books in existence. That would be impossible, not to mention a waste of time. I'm only interested in those whose themes and subjects apply to my own research."

"Correct me if I'm wrong, as I'm sure you will, but topics of discussion often overlap. This can lead to some confusion, sure, but reading every book at your disposal, and there are quite a lot here, would increase the likelihood of finding answers."

"No scholar could possibly read such a vast number of pages in so short a lifetime."

"Thus, my interpretation of your assumption presents itself," Roy said. "Completing all the books you read will never limit your options. It will only lead to the anger of a scholar leagues from the true answers they desire." He smiled, propped one hand on his hip, and put the other behind his ear, his fingers splayed. "Do I hear any points of disagreement?"

Percival narrowed his eyes, then poked Roy hard in the chest. "*Don't* interrupt my reading again," he said, then delved back into his research with a pointedly aggressive flip of the page that seemed to announce the conclusion of their argument.

Wiseass, Roy thought.

Roy's odds at convincing Percival to work with him were not

looking good. He had put his all into his aspirations, sacrificed his own well-being for the expansion of his mind. He had struggled for this, fought tooth and nail, even when it felt as though the city had sharpened all its blades and pointed them at his throat. Now, as he watched Percival settle himself back into his work, Roy could almost hear the drumming thunder of gunfire, the gurgles of dying men, women, and children. The din that preceded doom.

A memory came to Roy then, unbidden: Briar's two-faced carving, gripped between her palms. His kind-hearted sister, her face ashen with yearning and devastation. *What was once war may bring peace*, he had told her, and she had finished, her eyes welling up with tears, *Or war again.*

Roy *could* work alone and abandon his chances of accomplishment and survival. That was a possibility. He could sequester himself away in the shadows of another study hall. He could while away the next six months and wait for death to come to Northgard, for the Radiant Droves to drag him by the collar of his coat to the barracks of the Iron Citadel. He could resign himself to that fate.

But he wasn't a soldier; he was a scholar. He understood—by the Scribes, he *loved*—stringing together theories to articulate an answer, not tearing apart bodies to appease an autocrat. Maybe Percival would never agree to academic collaboration, but if Roy had to take a risk, now was the time to shed his fears and do it.

"Percival," Roy said, pulling out a chair beside him and sitting down.

Percival stiffened, his right hand grasping his quill. He looked askance at Roy, and Roy had to jerk his eyes away from Percival's sensuous lips, parted in a soundless sigh, in fear of losing his focus. Though Percival didn't say a word, he angled his head back, then rotated his hand in a *go-on* gesture.

Gathering the shards of his courage, Roy said, "This assignment is pointless without both of our input. We'll hardly be able to find answers in six months on our own. We..." He ran a hand over his face, then forced himself to look Percival in the eyes. "We need each other, Percival. We need to work together."

ROY WATCHED PERCIVAL'S FACE CAREFULLY FOR A change in his expression, something beyond his customary annoyance. Surely he would unveil his agenda to *some* extent.

Eventually, his narrowed eyes relaxed, then shifted back and forth. He seemed to be sifting through a catalogue of responses, assessing which best suited the situation. Or he was contemplating, depending on their surroundings and the items within his immediate range of movement, the most efficient method of murder. Roy wouldn't have been surprised by either choice.

"And what brings you to that conclusion?" Percival finally asked.

Roy should've known Percival would use some deflective technique, a shield to hide the truth. The past few minutes, and even the previous night, had shown Roy exactly what kind of person Percival was: an arrogant, self-absorbed fool more interested in his own ambitions than common sense and decency. Roy cursed himself for not having seen it before.

As much as he couldn't quell his anger, he also couldn't let Percival's poor excuse for conversational tactics sway him. Percival was *clever*; Roy couldn't deny that. And if he took Percival's verbal attacks too close to heart, then so be it. Roy had endured his brother's fists and knives for years; words were the least of his concerns, or so he told himself.

In some way, this encounter felt more like a battle than the last. Percival was testing Roy's limits to assert himself as the more educated scholar, though Percival was so conceited there was no doubt who he believed would win.

"You take me for a fool," Roy said. "You might even think me beneath your intellect, but I'm well acquainted with the lore and customs of the old world. Yet despite my education, you have declined the opportunity to collaborate with me. I can't see the sense in this; the Governor *specifically* ordered us to work together. The ticking clock is *finite*. So, would you care to elaborate?"

Percival grinned. "Oh, darling, I *would* care, in that I care little for your confusion."

Darling. That name again. Roy dutifully ignored the warm, confusing fluttering in his stomach. "And the part that *does* care?"

"Well, I have to be entertained by *something*, don't I? And I must admit, your curiosity amuses me."

"You didn't seem particularly amused when I was on the ground."

"Your screaming interrupted a perfectly good reading session. I can hardly be blamed for being unenthused."

"'A perfectly good reading session,'" Roy echoed. "Didn't we just discuss your antipathy toward Razkamun?"

"You're confusing a good book with a good reading session. I was content, absorbing line after dull line of text." Percival chuckled. "You can only imagine my utter frustration when I heard your wails."

Roy almost told the truth then—*I wailed, as you say, with good reason*—but instead replied, "You're deflecting my question."

"Am I?" Percival batted his eyelashes. "Oh, dear me, I'm terribly sorry. It must not have been a very good question."

Roy grunted. "This is *ridiculous.*" His voice broke, and shockingly, Percival went still with alarm. "Northgard is on the cusp of war, Percival. The Old Ones are annihilating this city as we speak. *No one* will be ready for the soldiers' full onslaught, not when they haven't a clue what they're facing. And here you are—"

"Gearing up for a little lecture for me, are you?" Percival said, then relented. "Yes, yes, fine. I know all about the war, or rather, all about the fact that we're *at* war."

"And that's why we're here!"

"That's why *you're* here, darling."

Roy was stunned. "You're not here to figure out who the Old Ones are, or why they're in Northgard? You're not reading to figure out how to stop them?"

"I didn't say that. I'm just saying the deal—or threat, I should say—the Governor and I made is not the same as yours. Moreover, I don't entirely buy the premise."

"What premise?"

"The one that says the Governor knows nothing about the Old Ones."

In that, Roy understood Percival perfectly. His own meeting with the Governor had confirmed his suspicions that Northgard's ruler operated on his own agenda, no matter what he might proclaim about defending the people. And the paucity of the information he provided about the Old Ones was now being brought into stark relief with every grating word from Percival's lips.

For fifteen years the Governor has been trying to find information, Roy thought. *And we have six months? There's no math in the world where that adds up. Even though he's not a scholar, surely the Governor must have made some inroads to obtaining intelligence on the Old Ones.*

And the truth was, even the information Roy and Percival had didn't give them much to start with. But perhaps it was a *place* to start.

Swallowing his anger, Roy decided to change tack, to see if he could somehow get Percival back on task. He remembered what Matron Dimestra had told him on their way to the Orphic Basilica. "I assume you know about the Old Ones' positioning, then," he said. "Five units on the southern coast."

Percival barely stifled a yawn. "Yes, yes, they've been posted there for three years."

"You don't seem all too bothered by the notion of war."

"What I'm not bothered by is the math. Most military units are quite similar in size and functionality." Percival drummed his fingers on his notebook. "Northgardian companies never exceed two hundred fifty soldiers. If we're estimating the size of the Old Ones' forces based on that scale, their numbers should amount to a thousand soldiers or so. The Droves number in the tens of thousands."

Roy shook his head. "But, once again, that's the point! You're making assumptions, when we have no clue whether the Old Ones abide by our customs—that's the whole purpose of our assignment! We just can't compare their perception of combat and military structure to our own. Don't you think the Droves have already tried that?"

"I have no faith in anything the Droves think up by themselves."

"Exactly!"

Percival paused. "You've intrigued me. Go on."

Roy took a steadying breath. "Forget the ethos of our own society, the rules of our own civilization. These are inconsequential. We are dealing with a foreign threat now—an *alien* threat—the nature of which we know frighteningly little. Ultimately, the distortions between our two peoples will be stronger than the reflections."

"And you've lost me," Percival said.

It took all of Roy's will not to grind his teeth into dust. "Where did I lose you?"

"War is fought in the same way on both sides of the battlefield, Dawnseve. Perhaps there are some exceptions—for example, their strange armor, which I cannot seem to find any information on in any of these military accounts. But as for their . . . killing methods, if you will, the distinctions are unclear."

"No, they *aren't*," Roy said, almost pleading Percival to see his side of the story, to see a perspective that was not his own. "If you truly believe the Radiant Droves and the Old Ones are utilizing identical battle strategies, then I'm afraid you're wrong. Consider our use of muskets, and the Old Ones' lack—"

"I consider everything, darling. I just don't care all that much about the logistics. The desire and ability to make war do not change from people to people. It's about power. So when I say the Droves and the Old Ones are the same, I mean it. The Droves are a squadron of tyrants dressed in the uniform of freedom fighters. They claim to side with the people of Northgard, but they themselves are the agitators. They might not look the same as the Old Ones, but I assure you, the Droves want war as much as the next army."

"I know they do," Roy said, remembering the female Drove with the bloodshot eyes he'd seen on the ride to the library . . . and the pink spray of brains when she'd cracked open that young boy's skull. He suppressed a shudder. "Civil war is imminent, Percival, I completely agree. But that doesn't mean we should avert our eyes from other threats. In fact, I'd argue that it means we should concentrate *more* on foreign hostilities, especially while we're cornered. And while I hate to agree with the Governor on anything, the Old Ones *won't* stop coming simply because we dislike the Droves. They won't stop coming until we have substantial information on their culture that we can exploit—until we find a way to *stop* them."

"Are you *belittling* me?" Percival exclaimed, sounding baffled. "I'm not *against* you, darling. I'm just trying to understand your stance here."

Roy held up a hand before Percival, his cheeks heated, his eyes wide, somehow frustrated and embarrassed at the same time. Ultimately the more timid part of him won out, and he found himself apologizing rather than asking why in the Above Percival was arguing with him if they agreed. "That wasn't a direct comment about *you*. I'm sure you're capable of figuring this out; I'm just . . ." Roy sighed, defeated. "I'm suggesting you—*we*—take the right approach."

"I *was* taking the right approach, but your interruptions continue to pull me away from my studies," Percival said, but there was no curtness in his voice now. He looked uncertain, nearly regretful of his past incivility.

Nearly.

Yet Roy was happy with any window of opportunity, and so he took advantage of Percival's lowered shield, not caring whether he caught Roy out on it. "Drop these pretenses, then, Percival," he said. "We must face the facts. You and I are the principal players in a game far larger than we anticipated. We were put on the game board and now we must make our move. The Old Ones have the answers, not us, but we have a lead. We have the library."

Roy truly believed this. There was no doubt the Orphic Basilica harbored thousands of years' worth of knowledge and that somewhere in here *must* be a way to at least understand the Old

Ones, if not outright defeat them. The trouble was that Roy was at a loss as to where he should start. Even the library's reputation confounded him. As he had seen when he wandered along its shelves yesterday, before he'd been chased by the ghost, there seemed to be no categorization system, no placards or labels to guide him around the maze of randomly assorted genres and topics. Every time he started to think he was close to discovery, something held him back; whether external or internal, he didn't know for sure. Maybe both. Maybe, in the deepest corners of his mind, he hadn't yet fully submerged himself in his research beyond perusing the bookshelves because he'd been waiting for Percival to concede, to give up his baffling moral code and unfathomable disinclination to assist Roy and instead help him sort through the mess. But either way, this was not going to be an easy task, and the feeling that the library was actively working to make it a *difficult* task wasn't lost on him.

He didn't need Percival adding to the obstacles and thus preventing him from finding an answer.

"Maybe I'm hoping for too much," Roy said, "but we would be foolish not to capitalize on this opportunity."

"I *am* capitalizing on this opportunity."

"But only for yourself!" Roy bit back.

"I'm not *working* with you; I thought I made that clear," Percival said, his expression a mixture of confusion and annoyance. Roy's heart plummeted into his stomach. "Don't you see, darling? We would only fight. We would only get in each other's way. Now be a dear and get out of mine." With that, he gathered his books, pushed the inkwell to the middle of the desk, stood up, and then stalked away.

Like a storm dousing a torch, Percival had snuffed out Roy's hopes. Roy had become so enraptured by the idea that he might actually convince Percival that he hadn't prepared for his rejection. He understood Percival's reluctance, but if they could only talk through their differences and see where, or if, their ideas might intersect, maybe they could be compatible. Even if it was not meant to be, it would have been worth a try.

That dream, though, was rapidly becoming a diminishing figure as Percival walked away.

Fear closed in over Roy's head like an oncoming tide. Faces flashed before his eyes: the Governor, the Matron, Briar . . . and the confined, winter-stricken city of Northgard.

Just then, Percival twirled about and marched toward him in a purposeful stride, hurling Roy back into reality. His deafening footsteps clanged through Roy's head. As Percival drew closer, his face glowing in the golden lamplight, he threw his books to the side, where they dropped to the ground with a booming thud.

Even as Percival clutched the front of his tailcoat, Roy stood firm. A gasp fled his lips, loud amidst the uncanny quiet. He closed his eyes. A long breath whispered across his parted lips. Warmth fluttered through the length of his body. He leaned into the heat, unable to draw himself away from the temptation. He could feel Percival's fingers brushing across his tunic and, as he took in a deep, uneven breath, Percival's heart beating frantically against his own.

Roy might have been in a dream, back in the dream he'd had last night of Percival's veiled hazel eyes, were it not for the clear and rational topography of the waking world. A hand shifted Roy's face to the side, and as a coil of warm breath skittered along his flushed cheeks, Percival whispered into his ear, "You should've paid better attention to me."

Roy opened his eyes.

Percival was standing right before him, his left boot pressing against the toe of Roy's right. Silver moonlight shone upon his high cheekbones, bathing the crown of his head in a glowing nimbus. He was gorgeous, a perfect graven image of timeless beauty. Roy didn't try to extract himself from Percival's grip. He knew it would be but a useless endeavor. And besides, he wasn't entirely sure he wanted to.

"*This* is the game," Percival said, nodding to his white-knuckled clasp on Roy's tailcoat. "*This* is the battle." His voice quickened. "I don't care for the war raging outside these walls. This island is going to fall, whether its people fight or surrender. The history of the enemy is insignificant."

"Then why are you here?" Roy spat, unable to keep his voice from trembling. "What the Hell are you fighting for?"

"Did you know you're one of the few scholars I've met?" Percival said. "And if you're here, then that means either you were ratted out or the Governor found out your treachery by himself. There's no in-between. But unlike you, Dawnseve, I'm unconcerned with being a principal player. And frankly, the fact that you think you're as important as that is downright laughable. What I want is to *beat* you, to root out the truth before you do, and if you're wise, you'll let me." He released his hold on Roy, though only to smooth the wrinkles rumpling his coat. "But something tells me you won't."

When he stepped back, Roy had half a mind to pull him back in—to do what, though, he did not permit himself to imagine. "You're mad," he muttered.

"Maybe," Percival said with a grin, shrugging. "But as I said, this is a game. And, darling, there is nothing I love more than winning."

A LITTLE LATER, WHILE HE WAS CONSUMING A LIGHT lunch of bread and cheese, Roy mulled over Percival's parting words from their encounter earlier that morning. He had tried reading for his own leisure to occupy himself, vaguely aware that he was procrastinating making headway on what he'd hoped to be his first full day of research, but he couldn't get Percival's voice out of his head. *But as I said, this is a game. And, darling, there is nothing I love more than winning.*

A game? What game? Roy thought, his confusion compounded by the memory of Percival grabbing him by his tailcoat and pulling him close when he'd mentioned this undefined competition, but perhaps that had been part of it—a distraction tactic. If that was Percival's current strategy, it might work temporarily, as Roy couldn't deny his voice had shaken when Percival had drawn him close, but Percival would quickly be proven wrong if he believed Roy would remain forever under his spell.

Roy couldn't puzzle it out. He had assumed, from the get-go, that Percival was competitive. He had essentially bragged about his knowledge of Northgard's military units and Razkamun's bibliography, and his overt reluctance to explain why he'd been studying the latter irritated Roy. But why had Percival marked him as an opponent? He'd mentioned only having met a few scholars, so maybe he *was* merely excited by the idea of cracking open the truth of the Old Ones before Roy got there... But why? What about Roy had struck such a nerve for Percival? Even that didn't really matter, though. Because as much as he welcomed the chance to prove himself to the arrogant young man, he was also fairly certain Percival had come up with nothing pertaining to the Old Ones thus far, either.

Which meant neither one of them was winning as far as he was concerned.

Once he finished his lunch, Roy finally shook off these thoughts and worked up the willpower to resume his studies. He found a reading den on the sixth floor—identical to the room where he'd argued with Percival—and browsed the bookshelves there. A hint of gray light filtered through the windows, and by its weak glow, he made out a diversity of manuscripts, from a romantic epic—*Arusvkia*—to a poem composed entirely of intricate hieroglyphs and swooping letters. This medley of literature looked like the stuff of alchemy captured on vellum and parchment and leather, and somehow, he was supposed to turn this lead into gold.

A burst of joy spread through him. Perhaps he ought to move to a southern bedchamber; like this chamber, it would provide some light. Only a little, yes, but that was more than what the rest of the Basilica offered. Moreover, even with some of his frustrations, he couldn't deny the surge of motivation that had greeted him as he'd crossed the threshold of this chamber. The momentary gloom that had descended upon the Orphic Basilica when he'd looked down upon the lower floors from above, escorted by Dimestra and Evan, no longer seemed to hold sway. *Had* that been an illusion, as he'd then suspected? A brief trick of the light?

After what he had intended to be a few minutes—but what

ended up being an hour—of perusing the books around him, slightly panicked and overwhelmed by the clutter but unsure how to go about cleaning it, Roy selected Louise Tungess's *Tracing Back the Past*, a memoir about cycles of history. Then a loud thud sounded from the back of the room. He jumped and whirled around to investigate the noise, half fearing that the shadowy apparition would emerge, poised to attack.

But it was Percival, his notebook, the same Roy had nearly gotten ink spilled over, tucked under his arm. "Ah, it's you." He ducked his head and squinted, peering at the cover of Roy's book. "It's rather early for Tungess, no? Her choice of subject matter is brave, sure, but the delivery of her research leaves scant room for imagination."

Roy looked back down at his book and muttered, "What are you doing here, Percival?"

Percival strolled over and dropped his notebook on Roy's desk. "And a wonderful morning to you also." He looked around with faint disapproval: the loose papers scattered atop teetering stacks of manuscripts, the pages curled from the meager sunlight and marked with the scribbled annotations of bygone scholars and theorists; the slender path of walking space between the piles, barely enough to shuffle past. At a second glance, Roy couldn't fathom how he'd maneuvered through the area. "Dawnseve, tell me you didn't . . . you didn't *sleep* in this clutter. Did you?"

Roy scoffed. "Of course not. I'd like to think I have *some* self-respect." He *had*, however, been having trouble moving documents around into some semblance of order, which had caused him considerable distress.

Percival bunched his lips to the side. "Yes, I suppose you would, wouldn't you? Well, if you ever *do* decide to doze off here,

I suggest trying a pillow. These books don't look awfully comfortable."

A smile tried to crawl its way onto Roy's lips, but he willed it away. He had to keep his composure, never mind how loyal Percival seemed in his plans to distract him. "Stop stalling, Percival. What are you doing here? Does this have to do with your so-called game? Do you want to keep an eye on my progress or something? And what *is* this game? Is it just a race? Is there a reward of some sort? Because if all you want out of this is to provoke me, then a competition is hardly necessary."

"Which of your myriad questions should I start with?" Percival laughed. "Have you completely forgotten everything I told you last night? I know I'm endearing, but I didn't think you were *that* doe-eyed."

Roy snorted. At least his theory about Percival's diversion tactic was correct.

Percival continued, "Yes, darling, since you want it simply put, that's the point of the game. We're racing against one another for answers."

"*Game*," Roy echoed, only now realizing how childish it all sounded. "Look, I see why you're frustrated by our differences, and why they might be a hindrance to the task, but frankly it seems absurd to me to throw away such a rare chance of collaboration simply because you felt discouraged by one brief, unexpectedly hostile interaction—if that's even what you're suggesting! Is that how you deal with most things in life? Twist them into some cruel form of entertainment and make a statement of them?"

A muscle twitched in Percival's jaw, but otherwise, he looked unfazed by Roy's remark. "Again—so many questions. Our differences are greater than you think, Dawnseve. I see the signs, as I have seen them in the past. Working together will not end well." His voice hardened. "Don't overcomplicate the situation. The rules are simple: We'll leave one another to our own devices, and whoever first discovers the truth to the Old Ones—"

"What, exactly, would be a more satisfying award than credit?" Roy interjected. "With *both* of our names attached?"

Percival blinked, amazed, then gave a small, incredulous laugh. "Credit? Roy, you yourself came to me and lectured me about the gravity of Northgard's situation. We weren't assigned this task because of our field of study, nor will we be rewarded for our efforts. The Governor can't understand what we have taught ourselves. He turned to *us* to decode the Old Ones' origins, then report back with our findings." He scoffed. "And here you are, talking about 'credit' as though the Governor could possibly care whose name is on a piece of paper only he will read. Is this just to persuade me? To get me onto your side? Well, if so, let me disabuse you of that notion. And if not, let me remind you: This is about *survival*, Dawnseve, pure and simple—as much yours and mine as the city's as a whole."

There are more of our kind than the two of us, Roy wanted to spit back. *Surely someone will discover our research. We could still be remembered, immortalized.*

Roy bit down on his back teeth, disgruntled. "My proposition still stands. We can overlook the variances in our research styles, combine them, and, using them, stop the Old Ones and prevent Northgard from falling into ruin. It's that simple." It didn't elude Roy that this was as simple as it would get—convincing Percival to view this assignment as a joint project—and that the hard part would be actually doing the research and somehow applying their united differences to their work.

He didn't think sharing this would help his argument, though, so he kept quiet.

"I am not your colleague, Dawnseve," Percival said, his voice firm. "I see a fire in you, sure; I saw it the moment I first saw you. But that's why I'm certain we would work better as opponents than as partners, why an alliance would break apart as soon as it's been forged. Because even if we would not last as allies, I'm still fascinated by you. To deny that would be irrational, and of all principles explored in philosophy, I am most drawn to rationality. It stands to reason that we will interact and cross paths, but just not as you'd hoped. I'm beginning to understand you, but I . . . I need more time."

"What's there to understand, Percival?" Roy asked. He tried not to read too deeply into Percival's words, but he also couldn't distinguish whether what he felt from them was anger or a confused sort of admiration. There *was* something there, to be sure; he just couldn't make it out, either. "I want to stop this war from spreading beyond Northgard, I want to find out who the Old Ones are, and I want to use the Basilica to do it. This place is an opportunity to learn more than we could've possibly imagined. That's all you need to know, isn't it? What would your game prove that the Governor's assignment wouldn't?"

Percival shook his head, either glum or disappointed. "You're looking through the wrong pair of eyes, darling. We were given an opportunity, yes, but that shouldn't mean we can't set some of the rules. He gave us six months, but maybe the deciding winner shouldn't be judged within a span of time but by *proof*. A demonstration of their findings."

"This is stupid," Roy said. "This is utterly impractical. Apart from our not knowing when the Old Ones will decimate Northgard, which could be a matter of weeks, not months, I think it's ludicrous you've completely discarded the arrangements originally set out for us. It's hard to come to terms with, I know, but the Governor—"

"The Governor doesn't know what's best for us," Percival cut in. "He doesn't know what is in our best interest because he's too preoccupied with his own motivations. Sure, we might get this done ahead of schedule, but I would rather use the . . . bond, for a lack of a better term, that we've made as momentum than the fear of extinction. I work best when I am hated, not when I am doomed to die."

"I don't hate you," Roy said, frowning. "I have no reason to."

Percival smiled, but it was cold and dismal. "Give it time, darling."

Roy shifted the conversation back to the topic at hand. "So, you want us to compete in a race. *That's* what this game is?"

Percival shrugged. "I suppose so, yes, but anyone can claim they're a scholar without irrefutable proof of their dedication." He mulled this over for a moment. "What about this? Whichever of us first unmasks the Old Ones shall display their findings, with indubitable evidence, in a practical demonstration. That way, there'll be no question as to who the winner is." Roy's face must have betrayed his suspicion, for Percival poked him in the sternum and said, "Conceding defeat before the game has even begun, are you?"

"No," Roy said, a tad too austere. "No, it's only . . . What would this demonstration entail?"

"Whatever befits the winner's conclusion, but that's not nearly as important as ensuring the opponent *believes* the research explained in the demonstration. Which is to say, of course, that this game caters not to liars but to the strong-minded. A battle of wills."

From somewhere deep within himself, Roy mustered the courage to smile. "Strong-minded, am I?"

Percival rolled his eyes and rubbed the back of his neck with apparent nonchalance, but his cheeks were burning red. "You're missing my point."

While Percival cleared the frazzled expression from his face, Roy deliberated upon the proposal offered to him. Two propositions in as many days, he thought, yet this one seemed somehow more intrinsically tied to his sense of identity than the Governor's assignment. *This is what I wanted,* Roy thought. *To prove my worth... But to Percival? Why would I need his approval?*

Although Roy knew he would never find it in himself to care for Percival—apart from, maybe, the fleeting flares of attraction his irritatingly striking looks induced—Roy could not repudiate his deeper curiosities. What could Percival *possibly* gain from this "race," as he called it? Had there been some ultimatum in the Governor's proposition that Percival was deliberately keeping from Roy? Or was he simply *this* obnoxious, *this* starved for attention and validation?

Roy doubted it. Gabriel had chosen Roy as his victim because he was weak, helpless, a flailing, brittle-winged bird whose dream to fly out of its cage was as lackluster as its ability to retaliate. Roy had shown none of the physical attributes that Gabriel had attained over the course of his twenty-seven years, and he'd been beaten and bloodied for it. Percival might not be so cruel as that, but from experience alone, the only guess Roy could hazard as to why this game was so crucial to Percival was that he wanted something from him.

"I don't know if this is what I want," Roy said now, and again, hoping it would cement his uncertainty: "I don't *know.* I like burying myself under books, not pressure. We have already bent to the Governor's whims. Why add to the weight?"

"Oh, don't *fight* it, darling," Percival said with tired but not dispassionate exasperation. He sounded like they'd had this argument many times before. "I know you like the craving. I know you long for that rush you get when you're fighting for something you love. Hell, isn't that why you're here? That's what led *me* here, at any rate. A chance to use what I know best, rather than scrabble for freedom in a city where my existence means *nothing*." His voice did not break, but it came quite close. Roy flexed his hands, fighting the compulsion to reach out for Percival. "*That's* what this little game between us is about, Dawnseve. You can try to hide it, but that fire in you will never die out."

Roy tensed, wanting with all the half-spent strength in his voice to express his denial, to show Percival's claims were unsubstantiated, but as Roy thought it over, his convictions were not altogether wrong. Somehow, Percival *saw* Roy. He knew what he felt, as bone-shakingly frightening as it was to admit, because it was exactly what Percival had experienced in the reading den on their first day in the Orphic Basilica, exactly what Northgard had dissuaded them from feeling: the fire of determination, ignited by academia. But although Roy and Percival were like-minded, their motivations were far from adjacent. Percival might've even initiated this game to feed his own ego, though Roy suspected that there was something else there inside Percival, a stolen part of himself that he hoped, through this assignment, he could reclaim.

"You can feel it, can't you?" Percival said. "I know you can. The Elder Scribes held that same flame in their souls. It was what moved them, *pushed* them toward the finish line of every novel, every thesis, every report and article and letter." He shook his head, his features tender and morose. "Darling, it was never about the obscurities, not the connotations or the contextual background. It was about *ambition*."

Percival's verdict held water. Around two millennia ago—in

the middle of the old world, a period of literary enlightenment—Northgard hadn't yet possessed the military strength to quash the academic community. But as the years passed, Northgard, the Northgard Roy had grown up in, gained the upper hand. They built war machines, ranging from vessels to explosives and, eventually, muskets. They went on weeks-long gruesome campaigns to weed out, publicly condemn, and then eviscerate as many scholars as their weapons could harm. According to a variety of historical reports Roy had found in Dawnseve Manor, those whose mythical beliefs hadn't been deeply entrenched had been brainwashed by the Radiant Droves, though the details of these brutal practices were undisclosed. Then, fifteen years ago, the Governor instituted a systematic raiding and purging of the havens to which those scholars had once flocked.

"Northgard destroyed every single establishment within the Hasdan Isles in which literature was praised," Percival said, as if to confirm Roy's historical musings. He looked around the room, then back to Roy. "Only this remains. If you ask me, our higher powers were *frightened* by the impact that scholars might have on their government because the Governor and his precious allies were so worried for their own survival, their own *lives*, that they spared no time to consider the people they're supposed to protect. Now what are we?"

Roy whispered, "Ostracized."

"*Condemned.*" Percival nodded, licking his lips. "We are shunned, mocked, and, at the end of the day, killed for what we believe in, for what we think is right. We hide in our holes, hope our secret correspondence isn't with one of the Governor's agents"—Roy swallowed at this—"and eke out the existence of our minds. But we can't help it, can we? Our ambition is our downfall. We don't have the privilege to avoid responsibility. Damn, nobody does in this world anymore, but unlike the rest of

Northgard, we aren't *fighters*." He scoffed. "We aren't meant to be on the battlefield. How can we go on like this, Dawnseve? Who would we be if we didn't defend ourselves? I don't want to find out. I'll give this life, this legacy I made for myself . . . I'll give it my all. I'll make myself heard, loud and clear, just to know that the Governor *sees* his blunder, where he was at fault for destroying all those precious books. All those precious *minds*." There was such misery in his eyes that Roy felt a chill. "I need it. Don't you? Or are you satisfied with this life?"

Roy inhaled deeply. He feared, for a split second, that he might smell remnant wisps of smoke from the burnings, orchestrated when he was only ten, on the day of reckoning when the Governor had dispatched a squadron of Droves across the archipelago to immolate the archives throughout the Hasdan Isles. Cold terror laced through Roy's bones at the grim reminder of Northgard's barbaric crimes, all committed before the construction of the Edict of Containment.

"I do," Roy whispered. "I need it more than I thought I did."

"*Nobody* could protest those burnings, Roy," Percival said softly. He shifted his gaze away, but before he could, Roy glimpsed the tears shining in his eyes. "Granted, there were more scholars then, but they knew any attempt at rebellion would be transient. Even if they'd had access to weapons, they were *creatives;* they didn't fight, just like the Elder Scribes."

Roy recalled an account he'd discreetly gotten ahold of, passed through several of his correspondents—Clive Lortan's *Neither Sword Nor Shield,* a historical analytical essay on the Elder Scribes' code of nonviolence. "'Although schisms of faith and opinion are inevitable within a community, it must be noted that the Elder Scribes, and their disciples, all stood firm on this: Neither sword nor shield were they to wield.'"

Percival gave a slow, sad nod. "So too did the scholars of fifteen years ago adhere to this code, paying respect to the ancients. They watched—*we* watched—as the world that we had come to love, and all whom we loved in it, burned. Some of us died in the wreckage; some years later from the smoke caught in their lungs. Both fared better than the survivors."

Against his best wishes, Roy's harrowing memories of the burnings reared up before his mind's eye like a nightmare augury in some dark sorcerer's crystal ball: parchment pages scattered on bloodstained streets; students and artists and highbrow classicists kneeling before bookshops engulfed in flame; years upon years of accumulated research, turned to ash after days of endless fire.

And now, Roy thought, *Northgard has fallen victim to a similar fate.*

He remembered the military reports from Matron Dimestra's meetings with her soldiers. After storming Northgard's southern coast three years ago, the Old Ones had set upon the city in a blazing warpath, tearing towns asunder, scorching noble manors to piles of debris, butchering civilians, infant and grown and elderly, without mercy or reason.

Roy despised the higher powers of Northgard, sometimes so fiercely he could barely breathe, but if the Old Ones laid waste to this city, the guilt—which his mission had made Roy responsible for carrying—would be insurmountable. He dared to imagine the outcome, and when he did, he thought of the rubble in the wake of war, the scholars trapped within it, choking on the ashes of their own, waiting for a respite, however temporary, so that they might fight back.

He couldn't turn on them. How could he? Such a betrayal would make him just as bad, just as *monstrous*, as the governing bodies of Northgard. The dream seemed vague from even its best angle, but it was all he had.

"If there are barely any of us left, if we're at a loss as to how to rebuild this shattered community, then how did the Basilica survive those dark, awful days?" Percival asked, breaking into Roy's thoughts. "How can it still stand, after everything its dissenters did to tear it down?" He shook his head. "It's a mystery. When the Droves attempted to burn it down, it was as though some invisible wind blew out their torches. They were out there in the storm for *days*, trying to strike a spark, a single ember, but . . . nothing." He looked at the floor, an introspective expression on his face. "The Governor told me some of the Droves vowed they were accosted by the dead—departed relatives, lovers, friends. One saw his mother, who had been killed by the Old Ones, and later blew a hole in the side of his head on the ride back to the Iron Citadel. It's utterly bizarre."

It was more than bizarre, Roy thought; it transcended coincidence. But then again, he had seen and sensed evidence of the Orphic Basilica's otherworldliness. Even from his short time here, it was clear that this library wasn't just a collection; it was a phenomenon, as ethereal and dazzling as sunlight after years of darkness—a darkness which seemed ever-present since the storm had begun. There had been a shift in the air the first time he stepped inside, a transference of power from the Basilica's soul to his own.

Maybe Percival was right. This library might just be unlike any other. It had certainly shaken Roy to his core, for he wasn't a believer of superstitions. He trusted his instincts and cold, hard logic . . . but he also couldn't stop thinking of the creature that had chased him that first day. A shadow? A ghost? Whatever it had been, there was no point denying what he had seen with his own eyes, and the one thing that had truly shifted in his life, that had granted him a new and tantalizing perspective, was undoubtedly his entrance into the Orphic Basilica.

What he didn't quite understand, though, was why Percival was bringing this up . . . unless he, too, had experienced something similar—something that set scholars apart and connected them to this building that defied so much logic.

"I might sound mad," Roy said tentatively, testing out this theory, "but when I first came here, I felt . . . I don't know how to describe it."

"Voices," Percival suggested. "You didn't *hear* voices; you *felt* the vibrations of voices, not as the Governor and his Droves did but rather . . . You *sensed* that someone was speaking to you."

"Yes," Roy said, satisfied to hear someone else verify his conflicted thoughts. "Yes! That's *exactly* it."

Percival nodded. "I think someone was trying to communicate with us but they couldn't, for whatever reason. An obstacle was in the way, perhaps, a barrier between where we are and wherever they are."

Again, Roy's flight through the bookshelves flashed before him. The creature had followed him, a bright light flooding his vision . . . and then he'd been assailed by a cacophony of anguished cries.

Now that he thought on it, though, something had held back the full brunt of the voices, not unlike the Basilica's thick-glassed windows muting the roar of the storm. As for the creature itself, Roy was hesitant to confide in Percival. He'd admitted to believing in the voices, but would Percival accept the actual presence of another being? He had said this was all a game to him—so what if he was goading Roy, baiting him to confess what he'd truly seen, only to deem Roy insane? Just as he'd thought of Razkamun.

So he decided to probe Percival's original thesis, rather than risk being discounted just yet. "How does this have anything to do with the Old Ones?" Roy asked.

Percival rubbed his temples. "I'm not so sure that it does. Everything's so disconnected it's hard to even make an educated guess."

His chest tightening, Roy chose his next words carefully. "What would you do about it? How might you solidify your assumptions into something substantial, something you could, theoretically, work with?"

Percival sighed. "Well, that's the issue, isn't it? Because any good theory necessitates a good foundation, yet I've made no progress on acquiring any historical records pertaining to the Old Ones. And while we've both found research material"—he jerked his chin to *Tracing Back the Past*—"unless I'm mistaken on your behalf, thus far no direct, let alone oblique, correlations have presented themselves."

"So?"

"*So*," Percival said, "maybe it isn't the *books* within the Basilica waiting to be found. It could be, and bear with me here, the library itself. Oh, don't give me that look, Dawnseve. We've established we felt something when we walked through the front doors. This place is trying to tell us something. Something it has hidden from those it cannot trust."

A feeble spark of hope rose in Roy, and yet he felt he *had* to push back, to make Percival be the one to say what he was so afraid to voice out loud. "The Orphic Basilica isn't . . . It isn't *alive*—"

A bright, stark lucidity swam across Percival's features. He had the look of a man whose purpose in life has suddenly been revealed to him. "Well, why wouldn't it be? Have you ever considered *why* the Basilica couldn't be burned down? Maybe someone was protecting it, yes, or maybe it was protecting *itself*."

"Fine," Roy said. "But then can you explain to me, Percival, why it won't openly communicate with *us*? Can you explain why, when two scholars wander through the library's doors after *years* of neglect, it refuses to show its secrets to us, those it's supposedly meant to trust?" He had meant to sound sarcastic, but as the question left his mouth, he realized he was genuinely curious.

"It's scared," Percival muttered. "It doesn't *want* to place its trust in anyone else. Would you, after being hated, denigrated—*abused*—so viciously?"

Abused. Roy swallowed at that word, keenly conscious of his scar. "That's . . . definitely something to consider." He sighed. "Regardless, we're here so that we can avoid war, not unearth some great magical revelation. A revelation, mind you, that is based on nothing but conjecture." Again, these words didn't ring true.

"Is it really conjecture, or are you just afraid?" Percival shook his head. "I'm beginning to think our game is forfeit, considering I'm more mentally equipped for this task."

"Your constant resorting to idiocy as a subject of ridicule is childish," Roy said. He rose to his feet and began to peruse the room for another book, preferably something connected to the actual topic they'd been allocated. As much as he'd wanted to discuss the creature, he was certain that was a topic that would lead nowhere and take up time they didn't have. If the library was alive, if there were ghosts, they weren't helping him, and Percival pursuing this line of thought wasn't doing much good, either.

"It probably is, but it's also the truth," Percival said. "As is the fact that . . . Well, you're a good person, darling, I know you are. And that's why I can't work with you. Because if I do, then I'll use everything in my power to change you into someone you're not."

"Change me?" Roy repeated, turning to Percival, his pulse thumping rapidly against the undersides of his wrists. "What are you *talking* about?"

Percival crossed the distance between them, his stride slow, and rested his hand over Roy's heart. He looked at the area of contact, more intimate than it ought to be, then at Roy. "The game, Roy. *Ambition.* All I'm doing is giving you an opportunity. Would you rather take one from a tyrant who doesn't give a damn . . . or from a fellow student of the arts, someone who knows what you've been through, what you feel?"

Roy stood straight, his obdurate foot-dragging vanquished by a sense of noble determination. He couldn't quite pinpoint what had overcome his stubbornness. Percival's voice? His confidence? Whatever it was, a measure of that same recklessness now flowed through Roy, and so he lifted his clammy hand and placed it atop Percival's, which still lay on Roy's heart.

Around and between them, a wind rose, swirling and moaning. Everything took on an eerie gray cast. The reading room grew dim, the darkness of gathered thunderheads pressing against the windows. The breeze gained strength, augmented by something greater than they could both fathom, a force more enigmatic than human.

In his panic, Roy grounded himself with the variables presently before him, what he'd divined from this conversation with Percival. The more he thought on it, though, the simpler it was.

Percival wanted retribution for the freedom and independence which he'd been denied. If he thought magic was the answer, then so be it—let him travel down that strange road by himself. Roy wanted acknowledgement of his value to society, something Northgard would forever despise him for pursuing, something with which his memories of Gabriel would forever taunt him. He was now more and more certain he could find that sense of value on his own by doing what he'd always done: digging deep into the texts until the truth emerged.

"I accept," Roy said before he could change his mind. "We'll each go about this investigation in our own way. The first to discover the Old Ones' identity and plans, along with incontrovertible evidence to support their findings, will be awarded complete academic credit for the breakthrough." Before Percival could interrupt, likely to reiterate the triviality of credit in a city bent on eradicating scholarship, Roy added, "*Someone* is bound to read what we've discovered. Years ahead of us, yes, but that slim hope is what I'm banking on. And I know some small piece of you wants that, too. Don't we all?"

Percival regarded Roy for a moment, then nodded with resignation. "And as for the losing participant?"

"Their fate shall be decided by the Governor upon his return to the Basilica," Roy said. Where this ambiguous penalty had come from, he was not sure.

"Well, then"—Percival disentangled their fingers, turned his hand around, and then locked his fingers around Roy's slim wrist, pressing his hand to his hammering heart—"let the game begin."

10

REGARDLESS OF HIS FAILED ATTEMPT TO COERCE Percival into a partnership, and then his consenting to Percival's game—an incident which Roy wasn't particularly proud of—he was still hopeful about the investigation. He might be without assistance, but it wasn't as though he was some novice. He had dedicated his life to uncovering truths, and the Orphic Basilica would be no different.

He hoped.

Roy's first solitary exploration of the library, this time as an active participant in an academic trial, began with the hallway outside his bedchamber. An assortment of framed pieces lined the walls, illuminated by the torches regularly placed in brass sconces. These artworks were predominantly paintings—family portraits, garden landscapes, and abstract pieces.

He walked farther down the hallway, though nothing of interest leapt out at him. Nothing indicated a history of the library or its secrets. While his focus *should* remain exclusively on the Old Ones, it seemed ever more important—perhaps, in part, because of Percival's increasingly adamant superstitions—that Roy should understand this arcane relic. He would study the *building*, not the books.

As he approached the end of the hallway and came to three rows full of bookshelves, however, he couldn't resist his greedy impulses. He felt nowhere near as foggy as he had the other day. His thoughts were no longer fuzzy from sleep. And as the wind let out a muffled howl, like the growl of a muzzled hound, Roy strode on, anticipation curling down his spine. He didn't know where to begin, nor which author to start his aimless adventure with.

Roy was about to continue his exploration when he was struck by an epiphany. What if he started with what he knew best? He thought back to when Percival had scolded him for reading Razkamun, for appreciating and idolizing the philosopher's views. *A philosopher should never compare war to his own studies*, Percival had said to Roy. *It's unforgivable, it's vile. It's a gross violation of the entire field of study...*

Be that as it may, Percival had mentioned that he had begun the investigation by concentrating on philosophy, which was also Roy's own area of interest. He wasn't planning to revert to philosophy to chip away at the mystery of the Old Ones, however; he simply needed to locate a point of access. He wouldn't force himself through a wall of research; he would instead climb his way over, using the knowledge he'd acquired. Contrary to popular belief—that being of his brother and mother—years of ravenously absorbing information hadn't taught him nothing.

As if confirming his mission, Roy quickened his pace until he came upon a sprawl of bookshelves stretching much farther than his naked eye could see. They stretched on for days' worth of exploration. The Governor hadn't lied; without Percival's assistance, Roy could easily picture himself getting lost in the stacks. The redwood bookshelves looked about fifteen feet tall, the upper heights backlit by an unseen source of illumination.

The shelves were crammed end to end with every manner of literature, some titles even wedged horizontally atop the vertical volumes. There were parchment scrolls, vellum tomes, bundles of loose-leaf documents bound with twine then bound together again in a larger bundle, and glass cabinets, stored within which were loose sheets of paper propped on gold and brass pedestals. Several handwritten declarations of academic accomplishments were pinned to the ends of each shelf. One read, *The Protectorate of the Elder Scribes, and of the Orphic Basilica, proudly grants MAUDE CHASILE, student and apprentice of ATTICUS WALESTONE, a fully sponsored scholarship to study at a college of her choosing.* On another shelf was a monstrously large book, its pages clasped with a black lock shaped like a pair of huge teeth.

Roy rounded a corner and started forward into the next aisle of bookshelves, his eyes scanning each spine. After a few minutes, he grinned and swept *Nexus*, an enormous brown leather-bound book just short of a thousand pages, from its placement and into his hands.

Penned by Tarnan Eldreave, one of the Elder Scribes, *Nexus* detailed the objectives of human connection and the reasons behind mental conflict, alongside ways to find harmony in such bleak and dismal times of distress. A crucial manifesto for any aspiring scholar, *Nexus* had made a noteworthy impact on the academic community, serving as the muse for hundreds of scholars who had longed to work for or with Eldreave—which, Roy knew, included Razkamun, who had based much of his Warfare-Philosophy Principle on the ideas within.

The trouble was, even as Roy flipped through *Nexus*, his thoughts went back to Percival and his distaste for Razkamun. He wondered if Percival's true appreciation for philosophy, and academia as a whole, stemmed from the widely beloved writings of the Elder Scribes. If so, that would clarify his contempt toward Razkamun, whom the Elder Scribes had regarded as a disreputable outsider, desperate to blend in with his peers.

Of course, the Elder Scribes had received their fair share of scathing criticism, both from within the Orphic Basilica and from Northgard's general populace. The city's outraged citizens had vehemently disagreed with certain unjust allegories within the Scribes' texts, particularly the notion that academia deserved more recognition and served a proper function in society. Whatever fueled this antagonism to intellectualism, as the years went by—and as Northgard resorted to riots and, gradually, the threat of civil war—the Elder Scribes scrambled for a resolution that could temporarily thwart the city's belligerence. Then, before swords could be drawn, the Scribes hastily drafted and released a short publication in which they denied the supposed allegories of which they had been accused.

It had not mattered.

If only, Roy pondered now, the Elder Scribes had lived long enough to witness what the world had become. Society had changed so much within those two thousand years, forced to fit the calloused hands of callous soldiers.

Which was all to say how, once more, he had taken the wrong approach. He put *Nexus* back on the shelf, realizing the colossal mistake he'd made, and the true implications of his blunder struck him hard: that it was one thing to use an academic approach that had always served him well, but quite another to regress into who he had once been; that, again, he was just a desolate boy, reading by firelight to avoid the horrors on the other side of his bedroom door.

Roy stood, stepping away from the bookshelf. He couldn't keep loitering like this, couldn't keep dancing back and forth across the line between duty and desire. But there was something always there, always at the fore of his mind, and he hated that he couldn't shake it. Particularly, a memory.

You're remarkably brave, darling. Our first encounter, and you've already gotten on my nerves.

Roy was intrigued by the plan quickly taking shape in his mind. It was dangerous, of that much he was sure, and could possibly take on a snowball effect, leading to choices he might not have ever imagined himself undertaking. But it could be worth all the trouble.

As methodically as he could, he went over the facts. What Percival had been looking for in *Upon Attrition*, Razkamun's novel, was intelligence on the Old Ones. Had it been, then, his failure to find anything that enraged him? Or had Roy somehow been at fault, too?

This brought him to another train of thought—one he found he was contemplating more and more often in the past few days: Percival Atherton. Or, rather, what did he really *know* about Percival? Aside from the fact that he was a nobleman, he was still a mystery. He had sharp wits, but Roy suspected they were exclusively utilized in academic debates.

As he evaluated his musings, Roy came to this conclusion: Percival did not want to raise his fists and fight. In fact, he had spoken at length about separating philosophy from war, his passion for knowledge appeared almost religious, and, when he'd had his head buried in his books, he hadn't even noticed Roy until Roy had addressed him.

He despised the unexpectedness of their dynamic, how he never knew what spiteful things Percival might say next. He'd only known Percival for a few days, and he was already treading on a thin pane of glass, wondering when he would next get cut. But he wouldn't let it get under his skin. He wouldn't let a few failed attempts at conversation spell his ruin. Maybe Percival *was* exhausted from stress and overwhelm. If so, Roy sympathized, but he refused to be belittled. He would sooner debase, harm, and end himself before giving anyone else the privilege—Gabriel was the last person he would let do that.

Roy wrote his own destiny. He made his own misery.

There was just one approach to this madness, then.

Roy would have to work alone, yes. But he would—surreptitiously—let Percival's own research guide him. It was the only way to ensure that no blade, and no blood, ever touched his hands.

Over the following week, that was exactly what he did. He spent his days, a comfortable and productive nine hours, holed away in shadowy corners and at writing desks. For a while, he felt like a soldier in the trenches, inching along on his elbows and stomach, making progress but then being bogged down by the incalculable number of texts at his disposal and the crushing amount of work he had to do to narrow it all down. He read up on things he had previously cared little for, things that his survival, and that of his city, now hinged upon—battles, fictitious and real; recorded weapon inventories; the accounts of traumatized civilians and soldiers, returned from the front lines of ancient conflicts. Each story was as awful as the last.

He searched between the lines for any references to the Old Ones—a passing allusion, a description of their black armor and great, gauntleted fists, capable of shattering bone. There was nothing. He stocked up on books on foreign armies, two of which he'd covertly glimpsed Percival taking notes on, and then consumed them with increasing rapidity, though he didn't skim over any of the details. But again, nothing presented itself. It was all much of the same: grotesquely described accounts of the injured, the dying, and the dead.

He was beginning to think Percival had figured out what he was up to. Did he notice whenever Roy was near and swap one important book for a useless one? Was this all some elaborate prank he'd concocted?

Still, Roy had built up his resolve too much over the past week to lay down these proverbial arms. And so, with this resolve, he revisited the small, cluttered room where he'd been about to work before being interrupted by Percival. Here he discovered, to his supreme delight, that the interlacing of meager moonlight and lamplight on the sixth floor—where the room, which he called the Observatory, was situated—worked wonders for his mental endurance.

He seated himself against a tiny bookshelf in the corner of the chamber, next to an ice-glazed window. A tall, imposing cabinet stood over Roy, dusty trinkets lying abandoned atop it. To his far right was a piano, the gloss of its black top lost to untold years of disuse, blending morosely into the floral, murky gray wallpaper. Stacks of books were piled atop one another like bridges on the verge of collapse. Loose scrolls of parchment were strewn across the floorboards, and the expansive fox-fur carpet beneath Roy's feet was stained black with ink. Calamuses, quills, and fountain pens lay on broken, three-legged tables.

A sharp, twisting pang of sadness went deep through Roy's heart and he placed a hand lightly over his chest. He was oddly comforted by the decay, though. It made for a whimsical backdrop to his endless pursuit of the truth, like the misunderstood, scorned hero from a dark fable.

As the days marched on, passing him by, he slowly started to understand how true this comparison was. He frequented the Observatory far more often than anywhere else in the library. He listened to the muffled howl of winter winds and burned through book after book, the bags underneath his eyes as deep as his adoration for literature. Some mornings he would rise from his bed, mosey along from the first floor to the seventh, piling books in his arms as he went, and then walk back down to his workspace. Some nights, he would collapse from exhaustion at his desk and wake to the sound of stirring wind and the rustling of paper. He had gotten sidetracked before, by philosophy and by Percival both. Now he had to atone for his preoccupations by committing himself completely to his task, and though it was utterly exhausting, it was also the most stimulated he'd ever been.

He instantly felt grounded whenever he entered the Observatory. It dawned upon him, over time, that its tranquil, secluded atmosphere diminished most of his disquieting thoughts from the past week, making space for new considerations, new information. As much as he felt the compulsion to work, though, sometimes he forced himself to take a study break for no more than ten minutes. He would stretch his legs, his arms, and even doze off before getting back to work.

Even as he struggled to find answers, however, it seemed as though the Orphic Basilica was an active part of that struggle. He had pushed back on Percival's thoughts of the building being alive—mostly because he hadn't wanted to admit his own spectral encounter—but Roy couldn't help wondering sometimes whether the Basilica didn't *want* him to find anything, like a lover withholding evidence of an affair. Every book he'd read thus far had been either elusive or written in an unfamiliar language. And if there were any underlying messages or codes, he didn't have the skill set to uncover them.

Was it possible, as Percival had hypothesized, that the library *was* protecting itself? Was it holding its secrets close to its chest? Roy prided himself on his instincts, but how could he *believe* in logic when a ghost had pursued him on that first night, when all he'd heard about the library was based around myths and rumors whispered behind cupped hands . . . when there was no apparent logic to *anything* about this building?

These ponderings, though, were distractions he couldn't afford. If he became too caught up in the mysterious haven of the Elder Scribes, he would dither and all his efforts would be for nothing. He almost wished that he had a talisman—*something*, like his sister's carving—to bring him back to reality.

No, he *did* have something—or *someone*, rather—to keep him tethered to his mission.

But as I said, this is a game. And, darling, there is nothing I love more than winning.

And so Roy kept playing.

Realizing early on that there was almost certainly no book that would outright describe the Old Ones' cryptic motivations, he began looking for accounts detailing other peoples' motivations to invade their neighbor. Before him was one such report. It was loose and might tangle him in another mystery, but with no true concept of war, Roy would take anything to expand that knowledge base, all in hopes that it might point him toward the Old Ones' goals.

Originally written in Urswaelian, as stated beneath a bright red stamp, the scroll Roy had been examining was a grant approved by the Court of the Silver Robes. Once a long-ruling nation located far south of the Hasdan Isles, Urswaelia had been the first to adopt a democracy into its government, which had ushered in an onslaught of petitions to defend the nation from rivalry. Urswaelia's crude warmongering mentality was often seen by its allies as a source of suspicion. But Urswaelia, its court especially, had been clueless, misguided. That, Roy guessed, had likely been why they didn't expect the ambush from Wynair, a neighboring kingdom and their closest ally.

Upon intervening on Urswaelia's shores, King Archibald IV of Wynair had announced a duel by sword with Randyll, the Court of the Silver Robes's Councillor of Finance. As these two unlikely combatants crossed blades, Archibald asked Randyll why a grant for an import of Tussyki weaponry had been approved. By the age of the paper, the scroll in Roy's hands seemed to be the very grant mentioned by the King of Wynair, not a historian's interpretation of the affair. It must have survived the battle.

Soon after Wynair's brutal ambush, Randyll had been executed by King Archibald, and the long-prevailing alliance between the two nations persisted until both were felled decades later in an unnamed conflict.

Roy averted his gaze from the grant and looked at the large leather-bound book beside it, the title imprinted in gold lettering on the cover: *The Ordnance of Old Wynair*. It contained a litany of information regarding Wynair's weapon inventories, along with further additions to the text: poems, limericks, and ballads.

It was massive—extensive—and he intended to dig in later. But for now, there was something about this grant that pulled at him . . . almost as if a gentle hand had turned his head back toward the scroll.

Setting his eyes back on the grant, Roy determined that the Republic of Urswaelia and the Kingdom of Wynair had demonstrated their alliance through mutual trade routes. Councillor Randyll had used the Republic's coffers for years to coax Wynair into delivering books, weapons, and other priceless artifacts. In return, Urswaelia sent Wynair vessels full of their nationally regarded artwork. One item, though—the grant Roy was now holding—had quite nearly shattered the alliance: a list of weapons, forged in the borderlands of Tussyk, purchased and approved by Councillor Randyll.

Just as he was beginning to doubt the effectiveness of his methodology, wondering whether he had made a mistake in this approach, he scanned the list once more and realized not all the weapons were even of Tussyki make. No, there was one at the very bottom of the list, separated from the others.

Roy lurched forward, certain he was experiencing another hallucination. He blinked, his heart pounding. He could feel his mind drawing tight, as if an iron fist was clenched around it and squeezing, tightening, until all he could focus on was seven distinct words:

Black chest plate, country of origin unknown.

Roy stared at Councillor Randyll's purchases, mystified. For once, the enormity of the assignment did not seem so intimidating. It was a lot, yes, but when put into the perspective of the mystery of the Old Ones' hidden identity, he understood. The history of a secret world lay within his reach, if only he stayed on course.

If this is a game, I've finally made the right move.

A wind started up around him. The breeze wove through his hair, twirled about his torso and danced through the gaps between his fingers. He made out, from afar, the susurration of whispers, which steadily grew and then disappeared with the wind.

Roy glanced around. Despite the unmistakable intensity of the wind, there were no windows open in the Observatory. Nobody else was in the room. He wondered whether this apparently mystical wind was somehow connected to the ghost he'd encountered and, if so, what the connection implied. Were those voices he'd discerned, held at bay by some sort of unseen barrier, a part of it too?

Disquieted, Roy looked back to the grant. *Black chest plate, country of origin unknown.* No, maybe this wasn't the Old Ones' black armor. Maybe this was yet another half-baked idea for Roy to compile in his notes. Regardless, Roy scribbled it into his notebook, alongside an addendum referencing the original source. Because, coincidence or not, it was *something*.

If the chest plate *was* a piece of the Old Ones' armor, there were many possibilities to consider, the most significant being the durability of these soldiers. Roy theorized, on the basis that he hadn't heard or read anything on Wynair or Urswaelia before, that the grant had been drafted in an era predating the Age of Scribes. But perhaps the Elder Scribes simply hadn't recorded the allied lands in their archives.

Was it possible that the Old Ones' people, the ancestors of those currently decimating Northgard, dated back thousands of years? Even longer, maybe? Northgard *had* existed for millennia, but the Radiant Droves not nearly as long. Which meant the implications of the Old Ones' heritage were astounding. If these soldiers possessed thousands of years of military training, inherited from their forebears, what were the chances that the Droves could even defeat them?

If Randyll had issued this document, then he must have committed some other act of treason that invariably made the Councillor break his promise with his people and, by doing so, betray Wynair. Maybe Randyll's request for the black chest plate, potentially wielded by the Old Ones of long ago, had resulted in the *current* Old Ones wearing the same armor. But why did he require weapons from two different territories? Were the borderlands of Tussyk involved in some way in a clandestine three-party allegiance with the Old Ones and Randyll? Would Tussyk or the Old Ones be sufficiently gullible to join a coalition without moderate benefits? What, in other words, did Urswaelia get out of such a transaction, and why would Wynair object so vehemently?

There was something larger at play here, something he couldn't quite yet piece together.

Roy groaned. He had to walk around and stretch out the cramps developing in his wrists and the nape of his neck. Twelve hours of rigorous research had tightened the muscles in his back and scrambled his thought process. If he kept pushing himself, Roy knew that he would faint. It had happened before.

Just as he was making to depart the Observatory, though, he felt his attention pulled toward the dust-coated piano in the far-right corner. On its stand were the notes for an original composition, *The Ballad of Queen Genya II*, which was described beneath the title as "a restorative, soothing balm for the troubled and the inattentive."

Roy gaped at the piano, pressure building in the space behind his eyes. His family owned a piano, located on the second level of Dawnseve Manor, though its principal function had, over time, become a mantelpiece for the Matron's—and then Gabriel's—certificates and medallions. Besides himself, Roy had thought his family seldom played the instrument until one night, to his amazement, he walked in on Gabriel, slouched over the piano and slamming the keys, grimacing as he swung side to side in eerie tandem with the monstrous tide of noise pouring out of the opened lid. It nearly sounded like a scream being borne away on a cold wind. Roy had hurried out of the room before Gabriel could notice him.

Before that night, Roy had played piano with the fervor of a dying man, the instrument his elixir, his only way back to health. He would lose himself in hours of reading, followed by hours of playing, but after seeing Gabriel lost in the music, Roy had drifted away from the piano, too afraid to play, too worried that Gabriel's influence might seep out of the keys and into his heart.

Now Roy was torn between longing and a bone-deep loss. He hated Gabriel for playing the instrument, for beating him with the books Roy had ravenously absorbed. He hated Gabriel's casually vindictive manipulation, the cold-hearted ease with which he took and twisted the few pleasures Roy had. But above all, Roy hated himself. He was pointless, hollow. He had made no true efforts to break the curse laid over him, to wrest control of his own mind and reclaim it from Gabriel's clutches. How could he dare take part in wonders like music and literature when it was obvious that he didn't deserve joy?

He curled his fingers into a fist, not immediately noticing the tears that streaked down his cheeks. Roy stifled a sob, his vision blurred and his knees buckling, preparing to give out beneath him. Yet for all that, he pulled out the stool and sat, a great mantle of sorrow splaying out across his shoulders. He didn't bother to walk back to the desk and retrieve the book. It was meaningless, no more consequential than his own existence.

Roy leaned forward and wiped away the dust on the piano with the sleeve of his tailcoat. He studied his reflection, revolted. "I wish you were dead."

11

Another week passed, and while Roy's wish for death didn't come true, it somehow inveigled itself into his routine.

Everything, from the books he read to the food he ate to the dreams he had, acquired a dreary and lifeless quality. The barbaric war stories he'd researched days ago, teeming with sickeningly vivid imagery and hyperrealistic interpretations of historical events, no longer affected him as they once had. He was utterly unfazed by the details. He even tried to locate some volumes on hoplology and metallurgy, the studies of armor and metal respectively, but once he realized this was getting him nowhere, offering him no insights into the black armor he'd spotted in the grant, his depression only deepened.

Amidst these long intervals of monotony, he remembered events from his past that he thought he'd shoved down, deep in some mental cavern where they couldn't haunt him any longer. These memories were mostly of Gabriel: his knives; his horrid grin; his blue eyes shining in the moonlight, cold as frost. The memories struck without warning, though Roy found he could endure them best when he was working. He never gave himself the chance to disassociate, either. He would simply let the memory do its work and drain the momentum and enthusiasm with which he'd come to his studies, and then, when it was over, he dove back in.

He didn't notice the effect this coping mechanism was having on him until later. It was astounding how one discouraging day could unravel your composure, how a single moment of emotional collapse could cause a change in the week to come. The change was subtle, almost leisurely, and so Roy didn't recognize it at first. He just started eating less, declining the meals that still mysteriously materialized at his doorstep, but chalked it up to being a symptom of overwork. He slowly lost interest in spying on Percival and sneaking glimpses at the books he had left in various study halls. It all seemed so pointless, so draining.

His dreams of Gabriel grew increasingly convincing, too. He could distinguish between reality and nightmare, but only because he reassured himself, day and night—and in the strange hours between them—that the Governor's letter had confirmed Gabriel's absence, that he was missing. But Roy's mind only took this to mean that, out of all places in Northgard, he was *here*, in the Orphic Basilica. He saw Gabriel in its darkest shadows, setting fire to book after book, his eyes peering out at Roy from behind a shelf. Roy would stop, his hands trembling, and then as Gabriel broke into a sprint and dashed around the corner, a silver knife gripped in his fist, Roy would jerk awake, panting, a hand clutched against the grooves of the scars on his chest. Sometimes, he wondered if Gabriel was the ghost he had first seen all those days ago, if he was chasing Roy in death, as he had in life.

Percival appeared unaware of Roy's worsening state of mind, or if he *was* aware, then he did not show it. Curiously, nothing really changed in their interactions. They didn't converse. They didn't bid each other a good morning or a good night. They occasionally crossed paths, because while the

Basilica was seven stories tall and as wide as three manors, it was still only one building. Moreover, their chambers were on the same floor, the sixth, whose books Percival seemed to have taken a liking to. And despite his incident with the piano, Roy hadn't stopped frequenting the Observatory, located on the fifth floor, so there were days, sometimes, when he would pass by Percival after a long day of studying and steal a furtive glance. Not at *Percival*, of course, or so Roy continued telling himself as he slowly crawled out of the fugue state he'd fallen into.

No, he was more interested in the books Percival was reading. He read fast, Roy noticed, faster than Roy. One day he was huddled over a half-crumpled manuscript. The next, he was scribbling annotations in his notebook about a leather-bound manifesto concerning etymology.

Percival looked perpetually focused, brows drawn, concentration unwavering, even when there were lines of unease inscribed deep into his forehead. His casual posture, his feet crossed atop one another or one arm flung out over the back of his seat, indicated affability. His straight back, however, denoted stern contemplation. But whenever he got so close to his book that it was like it had caught him by the hand and pulled him into its pages, that was when Roy tended to back away and find another spot to study. Because somehow, he knew that if he was to walk in on Percival in this state, he would get distracted by his deep blond hair, his irksome witticisms, his beauty.

He had never met someone so deeply affected by academia. Then again, he hadn't ever met anyone in academia, only corresponded with them, so perhaps this was natural. But he couldn't help but think this was specific to Percival, and Roy just wished he had the strength to ask.

The days and nights blurred past, abstract and bleary, like a watercolor painting. On one such night, Roy was only a short walk from his bedchamber, fatigued from hunching over his workspace for fifteen hours or so, when he spotted Percival sitting at a lamplit table propped against the wall, his knees drawn up to his chest, his eyes wide and disbelieving behind his glasses. On the cover of the massive book he was making his way through was the title: *The Lost Records of Old Wynair.*

Excitement and recognition crashed over Roy. His heart was palpitating, beating triple-time, and his hands had grown clammy. Instinct took over, and he walked forward but then, just as quickly, ground himself to a halt.

What are you doing, you fool? Roy chastised himself. *You're so tired, you can barely walk to your bed; how in the pits of Hell are you planning to convince Percival to discuss a text with you? That certainly worked out splendidly the last time, didn't it?*

After a moment, Roy conceded, withdrawing from the alcove and stealing toward his bedchamber, his footfalls whisper-soft. Yet as he settled beneath his silken sheets that night, he resolved to speak to Percival in the morning... but it wasn't until the next night that Roy mustered the courage.

He was working in the Observatory. A chill permeated the room, and though a lamp was resting atop Roy's desk, its heat did little to warm his bones. He wrapped his coat tighter about his shoulders, then retrieved a book from the stack in front of him and caught a quick glimpse of Percival, sitting on the other side of the desk. He had entered the Observatory without ceremony or greeting, deposited a stack of manuscripts on Roy's desk and proceeded to prompt Roy with a question regarding the power imbalance embedded in Northgard.

Percival clicked his fingers in front of Roy's face. "Darling? A response would suffice."

Roy drew in a tight breath and dipped his head, glancing down at the book on metallurgy he'd been revisiting. "Sorry, I was thinking," he said. "What was your question?"

Impatient, Percival sighed. "I've attempted to determine Northgard's stance on power so that we might separate them from the Old Ones, but I think I'm missing something."

Roy met Percival's eyes. "And you were hoping *I* might fill you in on the rest? Doesn't this violate your game?"

"Maybe, maybe not. But that's part of the game, too, darling."

Roy almost got up and left at that, but instead said loftily, "I figured it was rather obvious. The lower class is condemned by the upper class for their existence, and the upper class remains ignorant of their own cruelty, as they're too busy trying to obtain more power."

"It's not even ignorance; it's just frank, unguarded dehumanization. The bodies of government who lay their affections onto communities, like the aristocrats of Northgard, have no respect for their peoples. All their fancy meetings and delegations and whatnot are a statement of autocracy."

"Northgard isn't autocratic, though. Despite the Governor's total authority, he still relies on his advisers, most notably the Masters and Matrons, to do his dirty work."

"And yet none of his advisers are academics," Percival said. "We can deny it until the day when our kind is truly no more, but conflict is still a historically integral component of the academic world. For years, Northgard has changed their system to please their people—those who attack our community specifically—as has been the Governor's intention, but as this author states"— Percival pointed to a passage in the book he was holding—"'Power is a gift. Power is a curse. But the damned can weaken the blessed.'"

"Scholars have no hope of weakening the Iron Citadel. We

cannot speak our mind. We cannot say no. We have no chance at rebellion."

"You're misinterpreting the text. This book was written from an academic perspective, and so in this case, *we* are 'the blessed,' blessed with knowledge, history, and love. We love fiercely, boldly. We love with a strength hate could never dream of. Those who condemn us, who deprive us of this love, are the damned. But this book portrays power as inherently bad, an ideal whose nature, no matter its wielder, does not change."

The notion of like-mindedness went against Percival's conditions for their game—although so did this entire conversation, so Roy didn't bring it up. Rather, he said, "Good people survive. Evil people suffer."

"Look at the world around us, darling," Percival whispered. He sounded haunted, distressed. "Has the Governor suffered for his crimes? Have the Droves? Everything, good and evil and right and wrong, died beside the Age of Scribes. 'Now we are but shades, this world our haunt, these nights hereafter our long rest.'" Roy knew the quote. It was the epigraph of the twenty-eighth chapter of Meha Torazkeer's *In Night's Arms*.

Percival cocked his head, his jaw tight, and looked out the window beside the desk, his features gone soft and tender yet pensive. There was also a sort of restless energy to him, as if a million rushing thoughts were trapped within his stiff body. Roy wondered if Percival preferred patching his wounds up to exposing them . . . or perhaps he was waiting on the right person to show them to.

Percival didn't want assistance, though; he wanted to avenge the near-death of academia by his own devices, to disassemble the violent society the Governor had established over years of oppression. Roy was tired of being afraid, however. Tired of seeing Percival in a hall or a reading room and recoiling. Not everyone wanted him dead. Not everyone was a new fear to conquer. Besides, there was a world at war, and Roy couldn't help wanting to assist those who needed it most. After weeks of little to no progress, he was once again sure he *needed* Percival to make that happen.

And that, perhaps, Percival needed him as well.

He rose to his feet, resolute, then searched through the piles of books and scrolls lying about the desk.

"I'm afraid it'll take some time to find your wits, darling," Percival said.

"Don't make me regret this," Roy muttered, then found a sheet of parchment. It was the grant he'd discovered a few days ago.

He felt a moment of apprehension, but he couldn't turn back now. What if this was the turning point? What if this game could coexist alongside his desire to share information with Percival? Maybe it contradicted the proposition, but the relationship between *The Ordnance* and *The Lost Records* was too auspicious to ignore.

Roy placed the grant atop *The Ordnance of Old Wynair*, sat back at the desk, and recounted to Percival what he'd unearthed: the grant, the difference between the Tussyki weapons and the black chest plate, and the history of Wynair and Urswaelia.

Percival lifted his head from the grant. He looked to be in utter disbelief, his mouth parted. *This isn't how the game works*, his perplexed expression seemed to say. *These aren't the rules I made.*

"I know you don't want me to do this," Roy said, "but I had to say something, Percival. This must mean *something*."

Percival picked up the grant carefully, as though applying any additional force might disintegrate the document. He whispered, "'Black chest plate, country of origin unknown.'"

"It might not be referring to the Old Ones, but—"

"But it sounds like a damn good possibility." Percival gulped, sighed, tapped his fingers on the desk. Roy had never seen him so frazzled. "Where did you find this?"

"Here. This room. I didn't notice it at first; I didn't think it would yield any valuable information, but I . . ." He debated explaining what had compelled him to share this discovery, then decided that if he had come this far and shown Percival this much, then what was one more truth? "I saw you reading something like *The Ordnance* last night. *The Lost Records of Old Wynair*, was it?"

Percival nodded, not at all upset at Roy's surreptitious observations. "Yes, that was it. There were a few accounts written by geographers who'd researched Wynair. I didn't come across anything terribly significant, but there *was* this sketch of a shipwreck that stuck with me. A black chest plate was found in the wreckage, though whether the piece was salvaged wasn't recorded—"

Roy stilled, ignoring Percival's annoyed expression as he cut in, "Wait. A shipwreck? Was there any mention of its sails catching fire?"

Percival blinked. "Well, yes, but I didn't think it was important . . ." He straightened, recognition sparking in his eyes. "Why? Did you find something?"

"The mural around the skylight," Roy said, unable to hold back his smile. "One of the bas-reliefs depicts a ship sailing toward a land. A small island, maybe. Perhaps it contained the black armor and somehow crashed ashore." His heart was racing.

"Perhaps it's a coincidence," Percival hedged.

"Does it feel like one, though? The details *and* the fact that these texts and sources are leading us here?" *And maybe,* Roy thought, *something else is leading us here as well . . .* He shook that thought free. "I'd have to get a better look at the painting. There might be an inscription underneath the scene that I missed when I first came here." A small grin was forming on his face. "This is earth-shattering, Percival. *Everything* could be connected to the Old Ones, even this library. I mean, why else would that artwork be shown here?"

Again, Percival nodded with satisfaction, silently considering their breakthrough and, almost certainly, the fact that although *he* had set the game board and put down the pieces ... it had been Roy who made the first move.

"It appears the Old Ones are associated with forgotten lands," Percival said. "The specific date of that shipwreck isn't certain, though as it's ostensibly related to the grant, perhaps you were right, in that the current Old Ones' ancestors existed *before* the Age of Scribes."

"If they provided Randyll with a set of their armor, as he requested, they must have been in league with Urswaelia," Roy assumed.

"Councillor Randyll was a traitor, though. King Archibald ordered his execution. The alliance between Urswaelia and Wynair persevered, and yet there's nothing in this grant, nor in *The Ordnance of Old Wynair*, about the Old Ones other than this reference to armor. I doubt what we know of them might be useful."

It was true ... to a point. They knew enough for speculations to germinate, but they had nothing with which to ascertain a firm correlation. But Roy had faith in what he'd claimed: everything was connected.

He hoped, then, Percival would forgo this whole game right now, right as they'd made this discovery together. He could stand Percival's self-absorption in mild doses, but Roy was loath to bear Percival's inexcusable caginess. It was clear he'd only discussed what he had unearthed in *The Lost Records of Old Wynair* because Roy had brought it up, but now that he had . . .

Roy straightened in his chair, then snatched the grant out of Percival's hands and stared at it. He looked up at Percival, excitement stirring through him. "Percival, the *armor*. I think it's what separates the Old Ones from any regular soldier. Why else would Randyll request a chest plate? Why else would this warrant his execution? Maybe the Old Ones were a rival to Urswaelia *and* Wynair. Randyll's treachery might have been the breaking point for the alliance, but there must be something about the chest plate that created such a debacle."

"As in, the properties? The metal used to forge it?"

"Or its specific placement on the body. Either way, it's unusual for this grant to include a single piece of armor without requesting the rest. Perhaps Randyll had intended to study it, to learn of its construction? I'm not sure."

"I haven't seen anything else on it in the Basilica, either," Percival said. His tone became grim and cold as a frostbitten corpse. "But back home, there were rumors of the Old Ones' strength. I got a letter from one of my cousins one night, long before the Governor sent his missive. A division of the Old Ones had passed through her village. She watched from her kitchen window as a soldier shattered two of her neighbor's children with their fists, then burned their manor to a crisp. The smoke hung heavy for another week." He shook his head, a grimace twisting his lips. "The Droves could do nothing against them."

"I know."

"But think: What *else* could the Droves do nothing against?"

Roy shook his head, not seeing where Percival was trying to lead him.

"What about the Basilica? This library has stood for *years*, untouched by time." His eyes widened. "Darling, don't you see?"

Roy cocked his head, a lock of black-silver hair draping down his face. He watched as Percival's eyes followed it, then darted back to Roy's face. Roy kneaded the left column of his neck, gulping at the splotches of heat he could feel marking his throat.

As Percival studied him, Roy froze, his breath caught as if on a hook. He'd once thought Percival wielded his beauty like a blade, but whatever the warmth in the pit of Roy's gut was, he was not pained by it. He almost thought he might be in more pain without it.

"Tell me, Percival," Roy said, and this time, he found it impossible to hide the hoarse edge to his voice. Then, as he reviewed the direction their conversation was taking, he chose a new course of action, a way to—hopefully—convey that the game, as evidenced by their exchange of research material, was over. He hesitated, then took the leap. "But if you tell me what I'm missing, then it's as much as acknowledging that this competition between us, this race for answers, has no place in our investigation."

After a moment, Percival surrendered. "All right, darling. The game is done. Maybe together, we can finally make some progress."

Roy let out a relieved sigh, grateful that Percival had at last given up his decidedly useless choice to drive a wedge between them, and moreover, that he had actually admitted to the effectiveness of their collaboration.

Percival held his hand up at Roy's sigh, a strange expression on his face. "I'll warn you, though, I'm not sure this will work."

"But it's already working," Roy said, confused.

"For now," Percival said. "I've just seen it fail too many times." And somehow, Roy knew what Percival was saying—he himself had failed at this too many times. But what could have possibly caused Percival to distrust others and himself so deeply?

"So," Percival said brusquely, "now that we're in on this together, here's my thinking: There are several similarities between the Orphic Basilica and the Old Ones. Both of their histories are now mostly lost to time. Thousands of years have slipped by since the foundation of the Basilica and the first of the Old Ones. This *must* be a sign. A portent."

Roy had to say, it did strike him as odd. An ancient enemy and an ancient library, their alleged significance resurrected by a new, deadly war. And yet . . .

"I am not accustomed to working with folklore, Percival, or conjecture."

"Please, darling, try to hear me out," Percival implored. "I am willing to hear any points of disagreement that you might have, but at least allow me to explain myself. Just . . . Just trust me on this."

Roy flinched at this last plea, but who else did they have to turn to? Who else could they present their theories, fears, and worries to, if not each other? Roy *had* wanted this, hadn't he? At last, he nodded, gesturing for Percival to continue.

"Right," Percival said, looking significantly more at ease now that he had Roy's assent. "So, as you said, everything is connected. The Elder Scribes praised the Basilica, though after they ordered its construction, they worried that it wouldn't meet Northgard's approval. They were scared, but they did it anyway. However, those against their cause, the supporters of Governorship, *did* try to accomplish what the Radiant Droves attempted—to destroy the Basilica and burn these legendary books. None prevailed. What *we* need to do is compile all we have on the Old Ones into our notebooks and string together as much intelligence as we can—battlecraft, war negotiations, peace treaties, anything that might pertain to the lore of the Old Ones *and* the Basilica. Maybe then we can find something concrete that connects the two, and therefore find a way past all"—he waved at the shelves—"this."

Finally, Roy thought. Finally, they might actually get something done. And it echoed how this had all started for him in the first place: looking for the Old Ones obliquely, coming at it from different points of view and academies of thought. Roy had been studying other invasions, and the Old Ones had reared their black visages in those indirect texts when days of just searching straight on had yielded nothing. In just a half hour, they had already accomplished more by approaching the topic sideways.

And all Roy had to do now was stop his breath from catching and his heart from thrashing whenever Percival did something as simple and mundane as walk into a room.

Maybe then Northgard might survive the war.

Percival looked around the Observatory. "I do think the Basilica will test our patience, though, especially since what we're looking for would ultimately lead to the library's own demise. We might be old crones before we get through half of these books. It's a shame the Droves lost their minds before they could thoroughly search this place. It would've been courteous of them to clear the mess."

Roy knew Percival was jesting, although it made him contemplate what he had not long ago believed strange: the affliction that the Governor had described, which had come over both the Droves and the Matron. He had pushed the thought into the dark waters underneath his mind, primarily out of disbelief in, and perhaps an aversion to, superstition. But now, with the shadow of so many other inexplicable occurrences suspended over his head, was it truly that far-fetched to believe that *something*—some force beyond his reckoning yet undoubtedly sharing the same space as him—had made the Matron uneasy, had made several Droves kill themselves? He didn't think so.

But who might have been responsible for this affliction, Roy couldn't be certain. The phantom that had accosted him? The library itself? Some other sinister entity? Indeed, it might be possible, but despite the conclusion of his and Percival's game, Roy couldn't yet bring himself to confess what he'd seen. He was almost there, quite nearly, but he couldn't stop thinking about how Percival had spoken about Razkamun and his apparent insanity.

"Sure," Roy said to Percival, "it might have been helpful, but sitting here and complaining about it isn't going to get us closer to the truth. Moreover, it won't stop the madness out there." He gestured to the snow-blasted world past the window. He felt a surge of frustration at Percival's joke, because it felt like a delaying tactic—a defense against fully collaborating. *Already,* Roy thought angrily. "What's done is done. What we do, we need to *do,* now. I don't know about you, but I want to *do* something. I want to—"

Percival smiled. "You want to be a hero."

"Our heroes are dead, if they were ever heroes to begin with. No, I . . . I want to see my sister again."

Percival's eyes softened at that, and once again he nodded, a gesture Roy was starting to see was as powerful a confirmation as he was going to get.

Emboldened, Roy said, "Somebody is good at keeping secrets. Whether it's the Governor, this library, or the Old Ones themselves—it doesn't matter. You and I are here, and those secrets are ours to find. That's all I know." Roy jabbed a finger into the grant. "This report, and *The Lost Records,* is a good start."

"It is indeed. So let's take a look at that artwork you mentioned, then," Percival said. "If the scene it's portraying and the event described in that grant are one and the same, then I'm suspecting it will give us at least a little more insight into these soldiers. From there, any details we pick up on, we'll add them to our compiled notes." He sounded determined, perhaps somewhat eager, too, but there was a kind of subdued reluctance on his face, like he was halfway to dropping some thought that had been lingering in his mind.

Before he could, Roy said, "What's the matter?"

"It's as I said earlier, darling: Don't read too deeply into this," Percival said. "I don't want you to mistake my cooperation for kindness or an attempt at friendship, because my earlier point still stands. We *will* argue. We *will* disagree. That's inevitable. I'm giving you as much collaboration as I will allow, and I mean that solely in the professional sense." He looked at Roy, and his expression turned a shade darker, like he was glaring, but it was weak, as though his last few scowls had lost their power. "There is a line between us, Roy, and crossing that line would not do well for either of us. I can't let you get in my way."

In your way? Roy thought. *Or close enough to actually know you?*

After Roy and Percival had reviewed their notes and assembled them into their notebooks, the two of them walked up to the seventh floor in a slightly uneasy silence.

Roy attempted to distract himself with thoughts of their theories and the grant, from which he'd gleaned no further information on Randyll's prized possession, but nothing worked. Nothing chased away his conversation with Percival, nor the way he had spoken Roy's name. It lingered, clinging to his mind like a nightmare upon awakening—frightening, yes, but enticing all the same.

I can't let you get in my way.

He massaged his temples, but it gave him neither aid nor succor. Perhaps this entire time, Percival had been *waiting* for Roy to openly ask him to finish their game, to rip off all the masks and do away with all the pretenses. And when Roy had unwittingly exposed his desire, Percival had lunged at the bait, eager to *see* Roy, to make him feel what Percival felt.

The only problem was Percival's interest in Roy seemed more personal than he'd first assumed. He didn't want to *hurt* Roy; he wanted to strip him of his armor, lay his heart bare. Roy would have rather died, taken a knife to his heart and done the deed himself, than allow that to happen. He had thought of it, too. He'd considered it when he'd sat down at the piano. He could've run from those morbid compulsions, and from Percival, too, and saved himself the mortification of vulnerability.

But for some sadistic reason, Roy couldn't resist the fight.

Once they reached the seventh floor, Roy tipped his head back, squinted, and inspected the painted bas-reliefs wrapped around the skylight. The scene closest to him and Percival, above the bookshelf they'd stopped alongside, was the burning ship sailing across a churning black sea. There *was* an inscription beneath the piece, as Roy had hoped, but from this vantage point he could not distinguish the words engraved in gilded lettering. He grunted, frustrated, and rose onto his toes, but it didn't clarify the text by any measure.

"Of course," Roy muttered. "Maybe I was a little too hopeful." *Or maybe*, he thought, *this damn library really* is *out to get me.*

Percival looked at the skylight, his lips pursed. "No, darling, we can't give up that easily. Some answers could be *right* there, just within our reach."

"Poor choice of words," Roy remarked.

Percival rolled his eyes. "Wait here, would you? I'm going to go look around for something that could give us a closer view."

Roy admired Percival's perseverance, though he didn't know where it came from, nor what had made him so confident in the Orphic Basilica's resources. All of the seven floors, from what Roy had seen, contained bookshelves and reading rooms but not much else—

There was a rattling sound from behind Roy, becoming progressively louder. This was accompanied by the hollow whistling of a wind, akin to a deep note being played into a flute, but there was a calming quality to it, something friendlier and more companionable than the feeling of disorientation he'd gotten when the red-eyed ghost had accosted him. No, this, he realized, was the wind that had swirled around him when he had made the discovery of the black chest plate.

"Darling!" Percival shouted, his voice casting a resonant, unsettling echo throughout the seventh floor. "Darling, look out!"

Roy turned on his heel, shaken out of his musings, just in time to see one of the rolling ladders set against a bookshelf rushing toward him. Its wheels clacked and clattered against the floorboards, and initially, Roy could not determine what had set it into motion. Percival clearly hadn't pushed it; he was standing a few paces from Roy, where he'd been observing the skylight. Then a blast of wind roared toward him, blowing back the hair dangling over his brows.

Percival cast a panicked look at Roy over his shoulder, his eyes widening with frank disbelief, then whirled around and tackled Roy—who had been rooted in place, wordlessly watching the rolling ladder's quickening approach—to the ground.

Roy gasped, the breath driven out of him. Once he'd managed a deep inhale, a residual feeling of curiosity stirred in him, and he weakly shoved Percival off his chest, then staggered to his feet.

Rolling over onto his back, Percival groaned, "Not exactly how I expected to be thanked for my daring sacrifice."

But Roy paid no heed to Percival. He was too entranced, too *hypnotized* by what the previous few seconds had confirmed. He wandered toward the ladder, which had come to a halt at the end of the bookshelf. He waited impatiently for the wind to make a reappearance, though it did not. It had done its job. All he could register now was a creeping coldness; not the ethereal kind, but one of revelation, of suspicion calcified into clarity.

Roy set a hand on the ladder, looking down through the unoccupied bookshelf. "It's *listening* to us," he whispered, then gawked at Percival, who was now standing. "That wind. It's the library *guiding* us."

Percival looked mildly perturbed by being pushed aside, but once he regarded Roy, he nodded solemnly. "Finally accepted it, have you?"

"I . . ." Roy fumbled with his words. "I suppose I have. I felt it when I found that grant, you know?"

"And even then, that wasn't enough for you?"

"It was, but I guess I overlooked the experience too quickly to look into it, unlike my reaction now," Roy said. He lifted a hand, and though the wind did not rise to his summons, he felt lighter, calmer, like there was another presence at his back, quietly monitoring his progress and wishing him well. He grasped the ladder with both hands and looked up at the inscriptions under the paintings encircling the skylight, which, he gathered from the soaring height of the shelf, would certainly be visible from the top of the ladder. "It's calling to us, Percival." He felt exhilarated, empowered, like he could absorb the most challenging texts known to mankind and never tire. "Something's there, written on the ceiling, and it's been there a very long time."

Percival seemed reluctant to agree, but as he looked between Roy and the ladder, it became clear that his reluctance was, in fact, concern. When a crease appeared between his minutely raised brows, Percival asked, "Are you sure?"

"I am," Roy said, stepping onto the ladder and then echoing what Percival had said moments ago, "if you can just trust me on this."

Percival watched him for a long moment, his features more open than ever before, and Roy momentarily thought, and secretly hoped, that some bridge had been lowered to span the chasm between them. Perhaps that closing of spaces had begun minutes ago, when Percival had accepted the game was done, a thing of the past, but Roy couldn't banish the feeling that this was their first demonstrable, practical step forward.

Percival said nothing. Rather, he grasped either side of the ladder, holding it rigidly in place.

Roy swallowed, his heart swelling with not a small amount of gratitude, though it was only once he'd averted his eyes from Percival's earnest stare and fixed his gaze upward that Roy was overcome with the enormity of what he'd gotten himself into. He wasn't scared so much by whatever the inscription might reveal of the Old Ones than by the daunting stature of the bookshelf.

By the Scribes, he thought, his stomach churning. *Have they always been this damn tall?*

"Well," Percival said from beneath Roy with his usual sardonic tone, "no dawdling about now, Dawnseve. Up you go."

Percival's half-hearted attempt at encouragement, however, had no effect on Roy. He felt immobilized, like his feet were encased in blocks of stone. He kept telling himself, in a sort of cyclic self-deprecating mantra, that he wasn't fit for this assignment if he did not take this next step, that the Elder Scribes had likely done what he was about to do—daily, with ease and without reservations. This motivated him to rise one step, and then he stiffened at the intimidating thought that it was the first of what seemed to be thousands.

Then Percival whispered, "Come on, darling." He wrapped his fingers gently around Roy's right calf and squeezed. "I'd take over if you wanted, you know I would, but I *know* you want this."

Roy had closed his eyes and hung his head, but now he looked up again, his hesitation dispersed by the casual tenderness in Percival's voice. He nodded, once to Percival and then again to himself with conviction. Percival released his calf, and Roy ascended the ladder, his eyes trained on the skylight.

But after a few minutes, he noticed that his considerably elevated position afforded him a spectacular view of the Orphic Basilica. The arrangement of bookshelves, reading halls, and study nooks looked painstakingly methodical, which was a jarring contrast to the absence of a cataloging system.

Focus, Roy reprimanded himself, tightening his grip on the rails. *Find your focus and maintain it.*

Thankfully, he reached the top of the ladder without incident. The air felt strangely thinner, and he couldn't tell whether it was from the remarkable speed of his ascent, but his head was spinning and he couldn't string together any coherent thoughts. But at least all he had to do, at this stage, was read.

Roy clutched the uppermost rung of the ladder and hoisted himself up. The paintings were still quite far, but as he squinted, he made out the inscription beneath the piece of the ship, its sails aflame:

> DEPICTED: An unnamed artist's dramatized interpretation of the Old Ones' voyage to Wynair, preceding their banishment by the gathered intellect of the Elder Scribes.

Roy dropped back onto the balls of his feet, still gripping the top rung. It took all of his mustered strength to hold on. "Banishment?" he muttered.

"What does it say?" Percival called out from below. Roy heard the distant riffling of paper. The notebook in which Percival had been recording his half of their findings, Roy suspected. "Read it out!"

Once Roy did, his recitation earning a shocked exclamation of disbelief from Percival—who, after scribbling in the notebook, shouted at Roy to descend—Roy inched his way down the ladder. Despite his earlier promise to himself to clear his head, he couldn't put his overworking mind to rest.

The Elder Scribes cast the Old Ones out of Northgard, Roy thought, letting the weight of that revelation sink in. But how? How could they have been capable of banishing an entire army? With knowledge? With ... He felt a horrid sinking in his stomach, like he'd swallowed a hot stone, as a thought emerged in his mind, something he'd never believed he would have to consider. Had they done it with force?

With weapons?

He blanched, the speed of his heart doubling and his dread deepening, and before he could process what had happened, Roy was falling.

A familiar gust of wind swept toward him from underneath, then rose higher and higher, keeping him airborne. The wind thickened, unfolding out across his back until it felt as though he was being carried on some imperceptible mattress. He dared a look down and was relieved to see that only a small distance separated him from the floor.

Percival jammed the notebook into his pocket, stuck the nub of charcoal he'd been writing with behind his ear, and reached up to grab Roy from underneath his arms. The wind thinned, then disappeared, leaving in its wake a trail of loose pages that swayed and fluttered out of the nearest bookshelf.

Percival deposited Roy on the ground, and while Roy determinedly refrained from memorizing the contours of Percival's body, Percival laid a hand on his shoulder. "Are you all right?"

Roy nodded, though he was well aware how evidently he was lying; his entire body had gone limp, his muscles trembling from the discovery and the dizzying fall. Once he'd caught his breath, he said, "That's it, Percival. That's the confirmation we needed. The Elder Scribes did it. They *drove out* the Old Ones."

Percival got out the notebook and read what he'd transcribed. "'*The gathered intellect.*' That could mean anything."

"It could," Roy said, "but it's a connection between the Old Ones and the Basilica nonetheless, and we don't have many of those. Now we have sufficient reason to believe the Elder Scribes discovered, or possibly contrived, a way to push back the Old Ones."

Percival seemed unsatisfied with this response. "Why do you look so upset, then?" he asked.

Because if my assumptions are correct, then the image of the idols I've built in my head—throughout the entire course of my childhood—is completely wrong, distorted by my naive hope of old-world pacifism. Because this image is one of the only pillars of stability I have, and if it comes down, if it crumbles, then everything I've been told, and have told myself, is a lie.

But he had *heard* of scholars rebelling, and not too long ago, either. He had even spoken with some of them, stuffed their letters of correspondence beneath a loose board under his bed. He had shirked any and all allusions his contacts had made to resistance, yes, but they'd only informed Roy of the small-scale acts of insurgence they had been planning, like riots and sermons conducted in alleyways where academics would pontificate on the political significance of literature.

But exile? Roy thought, his mouth dry and his hands prickling with sweat. *How could a scholar even accomplish that?*

"Never mind," he said to Percival. "Come on, we've been here long enough. It's time we get back to the books."

12

IN THE DAYS FOLLOWING THEIR BREAKTHROUGH ON THE seventh floor, the most baffling thing happened to Roy. Every time he saw Percival, Roy could think of nothing and nobody else. Every time he knew Percival was nearby, he felt addled and weak, as though he'd drunk to the bottom of one too many glasses. He thought about him far too often and, because of this, he studied far too little. He lost his rhythm. He slipped up in his notations. He forgot idioms and aphorisms that had once come easily to him.

I can't let you get in my way.

He thought of that frequently, too, how *can't* wasn't *won't*, how, to Roy, it sounded like Percival was *stopping* himself from the affliction that had come over Roy. Was that not what this was? A sickness? He didn't *feel* ill, at least not physically, but his imagination, reason, and perception were unquestionably impaired. Once more he wondered if this sickness was in any way connected to what the Droves who had unsuccessfully investigated the library had experienced, if the library had anything to do with how recurrently Roy's thoughts snagged on Percival, but the latter especially seemed highly unlikely. Roy could be outside the library, shivering and frozen down to the marrow in his bones, and Percival would still be on his mind.

Roy attempted, for a while, to view this strange infatuation—a feeling he had not once encountered in his twenty-five years—in an analytical light. He thought of how he'd felt whenever Percival looked at him, whenever he spared him a glance that held longer than was strictly necessary, but in his endeavor to define this host of emotions twisting and tumbling in him, Roy found himself remembering Percival's crooked smile again, and the intricately detailed brown flecks in his hazel eyes, and the unexpected strength he'd displayed when he'd caught Roy the other night, borne up on that mysterious, whistling wind. Then he was back to where he'd begun—falling for Percival, with no clue as to how to get back up.

The nights wore on, seeming to darken with time, and his feelings deepened, sitting restless in the pit of his stomach. He didn't know what to do with them, how to study or read or cope in such conditions. How did one go on with an attraction so distracting? And yes, he could finally admit that this *was* attraction. Perhaps a ruinous sort of attraction, but a pull he felt nevertheless.

The question lingered, then: How did one distract oneself from a distraction? The same way he had with the repulsion he'd felt for his brother: He read and worked on and examined texts into the smallest hours of the night, until reality became intangible, a gray pool of water he had to wade through. He surrounded himself with books. He absorbed encyclopedias and pamphlets, poems and articles, anything distantly or closely related to the Old Ones and how they'd been temporarily banished from Northgard by the Elder Scribes. He did not care if he came up empty. He only wanted these thoughts out and gone before they could do him further harm, before he dawdled for the next six months, lost in Percival's eyes, enchanted by his smile.

Roy knew he was not alone in his thinking. Something had

formed between them, not an understanding but something undeniable nonetheless. He could feel it, sense it—the stretches of taut silence, the stealthily stolen glances they exchanged while Roy wrote up his personal report of their progress for the Governor (*found some mentions of black armor, will follow up later; researching historical battles to find references of tactics and patterns similar to Old Ones*), the resemblances between the books they leafed through and the notes they jotted down. He liked it sometimes. It gave him a thrilling rush. Whenever he caught Percival's eye, he could not tell which of them had won a round.

But these pleasures were temporary, and they left Roy feeling a selfish, petty sort of spite. Hadn't Percival shown moments of weakness? If so, then wasn't there an event from his past that must have been responsible for the crease in Percival's brow and the set of his shoulders? These questions shifted Roy's spite into concern.

If Roy could not change Percival, then perhaps he could understand him. Perhaps that was what *Percival* was doing in return, and Roy was too broken to see it.

It was foolish to let some wild-mannered man affect him so, Roy knew that. But by the Scribes, he'd never been so eager to do right, to prove his competition wrong so that he could stop thinking of him, of the small joys he couldn't have.

About a month into the investigation, Roy was in the Observatory, in the middle of reading a thesis on the Warfare-Philosophy Principle, when three rapid knocks sounded from the first floor. Once he finished the sentence he'd been reading, he stood from his seat, exited the Observatory, and then paused at the railing of the nearest balcony.

Down below, Percival handed several torn-out sheets of notebook paper to the Governor, who then looked over them with a stern nod before folding and tucking them into an inner pocket of his suit. Behind him, three Droves were carrying crates packed full of supplies—inkwells, quills, notebooks, waterskins, loaves of bread, cheese, and several types of fruit—and bringing them up to the sixth floor, where the Governor had told Roy at the beginning of the assignment to select his personal chambers. As the Droves passed Roy on the fifth floor, he noticed that they moved with mechanical exactness, their shoulders stiff and their bloodshot eyes ringed with shadows.

With an affirmative grunt, the Governor dismissed Percival, who silently turned on his heel and headed back to wherever he'd been studying without acknowledging Roy. Or maybe he didn't see him.

The Governor did, though. He looked up at the balcony where Roy stood, holding his gaze, an expectant expression on his face.

Roy swallowed, then nodded and walked back into the Observatory to retrieve his own report, which he'd been working on over the last few days. It was not an extensive list by any means, for they were only a month into their investigation, though it was also evidence of their labor.

It was proof that they wouldn't just take the Governor's supplies without recorded progress of their research.

Still, when Roy got to the first floor and gave the Governor a sheaf of several papers, torn out of the notebook he'd been writing in, he could neither hold back nor explain the frisson of unease that went through him.

"If the weather wills it," the Governor told Roy, one of the Droves opening the doors to the Basilica behind him, "I'll be back in four weeks." He tucked Roy's sheaf of papers in the same pocket where he'd placed Percival's. "Best of luck to you both."

A little later that day, Roy went up to the sixth floor, where he had been tailed by the creature, in the hopes of finding an artifact from the Age of Scribes that might hold relevance to the Old Ones. This floor, like those beneath it, *was* crowded with manuscripts, but it also featured the exhibition of relics Roy had looked through on his first night. After seven hours of picking through the shelves and cabinets, he almost *wanted* the Old Ones to raid the library, if only so he could be reminded they existed and maintain his sanity.

"Do you plan to stumble and fall again?"

Roy looked up from the astrolabe he'd been observing, which he'd placed on the low-lying table in front of him.

Percival strode toward Roy, his boots rapping against the floorboards. He pointed at the bookshelf past Roy's shoulder. "It happened over there. I would know; I remember it quite clearly."

Roy remembered it, too, almost as well as he remembered what Percival had said some few days ago. *There is a line between us, Roy, and crossing that line would not do well for either of us.*

Roy had skirted that line by admitting that he'd heard whispers when he'd entered the Orphic Basilica, and although the game was over, discontinued shortly after it had begun, he couldn't remember being accosted by the ghost without remembering the brief impression he had seen of Gabriel's leering grin. He *wanted* to tell Percival about the ghost, because he was sure it had its own place in this conspiracy somehow. But each thought and memory of Gabriel drew a new line of blood over Roy's scars, and he didn't think he could go through with it if Percival saw and knew what evil had been done in that old, cold manor Roy had once called home.

Just tell him about the ghost, Roy told himself. *Just the ghost. That's all you have to do. Simple, no?*

Not so, he thought, because he had only now fully come to terms with his attraction for Percival. These feelings were fresh and therefore fragile, and he could not trust himself to tell Percival the necessities without letting slip something about Gabriel, *something* about the true thing haunting him.

So he said nothing.

Percival surveyed Roy from head to foot, then dropped his gaze to his book again. "You haven't found anything, have you?" He sounded accusing, but also faintly sad.

Roy saw no reason to lie. "Nothing."

Percival nodded, the palest shade of red forming on his cheeks. "I've been looking for any more references to black chest plates in *The Lost Records of Old Wynair* and any reports on the Elder Scribes' agenda with, and banishment of, the Old Ones. But that's about as much as I included in my report to the Governor. Otherwise, all I managed to find were other books on Wynair, but—"

"*What?*" Roy exclaimed. "Where are they?"

"That stack over there," Percival said, pointing over his shoulder to a pile of books on one of the tables lining the nearest wall. He smirked at Roy, whose eyes had gone wide. "Oh, don't bother, darling. I've already checked; I couldn't find anything. They're purely there for safekeeping, should I discover any other connections that link back to those books. Besides, I wouldn't want anyone to misplace my research materials." He quickly winked at Roy, then looked around, his expression introspective. "There are quite a few ancient documents here, though. Here's hoping this library is willing to be a tad more lenient."

Percival took his feet off the ottoman, stood, and walked toward the glass displays surrounding the star-shaped reading benches. Above the benches, the orrery emitted bright bangles of orange light, which radiated from torches mounted on the walls.

Roy stood and followed Percival. "The last time I was here, I..."

But he stopped. For some reason, contrary to what he'd *just* thought, he felt compelled to tell Percival, to blurt out, *I saw something I cannot properly explain, something I have not yet fully wrapped my mind around.* Was that impetus because he wanted to ingratiate himself with Percival? Guilt? Or, perhaps, something else. Something Percival had said, about the library being a tad more lenient...

And also *insistent*?

But then Gabriel's face sprang into his mind again, his smile as wide as the cuts he'd made in Roy's skin, and the words died on his tongue.

Instead, Roy said, "One of the first times that I came here, I was drawn to the relics—the abacus, the journal... I think this level houses the oldest manuscripts of the library."

Percival, who was poring over a half-crumbled journal, raised a brow. "Why have you returned to this specific area, then, if you weren't as successful as you'd hoped? Trying your luck again?"

Roy shrugged. "I've been thinking recently about how many books I must've walked past, books that I once thought would hold no pertinent information, while wandering about these shelves the first time." He deliberated cautiously on the phrasing of his next words, believing there might be some way to state them without sounding irrational, then decided he was overthinking it. The truth was hard to admit, but there was no other answer. "Earlier, I thought there weren't any visible systems of organization in this library, and to a point, I was right: There aren't any *visible* systems. It's unseen. It's intangible. And it's ludicrous, but maybe with each crucial piece of information we uncover, the Basilica guides us, *pushes* us, toward our intended destination. The place we *need* to be."

"Nearly being trampled by that rolling ladder truly convinced you that the library is alive, then?"

"Yes," Roy said, and in spite of the unshakable confidence with which he'd once claimed otherwise, he felt his answer to be deeply true. "And I'm not sure if it or the Elder Scribes are responsible for the layout of the building and the placement of the books and the artifacts, but regardless, a design exists and we just have to find it."

Percival glanced over his shoulder. "Do you feel the same as you did when you entered the Basilica? Around this level, I mean?"

Roy is running, sprinting. His hair blows and whips about him in the air, so stale, so dry, not because of this antiquated building and its old, yet seemingly pristine, walls but because of the thing gliding after him on its silent shadow-feet. He senses its nearness like the stench of a corpse in its later processes of decomposition. His heart is pounding with a feral terror. He is an animal. He is prey. He sees books and moonlight and other wondrous, holy sights, but the thing advancing toward him spoils it all. It is his doom, his dark mirror, and once it has its hands on him, he will have no breath with which to scream—

Roy turned away from Percival, wrapped his arms around his waist, and shook his head. "No, I haven't felt it since."

Percival did not see through Roy's lie. He strode toward a display showcasing a book twice the size of his head. Its pages were stained black. "Neither have I," he said. "I've been trying to find it, though, to see if those strange whispers say something about the Old Ones. It's a flimsy idea, but..."

"But it's the only idea you have," Roy finished. He looked up at the orrery, at the slow but inevitable rotation of worlds and moons orbiting around one another, and wondered if, on one of those distant civilizations, any of them, they were fighting battles as great as—or even greater than—this. "Any idea is a good idea now."

"With the exception of the idea that doesn't work," Percival said. "You say you think they had to have had a system, but what? How did the Elder Scribes study in this cesspit? For the sake of progression, let's say that your theory has a grain of truth to it, that the Basilica is steering us toward our destination like a compass or . . . or a pathfinder. How did the Scribes know what they were researching would lead them to the same path? How many years would it have taken them to deduce this, let alone design it? And once they *did*, why didn't they take the time to save us the effort of plumbing for answers? Why keep up this aggravating treasure hunt?" He sniffed. "They're selfish, that's why. They wanted it all to themselves."

Roy started forward. "I see where this line of thinking might originate, but . . . the way I see it, the Elder Scribes wanted future scholars to seek the truth on their *own*, to discover the world through their own experiences, their own lives, to enlighten but not entirely give away all the secrets of academia to students of philosophy like you and me."

Percival laid a hand against the display in front of him. "Glorification is the nemesis of authenticity. They left us, Dawnseve. If the Scribes were meant to be our leaders, then what does it mean that they left us to fend for ourselves?"

"Did they leave us, or were they eliminated?"

"In my eyes, it's the same thing." Percival went silent for a moment. "So far as we know, we are the last scholars standing. The last who give a damn, at least, who believe an overthrow of the Governor and the Iron Citadel is still a viable option."

Roy stared; he was certain he'd heard Percival wrong. "An overthrow?"

"You might be a little ditzy, darling, but you're not blind. Northgard is sitting on the edge, the very fucking *precipice*, of a revolution. The city has been quiet for too long, and not without reason. The Old Ones intervened when the Governor signaled the call to war—not that Northgard had any hope then of insurrection."

Roy remembered the sled drive along the winding streets—the families pleading for food, their frostbitten fingers hooked in desperation like gnarled icicles. He had not seen a single spark of mutiny, however, as any budding ember of insurrection had likely been extinguished by the Radiant Droves watching over all like sharp-eyed shadows, but despite its light, fire could hide. Embers could lie warm yet dormant, smoldering until the right kindling, the proper breeze, sparked a greater flame. It could be hidden, indeed, underneath generations of systemic oppression. But if that pale hope ignited into a full-blown revolution, there *were* still the Old Ones to contend against. But now, Roy figured that revolution would only mean changing who was in charge of Northgard's downfall.

Not that any of it mattered—there was no chance of rebellion.

"The Governor wields far too much power," Roy said, his voice shaking with hatred and denial. "He has the resources to destroy his own people."

"But not enough to destroy the Old Ones," Percival countered, reading Roy's own thoughts. "And, as history has shown, not enough to destroy the Orphic Basilica. If things had not turned out as they had, we wouldn't be here, the Edict would serve no purpose. That damn iron wall would be gone." His voice was quivering like Roy's, but there was an undercurrent of personal conviction in it, as though he had some long-held grudge against the Edict. "If he was unstoppable, *unconquerable*, the Governor would have completely mastered his control over the Hasdan Isles."

"He doesn't have to master the Isles, though. He has mastered *us*. He's powerful enough that he can force us here and call it an assignment when we both know it's a death sentence—need I remind you that if we don't find anything, we'll be dragged onto the front lines?"

"That might have been the ultimatum *you* were given, but I . . ." Percival pursed his lips, which stopped trembling, but then a quiver started in his hands. "I *was* punished, Roy. My family knew of my treachery, that I'd harbored contraband and dedicated myself to old-world lore to escape the rules of this society, but I went too far. I sacrificed too much. That's why I'm here."

Roy stilled at the allusion to Percival's past. It made him yearn to know more, yet, at the same time, haunted him with memories of his own suffering, of Gabriel, of H-I-S-T-O-R-Y, of the inexorable dreams that, night after night, thinned the barrier between nightmare and reality. He felt entombed, immobilized by both the weight of his burden and the knowledge of Percival's. He wanted to approach the matter with caution, but he couldn't wrest control of his own emotions, nor put a damper on them. He wanted to lash out, to scream his fury, to let his fists swing and have them land right where it would satisfy.

On sheer impulse, Roy retorted, "And you think that I haven't sacrificed enough? Is that it? Do you think that your sacrifices and suffering exceed my own?" He rubbed at his chest and let his hand linger there, afraid that if he lowered it, Percival might see his scar, the part of himself that had never healed—and never would.

Percival stared at him, vulnerably soft and piercing all at

once. "I don't *know* your suffering, Roy, and you certainly don't know mine. Even if I opened up to you, bared my soul to you, right here, right now, it wouldn't change a thing."

"Nothing needs to change," Roy assured him. "We can forget this ever occurred, if you prefer, but for this brief moment, this one time, I . . . I wish you would just let me in." His voice softened, turning tender and glum. "What did you sacrifice, Percival? What did you lose? And how did it land you in the Basilica?"

A shadow of devastation crossed Percival's face. He hung his head, as though he could hide it, evade the truth by cowering, and for a while, Roy thought that was exactly what he'd do: close off and continue this shared existence of forced separation.

But then Percival said, so quietly at first that Roy wasn't sure when he started, "I lost someone not too long before I was sent here. I made a mistake that I initially thought was a good, moral decision, but when the plan went to ruin, it wasn't I who stood in the line of fire." He brought his gaze to Roy's, his eyes glittering with tears. He wiped them away with the back of his hand, his jaw hardening. "The aftermath . . . I'll spare you the details, but the Governor wasn't happy."

A thousand questions cascaded through Roy's mind, but he only asked, "Why would your . . ." *Friend? Lover?* He cast that aside and pressed on. "How could their death affect the Governor that personally—"

"Never mind that," Percival said, assuming a contemplative expression, erasing whatever emotion had caught his breath and made his voice crack moments ago. "Just know that I know, from experience, the next steps to take. We need to even out the power balance and make sure we're on an equal level of standing as the Governor. Yes, he forced this mission on us, but he didn't say we couldn't also pursue our own mission."

"But I have no other mission!" Roy shouted. "I just want—"

"You don't know what you want," Percival said smoothly, and that stopped Roy in his tracks. "But, as I insisted during the game, what you *need* is to stoke that fire inside you. To not be led, but to lead."

Except you're conveniently leaving out that you're leading me right now, Roy thought. Yet, even with that truth, he wasn't sure he minded all that much.

Percival continued. "We've been accepting it for years. Now we're doing what Northgard hasn't had the drive to do. We have no choice but to embrace it."

At that, Roy snapped, "It's a shame you had to stoop so low and make it a competition." He was truly angry, too, because instead of the last month of farce, they could have, possibly, been working toward the same goal. Roy was aware enough to know he probably would have resisted initially—even as he resisted now—but the allure of this idea...

The allure of *Percival*...

Percival chuckled, rough as war, his eyes like dying flames. He flexed the hand that wasn't holding the book, his veins standing against his fair skin. Though his arms were thin, they were bound with muscle, their strength evident in the orrery's glassy lights. He canted his head at a minute angle, and as his intent gaze met Roy's, Percival raised a hand and dragged his fingers through his own hair, his lean biceps bulging.

Roy watched the slow and determined trajectory of Percival's fingers, the transformation of his hair from bristly to tousled. Roy stood still, the air stolen from his lungs. He thought of rumpled bedsheets, of midnight breezes and clandestine kisses. He thought of the days they'd passed one another, not a single word spoken or exchanged, and how many times after these incidents Roy had envisioned Percival huddled over his books, his lips curved into the same roguish smile that they were curved into now.

The air between them seemed alive, shuddering, like the air on a blazing summer's day. He inhaled and tasted it on his tongue, and although his lungs felt swollen and hot, as though they'd taken in a vat of steam, he had not nearly reached his fill.

At the corner of his vision, Percival took another step forward. Even while Roy tried to retain a frightening lack of self-control, he knew too well he would look up and find himself staring at Percival, a young man so burdened with untold misery and rage it had become a weapon. But as Percival walked closer, Roy didn't think he'd ever been Percival's intended target. He was cross at times, yes, but he could simply be opinionated, afraid he wouldn't be heard unless he shouted from the top of his lungs. That was not so with Roy, though, not at all. Percival could whisper and Roy would only lean in, eager and defiant of his rational mind.

We have no choice but to embrace it.

Had it been not their circumstances Percival was speaking about, but *this*? Their mutual urge to be aware of the other's every move, whether asleep or awake, working or resting? He was astounded by the implications, all of them too terrifying to acknowledge or to name, so he discarded them, let go of his bearings, and then looked up.

Percival crossed the distance between them. They were either a chasm or a hairbreadth apart; Roy could not discern the difference. But when Percival stopped before him, all Roy's thoughts of proximity and distance were cast by the wayside. Percival was a storm, and Roy was caught in his eye. His coat, a green riot of brocade and velvet, brushed against Percival's raggedy tunic. Percival inched closer, their stomachs nearly pressed flush together, and Roy fought to contain his sigh, yet when he exhaled, his breath still came out wavery and stilted, as if he were exerted, pushed to the brink.

Roy tilted his head to the side, and Percival complied to his tacit request, no matter that he was striding past the line he had only days ago forbidden them to cross. He leaned in and slowly exhaled, his hot breath rushing along Roy's cheek. Roy immediately bunched his hands into fists and even fought the urge to scratch his own skin, initially discomforted by Percival's nearness, but not long after, a delightful shiver ran through him. Percival laughed under his breath, too rough to be a chuckle, and tucked Roy's hair behind his ear, exposing the column of his neck.

Was one of them leaning in or was the world tipping on its axis? Roy could not tell. His heart was pounding too loudly in his ears, and he couldn't keep his eyes from fluttering shut, enclosing and drawing out every moment of this, whatever *this* might be, within the darkness behind his lids. Percival dragged his finger from Roy's neck to the shell of his ear. Roy ached to know what the next moment might hold and longed even more for its unexpectedness, its dark mystery.

And when Roy opened his eyes, Percival appeared just as spellbound, studiously watching each movement of his own fingers. A secret smile tugged at his lips, and if Roy was not so beguiled by the spell laid upon him, he might've divined Percival's thoughts from his crooked mouth.

I can't let you get in my way.

But there was only the palm now cupping his cheek, the closeness of their bodies, the arduous, and ultimately impossible, challenge to withdraw. Roy leaned into Percival's warm skin, his face flushing beneath the contact. Percival dragged his thumb along the underside of Roy's jaw, just above his pulse point. The loose sleeve of Percival's tattered tunic hovered near Roy's shoulder. Yet another layer dividing them, another reason why this ought to stop, to promptly cease before their deadline passed them by.

Roy stiffened; his mouth frozen into a thin, bloodless line. But if he tried to speak, he might rip away the curtains of Percival's illusion. And though his heart was still pounding in frenzied abandon, Roy was still aware of who stood before him, of the man who strove, day after day, to outshine him, to manipulate him. Had their game not come to an end, he would have suspected that *this*—Percival's palm on his cheek, their bodies a breath apart—was the next move on the game board.

But he wasn't sure if that bothered him in this moment.

Percival ran his thumb over Roy's jawline, then across to the divot between his nose and mouth. He quickly looked from Roy's lips to his gaze, then back again.

Anticipation coiled tight in Roy's stomach. He drew in a deep breath, the soupy heat of Percival's skin filling his lungs like a cloud of fog. Percival moved his thumb down, stopping only as he pressed it against Roy's mouth. Percival nodded at his thumb, at Roy's lips, and it came over Roy, what Percival was offering him: He was holding the game piece in play, and now it was Roy's choice whether to tip the scales in his favor or, for a moment, relinquish control to his opponent. He didn't want to consider the consequences, but regardless, a series of progressively vivid thoughts cycled through his mind.

Roy would part his lips and Percival would slide his thumb into his mouth, gliding it along Roy's tongue. Roy would tip his head back in exhilaration, but Percival would want nothing of it. He would want to claim his prize, to prolong his grasp of power. And so, he would take hold of Roy's jaw with the side of his index finger, then pull him forward, their mouths only inches apart but steadily drawing closer—

Roy shoved Percival back, his hands briefly touching Percival's midriff, then stumbled away. The absence of their proximity was as disorienting as awakening from a deep dream.

Unlike Roy, Percival appeared entirely unperturbed by what had just transpired. He clasped his hands behind his back with nonchalance, though Roy couldn't make out whether it was affected. "You really ought to control your breathing, Dawnseve," he said with a scoff. He nodded to the table where he'd deposited his research material. "Come, darling. Maybe my company might help you find some answers." He walked toward his desk, rolling back his shoulders.

Befuddled, Roy looked after him. He had not been deceived; he knew that much. What had happened had not been a conjuring of his imagination, a mirage of his own fantasies, but a moment grounded in reality. And he'd found the courage, the *discipline*, to extract himself from the test. But it was impossible not to feel that Percival still had a hold of him, that no matter how Roy looked at it, something was still in play. A battle, perhaps, between his heart and his instincts. But the two were so entangled, they were almost indistinguishable, and he couldn't help but feel that some lonely, wanting part of him was at fault.

13

ROY DECLINED PERCIVAL'S REQUEST TO STUDY WITH him at his table, and instead they separately pored over their respective texts, but it didn't stop Roy from gathering his own texts in his arms and sitting at the desk opposite Percival's.

Thankfully, Percival didn't argue; if anything, Roy could perceive a slight smirk on Percival's beautiful lips—

No, Roy thought. *I will not go down that road right now. I've already trod down that path, to nothing but frustration. In fact, I should get up and leave, get him out of my sight, while I still can.*

Why would he leave, though? He wasn't bowing to Percival's every whim and he *certainly* wasn't being led by a leash to do Percival's bidding. Roy was a scholar, too, and as far as he could tell, he was the only one to have actually discovered anything.

More, to go somewhere else wasn't an option. Definitely not the Observatory, which he couldn't quite convince himself to go back to anytime soon. No, Roy couldn't put his finger on precisely what it was, but the sixth floor felt vital, like the linchpin to all that he'd uncovered thus far—and all they'd yet to uncover.

The ostensible importance of the sixth floor, however, did not discount its absurd texts, nor the maddening warren of ambiguities and dead ends therein. Self-styled "history books" concerning the exploitation of old-world magic misquoted one another, which led Roy on a hunt for references, only to end up with the same book in his hands he'd been studying for the past several hours. One tome, Gideon Argell's *The Bandits of Sorcery*, seemed at first to hold decent information and possibly some answers regarding the Old Ones, insofar as there were several diagrams of men, women, and those who identified as otherwise clad in dark armor, but he got halfway through the text before flipping to the author's note (unwisely placed at the *end* of the book) and realizing it was a work of fiction.

This happened no less than fifteen times, but at least by perhaps the eighth book, he grew more aware of the regularity of these obstacles. The next time that he forced himself to take a break, return his previous stack of books to their respective locations, and then gather a new stack, he chose carefully. He glanced over historians' interpretations, tables of contents, footnotes, epigraphs, authors' and editors' notes, and biographies; deciphered whether the content of the book was true to life or fictitious; then sat down and got back to work.

He understood, of course, that fiction was partly modeled after reality, but that only helped so much; it was crucial he be able to go directly to the source. If he wasted time disentangling truths from fabrications, that would, he feared, increase his workload. And he already had no way of knowing when this search would end.

After another six hours' work, Roy lifted his head up from the book he'd been hunched over, a collection of expeditions recorded by a band of seafarers. He groaned, kneading out the knot in his left shoulder.

Percival chuckled without raising his gaze from his own work. "Having some trouble over there, darling?"

"No more than you," Roy said, regarding the disarrayed scrolls strewn across Percival's desk. "Are you doing research or constructing some sort of flimsy tablecloth?" Roy feigned a look of fervid concentration, as though he wasn't fumbling aimlessly through his own studies. "Now, limit these interruptions, would you?" He waved in dismissal at Percival, despite that he wasn't looking at Roy. "I have far too much work to do."

Percival rolled his eyes.

A half hour later, Roy was skimming through a nautical analysis of the chapter he'd just finished reading, which mainly contained coordinates he didn't understand nor had any care to, when he flipped to a page that had a folded, crumpled piece of parchment wedged into the binding. Frowning, Roy unfolded the parchment, then smoothed it out and surveyed its contents.

The diagram was simplistic, almost deceptively so. Eight rectangular blocks, each outlined in deep gray charcoal, were stacked atop one another and labeled: *FLOOR ONE, FLOOR TWO*, and so on. Scribbled into the topmost of these blocks was another column of rectangles labeled *BOOKSHELVES*, above which were a sequence of overlapping circles, although these Roy couldn't make sense of. The six blocks below were identical, excluding the circles, but the lowest contained a winding network of curves, like a descending spiral of some sort. Underneath the illustration was this inscription, also scrawled in charcoal: *THE ORPHIC BASILICA—FRAMEWORK—DRAFT.*

Roy gawked at the piece of parchment, excitement bursting within him, then slipped it under the book and continued reading, enthralled. The next chapter, "The Treacherous Passage to the Orphic Basilica," unfortunately exclusively addressed the details of the actual seafaring expedition, not the journey to the library thereafter. If there were any references to black chest plates, or anything remotely linked to the Old Ones, Roy didn't pick up on them.

He reviewed the illustrated framework of the Orphic Basilica again, curious as to the eighth block, which he assumed to be the artist's hastily drawn interpretation of an eighth floor. It was this that puzzled Roy. There were definitely only seven floors; he had counted them when he'd first been brought here. Had another been in the drafting stage at the time of this expedition, then? Had the architects of the library rejected the propositioned additional floor, explaining the current absence of the eighth? Or could the eighth floor not be *seen* from outside, nor even inside, unless properly accessed? Was it . . .

A soft breeze whisked through Roy's hair. Whispers rose from beneath the muffled grumbling of the winter storm, then twirled around him and hissed in his ear, rising as the question formed shape and substance in his mind.

Is the eighth floor underground?

Roy shot to his feet, knocking back his chair and startling Percival, who was ogling him with marked bafflement. Roy stalked toward Percival, then slapped the parchment down onto his desk, his chest heaving.

"Go on," Roy panted. "Read it."

After a long moment, Percival obeyed, then slowly straightened in his seat as the truth of the Basilica's hidden and unknowably vast scope settled in. A cold wind twined around Roy once more, swirled through the air, and ruffled the scrolls on Percival's desk.

"We're heading to the first floor," Percival whispered, his eyes sweeping across the disturbed papers, one of which had drifted toward him. "Right now."

"*Now?*" Roy echoed. "We don't even know what we're *looking* for—"

Percival snatched up the small scrap of paper that the wind had seemed to deliberately stir toward him, then thrust it at Roy.

Roy took the paper and surveyed it. "This is a poem."

"Written by Charles Patiny, yes," Percival said. Roy had only read Patiny's novels, though his poems were considered to be some of the most hard-hitting, all concerning an unreciprocated love. "He wrote chiefly about this man he fancied, but there are a few about his love for the Basilica."

Roy shook his head, dubious. "I don't see how—"

"This is what the wind is getting at," Percival interrupted. "You don't see how *now*, but read it and we'll know." He jerked his chin at the paper. "The first, second, and third stanzas. At first, I thought Patiny was making some sort of metaphor, but perhaps not."

"This damn wind," Roy said, shaking his head. "I'll admit: As averse as I once was to it, it's remarkably helpful."

"You've felt it before?" Percival asked, intrigue glittering in his eyes. "On the seventh floor, you mean? With the ladder?"

Roy supposed it was too late to hold his tongue now. "When I found the grant in the Observatory."

"The Observatory?"

"The room on the fifth floor, the one with the piano."

"Ah," Percival said. "Well, that's all the more reason to trust its guidance once more, right? Go on, Dawnseve. First, second, and third stanzas."

The breeze picked up again, making the scrap of paper in Roy's hand flutter back and forth like a bird testing its recently repaired wings. Roy looked down, then found the stanzas Percival had indicated and read them aloud:

> Too many voices, too many words
> this hall of memories does hold,
> that under flesh, warm forevermore,
> further stories are kept on walls of old

"The red-eyed devils!" the pages call,
"the bringers and keepers of death!"
whose eyes of burning light do glow
upon their prey's final breath

'Neath the wise eyes of the Oracle,
there yawns a dark and winding cave;
the lips know only dust and earth
but its limit holds relics saved

Roy raised his wide-eyed gaze to Percival. "A tunnel network?"

"It seems like it," Percival said, then snatched the scrap of paper off Roy and pointed at the first line of the third stanza. "And the Oracle. Darling, that was one of Patiny's names for Walestone. He thanked him in the acknowledgments of *Hearts Unsung*, his last novel. '*My greatest blessings to the Oracle, he whose insight—*'"

"'*—is as effulgent as his heart,*'" Roy finished. He'd always wondered what that moniker had meant. "By the *Scribes*, Percival, there must be something underneath us. Under the library itself." He blinked. "The bust of Walestone on the first floor. I saw it when I was first brought here. That has to be it. It *must* be, Percival. Don't you think?"

"''Neath the wise eyes of the Oracle...'" Percival grinned. "Oh, I don't just think it. I would *bet* on it, Dawnseve."

After exchanging an incredulous look, they sprinted down to the first floor.

Roy bounded off the last step of the staircase that led to the first floor, then raced over to the elaborately sculpted bust of Atticus Walestone.

"Give me a hand, would you?" asked Percival, who had his sleeves rolled up and his hands braced on one side of the plinth on which the bust was resting. "I have a feeling this won't be accomplishable with only one of us."

Roy looked around him, half-afraid that Walestone's ghost might come soaring out of some shadowy study hall and give them a tongue-lashing for plotting to destroy the statue of his likeness. "We don't have to break it, do we?"

"This thing is damn heavy, darling," Percival said, then grunted as he grabbed hold of the crown of Walestone's head and shook it a little. "And I'm pretty sure the bust is welded to the plinth. So, yes, we do have to break it."

Roy stood there hesitating for a long moment, then muttered, "I doubt this is how the Scribes opened it in their time," and finally assisted Percival. They each took hold of either side of the plinth, which was flatter and therefore less cumbersome to grip than the bust, and then heaved it to the side. Roy let out a whooshing breath at the staggering weight of the plinth, and Percival's face, which had turned a dark shade of red, was slathered in a gleaming veil of sweat. Then, once they'd pushed the plinth off the ground to such an angle that it was slanted more backward than standing upright, the two of them let go on Percival's murmured count of three.

The bust crashed to the floor with a disconcertingly loud crunch. It and the plinth might have been fused together, or had maybe been seamlessly crafted from the same marble block, but Roy and Percival had toppled it with enough force to send a splinter, loosely resemblant of a lightning bolt, zigzagging down the middle of Walestone's scalp. He looked like a felled warrior, but that thought only made Roy think of the inscription he'd read under the painting, which in turn brought back the unsettling image he'd had of the Elder Scribes all bearing swords. He shook off these memories and bid himself to focus.

Though nothing moved, Roy could feel the world slowing in the air around them, a grinding, then a halting, of clockwork. A long pause, which he waited through with bated breath. And then the cogs began turning anew.

He knelt before Percival, who was crouched in front of the floorboard where the sculpture had once stood. Between them was a small square wooden platform, slightly raised above the surrounding redwood. It was the size of a fist, its edges flat and smooth, and was encompassed by a gap as thin as paper.

Percival licked his lips, sweat dripping down his face. "This is it, Dawnseve," he whispered. "This is it." He looked directly at Roy, then, and smiled.

Roy, despite himself, smiled back.

Before Percival could move, Roy pulled his gaze from those captivating hazel eyes, reached over, and pressed his palm into the block, the tips of Percival's fingers grazing his shoulder. Roy recoiled with a small cry, acutely aware of the scars that had been so near to Percival's touch, but Percival did no more than frown at Roy's reaction before the piece of wood clicked into place. A hidden compartment in the block sprang open, covering the gap that surrounded it. The block now created the barest dip in the floorboards.

A sound rumbled from beneath their feet, rising higher and higher, and then exploded outward in a cacophony of discordant noises. Roy was unprepared for the assault. He could not pick apart the sounds at first, but as he gritted his teeth against the racket, they clarified: the grinding of stone against stone; the grating sound of scratched sandpaper, its volume increased tenfold; and a clamor of tortured, grief-stricken screams. The noise didn't seem to affect the library; no books toppled from their shelves, none of the remaining busts trembled on their plinths, and none of the curtains swung.

Still, Percival grabbed Roy's wrist. "Get back. *Move.*" He pulled back Roy, who let out a muttered "Fuck" when the ground abruptly opened out beneath them.

The floorboards rippled apart, revealing a descending passage of stairs. Wide slabs of stone, uneroded by time and unmarked by footsteps, led down into an untold length of pitch-blackness. A terrible stench wafted up from the void, borne aloft on a dry breeze: graveyard dirt and dried wallpaper. Roy closed his eyes, and somehow, in the darkness behind his lids, he glimpsed a history cloaked in shadow: the skeletal remains of scholars who had suffered far beneath his feet; their eyes bulging out of sockets, liquefying and running down their cheeks, aghast—in the last moment of their lives—by the deplorable things they had seen down in the dark.

Roy was struck with terror, now stronger than ever. He tried to swallow, but his tongue felt dry and compact, like a block of hardened sand. He wanted more than anything to give in, to run from the pursuit of knowledge, the one prospect that had provided him clarity throughout a lifetime of questioning his identity and determining his future, but . . .

But something had called to him for all those years as it was calling now, echoing from the darkness.

Find answers for this city, it said to him, *or march into battle for this city.*

He looked deeper into the dark, but perhaps it wasn't just that. No, perhaps he was crouching before the fringes of an unfamiliar land. He knew not what might wait ahead . . . unless he took the first step.

Roy stood and hovered his left foot above the first slab of stone, hesitant, afraid some grave fate might befall him upon contact. It didn't seem far-fetched that the Elder Scribes had hidden traps in the stonework to maintain secrecy and protect their manuscripts. He bore his weight into the step, and when he was certain he wasn't about to become one of those bodies he'd envisioned, Roy exhaled.

Hurried footsteps sounded beside him. Roy went to give Percival a sidelong glance but Percival was already walking toward an unlit candle perched upon the edge of a pedestal. Not a second before he retrieved the candle, it sparked alight.

Percival strode back to the passage of stairs. The candle in his hand cast a fine glow through his blond hair. He returned to Roy's side, his gaze flicking from the candle to the void. Only then did Roy catch Percival's expression, an emotion rarely seen on his face: sorrow.

Roy took hold of Percival's shoulder, tensed when Percival did. When neither of them broke away, Roy said, "Whatever your past may be, there's no need to hide yourself. You don't... You don't have to *keep to* yourself. This might not be the time to share, but you don't need to live in constant fear. And neither do I. I know you said we're shunned for what we believe in, for who we are, but the world doesn't always have to be like that. It wasn't before... well, *before*."

Percival gave no response, and Roy practically screamed: *Can you tell me what you're thinking? Can you show me what you're hiding?*

But Percival couldn't answer what was unasked. Instead, he walked on, his slow stride jarring compared to his earlier excited stroll. He cupped his palm around the candle, a small length from the leaping flame. He took a step forward, and another, and another, every step bringing him deeper into the darkness.

As Percival disappeared into the void, an inexplicable sensation seized Roy, like a foul, ungodly presence had invaded his mouth and inhabited his limbs. He could feel his body as if from spans away. For a moment, he saw himself from afar, and then the darkness was rushing toward him, and he was well past Percival, a breeze squalling about him, the sound of bones clacking and the stench of moss and dirt hanging thick in the air and wrapping tightly around him—

He blinked, and instantly, he was dropped back into reality. He looked around and saw that he hadn't moved an inch.

It's nothing, he told himself. *It's fear, and fear can manifest in a thousand different forms . . . and if there's one thing you know how to do best, it's being afraid.*

Then Roy followed after Percival, toward his fear and—hopefully—his salvation.

THE ELDER SCRIBES

Part Two

14

AFTER A FEW MINUTES OF DESCENDING INTO THE darkness, the planks of redwood that had hidden the passage covered the entrance once more. Roy started, his heart pounding unevenly in his chest, though it returned to its steady beat as he took in his surroundings.

The walls were painted in a honey-gold glow, stretching four steps ahead of where Percival was walking, the candle held in his outstretched hand. Beyond that, the stairs were visible. The farther down they went, the more convinced Roy became that his strange vision had been only that: his imagination fueled by exhaustion.

Roy proceeded downward, each of his footsteps accompanied by the smell of dust. Frowning, he drew to an experimental halt, making Percival glance interestedly over his shoulder, and the smell faded. Wordlessly, Percival resumed his stride and Roy followed—and the smell came once more.

It would have been easy to dismiss the scent as just the thin film of dust coating each slab of stone being disturbed. A sign, as he'd imagined, of a history secreted within this tunnel. But there was something else. Distantly, the odor of the forgotten dead assailed his nostrils, hauling up before his mind's eye a sequence of grisly images—limp tendrils of flesh hanging from rotting bone, gaping jaws, and hollow sockets. He wrinkled his nose and groaned, a deep revulsion crawling through him. He could *feel* those skeins of flesh scraping across his face, brushing over his cheek like scabrous fingers—

With a sharp gasp, Roy tried to shake this dark flight of fancy, focusing instead on a rational connection between the scent and the flashes in his mind.

On a logical plane of thought, this tunnel *could* lead to the burial chamber of the Elder Scribes. Several sights within the Orphic Basilica had hinted at death, memory, and reflection: on the sixth floor, a museum of old artifacts; in the Observatory, whose dust-coated surfaces alluded to forgotten objects; and throughout, the various art pieces displaying certain figures and events throughout Northgard's history. Even the appearance of the Orphic Basilica, from outside, seemed like material for suspicion—of what hid behind those massive double doors, of what secrets the Scribes had augured all those years ago, of what, beyond the supposed hallucinations, had stopped the Radiant Droves from reducing the library to rubble.

It's reasonable enough, Roy mused. *If the Scribes wanted a place to be remembered, they wouldn't have risked a cemetery above ground.*

But if the Elder Scribes had wanted to preserve anything, it would have been their manuscripts, not their bodies. Life was finite and death was eternal, but a book could outlive its creator and the ideas within could prevail over even the greatest calamity. Perhaps the Elder Scribes had been aware of this and created a guaranteed method of survival when pitted against those who meant to harm their work: an escape route from danger.

But isn't the Basilica protected enough? Roy thought. Every person who'd tried to burn the library to ash had faced madness and defeat. Something, a shield perhaps, had protected the Basilica from harm. So why would the Scribes feel the need for such an egress?

But he stopped himself there. Conjecture would get him nowhere. Only moving forward, onward, held the answers. Whether mausoleum or manuscripts, or something else entirely, this tunnel held a great secret. Roy could feel it in the walls around him, like coils of mist seeping from stone. Because of this, his eagerness warred with his hesitancy.

You're getting ahead of yourself, you dim-witted fool. You don't entertain theories. You relish facts.

It's Percival's fault. He's letting you forget who you are, changing you into someone who protests evidence. You don't make spontaneous decisions; you make careful ruminations. When have you ever resisted the traits so fundamental to your own existence?

But there were multiple examples of this sort of resistance: when he'd accepted Percival's game, when he'd deemed the Urswaelian grant for *Black chest plate* indisputable evidence of the ancestors of the Old Ones . . . and when he had wanted, *longed* for, Percival to slide his finger into Roy's mouth.

A cool shiver trailed up his spine. Beads of perspiration formed on the nape of his neck.

Roy furrowed his brow, his longing and frustration interchangeable, as they'd been before. But even now, he couldn't distinguish which emotion had shone brighter when he'd stood a breath from Percival. It would have required no further effort to lean closer and taste Percival's skin. Yet Roy had pulled away, and even after the infectious desire that had swept through his body when he'd felt the contours of Percival's own, Roy didn't know if he could survive another similar encounter without giving in. He would melt. He would burn.

Roy looked over at Percival now. He held the candle near his chest, firelight fluttering over the angular planes of his face.

The only suggestion of his bitterness lay hushed in the air like an unwelcome visitor.

You don't... You don't have to keep to *yourself.*

Gone was his vulnerable sadness; Percival wore an expression of fearful resolve, severe lines marking the skin beneath his lips and around his narrowed eyes. While Roy knew it was a mask, his hands were still clammy with sweat. He tried to keep his attention on the firelight flickering across the walls, but Roy was no soldier. He could not win this battle.

"I hear them," Percival murmured. "Not voices, but those... vibrations."

Roy heard them, too. They were quiet but rhythmic, like the fluttering of butterfly wings.

He wanted to keep silent and show Percival he was capable of not giving him the satisfaction of a response. Percival had done the same. When the descent into the catacombs had been too much for him to bear, owing, perhaps, to the tragedy he'd hinted at, he had gone silent. Roy knew he could do it himself. Why not? He didn't have the willpower to coerce Percival into a false sense of security or form replies full of gilded trickery. Maybe silence was the better option. But the tension that had risen between them was receding, and the whispers were getting louder, so Roy eventually broke the quiet.

"What is this place?" he whispered.

While the candle provided a warm glow, breezes of cool, crisp air kissed his cheeks. A second scent lurked beneath that of rot and decay but he couldn't determine the odor; the first was too potent, clogging his nostrils. It sneaked inside him, then came back out, up the back of his throat. He gagged, swallowing the vomit pressing against the inside of his mouth.

Those whispers, the voices Percival had mentioned, sounded more than anguished; they sounded *trapped*. Muffled pleas scuttled through the eerie silence, just beyond his reach, like sobs stifled by a damp rag. He remembered those agonized screams when the ghost had chased him and tried to draw a comparison, though these voices were much quieter, softer, but just as terrified.

Before Roy had been taken to the Orphic Basilica, he'd walked down a hallway in Dawnseve Manor and seen Northgard from afar. Only then had he realized how tiny the city was and, with this in mind, how much misery could be compressed into a single pocket of civilization. Distraught, he'd listened to the desperate appeals of frostbitten families, begging for food and mercy, their screams carrying on the shrieking winter wind. He had tried several times to give the Matron a written petition to deliver to the Iron Citadel, requesting bread and jam and other amenities, but she had burned Roy's letter seconds after reading it.

The familiarity of the citizens' screams struck a chord in Roy's chest now. Phantoms hissed within his head, and though he wished to help them, Roy was powerless to do so. The innocents, those in his mind and outside these walls, had no savior.

"What is this place, Percival?" he asked again.

"No place for the present. You can feel the age in this tunnel, yes? It feels so . . . so *old*, like the stones might crumble at any moment."

Roy stopped and looked at the walls. Percival circled back and followed his lead.

There was truth in what Percival had said. The age of a building reflected the shadow of its past. Architecture had an uncanny way of depicting history so that later generations could understand their ancestors, ruminate on their triumphs and misdeeds. Yet this tunnel was more akin to a warning, a place best left undisturbed. Indeed, Percival was right. This *was* no place for the present; whatever cataclysm had caused such dread here did not belong in this age—or, possibly, this world.

Roy exhaled, his breathing ragged. He needed to be here; of that, he had no doubt. He had to save the damned people of Northgard before they became the dead.

He pressed his hand against a flagstone, and a chill rushed through his palm. A thick substance coated the stone, sticky as sap. He pushed his fingertips deeper into the liquid, then slowly pulled his hand away.

Roy frowned, confused. Perhaps his vision was failing him—he had been subject to odder occurrences in this library—but he couldn't seem to locate the substance. He rubbed his fingertips together, cringing at the unusual sensation, and, sure enough, he felt its resinous consistency. But the wall was clear as the slabs of stone beneath his feet.

Despite his deepening disgust, Roy was unable to suppress his curiosity. He raised his fingertips to his nose. A sudden wave of disorientation came over him . . . and then a rush of familiarity. Certainty rose and hardened in his chest. He had felt this before; he *knew* it. The smell of the substance overpowered the reek of dead and rotting things.

This must be that smell, he thought. *The smell that put those visions of rot and death in my head.*

The discovery was far from an indication of what purpose this tunnel had, but all the same, he inhaled again. Something lingered beneath the mildew. Charcoal? No, burnt meat. Or burnt *flesh*, for all he knew.

"What are you doing?" Percival asked. He was looking at Roy's hand, a questioning look on his face.

It could've been the inquisitiveness in Percival's voice, but Roy didn't hesitate as he held out his hand and said, "Smell this. There seems to be some substance on the walls."

The candlelight illuminated Roy's fingertips. Although he couldn't see anything, aiding his theory that the substance was a figment of his imagination, warped by hallucinations, he also couldn't doubt its existence.

Percival shuffled a step closer and bowed forward. There was a scent drifting about his hair, a crisp and woodsy aroma. He lifted his head and nodded. An expression of resignation settled upon his features, as if he'd finally given in to the prospect of Roy finding something worthwhile.

Roy surveyed the area for a surface to relocate the residue. He looked down at his trousers, but the fine, soft cloth seemed too expensive to be marred by a stain, albeit an invisible one.

"You have quite the attitude about maintaining an image," Percival said, his voice tinged with careful curiosity.

His cheeks hot with mortification, Roy cleared his throat, resuming his search for a place to remove the substance. "I don't do well with unfamiliar textures and sensations. Sometimes, *most* times, it gets under my skin, and even when I can't see it, it still feels like it's there." It was a severe understatement of the feeling—he had sometimes scratched his arms for hours because the elbow pads of his coat felt like they were burning through his skin—but he was anxious that Percival would deride Roy or use his experiences as blackmail.

But Percival was fortunately quite understanding. "Ah," he said. "Yes, I've noticed you scratch your hand on occasion. Here." He proffered a corner of his tunic. "It's not as though it hasn't been scuffed and torn already."

"You wouldn't mind? I know it seems a little unnecessary, but . . ."

"Darling, I am a man of limited charitability and great impatience. Standing here talking about it won't make it any less awkward—"

Roy swiped his fingertips down the front of Percival's tunic.

Percival went still, his jaw dropping in mock outrage. The streak of invisible residue clung to his abdominal muscles. "You're wrong. That was *entirely* unnecessary."

A small smile on his lips, Roy continued walking down the stairs, and after a moment, Percival followed.

"It's mildew, isn't it?" Roy asked. "The substance."

"Not as strong as the smell of rot, but yes, I believe so. But if the Basilica has spent millennia in disuse, how are there meals brought to us every morning?" Percival asked, a note of intrigue in his voice. "How has this building not fallen into a state of complete disrepair? I mean, parts of the library *should* be decaying, if these scents are any indication, but it's kept upright for generations."

"You're the one who first said the Basilica could be alive."

"Yes, but not *feeding* us, as you've asserted," Percival replied. "I *did* think it was sentient, but this tunnel disprove that assumption." His voice deepened. "All I feel here is death."

As if in confirmation, another flicker of visions descended over Roy's opened eyes: skulls lined up in a row; moss spread over skeletal jaws and foreheads; a blindfold made of cobwebs. He swallowed. "As do I."

The passage of time felt broken, somehow, furling and unfurling with disorienting rapidity. The darkness of the tunnel stretching beyond the candlelight seemed to go on either forever or not at all. They were stuck in a moving diorama of echoing footsteps, firelight dancing across stone and the ever-thickening stench of rot.

Then, just when Roy had begun to think this labyrinth might never end, a large chamber appeared out of the dark. He felt a momentary sweet relief flood through him, but it was secondary to the visceral terror underlying all his senses. He knew not what existed beneath the foundations of the library, what age-old horrors had lain here in perpetual slumber. He skidded to a halt, terrified, and Percival stopped beside him, then raised the candle to fully reveal the room.

The stairs ended at a long expanse of mist-blanketed flagstone. Cobwebs hung in the corners of the low-ceilinged chamber. In the center of the space was a tall-stemmed chalice perched upon a marble plinth, the water within shrouded by a thick film of algae. Skeletons were sprawled across the ground, age-yellowed bones protruding from the mist. A miasma of cloying rot and coppery blood hung fresh in the air, as though these bodies had been dead for hours, not thousands of years.

Tears welled up in Roy's eyes; whether from overwhelm or fear, he could not say. Through his bleary vision, he perceived a bend at the back of the chamber. Tendrils of mist swept through the archway and around the corner. It wasn't until he watched the fog stir that Roy realized an icy breeze had been whispering across his skin. Even the overcoat he'd chosen this morning couldn't dispel the cold gnawing through to his bones. Reluctant, he stepped closer toward the warmth emanating from Percival's candle.

"Be careful," Percival whispered. Flickering shadows endowed his face with punishing beauty. "If we lose that light, something tells me we won't be getting it back."

Roy prepared a retort, but by Percival's tone, Roy didn't think it would win him any favors. It seemed Percival was smart enough to know they should, at least right now, remain civil.

Roy started walking again, but slowly, his footsteps sending plumes of bone-dust into the air and rippling candlelit mist. He licked his dry lips, his throat tight with fear.

As the mist swept aside, Roy beheld the dead, at first terrified, then enraptured. One skull was perched on its jaw and cranium, its hollow sockets staring eternally into the eyes of the Reaper. A fat-bellied mouse scurried out from the skull's dark, gaping jaws. About a foot away was a skeleton, its sinister grin like a macabre mimicry of a smile. Its chest was caved in, its shattered ribs like a mouthful of notched teeth.

Roy flinched, his arms covered with gooseflesh. "What happened to all these people? I know the scholars of the old world were frowned upon, but I . . ." He found another skeleton, its skull craned back in horrific agony. "I hadn't realized they were slaughtered, *massacred*."

Percival, beside him now, regarded the dead with a dour expression, the corners of his mouth pinched. He might have been frozen, if not for the minute twitch in his left eye. "This is what happens when we dare to dream, darling," he said. "This is what *will* happen if we're sent into the front lines. We'll die before we can even fight back, and this entire fucking city will praise the day."

Roy gulped. "Millennia of debasement and humiliation."

"It's not *humiliation*. It's sacrilege and societal desecration. The Iron Citadel strips our people of personal identity and manipulates what remains to their own perverse satisfaction. We're forced to sacrifice our beautiful purpose for a violent cause. I refuse to see this dark age as anything but an avaricious resurrection of the past."

"And the Governor is orchestrating the full scope of it."

"He's not the only one to blame, though." Percival gestured around them, at the scattered bones and the smog of death filling the air. "I don't know what this place is, but . . . It reminds me of everything our people have fought through. Everything they've endured. No, it's not just the Governor. Thousands of years, you said. That equates to hundreds of rulers. *Hundreds* who made it their life's goal to abuse and kill us. Why they think this way is beyond me. I've gone too long considering the hypotheticals. This place... Oh, Dawnseve, this place is going to hurt me."

They stood in silence for a while, but as the minutes passed, whispers rose from the mist. The candlelight shuddered again, flinging shadows across the walls.

An anchor of years descended upon Roy's shoulders, a leaden medallion forged from time itself. His thoughts drifted and then flitted from one to the other, like a conspiracy of ravens migrating. The voices snaking through the tunnels continued whispering, subdued by some unfathomable pressure, yet he couldn't wring words from their wails.

Say something to Percival, Roy demanded of himself. *Tell him he deserves to be hurt, that his pain is warranted for all the things he's said to you, all the things he's made you feel, that your nightmares are his doing, that the scars on your chest are as much his fault as Gabriel's...*

But Roy held his tongue. He thought it might be for the best.

15

ROY DIDN'T MOVE UNTIL PERCIVAL DID, AND EVEN then, apprehension gripped Roy by the heels, as though he was suspended in hardened mud. He was still trying to process what Percival had said. *The Iron Citadel strips our people of personal identity and manipulates what remains to their own perverse satisfaction.*

Roy had experienced this sort of psychological change since the first time Gabriel had beaten him, but there'd been no actual recognition of it until recently. This change was different than what he felt around Percival, though; that was a kind of emotional echo, considering that Roy more recently expressed himself in angry outbursts. No, this deeper change—the Iron Citadel's manipulation of the larger academic community—was a reworking of who he was, who he aspired to become.

When Roy had first met the Governor, the man's rheumy eyes had flashed at Dimestra's plea to remain present in the room while Roy received the details of his assignment. Perhaps the Governor had hidden his shrewdness beforehand to seem unaware, but in truth, his insight was broader than Roy had known. Now he could see it for what it was: The Governor could somehow, and not by magical means, *see* someone grasping for power before they even moved a muscle. If not from sorcerous practices, then had he learned this talent from his predecessors, the previous Governors?

Percival glanced over a shoulder, silently bidding Roy to follow. He did, his tread slow, and his fear went with him.

They both rounded the corner, wisps of mist threading around their boots. The air was heavy with petrichor, lichen, and the substance that Roy had encountered in the last chamber. A narrow tunnel stretched before him, winding like a hollowed intestine. Golden candlelight and the long shadows cast by Roy and Percival shivered in tandem as though in some tenebrous waltz. As they passed through the tunnels, burnt orange light pierced the mist and illuminated the skeletons lying sprawled upon the earth. With each one he passed, unease twisted tighter and tighter around Roy's stomach, cinching it closed. The dead watched him in the cold, grim quiet, damning all he'd accomplished, paltry though those accomplishments might be.

Cobblestone eventually gave way to gravel, which was, again, strewn with remnants of the fallen. It never seemed to cease. Bones lay scattered upon the ground, a trail leading into unhallowed territory. Femurs, ribs, and clavicles gathered among the mist, other bones jutting from the fog like shark fins rising above the ocean. It looked like a murder interrupted, some simple tragedy made messy and complex by unforeseen complications.

Roy couldn't turn away, so terrified by yet oddly curious about the events that had transpired here. How long ago had this happened? How many people had been involved in this ambush? Was that what had occurred here? An ensnarement laid by a trespasser? A voyage into the dark gone awry?

These souls will find no release, Roy thought. *No answers and no Above. This silence is their purgatory.*

A dry hacking sound interrupted Roy's musings.

Percival was hunched over, his back muscles straining through his tunic. He shivered, shadows fluttering along the slope of his neck and through his hair. His skin fluctuated between shades of sunset and relentless dark. He cleared his throat, and his breathing soon steadied into a healthy rhythm. Roy reached out, as if to pat him on the back or console him—he wasn't quite sure himself—but pulled back, not sure if Percival would welcome such succor.

Instead he strode onward, but came to an abrupt stop himself when a burn crept through his chest like a wildfire. He coughed, his heart slamming against his rib cage. Skeins of dust shot out from his lips in bursts and trailed through the air in ribbons. He bore the pain for a moment, but it soon subsided.

He inhaled deeply, and like a dreamworld covering reality, the insides of Roy's eyelids projected episodic visions, as had happened before. He saw green splotches of moss splayed over skulls and bones. He saw the mouths of blurred faces stretched out into screams which rippled and warbled, reverberating against the stone walls. He saw hundreds upon hundreds of scholars dead and dying, throats cut to the bone, fingernails torn and bloodied, widened eyes gouged and dangling from bleeding sockets.

And there was something far beyond, some spectral figure he couldn't quite see.

Then the world rushed back to him, his vision distorting and bending at the corners. He bent over and grasped his knees, panting, pulling in deep breaths, only for bone-dust to catch in his lungs.

Roy coughed. "The visions, Percival . . . I can . . . I can see them now. They're becoming clearer."

"We might be *seeing* the visions," Percival said, "but they're not *showing* us anything. It feels more like a closer view of our surroundings, but nothing more."

Roy shook his head. "No, there's something about these new visions. I felt a pressure behind it, the same as within the walls. Some sort of force? I'm not certain. Maybe . . . Maybe that dust has something to do with it. I didn't see the visions so vividly before as I did when I was coughing."

If Percival registered that, he didn't let on. "We'll wait until we get deeper into the tunnel. That chamber can't have been the only one down here. Share all the theories you like when we arrive someplace worthwhile."

Footsteps sounded ahead of him, and Roy lifted his head from where he'd been bent over, clearing his throat, and saw that Percival had already walked on. He looked somewhat like a wraith in the gathering dark.

When Roy quickened his pace, Percival laughed. "I was wondering when you'd stop trailing behind me like a hound."

"I haven't a clue what you're talking about."

"Oh, please, you've been slavering for my attention since you caught me in that reading room. That *was* the look in your eyes, wasn't it?"

"I was once convinced that you were arrogant and in need of a smaller ego, but I judged wrong. Perhaps all this time, throughout the entire game, you've just been delusional."

"*I'm* the pragmatist between the two of us, darling." Percival pinched Roy's cheek and shook it. "Don't forget it." Roy shoved him in the chest and Percival stumbled back, a wild grin stretching his lips. "And *you* are in denial."

"Of what? Your self-obsession? Your infatuation and satisfaction with having made a game of our survival? Of *using* me only to further your own ends?"

Percival seemed a little flustered, his cheeks splashed with a deep red blush, but he only propped a hand on his hip and said, "By the Scribes, you're no fun. Come on, darling. I'm here at your disposal. What other witty remarks have you prepared for me?"

"Even if I had any, I'm sure you'd find some way to knock

them all down." Roy smiled. "Or at least try to. So, if you would be so kind, I'd appreciate your silence on the matter."

"Unfortunately, kindness is not in my repertoire."

Roy rolled his eyes. "I could have told you that."

He expected a sudden shift of behavior, a chink in Percival's armor of good cheer, but he was as amused as before. "Not the most convincing remark, but I've heard worse. Mostly from you. And you may try to paint a different picture, but years of having a charming personality has won me great insight into others' minds." He winked. "And yours is clearer than a pane of glass."

"What do you see, then, Percival?" Roy asked. He knew Percival wasn't yet done donning his masks and hiding his past, even with the game over. But, in the darkness, Roy didn't feel nearly as tense as he did in the library. He found himself envious of Percival's ability to conceal himself at any given time. "What do you *claim* to see?"

Percival regarded him sidelong, his mouth frozen in that unrelenting smirk. "A liar."

Roy snorted, exasperated. "Nonsense. The best method of academic approach is an honest mind-set."

"You lie to *yourself*," Percival elaborated. "About who you are, what you want, and why you're here."

"I was brought to the Basilica by the Governor. I stayed here because it is *right* to save this city."

"I am not speaking of the Basilica, darling," Percival said, soft and tender as a chaste kiss. "You know that. There's no need to lie. You keep looking away from the truth. You don't need to hide yourself *or* your desires, Roy." His name clanged through his body like a pealing bell. "Don't listen to those instincts."

"I'd rather listen to my instincts than to *you*, Percival."

"Is that what you were telling yourself on the sixth floor?"

The question tightened the air between them, weaving an illusion of bodies pressed together, of Percival holding his thumb against the seam of Roy's mouth, waiting patiently for a request that did not come. Roy shivered at the juxtaposing warmth of Percival's skin against the chill of the tunnels.

"I pulled away from you," Roy murmured, though his words were slurred. He repeated, enunciating this time, "I pulled away from you. You know I did."

Percival rolled his eyes. "I thank you for recounting what I saw with my own eyes. You walked away, yes, but there is something to be said for your reluctance to do so."

"You're no better than me, Percival. You said you can see into my mind, but I could be blind and still know who you are."

"Tell me what you see," Percival whispered, his eyes agleam with delectation.

Roy shook his head. "No. I won't tell you what you already know. What would that do for me?"

And yet as he made to turn away, when Percival strode forward and bent his head intently toward Roy, Roy neither recoiled nor froze. He leaned in, tilting his head back and baring his throat. Percival closed his fingers around Roy's neck, his eyes darting between the wall, slick with its invisible coating, and Roy.

Roy hooked his foot around Percival's leg and pulled. Percival lurched forward, his hand still around Roy's throat, pinning Roy to the wall behind him. The greasy, sap-like substance coated his hair and drenched the back of his coat and trousers. For a long while, in a deep silence, Roy hung his head and squeezed his eyes shut in discomfort at the alien, unsettling consistency of the sludge, his jaw clenched so tight that it felt permanently locked in place. He was about to scratch his arms to distract himself from his distress, but then he looked at Percival, and while Roy's unease did not fade away, it was at least temporarily forgotten.

Percival watched him with incendiary fervor. Roy met that searing look with a half-hearted glower. It was a light blow—he *was* drawing in Percival's breath with each of his own—but Roy refused to lay down his only weapon: denial.

Roy swallowed, his heart tremoring, a sheen of sweat gathering on his forehead. At some point, he thought his vision was swaying. But it was the candlelight, distorting the outlines of Percival's face. Percival stood uncannily still. Two droplets of sweat coalesced upon his left temple, then streaked down his cheek and splashed onto the gravel. They both started at the small sound, and as they jolted forward out of instinct, their lips brushed.

Percival tightened his grip, just a fraction, but Roy strengthened his resolve.

Yes, your resolve, he chastised himself. *Your resolve not to kiss the bastard right on the mouth.*

But if this was a battle, then it would be executed as such: meeting a jab with a punch, a punch with a bloody wound.

Percival brought the candle closer to his own face, exposing the blush staining his fair complexion. The shadowed hollows above his clavicle peeked through the collar of his tunic, the laces half-done. Blond dots of day-old stubble were speckled across his jaw and the lower half of his cheeks.

The scent of musk and pine filled Roy's nostrils, overwhelming him with a baser need from which he *had* to tear his gaze. He was about to do exactly that when a voice entered his mind. *Oh, please, you've been slavering for my attention since you caught me in that reading room. That* was *the look in your eyes, wasn't it?*

"That's quite enough," Roy said, even while he was curling his fingers around Percival's trim waist. "Let me go, you bastard."

Percival grinned. "What pretty names you have for me, darling."

"Stop calling me that," Roy spat, grasping Percival's waist. "Let me go."

Percival frowned. "Oh, I don't think I deserve *that*."

"You deserve *nothing*, you—" Roy stopped himself, the word sitting on the tip of his tongue.

"Say it, love," Percival whispered, his voice echoing through the tunnels. "Say it with every bit of hatred in your soul."

Roy wanted to. No, he wanted silence. He wanted to freeze himself in this moment to avoid moving forward and accepting what Percival was.

Instead, his pulse racing, Roy observed the man who occupied the better half of his thoughts, whose beauty and spite had ensnared Roy like forbidden sorcery, binding him in its cold clasp. Even when he looked away, the impact Percival had on him was undeniable, and that was why Roy despised himself when he said the words, an inevitable untangling of his tongue.

"You're a distraction," Roy hissed. "Nothing more, nothing less."

Percival recoiled, a barely perceptible, surprised hurt shuddering across his face, but he covered it with a grin, a ferocious hunger in his eyes. He ran his hand slowly from Roy's neck and up to his jaw, the sides of his fingers hot against Roy's parted lips. "There you are."

Roy shot his hand up and grasped Percival's. "You make me want to intimidate you, to see fear on your face, to—"

"Look at you, Dawnseve," Percival said with a smile, his warm breath on Roy's cheeks. "You're shaking. I know what you're feeling, darling. I know what it's like to succumb to desire. That might be just what you need. To stop lying to yourself. To stop feeding your fears and give in. You need to open that heart of yours."

"Stop talking in riddles or I'll—"

Percival leaned forward, and with no room to move his head, Roy could not retreat. Their noses brushed as Percival angled his head forward, his forehead pressing against Roy's. "Just what will you do, darling? I doubt you wish to wake the dead."

"I'd take that chance if it meant you would join them."

Percival chuckled. "Believe me, you're the last person I'd consider capable of murder, especially my own."

"I'd wager that I'm not the first person to threaten you with murder, though."

"An interesting method of flirting, to be sure."

Roy snorted, ignoring the heat pooling through his stomach. "Don't be ridiculous. I have a long list of priorities and nowhere on it have I planned to flirt with anyone, much less you. Now, get your face away from me—why are you smiling?"

"Well, either my eyes are deceiving me," Percival said, "or yours have been on my lips for a rather long time." He placed a finger on Roy's mouth. "Regardless, I think I'm growing quite fond of your plans to murder me. In a crypt, no less; have you no respect for the dead?"

Roy wrapped his fingers around Percival's, which was still against Roy's lips, and drew his hand down. "Don't do this here, Percival. Anywhere but here."

Percival exhaled softly through his nostrils, his smile fading. "I said this place was going to hurt me, not that I would commemorate the dead."

"These are your people. *Our* people."

"And they died for what they believed in, I know, but maybe they weren't as brave as the legends claim. They could have lied as much as you do," Percival murmured, his voice heavy with that familiar but nameless sorrow. He took a small step back. "I can admit who I am, Roy. *That's* the difference between us. The competition has come to a close, and *still*, you won't confront the truth."

Roy dragged his fingers through the slick snarls of his hair. "I know who I am."

"There's that lie again; the denial. No, darling, you know who, and what, this world has made you become, what they've shaped you into," Percival retorted. "But that's not *you*. If you live in ignorance long enough, you grow accustomed to *their* lies. And those lies will soon be your own."

"That's preposterous."

But Roy could not help the surge of memories that rushed through his mind: Matron Dimestra, her steely gaze like a blade; the grapple for power shifting between two evils; the identity and belonging that had been absent throughout his gray-toned, half-lived life. He'd been searching through the dark with nobody to guide the way, and now there stood somebody before him who was offering him a choice to light his path, and still, Roy couldn't do it.

"And there might come a time when you try to gain control of your future," Percival said. "But there's no hope for those who refuse to make a stand."

"This is me making a stand." Roy gestured around him. "I am doing what's right for my country."

"But not for *yourself*," Percival exclaimed, true anger contorting his features. He seemed another person entirely, not even a shadow of the man whose lips had brushed Roy's. "You haven't changed since you entered this fucking building, Roy. All you do is weep and wait for an angel to rescue you."

"What in the name of the *Scribes* are you saying? I don't need to be saved or protected or *coddled*."

Percival gave a rough, dry laugh. "No, you just need to be

told exactly what to do and how. And you know damn well I'm not speaking about the Old Ones or the war; I'm talking about *you*."

Roy held back the urge to shatter Percival's clenched jaw. Maybe that would disperse the puzzling emotions he felt toward Percival, all in one fell swoop. "You're a manipulative *ass*."

"And you're a liar. You're a *fucking* liar."

"You don't want to save humanity," Roy said, scowling. "You don't care for anyone but yourself. Whatever happens in this world, whatever happens to *us*, you just want to ensure it benefits *you*."

"Thank the Above," Percival said, clasping a hand over his heart. "He understands! How thoughtful of you, darling. Truly thoughtful." Roy scanned Percival from head to foot, and Percival snapped, "Ah, the predatory assessment. Before you murder me, Roy, should I swoon, or would you prefer I put up a fight?"

Roy seized the candle from Percival's hands, set his jaw, and walked away.

16

THE DEEPER ROY WENT INTO THE TUNNEL SYSTEM, the more difficult it became to determine the length of the passageway and the direction in which he was headed, or even to deduce the duration of time for which he had been traveling. He guessed an hour or two, based on the persistent burn spreading through his thighs, the strain that had developed in his eyes from staring too long into the darkness, and the sluggishness of his arms, despite switching the candle from one hand to the other.

There was also the uneasy feeling that had snuck up on him ever since entering the catacombs of the Orphic Basilica—the feeling of *sameness*. It was as though he was treading through a maze of cave walls reflected upon one another. There were no distinct markers of progression. Even the bones lying among the mist began to assume an uncanny resemblance to those he'd seen hours ago, but Roy wondered whether this was due more to the process of decomposition than to the hallucinatory effects that sustained darkness had on the human mind. Either way, he was too scared to voice his concerns.

Percival had grown quiet, too, but regardless of their recent argument, he looked introspective rather than mad. He was walking slowly, his head tilted back and his eyes alight with faint shimmers of candlelight. He looked to be observing the irregularly placed recesses embedded in the tunnel walls and the agape-mouthed skeletons of ancient explorers sleeping within them, but he kept gnawing at his bottom lip and tugging on the hem of his tunic.

Not for the first time, Roy wished he could better recognize emotions. If he could at least make out what was on Percival's mind, then this whole damn mission might go ahead a lot more smoothly. He had no immediate compulsions to dredge up the entirety of Percival's past, but it seemed more than unfair that, in spite of Percival's obstinate insistence that Roy should open up and bare his heart, Percival could still intuit the smallest measure of Roy's history while never divulging in kind. He didn't know if it was selfish or impure to want the same, to see Percival to the extent that Percival saw Roy.

These thoughts did not so much as flutter through his head before a powerful, howling squall came racing toward him out of the darkness, trailing a whipping cloud of dust, grit, and the powder of trampled bones.

Roy yelped, his overcoat billowing about him in the breeze, his breath momentarily stolen from, and then rushed back into, his lungs. Percival uttered an indignant, stunned curse, but the wind was much too loud for Roy to hear what he said. Startled, Roy fumbled with the candle for a moment but lost his grip, and the dish upon which it sat plummeted to the ground and shattered on impact, plunging them into darkness.

Roy reached out for Percival, and when he caught the sleeve of his tunic, Percival didn't push him away but instead pulled Roy closer, against his heaving chest. Roy rooted the soles of his boots to the ground, overwhelmed with an odd mixture of terror and gratitude. Then the wind started anew, shrieking shrilly, and he gritted his teeth against the blustering gale. Tears streamed from the corners of his squinted eyes, running down his cheeks like chilled water. A numbness crept over his skin, stealing the warmth from his blood.

When the squall finally disappeared, all at once as if vanquished by the incantations of some unseen wizard, Roy was still shivering, his skin speckled with gooseflesh. He let out a series of deep, ragged breaths, Percival doing the same as they gracelessly held on to one another.

Although he knew better, in the endless gulf of darkness, Roy felt terribly alone. He felt, too, that he had no accurate sense of reality, like everything he had been told about the world had been as real as his hallucinations of his dead brother. Timeless horrors of unknown origins could be crouched here, watching Roy, with their thousands of lunatic blood-filled eyes, without his knowing. And though Roy felt so near to the truth, the reality of Northgard's looming downfall, he also felt like a fool, like he'd learned nothing throughout his month of huddling over dusty books.

You're a liar. You're a fucking liar.

He wasn't only a liar; he was terrified beyond his wits. Now that he stood here, his arms covered with prickles and his legs watery and wobbling, he realized that the Governor had never known the complete extent of what he'd assigned them, that it had been up to Roy and Percival, two scholars towed out of their homes by the scruffs of their necks, to unearth what had been lying beneath them all along.

Northgard was sitting atop a necropolis.

A city of corpses resting forgotten underneath a city of impending death, he thought, but he knew the truth ran far deeper than that. He'd assumed earlier that the chamber somewhere ahead of them contained the tombs of the Elder Scribes, as there had to be a reason why that block of wood had been installed and a mausoleum seemed a good one, but exactly how the Old Ones were connected to the Elder Scribes, *how* they'd been cast out of Northgard by the Elder Scribes, far surpassed Roy's knowledge.

"Percival, I believe that wind might be the least of our worries," he whispered.

"Don't move too far from me," Percival demanded, though his voice was as soft and low as Roy's. "I'm not going to chase after you—" He stilled, his eyes wide. "What is that?"

Roy murmured, "Don't do that."

"No, I'm quite serious," Percival said. "Look ahead. *Look*."

Gingerly, Roy stared where Percival had indicated. Nothing materialized initially, but it was as with any dark space: The longer you looked, the more you saw. His surroundings grew clearer, his vision sharpened, and as he squinted, a ghostly gray light appeared in the distance, swaying and rippling like murky water. He appraised the illumination, vaguely unsettled by its hypnotic quality, but it began to soothe him and, after a while, drew him forward.

Without thinking, Roy complied. He drifted toward the dim gray light, by which he made out Percival's features. He had a hand cupped over his brow, which was gleaming with sweat, and his mouth was twisted into a sour, mistrustful grimace. He looked askance at Roy, a small divot between his brows, but kept up his pace without complaining. A part of Roy wished that he would have, but a bigger part, the part that was under the thrall of the mystical light, was unfazed.

After about five minutes, they came to the source of the light. Roy gasped. The ceiling of the narrow, low-ceilinged tunnel widened into a gargantuan domed chamber, which appeared about fifty feet wide and made of sandstone. The walls were bare of decorations, tapestries, or murals—startlingly naked compared to the gaudy embellishments, portraits, and artworks hung on the library's upper levels. The air was thick with dust and damp, along with the familiar scent of crumbled bone. A quick look around revealed no adjoining chambers except the tunnel through which they had arrived.

Carved into the walls were rows after rows of stone alcoves, each twice the size of a skeleton and inside of which were chipped mahogany coffins coated with grime. The ground was scattered with clumps of earth and furred moss, which sprouted from the untouched soil. No bones rested upon the cobblestones underfoot, yet a horrid stench swirled up from the floor nonetheless, something noxious like fungi or rotting cabbage.

A coffin hovered in the heart of the chamber, hewn from misshapen bits of crumbled cobblestone and hardpan, surrounded by six others of identical material. Gray light escaped from underneath the middle coffin, coiled out of the earth and stone like blood from a wound, and then passed through crevices in the ground, pulsing from the outer coffins to the inner, like a call and a responding cry.

Gold, silver, and bronze glinted in Roy's periphery. Ancient relics lined the stone slabs upon the walls: amulets, necklaces, wineglasses, and vases. A small gilded chalice was filled to the brim with ash and beads of crystal. A reliquary housed a grinning skull, its huge, jagged teeth looking like shattered bones in the cold light.

On the far left wall, bordered by a column of coffins, was a glass bookshelf containing only four volumes. Engraved on all their covers were weird, arcane symbols. Hieroglyphics? Cryptic motifs? Runes? Roy could not say. Curious, he traipsed forward, close enough to make out a name inscribed in miniature stenciled letters underneath each of the four different symbols: *Jocelyn Kallard, Neil Eldreave, Tarnan Eldreave,* and *Atticus Walestone.*

Roy walked around and touched one of the coffins in the wall, disquieted. "Who are all these other people? The seven sarcophagi in the middle here must have been leaders of the library—certainly all scholars of the highest repute, anyway. But the rest? Other scholars? Librarians? Students? And if so, who buried them here? Who *built* all this? It looks like these coffins were made from the catacombs themselves."

"What does any of that matter now?" Percival asked. "The Elder Scribes left us here to fend for ourselves. Either they couldn't find an answer, or they *did*, but were too cowardly to use it. And now here we are, living with as much purpose as the dead around us." Roy was startled at how matter-of-fact he sounded.

"Men, women, and children are slaughtered every day by the hundreds and, if the Old Ones go on as they have been, by the thousands," Roy said with finality. "There is no god, no deity who metes out death; there is only circumstance and consequence. The Elder Scribes might be our idols, but they weren't immortal. This chamber is proof of that."

"And so, what?" Percival asked. "We just pick up where they left off, as if it's just a matter of *reading books*?" He swirled his finger in a circle through the ash that had settled on one of the coffins. "Maybe they weren't truly divine, but the Scribes were considered gods by those who paid tribute to their guidance. They weren't immortal, no, but they were blessed by other means. They built the Basilica—they built *this*—and if that isn't testament of their power, what is? The problem, however, is that this room is also testament to their failure."

"Then they did not leave us, Percival," Roy said, "and most importantly, they did not leave nothing behind. We are standing in the last stronghold of knowledge."

Percival scowled. "Or we're just in the place where that knowledge died."

"I have to believe that isn't true."

For a long time, there was silence. Then, sounding frustrated when he replied, Percival said, "Then we better find some damn answers."

They paced around the circumference of the silver-lit crypt, searching attentively for anything that immediately jumped out at them. A correlation, whether express or extraneous, to what they had happened upon in their studies thus far: a line of archaic scripture; a passage from a book either or both of them had researched; a portrait of a historical figure, perhaps a knight-errant, or even an Elder Scribe, riding back home on horseback from some grisly skirmish against a division of the Old Ones. Nothing could be ruled out. Nothing was beyond the realm of possibility or practicality.

There were about a hundred coffins in the burial chamber, including those of the Elder Scribes. Roy supposed the wooden caskets, those on the wall, contained the remains of the members of the Protectorate, the private association that had answered exclusively to the Elder Scribes' demands. Chief among these had been administrative tasks—relocating contraband and gathering scholars' reports and theses into anthologies. They didn't write the books; they tended to them. In the latter days of the old world, they had been considered the last voice of hope, the last defense against the anti-Scribe movement, but they had been purged and afterward forgotten alongside their proprietors. Beyond this, Roy hadn't gleaned much from the books in Dawnseve Manor.

"The Basilica brought us here. We know that," Percival said, his voice quickening. "And I don't think it's a coincidence that it brought us to the Scribes' burial vault. It knows we're here. The library, I mean to say. That must be why we feel so connected to it, and maybe when we came here, it awakened."

"That's not our primary concern right now," Roy said. He nodded to the coffins, and to the ethereal light throbbing from stone to stone like a pulse. "*This* is."

He surveyed the seven sarcophagi, an air of foreboding suspended about him. Pinpricks of light raced among the crevices in the cobbles, like stars arcing through the night. With each pulsation, the light converged at the middle sarcophagus, which hovered five feet from the ground.

Roy ran his tongue along his lips, which had gone dry from fear and uncertainty. "This doesn't look like a summit, Percival." A breeze, much softer this time, eased out of the crypt's entrance and ruffled through the snarled curls of Roy's hair. He tensed, his nerves strung tight. "It looks like a trial, like the Elder Scribes, interred at the bottom here, are the defendants."

Percival shivered, his apprehensive gaze flicking from one sarcophagus to another. "The one hovering in the middle there . . . It *must* be connected to something."

But that contradicted the surreal atmosphere of the high-ceilinged space, the sense of unseen terrors moving around in the dark beyond. Regardless, Roy doubted a rope or string could suspend the stone coffin at the height at which it was positioned. Beneath the middle sarcophagi was a round pool of the silver light, its depth indiscernible.

Roy started forward to inspect closer but was drawn to a halt by the crack in Percival's voice as he commanded, "*Stop.*"

"My humble apologies; I forgot your position as the keeper of the crypt."

Percival narrowed his brows. "Be grateful it isn't your skeleton in one of these coffins."

"Because you're so confident you can arrange that?"

Percival gestured to the coffins. "Maybe walking near those will kill you first."

"You said you wanted answers." Though Roy was some distance away from him, he still heard Percival's sigh of resignation. "We've had no luck for almost a month, Percival. I don't know if the Basilica showed us the way here, but *something* did." He lowered his voice. "The Protectorate is gone. The Scribes are gone. But we aren't."

Remnants of hesitation scudded across Percival's face, but he smoothed out his features, pressed his lips into a rigid line, and then blew out a short breath. "I'll do it."

Roy didn't think it mattered either way, but still he asked, "Why?"

Percival shrugged, his expression of uncertainty becoming one of fathomless sorrow, a soldier who'd fought one too many battles. "Everybody wants something to be remembered by."

With that, he burst forward in a flurry of movement, his boots crunching through gravel and stone. The closer he drew to the central sarcophagus, the faster the light traveled, until it seemed that the crypt was ablaze with starlight. Silver and shadow flickered upon the walls, incandescent and divine. Despite the dust layered upon the relics throughout the burial vault, they were still gleaming as fiercely as if they had been set afire.

As Percival entered the inner ring of the six sarcophagi, he slowed his pace, cautious. Though his gaze was locked onto the central coffin, he wove around the luminous cracks in the stone floor with perfect facility. He looked like a wingless fallen angel, his blond hair uncombed and his shoulders heavy with despair.

Above the merciless beating of Roy's heart, and the roaring of the blood in his ears, there came a distant melody. It grew louder and louder by the second, from a strident whining to an orchestral chorus of whispers. He clamped the heels of his hands against the sides of his head, jamming his ears shut, but the noise persisted, building into a shriek that swooped and wheeled around the inside of his skull like screeching bats.

Percival gave him a shadow of a smile, there and then gone. Then he curled the fingers of his left hand around the top of the coffin, his thumb pressed against its lid. It did not budge. It was nailed firmly shut. He drew back and clenched his jaw, as though about to give it another go, but stiffened when a deluge of light blasted out from the small pool under the coffin.

Roy watched with increasing fascination, his tongue pinned between his teeth. His heart was racing with anticipation. The light rose and rose, halted just before it could overflow and spill across the cobbles, then swept back toward the middle coffin.

A faint rumble went through the earth, like a faraway stampede of beasts trundling by, which was then followed by utter silence. Wisps of mist united at the light-pool, twisted and whirled into a wind-whipped frenzy. The fog rose higher into a cylindrical pillar that speared through the foundation of the sarcophagus. Trickles of liquefied light spiraled up into the coffin and disappeared. Inky darkness swamped the crypt for only a moment before silver light seeped out from the edges of the sarcophagus and cast a celestial glow.

Roy yelped and staggered to the side, his balance unsteadied by the pressure mounting swiftly in the air. He felt trapped, like the walls were closing in on him, yet nothing beyond the light and the mist was moving. Not even Percival, whose hand had gone still on the side of the sarcophagus and whose mouth was agape with astonishment.

Operating on sheer impulse, Roy joined Percival in the central ring of the crypt, and once he came to Percival's side, he could see the muscles in Percival's back bunching and shifting, as if he was carrying some tremendous weight. He uttered a low, nearly breathless grunt and, with a fierce tug that sent a bolt of heat through Roy's stomach, relieved the sarcophagus of its lid. Although he didn't move it aside.

Instead, Percival looked to Roy and muttered, "The light. It looks like it . . . I think it loosened the nails hammered into the coffin. The Basilica wants us to do this, Roy. It's been showing us the way the entire time."

Roy shook his head, sinking his teeth into his lower lip. "Why didn't it show us a month ago? Why were we shown this crypt only now?"

Percival froze. The idea, Roy realized, had not occurred to him. "I believe there's only one way to find out."

Yes, Roy believed so, too, but he was so scared—so horribly frightened—of what might be lying in the coffin, the tomb of one of his childhood heroes. However, the toughest part was that he could not even bring himself to imagine the worst scenario. He was afraid to. Now that he found himself at the edge of what he predicted to be their greatest discovery yet, he was struck by the totality of his duplicity. He had never felt so much like a hypocrite, a fraud.

Percival braced his hands on the lid of the coffin, apparently oblivious to Roy's self-haranguing, and then unceremoniously thrust aside the large slab of stone. It smashed into the cobbles on the other side of the coffin and shattered. Thick chunks of crumbled stone jutted skyward like the cracked spine of a titan. Another cacophonous thud went through the ground and set it trembling.

Once the air stilled, Roy became conscious of the heady, pernicious stench rising out of the opened coffin. Attempting and failing not to gag, he pushed up onto his toes, the palm of his hand clamped against his mouth, and peered inside.

There was indeed a skeleton inside the sarcophagus. Its jaws were ripped wide open, as if its last scream had torn it in two. Its fingers were crossed over its chest. The cracked bones of the rest of its body had long decomposed after thousands of years and fully decayed. Only the brittle frame had been left behind, like that of a burnt house.

Roy was more interested, however, in what lay next to the Elder Scribe.

By its right hip was a slightly curved sword sheathed in a dark scabbard, the cross hilt resemblant of the upper half of a skeleton: the pommel was the head, the cross the chest and arms. Even sheathed, the sword radiated an aura of vicious, savage power. In his mind, Roy imagined releasing the sword from its scabbard and a thousand untold stories of unbridled carnage pouring out.

By its left hip was another sword, and though the scabbard had seemingly been forged from the same dark metal, it was much narrower than the first sword. Yet it still discharged a sense of barely bridled malice, contained within the scabbard.

"By the love and mercy of the Elder Scribes," Percival exclaimed, his voice thick with betrayal and terror, "what the *fuck* are swords doing in a philosopher's coffin?" He lurched sideways and nearly staggered to the ground, but Roy caught Percival by his armpit, hauling him up as they both gawked at the skeleton.

Roy could not speak; shock had rendered him mute and jammed his tongue against the bottom of his mouth. He managed to keep his hold on Percival, who had buried his head in Roy's shoulder and was now weeping quietly, but only through the sheer force of willpower and desperation.

"I—" Percival choked out. "I can't—"

"Percival, would you stop it for a moment?" Roy demanded, shocked by the stern authority in his voice. Percival took a second to recompose himself, then looked at Roy, who went on,

"This is troubling to see, I will not lie about that, but it's nothing we didn't suspect before. It's completely contradictory to the notion of pacifism we once believed the Scribes to have upheld, and to Lortan's *Neither Sword Nor Shield*, but don't you remember the painting we saw? The Old Ones—"

At some point while Roy had been speaking, something close to acceptance dawned upon Percival's face. "The Elder Scribes cast them out of Northgard." He appeared mystified; his eyes wide as he scrutinized the entombed weapons.

Roy nodded vigorously, then gestured to the swords. "With *these*."

A noise coalesced in the air around them then, borne aloft by the wind.

"The whispers, darling," Percival said. "They're trying to communicate with us. I can *hear* them; they're calling out. It's so beautiful." His eyes were filled with tears, though Roy doubted this was purely out of his awe at the whispers, because Percival's gaze had shifted back to the black-scabbarded swords.

But to Roy's ears, the whispers were far from beautiful. He detected, though he could not completely pick apart, the shapes of voices, like tremors passing through the air. Emotions that were not all his own tore through him: misery and despair, heartache and anger. But underlying them all was the deepest, most profound anguish he'd ever known. He could not tell who these phantoms had once been, only the unimaginable torture to which they had been subjected.

A refrain of screams exploded inside his skull. *See me! Heed me! Witness what they did to us, what they took from us!* An iron clamp took hold of Roy, its grasp tightening. *See what they made of your kind! Oh please, I say! I plead to the Above! Heed me! They butchered us and killed our young—*

The voices vanished as quickly as they'd appeared, concealed behind the barrier he and Percival had sensed when they'd first entered the Basilica.

Roy didn't know if it was his proximity to the sarcophagi of the Elder Scribes, or some other anomaly, but he could *feel* the dissolution of those intellectuals, the knowledge that Northgard had cut off at the legs and replaced with the disease that was war. It had infected the Governor first, then the Radiant Droves, and—

And then Matron Dimestra, Roy thought. *This city and this war changed her.*

While Matron Dimestra had always prioritized her squadrons before her children, she had once demonstrated moments of kindness. She would offer to wash Roy's hair, even when Roy decided to grow it out to seek some independence, and she would request that their chefs make him his favorite meals. But any reminders of his literary interests had slowly stolen the love from her heart.

Tears rolling down his cheeks, Roy murmured, "All those people. They're restrained by something, imprisoned."

"The swords."

Roy wiped away his tears with the back of his hand, then asked, "The swords? What about them?"

Percival swallowed. "Where else could those whispers be coming from? They were so soft before, so *quiet,* but now . . . Now I can hear it all." His expression turned glum but still determined. "We need to study these weapons, darling. We'll start first thing tomorrow. It's obvious that something is missing here."

Roy agreed. Besides, he needed to work, to dive back into the books or otherwise do *something* to put to use what he had seen and learned.

Nodding decisively, Percival reached for the sword with the skeleton-shaped hilt, and once he'd hefted it out of the sarcophagus, Roy retrieved its narrower companion. As he did, Percival tugged on the hilt of his sword, trying to get the blade out of its scabbard.

Panicked, Roy gripped Percival's forearm with his spare hand and drew it away. "Percival, stop. I don't want to do it here. These people have gone through enough. They shouldn't bear witness to this, too."

Percival looked at Roy's hand, which was still closed around his arm, then brushed it off. "Soon they will know peace." He hung his sword in a loop in his belt. When he was facing Roy again, Percival rested his hands on either side of Roy's face, pressed their foreheads together, and whispered, "And we will know war."

17

LATER THAT NIGHT—HOURS AFTER A TREACHEROUS walk up the staircase in the catacombs, which Roy and Percival had somehow managed in complete darkness on account of Roy dropping the candle—Roy decided to finish up on a bit of light reading alone, wanting to alleviate some of the anxiety that had been hounding him since he'd departed the catacombs. Percival, upon their return upstairs, had announced he was going for a nightcap, the weight of the experience more than the weight of the swords on his mind.

Roy, however, couldn't rid himself of the temptation to pass the swords a desultory glance. As he did so now, he noted again that there was something cruel and sinister about them. It was more than their appearance, more than *where* they had found them. No, it was what Roy had sensed when he'd first seen them: that if he relieved either blade of its scabbard, pure malevolence would come pouring out. He kept an eye on the swords, though whenever he looked back down at his research, he could feel them watching him. He imagined scores upon scores of eyes etched on the scabbards, flicking back and forth, monitoring him with baleful scrutiny.

Roy knew that he and Percival would need to examine them eventually, despite not having felt the wind around the weapons as guidance and confirmation of their importance to the mystery, but trepidation kept him at bay. Percival, too, Roy assumed; he *had* declared that they would look further into the swords tomorrow, not this night.

Realizing his concentration was drifting, Roy stood up with a sigh, stretched out the strained muscles in his back and neck, then made his way down the staircases overlooking the first floor of the Orphic Basilica until he heard the clinking of glasses.

He found Percival in a sitting room on the fourth floor. He was sprawled on a settee before a hearth, his short blond hair gilded with firelight. His legs were splayed wide: the left foot perched atop the back of the seat, the right dangling over the edge. A splash of liquid, which smelled distinctly like whiskey, stained the front of his tunic, the laces undone to expose his lightly muscled chest. He was staring into the flames with a look of glassy seduction, as if engaged in a wordless exchange with an unseen lover. The reflection of fire shivered in his spectacles.

"Percival," Roy said, striding over and standing in front of him, his hands set firmly on his hips. "This is what you call a nightcap?"

Percival blinked twice and squinted at Roy in befuddlement for a moment before his features brightened. "Ah, it's you! Have you come to join the festivities?" he asked. The last word came out slurred and a fraction louder than his usual volume.

"You're pathetic," Roy said, although as he observed Percival's state of inebriation, he was unpleasantly reminded of the string of delirious nights when he had dug himself into the same pit. He thought of the bottles of cheap wine he'd filched from the Matron's liquor cabinet, of waking up to the drumming in his head and looking through bleary, tear-filled eyes, of the events he'd been trying to drown out . . . and how it had never worked. He cast the memories out of his mind and glared at Percival. "You should be resting up for the work ahead of us."

A theory floated into Roy's head then. *Is this because of what we found in the catacombs? Did seeing and holding the Scribes' weapons wound him so deeply that he immediately resolved to lose himself in drink?* Despite reprimanding Percival, Roy couldn't say that he was fully averse to the idea. He wasn't fond of the taste of whiskey, having mostly indulged in wine, but the smell wafting out of that glass was still compelling, still unbearably intoxicating.

Percival waved one hand through the air, the other gripping his glass. "Oh, don't play the saint, Dawnseve. This spoilsport mentality is trite as they come." He furrowed his brows with intense concentration, then exclaimed, "'Weep not at the joybringer, Aphantus! He who holds the throbbing heart of elation is he who holds life!'" He took a swig of his whiskey. "Say, who wrote that nonsense?"

Unable to help himself, Roy muttered, "Aphantus. *Glory Mine*. The play was a satire on self-criticism."

Percival grinned at Roy and made to reach up and ruffle his hair, but Roy stepped back. "Darling, you smart angel, you! If I'd known you had even a basic interest in *The Nemefiran Quartet*, I would have incorporated more passages into our lively discussions. Here, this is an interesting one." He cleared his throat, then boomed, "'Hark, hark! The gates have opened; of whose accord, Aphantus does know; to what doom, fate does not tell!'" He laughed. "Sit down and have a drink, darling; I have plenty of these memorized. Come to think of it, how do you fancy pouring me another glass?"

Roy put his hands in the pockets of his trousers. "I don't fancy that at all, to be quite honest."

"Fetch me my drink, darling."

"You've consumed quite enough, *Percival*."

Percival swung himself into an upright position, a meticulous yet sudden maneuver. He sat on the edge of the settee, his boots thumping onto the redwood. He shot his left hand, the spare one, forward and clutched Roy's coat. "Pour me my drink."

Roy shoved him away.

Percival shook his head. "Oh, fine, *I'll* pour myself a drink." He stood from his seat, stumbled and staggered, then righted himself. Once he located the decanter on the table beside him, he filled two knuckles' length of whiskey, swallowed half of it, and then returned to his seat. "Rich taste," he said, as though he hadn't guzzled most of the decanter's contents. He lowered his lips to the rim of the glass, frowned, and tilted it toward Roy. "Be a scoundrel, Dawnseve. How hard can it be? We're already halfway there, being scholars and all. Here, I have a proposition for you."

"A proposition?"

Percival smirked. "A drinking game."

"Unfortunately for you, I'll have to decline," Roy said, though that sharp, smoky scent was still winding toward him, pulling him in. "I don't drink." His last bottle of stolen wine had been three years ago. *And I don't play games with you*, he thought. *How many times must I say that?*

Apparently he would have to keep saying it, because Percival asked, "Are you forfeiting?" He pushed his spectacles up the bridge of his nose. "Come, darling. I know the look of a man aching for a drink."

Roy knew he was being manipulated, but he couldn't shake the compulsion, couldn't look at that whiskey another moment without wanting to gulp it down, to experience once more that dizzying sense of euphoria. Just as difficult to ignore, too, was the fact that his desire to never play was far outstripped by his desire to do anything to cross Percival's lines, to connect just a little more. Besides, after the devastating intensity of what had occurred in, and what they'd found in, the catacombs, Roy felt the much-needed urge to blow off some steam. His light reading hadn't been nearly enough to disperse his tension, and if spending some time with Percival wouldn't smooth out his edges, then Roy was certain that a bit of whiskey might.

"I'll play," he said. He took the glass from Percival's hands and consumed the remainder of the drink. A malty, briny flavor coated his palate, and when he swallowed, the notes of oak and caramel lingered in the back of his mouth. He licked his lips, savoring the aftertaste.

"And I hadn't even specified the drinking game," Percival said.

Roy handed the glass back to Percival. "Proceed."

"We will each drink . . . hm, let's say a knuckle's length," Percival explained. "Then one of us asks the other a question. Simple."

Roy rolled his eyes. "Yes, simple. Infants have conceived more convoluted tournaments than this. Assuming we follow your deceptively easy rules, it seems only fair that I ask you the first question."

"It might suit you better once you've found a place to sit."

Roy shook his head in exasperation, not quite believing he'd consented to this madness, but then dragged over the ottoman in front of Percival's settee and sat down.

"He *can* listen to orders," Percival slurred, his jaw dropping in mock surprise.

"I'm going to ask you my question now, unless you haven't finished talking to yourself," Roy said. "What was your field of study before the Basilica?"

Percival was well prepared for this question, or perhaps he had done so much work in his field of study that the answer came naturally. "Many years of my education were devoted to understanding philosophers' stances on the connection between human emotion and art. What draws sadness from literature? How might the ideas of the past sour the soul or brighten the mind? I was around thirteen when I began unraveling these questions to try to contribute my *own* understanding."

Roy examined Percival's state of drunkenness. Although Percival was clearly finding it difficult to perfectly depict his thoughts, Roy couldn't identify what had cleared his mind so suddenly. "Drink," he said.

As Percival bent forward to retrieve the decanter, his cheeks daubed with fever-red splotches, a portion of his tunic fell free from his chest. Roy stole a glimpse of the shadowed cut of Percival's abdominal muscles and the hollows of his collarbones, accentuated by firelight, then glanced quickly away.

Percival sat back, seemingly oblivious to Roy's observation of his physique, and swallowed two inches of whiskey. A drop slithered down his chin. He wiped it away with the pad of his thumb, his eyes fixed on Roy. "Why are you so fascinated with Razkamun? I've gotten the notion there must be some deeper level of reasoning, but it escapes me."

"Because the Warfare-Philosophy Principle insinuates that the everyday soldier is capable of philosophical thought," Roy answered, "and conversely, that philosophers are as capable of defending themselves as the everyday soldier."

Percival nodded with grim understanding, the wrinkled lines between his brow smoothing out.

Roy wrung his hands. "I know that the greats, particularly the Elder Scribes, have looked down on—and in some cases, disparaged—Razkamun for peddling this notion, but the broad opinion of the public will never immediately, or perhaps ever, overturn the relatability which the minority feel toward such philosophies. But on that point, it *astounds* me how few of our people embraced and sympathized with Razkamun's principle. Shouldn't the idea that we, the undermined, be worthy of protecting ourselves from harm circulate through our community? It rings true to who we are."

"Perhaps truer to some than to others," Percival said. He sounded solemn, introspective. Somehow, Roy sensed he was thinking of the sword they'd found, and where they had found it.

Roy nodded. "That aside, there's just something about his style, and his approach to academia, that pulls at me. That *insists* he's not a—what would you call him?—a *crank*."

"That's all well and good, but it still doesn't answer my question, not quite. Why are *you*, specifically, drawn to Razkamun's beliefs?"

"Because pretending I'm brave," Roy said, "is as close to the real thing I'm ever going to get."

Percival crossed one leg over the other, tipped back his head, and rolled it slowly from side to side. "You don't mean that," he said. He was still slurring his words but was at least trying to articulate his thoughts more coherently.

"You asked, I answered," Roy said. He took the decanter from Percival's hand, poured, and swallowed, wincing at the burn that slid down and spread outward into his chest. "Why didn't you move when I moved my notebooks and texts to the sixth floor?"

Percival spoke as soon as Roy had finished asking his question. "Because I don't mind the view," he said, regarding Roy with intense ardor, "nor the distraction." He reached for the decanter, which Roy had put between his feet. Then he paused, his fingers curled about its neck, and looked up at Roy. "And I like the way your cheeks and your ears go pink when you come across something you don't understand, something you desperately *want* to understand. And I kept thinking that, if I stood up and walked away, the image would never leave me be. So I stayed." He hung his head, his own cheeks pink now, and settled back in his chair with the decanter between his legs. "I . . . I'm sorry." It was barely a whisper.

Roy gaped, every perfectly constructed thought washed clean out of his head. The whiskey had done its part, but the rest of it—the most of it—was Percival.

A fog creeping into his eyes, Percival sagged back, looked from the decanter to his glass, and, with a drunken, indolent shrug, took a long swig, imbibing far more than they had decided upon. Roy leaned forward, though by the time their boots were nearly touching, Percival had pulled himself away from the decanter, smacking his lips. He blinked, staring at the remaining mouthfuls of whiskey in the decanter, which refilled itself after a moment. Percival chuckled. "'*The night unfurls ever on!*' *the Phantom-Laird cried. 'Drinks for the youths, I say! Drink till we are again young!*'"

"Your question?" Roy asked.

Percival became suddenly serious, the dimple at the corner of his mouth gone. "What did Gabriel do to you?"

The question was so unexpected, and asked with such haste, that Roy almost lost his grip on his glass. He fumbled with it for what felt like a long while, then seized the wrist of his shaking hand with his spare one. A haze descended over his head and eyes like a red veil, and it took him a moment to realize his skull was pounding with a rage such as he had never felt before. It was oddly invigorating. Through the thumping in his head, Roy heard himself ask, "What did you say?"

Percival shook his head as if to clear it, then tried at a smile. It was not at all convincing. "Another question, I hear! Perhaps you should drink to compensate for—"

"I don't care how many times I must drink, Percival. *What did you say?*"

"What did—" Percival went quiet, then choked out, "What did Gabriel do to you? Who *is* he, as a matter of fact? You called out his name when I found you on that first night. You told him to stop, something about 'not tonight.'"

All at once, Roy was reminded of who Percival truly was, the man underneath the mask of feigned civility and elegance. He had planned his proposed academic competition, and so he had doubtlessly laid out the pieces in plain sight for this drinking game, too, arranging the rehearsed lines and responses. And Roy was left with only two choices, then: Answer and submit, handing Percival the knowledge of the torture he had suffered at the hands of his brother, or refuse and drink and slip back into the skin of the drunk who'd been slumped against his bed, his mouth dry and his skull throbbing.

Roy drew in a trembling breath. "I'm not answering your question. I *can't*."

Percival observed Roy, some softer emotion rising to the surface of his features, and then said quietly, "One drink for declining to answer. I'll ask another question."

Nodding, Roy took the decanter from Percival and acquiescently poured a knuckle's length of whiskey. This time, though, he relished the drink, savoring its smoky tones and how smoothly the liquor traveled from his tongue down to his throat. Once finished, he clumsily handed the decanter back to Percival.

"Careful," Percival murmured. He sat back, poured, and drank, studying Roy all the while with cold and critical observation. If not for the bleary cast of his eyes, Roy might have thought he had sobered up entirely. "On the night we met, I was interrupted from my reading by your screams. When I confronted you about it, your first instinct was to tell me that you'd fallen over. But the grief in your voice, darling . . . The *horror*." He looked troubled, as if he'd been woken from a night terror. "What happened? What *actually* happened?"

"I thought I'd seen something," Roy explained, the thoughts, the *memory*, that he'd kept at bay since that night now streaming freely from his lips. "Perhaps it was a trick of the light, or the Basilica tampering with my senses, but it felt simultaneously the realest thing to, and the farthest thing from, reality. There was a shadow, Percival." He laughed at the absurdity of the recollection, but a shudder passed through him nonetheless. "A shadow with glowing red eyes. It was chasing me, hovering like that coffin in the burial vault."

Percival sat forward, clutching the neck of the decanter with both hands.

"I fell over because I heard it . . . I heard it *screaming*," Roy said. He pressed his finger to his left temple, then drifted it over to the middle of his forehead. "It went from here to here; I could feel voices—those vibrations, as we've called them—inside my skull, demanding to be freed, to be let out of their cage, but I couldn't *breathe*, Percival." He clutched his own throat. "I thought the shadow had shredded my lungs apart or torn out my throat, simply by passing through me, but when you walked over to me, it . . . it *vanished*." Tears gathered in his eyes. "I don't know why it attacked me when it was clearly desperate for help, for someone to hear its pleas and if not obey then *acknowledge* them."

A flicker of curiosity and fear crossed Percival's face, but it disappeared the moment Roy saw it. Percival laughed, but it was too curt, too loud. "'*The Phantom-Laird frequented the ill-lit hours of the night, sparing secret visitations to half-mad fools and chroniclers.*'" He smiled. "I have no other choice but to believe you've gone half-mad, darling."

Roy was stunned by Percival's insouciance. "You believe most of the impossible things we've experienced, some of which I'm certain you fabricated yourself, but *this* is too surreal for you?"

"Is that your question?" Percival asked, nodding to the decanter. "I'd suggest you drink up."

Roy did, but as he licked the taste of the whiskey off his lips, it wasn't Percival's suddenly stunted suspension of disbelief he asked him about. They were veering toward the more troubling topics of discussion now, the intimacies and traumas that were too horrifying to elaborate on in broad daylight and with a clear mind. "You lost someone not too long ago," Roy said. "Shortly before you were brought here, you said—"

Percival straightened, a deepening red blush flooding his cheeks. "I'm not telling you who—"

"And I'm not asking you to," Roy said. He held up a hand. "Please, I understand this is hard for you, but . . . Please, let me finish." Percival nodded, and Roy finished, "Can I assume that what happened to this person, whatever mistake you made that instigated their death, resulted in your presence here? Is this assignment your punishment?"

Percival took the glass from Roy, the whiskey sloshing against the rim, and drained it without taking his eyes off Roy. "Ask another question, Dawnseve. You have your limits, and I have mine." Through his spinning vision, Roy tried to find a splinter of sadness in Percival's anger, a crack in the ice, but when he did, all he felt was guilt, not satisfaction. "Please, Roy. Another question. *Please.*"

After a long and heavy silence, Roy said, "During our game—not this drinking game, but our competition—you unswervingly pushed on this concept of ambition as the foundation of academia. Where does this concept, for you, stem from?"

Percival replied without hesitation, "My family."

Roy concealed his amazement at the piece of information

he'd been handed. It shouldn't have come as such a shock to him that Percival had—or had once had—a family, but Roy had begun to think of Percival's past as a myth, a legend he would never completely grasp. Perhaps Percival's origins were to blame for his inclination to construct a game out of every given scenario, but from which relative had this trait emerged? A ruthless brother? A heartless mother? Did he and Roy have more in common than met the eye?

The fragment of truth seemed to be too much for Percival. His face returned to its usual sardonic expression, and he said, "This is your opportunity for some leeway, darling. Take it." He poured, drank. "Do I intimidate you?"

"Yes," Roy whispered.

Percival snatched the decanter back and finished its contents. "What do I make you want to do?"

The question was brazen, and yet utterly justified based on how Roy had said "yes." So Roy reclaimed the decanter, his thumb brushing across Percival's fingers. "You make me want you," he said, his gaze involuntarily falling to Percival's lips. "It's off-putting. I get lost in my head, worried that I might lose track of time, of how much we have left to lose, and it's costing me because you make me want to have you against the wall." His breathing was uneven, heavy. "And I can't have that."

Percival rested his elbows on his knees, his fingers intertwined. "And how does it make you feel to know that I wove that web?"

"Drink and you may find out," Roy said, and once Percival did, without a complaint about Roy stretching the rules of the game, Roy went on. "It makes me want to know how you do this. How you can change my mind. How you *know* you will win. No, I know why. I've always known."

"Tell me."

"You're convinced you'll win because you've been corrupted by whatever happened to you, whatever brought you here."

Percival shuffled closer and placed his legs between Roy's. Their knees were pressed together, their trousers swaying from the sudden rearrangement of limbs. Percival cupped Roy's left cheek in his palm, stroking his skin, and Roy had no choice but to lean into the touch. With his other hand, Percival poured the remnants of whiskey from the decanter into the glass, civilized compared to his earlier debauched guzzling of the drink, and flicked his eyes back to Roy. He gripped the glass, the vein along his wrist standing out against his skin, then dipped his head low and whispered in Roy's ear, "Why haven't you kissed me yet, Roy?"

Roy stiffened, his heart hammering. He reined in the amorous craving to glance at Percival's mouth again. By the Scribes, he wanted more than a chaste kiss. He wanted to throw the glass into the flames and lace his fingers together against the back of Percival's neck. If Roy straddled him, he knew Percival would grip his ass, anything to hold him captive.

You want this, don't you? Roy admonished himself. *You want this, you lust-ridden fool, and it's costing you. He has you in his web, Roy. You cannot give in.* But since the day he had picked up Polisworth's *Ambrosia for Curses*, his first foray into old-world literature, Roy had set a precedent for defying what was right, what was deemed socially acceptable, and despite his own cowardice, he wanted this one wrong thing.

"Because you never asked," Roy whispered, his breath shuddering across Percival's arm.

Percival put the glass onto a nearby table, his palm momentarily leaving Roy's face, then staggered back to him, stood between his legs, and tucked two tufts of Roy's black-silver hair behind his ears. Roy could have been mistaken, but he couldn't seem to see even the briefest glimpse of arrogance on Percival's face, nor feel any hostility in his tender, affectionate touch. Percival traced his jaw with a finger, drawing a small gasp from Roy's lips, and tipped his chin up so their eyes met.

Percival kissed his forehead. "And I never will." But his hot breath was sprouting beads of sweat on Roy's temples, and his mouth was quivering against Roy's forehead, like he was holding himself back.

Roy closed his eyes, his face upturned. He didn't know how long he was sitting there like that, but when the cold swept in, he opened his eyes and saw that Percival was gone.

18

WHEN ROY WOKE, HIS MOUTH WAS DRY, HIS vision was swimming, and his skull was filled with an incessant, excruciating pounding. It felt as though soldiers were smashing the hilts of their swords inside his head. He groaned and gritted his teeth against the pain. He could tolerate it, he supposed, but the implication was more unbearable than the cost.

Memories of the night before broke through the fog. He remembered the descent into the catacombs and the necropolis snaking beneath the library. He remembered the swords, eldritch and forbidding, resting within the sarcophagi of long-dead Scribes; the anxiety that had followed him on his way back upstairs; and his drinking game with Percival, an attempt to take everything off his mind for a little while.

He hadn't been anticipating the end of the night to go as it had, though, but he couldn't refute that a part of him had secretly hoped for it. He laid the back of his hand on his forehead, and sure enough, he was instantly revisited by the memory of Percival's lips there. Nothing else came to him, though. Had he admitted to any other wild fantasies? It pained him to wonder if he had.

An hour later, once he'd pulled himself out of bed and

attempted to work out how to wiggle himself out of a conversation with Percival about the drinking game if it was brought into discussion—only to come up empty—Roy was walking into the Observatory and rubbing the sleep from his eyes when he skidded to a halt and gasped.

Gone was the decrepit, ghostly room where Roy loved to study; the Observatory was now spotless and beautifully organized. At the back of the room was an opened door, which Roy hadn't seen through the clutter before, that gave on to either another chamber or a hallway. Against the wall beside him was the piano where he had broken down and sobbed, now polished to a fine gleam and topped with gargoyle-shaped bookends. Along the window opposite the piano was the desk Roy typically used. It had been cleared entirely free of dust.

"The library did this?" Roy exclaimed, amazed. "By the Scribes, Percival, look how *neat* everything is." He pointed at the entryway at the back of the room. "I didn't even know that existed."

Percival swallowed and rubbed the back of his neck, which had turned a feverish shade of red. "This was . . ." He cleared his throat, despite that he sounded perfectly articulate, albeit a little nervous. "This was all me, actually. I've noticed how uncomfortable you get whenever your study space is cluttered. I know sometimes you design it that way, but I've still seen you fidgeting and moving papers around, trying to get things in order, so I put some drawers from my closet on the windowsill there. You can label them if you like; I would've done it, but it was nearing dawn and I couldn't find anything, and besides, I thought that you'd like to label them yourself—"

Suddenly, Roy cared not at all that the night before had ended the way it had; with Roy closing his eyes, waiting and wanting, and Percival already gone. He kissed Percival's cheek. "It's perfect."

Percival shrugged. "It just needed some flair." But Roy spotted the rosy blush spreading across his damp cheek.

Once they settled in at the desk together, reluctantly delving into research on the black-scabbarded swords, Roy and Percival retired from broader war books, fictional and non-, to books on the exact weapons wielded in skirmishes, duels, wars, and other forms of combat. There were axes, clubs, hatchets, bows and arrows, falchions, and war hammers. No muskets, though, since these had been invented in the new world and the Orphic Basilica housed texts specifically written during the old world.

And so many swords. Roy had not realized just how many types existed. He found longswords, scimitars, claymores, fabers, and cutlasses. Some belonged to warrior-kings and knights-errant, others to impoverished servants whose royal-blooded relatives were unbeknownst to them. There were depictions of swords being used on the battlefield, too, and of legendary swords hung on the glimmering walls of throne halls.

None of them, however, held even a vague resemblance to the swords they'd discovered in the catacombs.

Every so often, while he was becoming increasingly agitated looking through historical accounts that yielded no answers, he would glance at the black-scabbarded sword propped up against the side of Percival's desk, and then the narrower sword resting against his own desk, and shiver.

The third time this happened, as it had several times the night before, it crept up on him what was missing from all these books he was rapidly consuming, what he had been hunting for: the wickedness of the sword, not of its bearer. He had come across no shortage of stories about soldiers who had gone mad, who had luxuriated in the power that stole into their heads whenever they curled their fingers around the hilts of their swords. But there seemed to be no accounts on innately wicked *weapons*.

Roy knew it was out of the ordinary, but he couldn't stop toying with the theory that had begun brewing in his mind. He was rigidly opposed to the notion of superstition and the like, but was it rational to deny what was right before your eyes? How long could he blame every unexplainable phenomenon he encountered on its impossibility?

One avenue he and Percival had begun pursuing was the unsettling power that they suspected was contained within the swords' sheaths. Had the Elder Scribes been aware of it? What *was* it? How had they used it to effectively banish the Old Ones from Northgard?

On the desk in front of Roy, who had been working opposite Percival for the past few days, were five piles of novels, essays, articles, critical and expository analyses, literature reviews, and stray pieces of paper filled with nonsensical jargon. He went through each and divided some in two—on the left, those written in the common tongue; on the right, the remaining texts, twice as high as the other.

Roy normally liked to tackle the challenging aspects of his research first, but he didn't want to start the day struggling, so he started on the left pile. In it, he found many texts that had seemingly important but ultimately useless connections to what he had gathered over the past month or so. He discovered a history book about the Burnt-Eyed Centurion, a knight whose sword was reportedly cursed . . . but this curse was unfortunately only in name. He found a few poems exploring death, soul-seeking, and the afterlife. Roy read through a few and thought that he, a mediocre poet, could have written better with his hands bound behind his back.

Then Roy discovered a thick book with a dark green cover: Leopileus's *The Blades of Tangror*, a volume on weapons of historically lauded craftsmanship. Throughout the book were paintings of a variety of weapons, but mostly swords. These were accompanied by a succinct description of their history, previous owners, and material. Their names were written at the bottom in cursive lettering: *Malevoli, Kharuan, Cephius, Valusvar, Parlikeves* ... There were more names but considering only Valusvar resembled the sword from the crypt—which would have been a match, had the metal been the same color—Roy wasn't concerned with them.

As soon as the thought formed, though, a cool, serene wind played with his curls and snuck behind his ear. Whispers gathered within his mind, like a softened echo of the storm currently slamming against the window behind him.

Percival glanced around the room, looking disconcerted, then continued researching.

Galvanized by the Basilica's encouragement, Roy moved the texts he could understand closest to him, and the rest behind them. This way, he could refer to any that seemed important later, including *The Blades of Tangror*, which the library seemed to insist was significant.

He went back to the pile of legible writings. He saw a long-winded report, written by one M. R. Svadir, about an enigmatic, sickening odor drifting out the maw of the Macchylian Mines. *An odor of grime and the dead*, Svadir claimed, but after a monthslong excavation, no discoveries were made as to what had been interred within.

Roy was disappointed by this, but at least he had a similarity to draw upon. When he'd caught that scent of "grime and the dead" in the catacombs, he had been plagued by visions, either of the past or of his own vision but magnified. *It feels more like a closer view of our surroundings*, as Percival had put it.

Roy then made a third stack of texts, which held possible

connections to the Old Ones, and slid it next to the other two he had made.

The fourth pile held nothing but some old books on rare archaeological finds, none of which hinted at the Old Ones, so he moved onto the fifth and last pile. He started to pull down the book on top, then paused as he read its title: Mortys's *An Account of Thanatology, the Study of Death*. He glanced at the spines of the manuscripts underneath it, and terror gripped his gut and twisted hard, nearly making him vomit.

There was a detailed diagram and written analysis of a child's skull, which had been trampled in an undisclosed incident. Beneath this was a research paper, written by a novelist who had performed disturbing biological experiments on his husband to "accurately convey an evocation of fright, heartache, and turmoil." The next was a book teeming with perverse confessions, including a young man who'd admitted to a yearslong passion for consuming the blood and ashes of his relatives, certain it would grant him immortality. He died at sixteen.

On and on the texts went, each as macabre as the last. Roy skimmed through books on occultism, necromancy, and psychological experimentation. Interspersed among them were haunting artworks of tragedy, some moments before the event but most at the time of. A black-hooded man grinning lecherously, bearing a scythe above a teary-eyed boy. A faceless woman strapped to a chair, glittering blades dangling overhead like a silver chandelier. Two women embracing, the cut wrists of their interlocked hands weeping blood.

Roy paused at the final item in the pile, breathless with terror. It was a colored, hyper-realistic painting of a valley covered with human entrails. *The Massacre of Kaolon*, read the messily scrawled title at the bottom. Beneath it, someone had left an annotation. *As far as I can make out, this is an artist's interpretation, described by a survivor of the Old Ones. This is the most we've seen of their thanatological abilities on full display.*

Roy stared, finally catching his breath. He recalled Charles Patiny's untitled poem, whose allusion to the catacombs—and the whereabouts of its entryway—had directed him and Percival underground. But the second stanza seemed to focus on the subject of the books contained in the catacombs, and though Roy hadn't found anything pertinent to the Old Ones there, he couldn't shake the feeling that Patiny had been alluding to the soldiers.

Roy asked, "Percival, do you have that poem with you? The one by Patiny?"

Percival, who appeared disgruntled by the interruption, scanned the disarray he'd made on his side of the table and then procured a scrap of paper from underneath a literary analysis he'd been skimming.

Roy read the poem to himself, then stilled at the first two lines of the second stanza: *"The red-eyed devils!" the pages call, / "the bringers and keepers of death!"*

This, coupled with the annotation beneath *The Massacre of Kaolon* mentioning the use of "thanatological abilities," substantiated Roy's suspicions. The Old Ones were linked to thanatology, the study of—and, apparently, the power of—death. It was typically regarded as a scientific notion, and many philosophers of the old world had debated its concepts: the direction of life's beginning in relation to its end; the afterlife; and even, Roy thought with a shudder, which parts of the brain were completely, partially, and not at all responsive in the moments preceding and immediately after death.

"By the Scribes," Roy whispered.

Percival looked up, read the expression on Roy's face, and

then set his quill down. "What's the matter? Did you find something?"

Roy took one last look at the painting, then handed it to Percival, whose breath shook as he flicked his gaze hurriedly over the scene as though not sure what to look at first. "Thanatology?"

"There's something about these swords, Percival," Roy said. "I understand we've been putting it off in search of answers, but it seems to me that there's no better answer than what we have with us right now."

Percival eventually pulled his gaze from *The Massacre of Kaolon* and observed the swords. "We *did* feel some sort of power in them. A wrongness." He dwelt upon this for a second, then stood, twisting his back. "All right, let's have a closer look at them. I suppose we should have a break anyway; it's been almost eight hours." He slipped into his overcoat, which he'd hung on the back of his chair, and headed toward the doorway he'd cleared for Roy.

"We're not going to do it here?" Roy inquired.

"I need to move around; my limbs are stiff," Percival explained, retrieving the sword with the skeleton-shaped hilt from beside his desk. "Besides, there's something else I've been meaning to show you." Roy went to get his own sword, but Percival shook his head. "We'll just experiment with the one. I haven't a clue what these weapons do, but the power in them . . ."

Again, Roy shuddered. "You might have a point."

Percival tugged on Roy's arm. "Come on, this way."

He escorted Roy through the Observatory's rear door, shutting it behind Roy as he went through, and into a long corridor. It yawned before them, the left wall and ceiling made from cobblestone. To their right was a sweeping bank of windows. Above the wall of snow pressed against the glass, which appeared to have decreased in the past few days, Roy tried to make out the soaring summits and flat rooftops of Northgard's residential complexes, but there was only a howling white haze.

Regardless, from the diminished wall of snow, winter seemed to have loosened its leash on the land. For a moment Roy was heartened by this, but he had seen respites in the weather before. These never lasted more than a day or two, though, granting Northgard's teeming, panic-stricken streets some time to recover from the previous prolonged blizzard before the next struck—usually harder than ever. It had been rumored for years, ever since the snowstorm had launched itself upon Northgard, that the weather was a sign of great danger, a harbinger of doom. Roy had been skeptical, but knowing what he knew now, he thought that these theories might hold more truth than he'd originally suspected.

"I'll warn you," Percival said as they approached a black door set at the very end of the narrow hallway, "you may soil yourself when you see this." After a moment, he squeezed Roy's arm, twisted the knob, and pushed the door open, standing aside.

Despite his lingering apprehension, Roy clapped a hand over his mouth, containing his shrill gasp.

Inside the room was a circle of seven monolithic sandstone pillars, which surrounded an enormous book perched on a black pedestal. A chandelier dangled from the ceiling, casting an ethereal nimbus of golden light upon the mounted book. Seven marble statues—four women, three men—stood between the pillars like the sentinels of a high divine order. Some had their heads bowed and their fingers interlaced, others their chins tipped up and their hands clasped at their back. Only one, the statue of the woman directly adjacent to Roy, had her stony gaze set on the displayed book.

The construction was encompassed overhead by low-railinged balconies. There, Roy imagined the bygone residents and tourists of the Orphic Basilica would have clamored for an uninhibited view of the statues, standing on their toes and peering over shoulders. He pictured children crying, begging for their parents and caretakers to hoist them up on their hips so they could get a better look. There was a black iron staircase, identical to those in the atrium of the library, which gave visitors access to the viewing platform. Written across the balcony at the back wall were the words:

THE MUSEUM OF THE ELDER SCRIBES

"It's stunning, I know," Percival said, his voice full of awe. "But you can explore another day." He pointed to a door lurking in the shadow cast by the balcony on their left. "Let's go here."

Roy walked toward the door Percival had indicated, feeling like he was traipsing through a labyrinth, but the room they entered was simple enough: a mahogany desk, a bookshelf, and a harp perched atop a small podium beside a porthole window.

Percival released Roy's arm and gripped the hilt of the sword with one hand and the scabbard with the other, but before he could do anything, Roy suddenly got cold feet. "Wait, what are you planning to do?"

"Unsheathe it?" Percival said. He sounded faintly sardonic, as though Roy had asked him some laughably obvious question. "What else did you think I was going to do?"

"I know, but—"

"You said it yourself—we've been stalling long enough. It's time to dig deeper, like we did in the crypt. There is a secret here, something big, and I hate the idea of not knowing what it might be, and *damn* it, I know you do, too." He placed a hand on the hilt of the sword.

Roy stepped forward. "Percival."

"Let me," Percival said.

"Percival," Roy called out, a fraction louder, and when he received no reply: "Percival, *stop*! I know I suggested this, but . . . but you were the one who said there's a wrongness about them. I agree—I can feel it, sense it."

Percival ignored him and curled his fingers around the hilt of the sword, making a white-knuckled fist around the skeleton-shaped cross guard. He paled, his eyes wide and filled with dismay. "You're right. I feel its power, Roy. This is just one of these damn things. Imagine *two*—and in the same room, no less." His voice was unnaturally low, gravelly, and his features were frozen into a look of such dread that Roy couldn't repress the shiver that went through him. "So . . . so *vile*," Percival whispered.

"Don't pull it out, then."

"And do what? Contemplate it forever, never even looking at it? How does that make sense? How can you even call yourself a scholar if you're afraid to encounter ideas you don't like?"

"This isn't some theory that rubs me wrong—"

"No," Percival agreed. "It's not a theory at all. It's real. And it's in *our* hands."

"Step back from the sword," Roy said, not sure whether he was speaking to himself or to Percival. He could feel himself being pulled toward it, like an invisible hand had oozed out of the blade and was lassoing around his torso, tightening its grasp, drawing him ever forward. "Step back—"

"I *want* this, Roy!" Percival shouted, his voice cracking. "I *need* this." *Everybody wants something to be remembered by,* he'd said in the catacombs. He clutched the edge of the desk with his right hand, a pillar to hold his frame. He seemed trapped, enmeshed in a war between vulnerability and resistance. "You can't take this from me, Roy, not this. *Please*, damn it, not this—"

"Let me do it, then, Percival," Roy screamed, not caring how desperate he sounded. He wanted so badly to leap forward, to hold Percival back and away from the sword, but he was revisited again by the eerie, premonitory sensation that its scabbard was decorated with thousands—or millions—of unseen eyes, watching him with predatory, ravenous hunger. Then he staggered back, horrified. "How many times must I repeat myself?"

Percival sneered. "Enough to stop me. We came here to do this. You said yourself you need to be doing something. Well, this is it, Roy. This is the doing!" He looked back at the sword. He took firm hold of the curved scabbard and tugged on the hilt. The blade didn't come free, though it hummed from within its casing, as though in answer to his efforts. He tried once more, the muscles in his arm flexing, a trickle of sweat coursing down his forehead. Then he relaxed his grip. "Don't say a word, Roy. Please, don't do it."

Roy disobeyed, but instead of disputing with Percival, he gave him an instruction. "Try twisting them in opposite directions," he said, his pulse pounding at the hollow of his throat. "The hilt and the scabbard, I mean. It's what—it's what my brother used to do whenever he practiced his sword work."

Percival looked annoyed, but he followed the directives. Instantly, the scabbard fell to the ground with a ringing whine, exposing about four feet of midnight-dark metal outlined with a lambent silver glow. A faded hum, true to Percival's claim in the catacombs, issued from the blade. He hefted the sword into both his hands and grunted at its weight, astonishment sweeping across his face. He tottered back and forth for a moment, tracing an arc of light through the air.

As that slender beam of radiance came toward Roy, he was struck by a wave of disorientation so mind-bendingly painful that he blacked out for a second, or maybe it was a minute, and was then battered by a crushing vertigo. The world seemed distorted, twisted out of shape. He had no longer than a second to look through this shattered version of reality before that indistinct humming rose to a deafening, ghostly scream. The din went on and on, seemingly infinite, so wretched and feral compared to the clamor that had emanated from the walls of the crypt and from the creature that had first accosted Roy.

It came to him then that never in his life, until this moment, had he known real terror. As he thought this, Roy ran a hand down his chest, H-I-S-T-O-R-Y scarred into his skin, and still felt the truth of this feeling now. He had sensed the wrongness of the sword since he'd laid eyes upon it, yes, but now he knew the difference between sensing evil and seeing evil. Now he knew he was too late to do anything about it.

He took in a shuddering breath, so deep that he was sure there was no air left in the room for Percival to breathe. Somewhere beyond the tears blurring his vision, though, Percival was lurching from foot to foot, the sword clutched tightly in his shaking fists, his teeth gritted and his eyes firmly locked on Roy's. The look of mingled guilt, horror, and fascination on his face was almost too much for Roy to bear.

But he didn't have to, for not even a moment passed after he'd met Percival's gaze before everything went dark.

From within the darkness, however, a rapid succession of nightmarish images rushed by, all laid over Roy's vision. He was lying upon the summit of a mountain littered with corpses and toppled flags, slashed open from his neck to his groin. Crows were pecking at the flayed flaps of his stomach, partially masticated ropes of intestines hanging from their beaks. A cold, howling wind blew across the mountain, bringing with it the stench of blood, gunpowder, and smoke. His dying screams were swept away by the breeze.

The vision shifted. He was standing upright this time, strings of his blood-spattered hair tangled and knotted across his face. He clutched at his chest, protruding from which was the blunt head of an axe. With one hand, paralyzed by nerve damage, he brushed aside his fringe and saw a grinning man bolting toward him—

Another vision. An arrow whizzed through the air, too fast for Roy to thwart, then plunged deep into his eye and shattered the back of his skull—

Another vision, and another, and another. He was a victim of innumerable atrocities, a vessel for pain. He did not recoil or resist. There was no place for retaliation in this spectral world, no room for kinship or freedom or love.

In one vision, Briar was holding a knife to his throat, the same knife Gabriel had used to carve H-I-S-T-O-R-Y into Roy's chest, and had her fist wrapped around his hair. She pulled harder, and a drop of blood slithered underneath his tunic. Then she slashed the dagger across his throat. Crimson blood first frothed then flooded out from the parted skin, painting a red veil over Briar's face. Her lips split into a grin, and as that grin broadened, the blood darkened into a syrupy black sludge—

Another. Roy was kneeling before Percival, who was dressed in only his trousers. A belt, outfitted with an arsenal of well-polished blades, hung loosely around his waist. He pulled out a dagger from the belt, lunged forward without thought, and then rammed the dagger deep into Roy's left nostril. The cold iron burrowed through his nasal cavity, filling his head. Something must have given way, because a clear, flat *crack* echoed through his skull, and he tried to reel back and cling for life, but his entire body seemed to have cramped up and—

The world—the *real* world—rushed back with increasing clarity. He was back in the Orphic Basilica, in a room within the Museum of the Elder Scribes. Percival had brought him here so they could experiment with some weapon. A *sword*.

Scatterbrained, Roy scrambled to his feet, realizing only then that he'd crumpled to his hands and knees. He panted, his breath short and tremulous, his heart pummeling his rib cage. His vision had cleared, but his disbelief was so strong that for a while he could not properly discern what he was looking at.

Percival was standing in front of the desk, staring incredulously at the sword, which had clattered to the ground. He had one hand raised before his eyes. He shook his head, his gaze settling on Roy. "I didn't . . ." he whispered. "I didn't know what would happen, Roy, I—"

A cord of restraint Roy had not been previously aware of, but could now feel thrumming through his entire body, snapped. Not quite thinking of what he was doing, he ran at Percival, sidestepping the unsheathed sword, and grasped him by the throat with a strength he hadn't known he possessed. Then he thrust Percival down upon the desk, leaning over him.

Percival forced out a rough, half-drawn breath and attempted to claw at Roy's forearms but only succeeded in running his fingers down Roy's wrist.

Roy squeezed tight, tears streaming down his face. "What did you *do*, Percival? What did you *do*?" He clamped his fingers down harder on Percival's throat, sobbing. "Tell me! *Tell* me or I'll snap your neck, you fucking bastard!"

Percival scrabbled weakly at Roy's arm again, the light in his eyes dimming just slightly, his stuttering exhalations blowing back the sweat-dampened curls that had fallen across Roy's face. His bloodshot, bulging eyes swung from side to side with mad desperation. His fair skin was turning a distressing shade of purple. But it was the look of utter powerlessness upon his face, the look that Roy had worn every time Gabriel shoved pages torn from Roy's favorite books in his mouth to muffle his screams as he was beaten, that made Roy eventually see reason. It was that look that made Roy let go.

He slumped on top of Percival, who was wheezing and coughing beneath him. Percival wrapped his arms hesitantly around Roy, then tightened his hold as Roy started sobbing into Percival's shoulder. Percival lowered his head, his soft lips hovering just near the hairs at the crown of Roy's head.

Roy banded his arms around Percival, curling his fingers into his hair. "What . . . What did you . . ." He could not seem to stop saying the words. There were no other explanations within his reach, and so there was nothing else to say.

Percival clasped Roy's cheek, tipped his head up, and wiped away Roy's tears with the pad of his thumb, his eyes tracing the movement. "It wasn't me."

"The sword was in your—"

"How could I have done that, darling?" Percival whispered. "I am of flesh and blood. I am as human as you."

Roy sniffled and staggered back to his feet. He was about to topple backward when Percival pushed himself up from the desk and gripped the front of Roy's tunic, holding him upright. But as Roy regained his balance, Percival's left thumb slipped across the outline of his scar, the second or third letter of H-I-S-T-O-R-Y. Roy shoved Percival hard in his chest, casting his gaze away.

"What—" Percival got out.

"What did you do?" Roy demanded again, intercepting any line of questioning Percival might drag him into. He knew that he would have to tell Percival about his scar one day—someday too soon, no doubt—but he shrank at the idea of crossing that line. He had no clue how Percival might respond, whether he would cut ties with Roy and abandon the bond Percival himself had said was there . . . or if he could even trust Percival with the torment he had kept quiet, kept at bay, for so long. "You say you're human, but when you unsheathed that sword . . ."

Coughing into the sleeve of his tunic, Percival pointed to the sword lying on the ground, which had stopped its strange ethereal humming, and said, "The power I felt, it grew stronger as the scabbard slid off the blade, but . . ." He went silent for a moment, then asked Roy softly, "What did you see?"

"Visions," Roy said. "Hundreds of them, maybe, but they went by so quickly, some of them overlapping each other, that my mind could only process eight or so."

"And what happened in these visions?" Percival asked, gnawing at his fingernails, his elbow propped on one hand.

Roy picked at his bottom lip. "I . . . I was being killed—stabbed, torn to pieces, trampled by the boots of people who had some grudge against me. But sometimes, Percival . . ." He held a splayed hand over his mouth and spoke raggedly through his fingers. "Sometimes I was the one killing myself. Sometimes it was Gabriel and Briar, and once . . . once, I believe it was you."

"Darling," Percival murmured, rubbing at the faint purple handprint Roy had made across his throat. "You know I would never—"

"I know," Roy said, and somehow, in that exact moment, he did. Of course he knew Percival could never bring himself to inflict such fatal and irreversible harm on Roy. Nor would Briar, for that matter. But Gabriel? Even Roy himself, who had, from time to time, considered that the only conceivable way out of the terrors he'd faced was to erase himself from the equation? That sword might've shown him false, twisted versions of reality, but here, in the real world, his contemplations of suicide had never been false. Was that the power invested within this cursed sword? Could it infiltrate and manipulate the mind of its opponent? "I know," Roy said again to Percival, but there was no conviction whatsoever in his voice. All he felt was an all-consuming dread.

They stared at the sword lying on the ground in a heavy, perturbed silence. Nothing about it appeared to have changed. The faintest suggestion of orchestral sound, as of angels singing, was still issuing from the blade, now bare after Percival's struggle with the scabbard, and that strange silver light was still hovering about the metal.

No, the change wasn't coming from within the sword but from *without*. Color bled out of the maroon floorboards underneath the luminous length of the blade, turning them the gray of desiccated skin. It tracked across the ground, spreading from where the sword rested, near the podium upon which the harp stood, in every which way. The room, once saturated with deep browns and reds, was now slowly becoming as lifeless as the weapon that had infected it. The angelic chorus trickling out of the blade sounded different, *warped*, charged with some erratic and infernal energy, mingling with the familiar keening screams that Roy had heard a while ago.

He stumbled away from the desk, first scratching at his arms and then clapping the heels of his hands against his ears. A shrill whining was rising in the hollow space between, as though a gong had been struck inside his skull. Drawing in small, shallow breaths over his teeth, he tottered off the podium and then lurched over to the sword.

All the while, the room around him continued its chilling transformation. The crimson shade of the wallpaper was now drab and bleak, and the storm-blasted world out of the porthole window looked like some macabre wasteland where ash fell from chasm-black skies instead of snow. Beyond, a circular formation of dark, monolithic structures materialized, stretching higher into the thinning clouds. Roy had an idea that if neither he nor Percival did anything about it, whatever they *could* do, the world would just keep unraveling until the sword finished its work and made those visions he'd seen come true.

Then Percival pushed Roy aside, picked the discarded scabbard up off the floor, and walked over to the sword. Its humming grew in volume and pitch, fervid in its intensity. Roy thought he might go mad from the sound of it, thought he might dig his fingers into his ears and pull out his brains just to free himself. But then the room lapsed into silence and, after a moment, slowly regained its color.

Roy took his hands off the sides of his head. There was still a ringing in his ears, and a throbbing ache had crept into his skull, but these pains were pale next to the discomforts that had nearly leeched the remaining ounce of energy from his bones moments before.

Percival rose to his full height, the sword now sheathed once more and dangling from the belt about his waist. "What do we do with it?"

Roy took a second to recompose himself, then said, "We'll keep it in its scabbard and store it away."

"Are you *deranged*?" Percival exclaimed, incredulous. "You have no compunctions admitting that the Basilica brought us to the crypt, and you can even entertain the possibility of dark magic as a crucial element of this conspiracy, and *this* is where you draw the line?" He scowled. "How fucking asinine and contradictory can you be? Nothing about you makes a lick of sense."

"Nothing about any of this makes sense, Percival! If you saw what I saw, you would understand my misgivings," Roy said. He would've returned Percival's scowl if not for the recurring memories of the harrowing things he'd seen. "But you *didn't*, Percival.

You can't scorn me for my reservations when you didn't even see what—"

Percival gripped the hilt of the sword. He didn't withdraw it from its scabbard, Roy knew this was only to prove a point, but it still made him flinch. "Go on, then," Percival said with a hint of derision. "Take it. Point it at me. That's how this blasted thing works, no? Show me, Dawnseve. Show me what you saw."

These last words were spoken with such undeniable contempt that Roy looked down at his feet, mortified.

Percival removed his hand from the sword hilt, sighing with what sounded like resignation. "I know you're scared, but . . . you don't need to live in fear—"

Roy stilled. Hadn't he told Percival something similar prior to their descent into the crypt? "Don't use my words against me."

"Not against you. *For* you. They were words I needed, even if I denied it at the time. And correct me if I'm wrong, but I feel like the same rules apply here." Percival came over to Roy, brushed the back of his hand across the back of Roy's. "We can't turn our backs now. What you saw *will* come to pass if we stop right here." He shook the sword emphatically. "If we stow this away, we've all but given up."

"I was not born for war," Roy said.

Percival offered him a sad, wistful smile. "Nor was I. Lifting and swinging this damned blade is the closest I'll come to wielding one. But we were born *into* war. And we weren't dragged here to do battle, were we? *'Poet, linger near me,'* said Peace. *'My darkhearted twin is not your savior . . .'"*

"*'. . . for there are safer waters than these,'*" Roy recited, finishing the concluding passage from Gertrude Pothel's *Troubled Kin*. He swept his fingers lightly over Percival's wrist. "But these aren't safe waters, Percival. Not by far."

"No," Percival said, "but they're waters we can navigate, and we'll navigate them together. The going will be hard, but it won't be impossible. My brother Edgar used to tell himself something when placed under such conditions. I never got to know him well enough to understand what had him so distressed, but I found myself saying it under my breath whenever I was swamped with readings and classwork from Rasileus Academy, and with my own personal old-world studies."

"What was it?" Roy asked.

Percival wrapped his arm around Roy's shoulders, and when Roy drew in a sharp breath, startled by the unexpected contact, Percival let go. But his smile was radiant as he said, "Do it, then it's done."

Roy almost laughed at how obvious the statement was, how clear-cut. But as he turned the words over in his head, contemplating them from new angles, he realized he felt renewed, his shoulders squared, his mind honed to a fine point.

The work would not be as easy as the words promised. There would be sleepless nights aplenty. There would be days of labor and tedium. But it would be worth it, despite the costs and the consequences. He begrudged the efforts he had to go to sometimes, but that didn't discount the satisfaction he received from the completion of such large tasks as these. That gratification was his and his alone.

Northgard could not, *would* not, take that from him.

19

ROY AND PERCIVAL MADE THRICE AS MUCH PROGress combining their knowledge as they had ever made alone. Over the next few weeks, they amassed their recent discoveries—the catacombs, the swords, thanatology, and the apparent significance of these elements to the Old Ones' reason of invasion—and recorded these in their second progress report to the Governor, who returned with additional provisions at the beginning of their second month in the Orphic Basilica. He then declared that the next supply drop would be in three weeks.

Throughout all this, whenever Roy got stuck or lost or distracted, it reinvigorated him to know that someone else was there. All he had to do was reach out, and Percival would reach right back. But he could only sustain Roy's sanity for so long.

And their new subject matter, the study of death, put a strong damper on Roy's spirits. There were more books on thanatology than he knew what to do with. He initially focused on the core attitudes of the study, the ethical and political and clinical and whatnot. But most of the texts he and Percival found—typically by way of the odd wind—perverted these values, especially when it came to compassion.

Together, they pored over old volumes on nightmarish torture practices, complete with demonstrations drawn from history. They read dialogues between killers and inquisitors. One book, a diary written by an arsonist who'd butchered and incinerated his father and sister, Percival vigorously refused to look at, much less read. Roy took up the task instead, concerned by Percival's reaction, yet once he discovered there was nothing of import in the journal anyway, he moved on.

As a consequence of the workload and the distressing contents of their research, Roy slept less and less. Seven hours a night dwindled to six, then four, then two if he was lucky. Initially, it occurred to him that he was suffering from insomnia, but he soon realized that was ridiculous. There was a simple cure for his lack of sleep: work less, sleep more. He couldn't do that, though. *Do it, then it's done*, Percival had said, and Roy took that to mean one thing: *We work harder.*

So they did precisely that. They worked themselves to the bone, until their eyes were gritty and they were out of breath from coughing at the dust that escaped the endlessly growing mountains of texts before them. But especially Roy. From the morning to the evening, he and Percival chipped away at thanatology, the odor within the Macchylian Mines, and the sword's bizarre abilities. But from midnight to dawn, sometimes hours later, Roy retired to his bed and continued his research there. Eventually he realized he was wasting the five minutes this process took and kept working at the desk. Percival did not pry.

It was only as the days went by, though, that Roy understood just how bad his restlessness had gotten. He started to hallucinate Gabriel again, spying his brother lurching between the bookshelves, his knife held firmly in his bloodied hand, his smile cold and wide. Once Roy dropped the pile of books he'd been lugging around and sprinted to the next aisle, only to find Percival standing there. Roy had stammered an incoherent, illogical explanation and darted off, abandoning his dropped books.

The night after, Roy was cautiously perusing the bookshelves on the first floor, where the breeze had brought him, when a tall, dark figure materialized at the right end of the aisle.

"No," Roy whispered, squeezing his eyes shut. He'd gotten a decent amount of sleep and had thought, all things considered, he was doing reasonably well. "Please, Gabriel, get out of my head. Get out, just for the next couple of months, and—" He opened his eyes, looked over to the right. But it wasn't Gabriel.

It was a ghost. He had seen one before—and theorized the identity of the first creature he'd encountered, deeming it a shadow, a figment of his imagination, one of the hallucinations the Governor's guards had seen during their own conducted investigations—but something else struck him.

Roy remembered the agonized, terrified pleas in the burial grounds of the Elder Scribes, the screams woven into the stone like mortar and seeping out of the walls like dust. Were those ghosts trapped in the crypt, imprisoned? And if so, did they begrudge the ghosts wandering about the Basilica, free from the cloud of gloom that had taken shape and grown over time beneath them?

Roy covered his hand with his mouth, ignoring the frantic beating of his heart, and observed the ghost. Hovering about six feet from the ground, it looked eerily like a three-dimensional silhouette, its eyes of scarlet light blazing out of its sockets. It extended its long, crooked arm, and Roy bounced back on the balls of his feet, preparing to run, but halted when it brought up its hand to its face, like a man demonstrating how to put on a mask.

Something uncanny happened then, something that Roy knew he would lack the ability to explain for some time: the ghost covered its shadowy face with its hand, and through the semitransparent palm, Roy could faintly spy a horribly disfigured face. It took him a moment to connect the dots, but when he got there, Roy reeled back, grasping at the bookshelf he had been inspecting before he could fall.

"That's . . ." Roy murmured. He felt dizzy, bilious, and energized all at once. It seemed getting any sleep tonight would be out of the question. "That's *you*, isn't it?" he asked. "The shadow hides your face, your *true* face."

As if to confirm Roy's hypothesis, the ghost pressed its dim, incorporeal hand closer to its partially obscured features, which were now clearer than ever before. He made out a jaw, cracked in half and gaping; a pair of bulging eyes, the left one swollen and smeared with blood. Its skull had been crushed and trodden, speckled with a crisscrossing web of gory foot- and handprints.

Roy inhaled, horrified. "That's what you looked like when you died."

The ghost swung its hand back to its side, its eyes brightening and flooding the aisle with a lurid scarlet glow. Shadow once more engulfed its face, frozen in death.

Roy winced. "My apologies, I wasn't thinking straight; I . . . Well, to tell you the truth, I haven't been thinking straight for a month or so." He paused, struck by a sudden realization. He had been sleeping fine when he'd happened upon the first ghost, or fine enough, but that didn't stop him from wondering. "This is real, yes?"

For a long while the ghost watched him with interrogatory concentration. A long, uneasy silence fell, stretching across the aisle and then the first floor beyond. The moaning wind, and the gangly branches scratching at the arched windows high above, receded and then faded to a dry whisper.

With startling abruptness, the ghost looked up, and Roy followed its gaze. He could've been sidetracked by those burning red eyes, but he hadn't heard anything out of the ordinary. Then an amorphous blotch of darkness scampered across the top of the bookshelf on his left, smoke arising from the tips of its wispy black claws. It reached the end of the shelf, joining the more humanoid-looking ghost, and perched on the corner, glowering down at Roy with its red eyes, a shade or two darker than its companion's.

A wail sounded from behind Roy, followed by a low, inhuman sneer. He whirled, finding two slender ghosts hovering beside one another. They would have been twins had it not been for the left one's head, which drooped over the stem of its broken neck. The other stared at Roy, its expression impossible to read with its mask of gloom, then floated closer to him. The ghost with the twisted neck dawdled behind, like an inattentive younger sibling, but it glided toward Roy, nevertheless.

"Please," Roy sobbed. Tears were leaking out of his eyes and dribbling down his cheeks. "I don't know what you want with me, or what I can do for you, but if you would just *tell* me, if you . . ." He trailed off, raising his hands to the sides of his head.

The ghosts gained ever nearer, surrounding him, hemming him in at every direction. He could take his chances and make a run for it, maybe through the gap between the shapeless entity and its companion, but these creatures were fast, unpredictable.

In the few seconds that these thoughts had run through his head, the ghosts had gotten within reaching distance of him and were now glaring, fixing him with their insidious, garish eyes. Roy was saturated with their scarlet glow, as though someone had overturned a pail of blood upon his head. He scrambled back, the heels of his boots screeching against the floorboards.

"Percival," Roy whispered, his voice shaky, rough. He told himself it was the first name that came to mind because Percival was the only other person—*The only other living person*, he corrected himself—occupying the Basilica, but it didn't change the fact that

Roy needed, *wanted*, Percival here regardless. He repeated, shouting this time, "Percival! Percival, come to the first floor! The first floor!"

His screams dissolved into inarticulate garbling and crying, and he sank to the ground, his knees pulled up to his chest and his eyes swollen and flooded with tears. He closed them, and spectral impressions floated by in the darkness. Voices raved and screamed and howled, like the baying of insane beasts. He could feel himself, his *mind*, buckling under the pressure, tearing apart at the seams—

A hand came down hard on his shoulder.

Roy leapt up and scrabbled to his feet. "Just *tell* me!" he wailed. "Tell me what I can do to—"

"Darling." It was Percival, his hair mussed on one side, standing on end on the other. He looked half-asleep yet still deeply troubled. "What is it?"

Roy hesitated. He'd thought he was better than this, *braver* than this. He'd thought that it might be easier to talk about his recurring encounters with the residents of the spirit world, or whatever plane of existence the ghosts inhabited, but now as he glanced around and saw none of them there, he quailed at the prospect of Percival thinking he had gone mad, that insomnia and overwork had finally driven him insane.

But would he? Percival had been changed since Roy had shown him the grant—thoughtful. Not quite kind, but considerate at least. He'd cleared out the Observatory because the clutter would always get Roy into a panic. He'd held Roy in that room in the museum, his fingers inadvertently brushing past Roy's scars.

This will be one of the hardest things I'll have to do, Roy thought, but as he took in Percival's worried expression now, some of his apprehension slipped off his shoulders. He did not speak the next words that came into his mind, but oh, how he wished he had the bravery. *But at least I have you with me.*

"Roy?" Percival asked.

Roy considered for a moment. "Can we sit somewhere?"

They walked up to a reading room on the sixth floor, where they usually frequented when they needed a change of scenery from the Observatory. Roy went over to one of the armchairs set before the hearth, which was flanked by a huge painting of men, women, and those of both or neither sexes, all dressed in flowing white robes. The plaque at the bottom of the frame read *Pictured: The Protectorate*, and just beneath that, *Behold the eye of memory.* There were about one hundred of the librarians portrayed, roughly the same number of the wooden caskets he'd seen lining the walls of the Elder Scribes' burial chamber.

Percival closed the door to the reading room, then strode toward Roy. "How's this?" he asked. "Is this all right?"

Roy turned to face Percival and was about to quietly thank him when he perceived something unnatural, misshapen, about Percival's face. It took him a moment to realize that what was wrong with it was that it wasn't his own.

A ripple had begun to flow across his features. His short blond hair, which ended just shy of the nape of his neck, spilled out, turning into shoulder-length, blood-matted brown snarls. His hazel eyes, soft with concern and anxiety, were now an attentive and piercingly sharp blue, glittering with malevolent glee. They looked sunken, though, heavy with the weight of the horrors he'd seen.

"Get back!" Roy howled at Percival, at *Gabriel*, and again thrust his palms against his chest. Then he scrambled away, keeping a safe distance between himself and his brother. And while he knew that this was simply a hallucination, an uneasily realistic mirage produced by his traumatized mind, that some aspects of Gabriel's features were not quite right—his nose was too bulbous, his head too narrow—this did nothing to quell Roy's panic.

Gabriel staggered back and fell on the ground, then shifted his weight from his left elbow to his right and cocked his head. "My dear, dear brother, what has he done to you?"

Roy bit into his bottom lip, drawing blood that passed through the tears gushing down his cheeks. "Get *back*!" he screamed again, his voice rasping, cracking. Briar was still asleep, after all, a few doors down from his chamber, and Gabriel didn't like it when she was awake at this time of night. He liked it when he and Roy were alone, any possible disturbances dealt with prior to the torture. He liked it when he could see the mess he'd made of Roy, his scars still fresh and weeping blood.

He'd become inured to, and acquainted with, Gabriel's collection of knives: which ones hurt the most, which bled the most. Roy wasn't squeamish, nor easily fazed by blood; he was more troubled by Gabriel's derision—his attacks on Roy's failings and shortcomings, how he had exploited his own intelligence by putting it to use for a bygone world. It was nothing that Roy hadn't heard before, but now that he thought on it and cast his mind back to those bleak years virtually locked away in Dawnseve Manor, his understanding of his own insignificance had only solidified when it'd been written in blood. His deepest fear, marked on his body.

"Briar will hear us," Roy said, barely a whisper. "She will hear you."

Gabriel pushed himself up from his elbows and into a squat, his hands dangling between his spread legs. He looked almost animal, his face dappled with gloom and burnt orange light. "The same words on yet another night." He laughed. "When will you *learn*?"

Panic burned hot in Roy's blood. He choked out another scream, and again, it came out as a garbled cry. Yet still he couldn't help clinging to hope with feverish desperation, despite knowing that Briar had never interrupted and stopped Gabriel's ministrations. If, on the nights Gabriel tortured Roy, he had forgotten to prepare for such intrusions with a gag or some other device to quiet Roy, then he made do. A piece of parchment. A handful of coal. And once, Gabriel's own blood-slick fingers, shoved down Roy's throat.

"It's fortunate that what you lack in courage, you make up for with obedience," Gabriel said. He slowly reached for something behind him, hung on the waistband of his trousers, and took it out for Roy to examine. It was a kitchen knife, the handle worn and grooved, the same one he'd used to carve H-I-S-T-O-R-Y. "Fortunate, yes, but a shame. They say that the sturdiest of the Above's creations are made of bravery."

Sniveling, Roy scuttled back on his elbows and the heels of his boots, the floorboards scratching at and abrading the tough fabric of his sleeves. Blood slithered underneath them, dripped down his arms, and splatted onto the floor.

Gabriel hunkered down before the spilled blood, dragged his finger through it, and lapped it up. He inhaled deeply. "And what is bravery but overcoming adversity? What is adversity but the birthplace of pain?" He stood to his full height, his shadow enveloping Roy. He fell quiet, his head cocked and his eyes squinted, as though someone were whispering something in his ear. Then he boomed, "This isn't a lesson; I'm doing you a *favor*!"

"Name your price!" Roy cried. He retreated another foot or so, then could go no farther; he'd smacked the back of his head against the chair behind him. "Name it!" With a quivering arm, he wiped away the blood, tears, and snot that had pooled into the divot above his top lip. "*Please!* What must I lose to be free of this?"

Gabriel stalked toward the fireplace, oblivious to Roy's pleas. He began to stoop low and angle the knife near the crackling flames, which threw cavorting shadows upon the walls, but stiffened when he saw the poker leaning against the stone arch of the fireplace, unblemished by soot or smoke. He slid the knife back under the waistband of his trousers and ran a hand down the handle of the poker, caressing it.

"No," Roy croaked.

"I resisted the temptation too long," Gabriel said, an undercurrent of longing in his voice. "I was patient, Roy. I was servile." He took the poker into his hands, observed it. "I wanted to wait for the right moment, for some time to pass before I indulged." He looked at Roy. "But I can hardly *stand* it. The sounds you made, brother. That gurgling whimper when you saw the first letter." He stared, his mouth ajar, his gaze drifting down to the left of Roy's chest. "I still hear it, still see it."

"Please!" Roy screamed, bawling. "*Please—*"

Something whistled through the air, dark and swift as smoke billowing out the barrel of a musket. Then pain exploded across his face. His head cracked to the side. A gash tore open in his cheek, pouring blood. His vision blurred, fragmented, and then came back together in time for him to see Gabriel advancing toward him, his face crumpled and disfigured with rage. He swung the poker again, raving incoherently, his tongue lolling out of the corner of his spittle-flecked mouth.

Roy dodged but did not entirely clear himself out of the poker's range. It struck the side of his chin, hurling black dots up before his eyes. A strident whine started in his head, ringing higher and higher, then dissipated once Gabriel had prowled back to the fireplace and thrust the poker into the blue core of the flames.

"I see the Matron hasn't made it clear enough for you, that rutting bitch," Gabriel bit out, his upper lip folded back in a wolfish sneer. "This sick predilection for stories... It's immoral, unbecoming. You're nothing without them. You *cling* to them, as a babe clings to its mother's breast."

"This is who I am!" Roy screamed. He cradled his own cheek, holding up the flap of skin that had been pared away by the poker. "This is who I was meant to be!" The argument came out of its own accord, but there was no other he could make. *The same words on yet another night.* "I was meant to see what was taken from this world, Gabriel! To see what my kind, my *true* kind, were killed for!"

"What you have seen is *sin*, and far too much of it." Gabriel drew the poker out from the fireplace, scrutinizing its searing orange tip like a blacksmith marveling at his handiwork. Steam coiled up from the poker, trailing dim gray streaks across Gabriel's face. "But worry not, brother. Soon you shall see it no longer."

Roy went to call out for Briar, to shriek her name, but his voice was shot. How long had he been screaming for?

But Gabriel was already walking toward him, the poker clasped so tightly in his fist that blood dripped from the gaps between his fingers and splattered onto the floor, near where Roy had bled.

Either the room or his vision was growing hazy. He glanced to the left and, to his horror, found that the library beyond the two chairs and the fireplace was blurred and shadowy as if seen through a pane of frosted glass. And farther beyond, indistinct figures roamed the space, their eyes big as lamps and red as fresh fury. Screams and mournful lamentations drifted out to Roy from afar, chilling his heart.

But nothing was as clear to him as Gabriel. He was bending over Roy now, winding his fingers through Roy's hair and pulling his head back. The poker trembled in his upraised fist. Roy could glimpse the kitchen knife jutting from the back of Gabriel's trousers, but even if it was within his reach, he knew from experience that he didn't have the nerve to grab it or the strength to use it. He was quick enough, however, to raise one hand over one eye, looking at Gabriel with the other.

"Gabriel, please! Name your price!" Roy blubbered, a thick loop of snot hanging out of his nostril. Agony drummed through the middle of his forehead, as if he was being branded. "*Please—*"

Gabriel drove the heated poker through Roy's hand; it proved to be no obstacle to him at all. The thin membrane of skin on the back of Roy's hand sizzled and bubbled, then gradually melted away. The scent of cooking meat curled through the air and into his nose. His stomach turned over. Blisters formed rapidly across his flesh, spread and then burst, spraying clods of curdled and burnt skin across his forehead.

Somewhere, past his own screams, a faintly familiar melody floated through the air. He heard screams and exclamations. He heard whispers and cries. And far beyond these, a voice, fraught with distress. He couldn't decipher what it was saying, but it was there.

Percival was there. He had come for Roy, to pull him from the clutches of his brother.

But he had come much too late.

Gabriel seized the base of Roy's skull, clamping down on the spaces beside the upper notches of his spine. He rotated the poker, widening the gory hole he had made in Roy's hand, and pushed it deeper, thrusting it through his eye. Syrupy white liquid leaked out from under his hand, which was pinned to his face by the poker.

"Your bravery was my price," Gabriel whispered in Roy's ear, "but you're beyond bravery, and you have lived in fear too long." He plunged the poker deeper, and Roy felt something bend, then break, in his skull. "My price is your *mind*."

Darkness rushed in over Roy's eyes, rising high over his head like a churning black tide. He made an effort to wade through it, but with no luck. The darkness thickened, surrounding him, drowning him . . .

It was a voice, that same voice from before, that shot through the blackness like an arrow of light.

"Sit up, darling," Percival said. "Sit *up*. Sit up against the chair."

Roy moved his lips around the shape of Gabriel's name, but there was no sound to it, no air.

"*Roy.*" Percival placed a hand lightly on his shoulder, and Roy flung himself back, gasping, sobbing, his eyes sewn shut. "Look at me, Dawnseve, damn you." Percival grasped his shoulders again, shaking him. "*Look* at me."

Swallowing hard against the knot that had grown in his throat, Roy pried his eyes open.

Percival was kneeling before him, holding a wineglass by its stem. He handed it to Roy, who pursed his lips when the cold glass brushed his mouth, but Percival appeared indifferent. "You took quite the fall, darling," he said. "I'll coddle you as much as I please."

Hesitantly, Roy took the glass from Percival and drank the wine down to its dregs.

"You called out for him," Percival muttered, removing the glass from Roy's hands and placing it on the table behind him. "Gabriel—"

"Don't, Percival," Roy said. He ran his fingers gingerly over his eye, and though there was no pain there, none of the excruciating agony he'd suffered in his trance, he couldn't stop the tremor that went through him. "I don't want to do this with you. I thought I could, but I . . . I—"

Percival tentatively kissed Roy's forehead, and though Roy flinched, he did not pull away. "One word at a time, darling," Percival murmured. "That's all you need to do."

Do it, then it's done.

Every thought drew away from Roy's mind, like waves retreating from the shore, but memories swept in, demanding him to relive them, to recall that which he'd tried so hard to bury, and like the ghosts in the crypt, they were given a second chance, resurrected by forces outside of his control. They hadn't been laid to rest in their graves; the coffins of his demons rattled like loosened chains, and he hadn't the strength to tighten them.

Was Percival's offer a sign? Roy wondered. Was it fate urging him to move on, to endure the agony of recounting his trauma? Or was it not so momentous as that? Was he looking too deeply into shallow waters? Was it only that he had finally found someone outside of his own family who wanted to listen to his sorrow, his aches and hurts?

"He hated me, Percival," Roy said, then decided there was no point sugarcoating the truth, varnishing old and rotted wood, and added, "He was *repulsed* by me, by my dreams, my hopes, who I wanted to become."

"Out of jealousy?"

"No," Roy said, "never that. To Gabriel, jealousy was weakness. It was poison. If you weren't content with the role you were expected to play, then you were undeserving of *any* role and were better off dead. I envied the Radiant Droves for that very reason, for though they may be ruthless, they have a *purpose*. The Governor had given them a future, a portrait of glory they could step into if only they bent to his whim."

"And Gabriel interpreted your studiousness as a shortcoming," Percival said, a knowing, dark look in his eyes. He, like many other secret students of his profession, had heard this old story before.

Roy shrugged. "Shortcoming, transgression; whatever you wish to call it. He couldn't fathom a world in which I, the outsider, was unaware of my privilege. He thought I believed our elevated status would make an exception for me, that I would be exempt from all of the obligations Northgard had forced its citizens to endure. I wasn't blind; I knew my defiance was treason. I had escaped the repercussions of my proclivities for many years, but Gabriel wanted me to see differently, through whatever means necessary, so that I could accept my destiny, so that I could see my scholarship for the sin that it was. I was sixteen the first time he found me reading under my covers, and he nineteen. That night, I lost consciousness more times than I can remember. I'm shocked I can remember that night at all."

Percival let out a soft, broken cry and bowed forward, wrapping his hands around Roy's waist.

Roy spoke into the crown of Percival's head, his voice slightly muffled. "He hit me with his hands at first," he went on. "The palm, though sometimes he backhanded me. Initially, I did not know why. I thought myself immune to the consequences of my actions. I was wrong, so wrong it hurts now. Your family knows where it hurts most. Gabriel and I never got along too well to begin with, but he was the troubled one among the three of us, and I the timid one, so I took this to be why he went for me.

"He would most always stand when he used his fists on me. It gave him power over me, even though we both knew he didn't need more to make me submit. It was around then that I opted not to linger at our family dinners, always the first to leave the table. Seeing him using a knife and cutting into his meat was more than I could bear, and it almost convinced me that death by my own hands would be swifter and gentler than by his."

Percival raised his head from Roy's lap. "Didn't your family do anything about it? They must've suspected something amiss."

"My sister and my mother knew he was ill-tempered, and everyone—including the maids and butlers—knew he tended to misbehave. He wasn't two-faced. But as I grew older, things changed. He became more violent in his attacks, yes, but also more desperate to see evidence of his progress, while also more circumspect in his abuse. One week, when my mother was away, he conducted an experiment and struck me to unconsciousness for every book I finished. I didn't realize what he was doing until the week was done. Once I *did* realize it, I began to think it was my own way of showing him I was stronger, that the light of knowledge will always outshine the shadow cast by violence, but there's no point idealizing what he did. It was just easier to tolerate the pain."

Percival gripped Roy's leg, brushing his thumb across his thigh.

"It wasn't a month before the war when he gave me my last scar," Roy said. He could barely get the words out. He was coming upon the end of it now, nearing the present, and he was *still* too afraid to retell it. "There were weeks when he wouldn't hurt me. Other times, it was all he could do to keep his fists away from me. Once he barred the doors to my chamber just to stop himself, to tamp down the urge. And some nights, while he was using one of his knives on me, he kept telling me that I was nothing, no one. I was a mistake, an outlier in a society bred for struggle. So eventually he . . . he wrote it on my chest, in my blood."

Roy moved before he could change his mind. He shucked off his sweater vest and tunic, then cast them both aside. His black and silver hair curled down over his shoulders, framing the muscles of his chest. There were several other scars, burn marks and gouges overlapping one another, but H-I-S-T-O-R-Y stood out, prominent. Fruitless though Roy's resistance had been, the lettering of the scar was slightly lopsided. The *O* was distended, and the horizonal line of the *T* was disconnected from the vertical. But it was still as legible as it'd been on the night of its making.

"If I had it my way," Percival said, his voice rough and low, "if I could have my hands on him—"

"I would stop you," Roy whispered. "I would stop you before you could even lay a finger on him. Because that's not who you are, that's not what you were born to do, and damn it, I'd rather go through it all again than let this—*any* of this—happen to anyone else, but especially you."

Percival's face reddened. "I just want to help—"

"You want to carry this burden?" Roy said. "Then carry it elsehow. Bear it with your mind, not with your hands. Help me through this and I'll help you through whatever keeps you awake—because I *know* something does, Percival, as hard as you try to hide it—but if you expect me to stand aside and watch as you bloody your hands, then just forget it. Have me as I am or have me not at all."

"I'm sorry," Percival mumbled. "I crossed a line. I went too far." He sounded so brittle, like he could crumble away at the slightest touch. "I can't undo what I said, I know that, but maybe I could make amends." He regarded H-I-S-T-O-R-Y, his mouth pressed into a shaking white line. "Maybe I could lighten the weight."

"*How?*" Roy exclaimed, clutching at his chest. "He *ruined* me, Percival. I'm stained, dirtied. I'm an aberration. You can have my forgiveness, but you can't restore what he stole." Tears dripped off the tip of his chin.

"No," Percival said, "I cannot. But if I can have you as you are, then that comes with the scars. And while mine can't be seen as clearly as yours, darling, that doesn't mean they aren't there. A tired expression, sure, but true all the same." He laid his hand flat on Roy's chest, an inch or so to the left of his racing heart, but his eyes were fixed on his most recent scar. "You lie to yourself. Have I not told you as much?"

"Percival—"

"You're beautiful, Roy," Percival said, resolute. "You're gorgeous, and I wish I had the words to properly articulate it, but I've always said the wrong thing around you, so I suppose I'll just keep trying until something sounds marginally better. And I wish, sometimes, that the sun shone more in this blasted place. I didn't notice until our second week here that you had these silver streaks in your hair." He ran his fingers through them, a smile playing around the edges of his mouth. "I understand, as much as I can, that it's hard to take my word as gospel, but I wish you could see what I see. I know that's a long time from coming, though, and so in the meantime, I promise you this." He hung his head and reticently placed a kiss just beneath Roy's scar. "I promise to hold your hurts." He looked up at Roy, took his hands in his own, and squeezed his fingers. "And I promise my hands are yours to hold."

Roy held Percival's gaze, and all his previous anxieties and reservations, his worries that nothing good would come of this, dissipated like mist under summer sun. "Would you kiss it? My scar?"

Percival stilled. "You'd let me?"

Roy would, but this wasn't only a matter of allowance. "I *want* you to." Percival nodded and lowered his head again, then stopped immediately when Roy held Percival's neck and blurted out, "It might be more comfortable in my chamber." He glanced out the window and added, if a little reluctantly, "Midnight is drawing near, anyway, and I've been a tad short on sleep."

Percival widened his eyes, giving Roy a look of mock amazement. "You use your bed for *sleep*? I'm astounded, Dawnseve. I thought that was your second workspace."

Roy smiled. "Tonight, it's not." As the unspoken request settled in the air around them, he found himself looking at Percival's lips, though this time—unlike in the catacombs—Roy wasn't called out on it. This time, as never before, the quiet that grew and stretched between them was alive with an affectionate vow, not the aching desire they'd shared in the dark. He chuckled. "You can kiss me whenever you like, by the way—"

Percival rushed in, clasped Roy's cheeks, and kissed him on the mouth. Roy inhaled, parting his lips instinctually and then capturing Percival's with his own. Percival seized the back of Roy's head with a hand, his slender fingers cradling him as though Roy were made from carefully spun glass. On another night, Roy would have been eager to show Percival that he was not, but he was still spent and disorientated from his visions of Gabriel and the long hour of confession thereafter, and a great part of him just wanted his bed, and Percival there with him.

When Roy pulled away, his lips damp and tingling, Percival whispered, "Do you trust me?"

"Not completely," Roy said, then, seeing Percival's face drop, went on, "But trust is hard for me. I'm not opposed to taking the first steps, though. I'd like to give myself that, because if I don't now, when it feels like—or *something* like—the right time, I'm worried that I never will."

Percival nodded and, with tender adoration, clasped Roy's cheeks. "Then I'll make every second last and every moment worth it."

Throughout the night, Percival held true to his word. As they lay shirtless in bed, he kissed Roy's scar, the only one he still dreamed of, like it was a beauty mark. He wrapped his arms around Roy's chest and held him in a passionate embrace. Roy kept waiting for Percival to cower or grimace, to touch his scar for a second time and finally see the ugliness of it, but he did no such thing. He was warm, kind, whispering assurances onto Roy's scarred skin. His lingering touches were glimpses of tomorrow, his soft lips a dream from which Roy wished to never wake.

He still dreamed of Gabriel. Usually, it was that same terrible vision, the one with the kitchen knife, the heated poker, and the imploding sound that Roy's skull made when the heat melted his eyes and burst his brain. But now when he woke, it was to Percival holding him, his lips moving along the shell of his ear, again and again until Roy fell back asleep. *I'm here, I'm here,* he would whisper. *You're safe, darling, I'm here.*

20

"**L**ET IT BE SAID THAT IT WAS I, PERCIVAL ATHERTON, who brought an end to the great war," Percival said as he joined Roy in the Observatory one morning, then put three vellum-bound books on the desk between them.

A little over three weeks had passed since Roy had told Percival about his past with Gabriel, and things had become markedly different between them. They sat closer, their thighs brushing. They slept together, and while they had not progressed beyond kissing, Roy was decidedly more comfortable with Percival's fingers drifting near his chest and his ribs. But they hadn't yet garnered more intelligence on either of the swords. Ever since Percival had unsheathed one of them, they'd once more gotten skittish around the weapons.

The Governor had informed them when he'd visited last that the third supply drop and check-in had been set three weeks from then, which was any day now but he and his Droves hadn't yet made their return. Perhaps the storm had blocked their passage.

Now, Roy groaned with relief at Percival's declaration. "By the Scribes, I dearly hope so." He turned the books around, scanned their titles, and gave Percival a sardonic, dissatisfied look. "Volumes one through three of Taglian's *Astevian Jousting Techniques*? Somehow I doubt this will be beneficial."

"Is that so?" Percival countered. He opened to a page halfway through the book, embedded inside of which was a hidden compartment lined with lush crimson fabric. Within was a black wooden box whose shape perfectly resembled that of the Elder Scribes' coffins in the crypt.

Roy stilled. "Where did you find this, Percival?"

"The fourth floor. Well, I didn't *find* it so much as I felt *drawn* to it. Can you guess what else I felt, Dawnseve?"

He didn't have to guess; he knew. "The wind."

Percival nodded to the other books. "And these?" He flipped them open, revealing identical hollow spaces within the volumes. "The same."

Percival reached inside one of the opened books and flipped up the latch on the side of the compartment within it. Inside, shards of black metal, none larger than a finger, lay scattered in a heap like crushed onyx. The velvet-padded edges of the box were suffused with gray light, dreary compared to the blade of the sword.

"The swords," Percival whispered. "They were forged from this metal."

"Don't touch it," Roy warned, a cold numbness stealing over his skin. "Hell, we shouldn't even be looking at it." The metal did not hum, nor did any violent light stream out of it, but nonetheless, Percival obeyed Roy, who then asked, "Why is it shattered? And why did the Scribes keep it contained?"

"Both solid questions," Percival said, then suddenly leaned closer to the compartment and agitatedly slapped at Roy's arm. "I can see something on the metal. Roy, *look.*"

As Roy complied, he felt gooseflesh spread across his arms, prickling his skin.

Along the flat edges of the shards, inscribed across the black metal, was a series of alien symbols and shapes. Engraved on the disarrayed pieces of metal were squares and diamonds and ovals, dovetailed together in a seemingly deliberate order.

"Is this a *code?*" Roy exclaimed. "What—" He looked up, then noticed Percival had disappeared.

Only a minute passed before Percival returned, scabbarded sword in hand. He must've left it in whatever room he'd been using before coming to the Observatory.

Roy rose to his feet, his teeth gritted. "Put that forsaken thing away. I can't have what happened last time happen again." *And I can't bear seeing those visions again, nor the risk of making you see them.* He attempted to steady his breathing. "I can't believe you brought it here."

"Darling, don't you remember how *powerful* this is?"

Roy shuddered; he remembered all too well. It was why he'd stashed his own away in the closet in his bedchamber since Percival had unsheathed his.

Percival continued. "It's obvious from the presence of the swords, and whatever else might be secreted away in this library, that something made the Elder Scribes break their code of non-violence established in Clive Lortan's essay. Now, I have a theory, and I would like to see if it holds any merit. That's why I brought the sword here. The moment I held it, I thought the blade was... peculiar. Black metal, emitting a bright silver light."

Roy muttered, "Paradoxical."

"Precisely. You claimed to have seen visions of your own death, executed in various, horrifying methods. But besides the weight of the sword, I felt *nothing*. I only saw the room losing and then gaining its color, and that was *after* you experienced those visions. It seems that whatever gives this weapon its power had no effect upon me. The wielder, I think, could be *immune* to its power. The sword might have grown louder as a response to recognizing hostile threats. Maybe it marked you as its target."

"This is your theory?"

"No." Percival glanced from the metal shards in the box to the sword, then explained, "Before I unsheathed the sword, I was distracted. That silver light is *blinding*. Considering that the Scribes evidently used these weapons to fend off the Old Ones, or buy themselves some time at the very least, maybe there are some commonalities between them all—this broken one, mine, and the one you're keeping in our chamber."

Roy pursed his lips, then nodded. "All right. That sounds plausible." He began to stand. "Let me go grab mine—"

The door to the Observatory, which had been shut, abruptly banged open, swinging back on its hinges. A gusting, bellowing wind swept through, carrying the sword Roy had stood to retrieve and depositing it in his lap. He gaped.

Percival blinked. "Well. It appears we're on the right track."

Roy took up his sword, Percival mirroring him with his own. They nodded at one another, then twisted the hilts and scabbards of their respective weapons in parallel directions, making sure to point the blades downward. Then, as one, they unsheathed them.

As his sword fell to the ground, clattering, Roy pivoted, shielding himself from the force of its deadly yet intoxicating power. An unworldly hum, like the reverberations made by metal ringing against glass, filled the air and set the windows a-shiver. He heard screams from the sword too, rife with torment, but they were nowhere near as loud as that ethereal chorus.

Roy looked over at Percival, who had placed the sword with the skeleton-shaped hilt on the desk. The silver iridescence that had once outlined the entire sword now only gleamed dimly near its hilt and the tip of the blade. He hadn't seen it in the room in the museum, but there was a slight curve to the black metal, as though intended to carve around the waistline. And indeed, incised into the flat of the blade was a chain of luminous symbols, written in the same eldritch language as the symbols on the metal shards.

Almost as soon as Roy had made this comparison, the symbols etched into Percival's blade shone brighter and brighter, glaring furiously, and then the same happened to Roy's. He drew closer. After a moment, the symbols disappeared, replaced by a variant vaguely similar to its predecessor. Again, it faded and was substituted. The cycle went on, each symbol bearing an equivalent structure but with the slightest of modifications: an accent over one icon; a line struck through another. One of the variants was slanted and bold, while the next stretched along the blade, elongating like a whip unfurling. They seemed nearly similar to the cryptic symbols Roy had seen upon the books in the catacombs.

"Get back!" Roy ordered, grabbing Percival around the waist. "Get *back*, damn it! Get *back*!"

"The swords will not attack us," Percival said, placing a hand on Roy's, which were clasped around his middle. "I . . . I think they're trying to speak to us." He withdrew from Roy's hold. "Wait. Roy, look."

Reluctant, Roy glanced at his sword and saw that the alternating symbols had begun to slow. Rather than twice every second, the languages changed within every few seconds now: sleek and elegant; stout and dense; high and curvy. He hadn't known that there were so many languages in the world . . . *If,* Roy thought with a sense of deep foreboding, *these languages even belong to this world.*

At long last, the symbols stopped at a language and froze. One word was engraved into the blade, in the common alphabet learned across Northgard:

KHARUAN

And on Percival's sword:

VALUSVAR

He recalled both of the names instantly. When he'd skimmed through the piles of papers and texts which had ended with books on thanatology, he'd come across a volume he'd previously thought unrelated to the Old Ones. *The Blades of Tangror* by Leopileus. And the names of the blades themselves? Malevoli, Kharuan, Cephius, Valusvar, Parlikeves...

Roy grabbed his scabbard from the floor, then sheathed Kharuan. "I didn't tell you this because I didn't think it was important," he said to Percival, "but I have definitely seen these names before."

"Both of them?" Percival asked, observing Valusvar with an unsettled expression.

"I have no doubts about it," Roy said, then paused. "But why were they in the catacombs? Did the Scribes consider them memorabilia? Spoils of war?"

Percival picked up Valusvar from the desk, sheathing it. "All solid questions, darling. Why don't we go ask someone who might be able to answer them?" He smiled. "How do you fancy another stroll with the dead?"

Roy had feared that something might have happened to the crypt since they'd entered it, that it had collapsed beneath the winter-rotted foundations of the library, but everything remained the same: the books displayed behind glass, the congregation of the entombed Protectorate; the seven sarcophagi of the Elder Scribes, the cracked lid of the central one lying upon the great dais, where Percival and Roy had left it.

"We need to get their attention," Percival said, sidling up next to Roy. "How should we go about this?"

"It's safe to say that the Orphic Basilica repurposed this space in the crypt as a shrine to the Elder Scribes following their deaths," Roy said. "In my eyes, if something were to happen to the ones it buried, if someone were to trespass on their resting place, the consequences for such an act of sacrilege would be severe." He smiled.

"And . . . ?" Percival asked.

"And I intend to see what those consequences are."

His smile fading, Roy wrapped his hand around the sleeve of his tunic, curled his fingers into a fist, and then pummeled the glass, striking it over and over, hard and swift. Percival did not stop him, not with a hand on his shoulder or a cry of protest, but he did raise his arm over his face, sheltering it from the glittering shards of glass that soared at him and then fell at his feet.

Once the hole in the glass was large enough to thrust his arm through without cutting himself, Roy reached inside, grabbed one of the books—engraved on the cover of which was one of those strange symbols he'd seen, *Neil Eldreave* imprinted beneath it—then turned on his heel and hurled it at the wall. A cloud of bone-dust, grit, and ash ballooned outward, concealing the book as it crashed to the ground. He retrieved another from the shelf he'd ransacked and flung it against the lid of the nearest sarcophagus, which it struck with a loud thud.

"*See me!*" Roy bellowed. He pulled a third book out and threw it at the coffin of a member of the Protectorate. "*See me!*"

Percival cautiously removed a book himself, one only a little larger than his hand, and pitched it against the wall, where it exploded into a whirling confusion of ink-stained pages. He blinked in amazement at the destruction he'd caused, then returned to the shelf and ripped out another.

As the book smacked against the wall, sending up curls of earth and dust, Roy followed it with another. The breeze within the chamber stirred quicker and quicker, rising from their feet to their waists. He grew peripherally aware of a chorus of screams, then saw the pale gray fog ascending from underneath the ground. Fear twisted within him, sharp as thorns, snatching at his breath and roiling through his stomach, but he only gritted his teeth tighter and ran back to the shelf, hauling stacks of books into his arms and pitching them in twos and threes against the wall. Percival was right on Roy's heels, screaming and hollering with him.

"*See us!*" they shouted, nearly overriding the pandemonium of noise. Roy was half surprised that Percival was voicing the chant, as he probably had no clue what he was doing but simply felt good doing it, but Roy didn't let Percival in on his plan. Some reckless part of him wanted to see the look of bewilderment on Percival's face. "*See us for who we are, you cowards!*"

They did not cease their looting and littering until there were no more books on the shelf, and even then, they carried on with their summoning. They reprimanded those who were unable to respond to their grouching, those whose souls had long departed this life.

Perhaps most egregious to the sanctimony of a library, they made a ruckus. Percival dashed to the lowermost of the coffins of the Protectorate, which were on the walls surrounding the sarcophagi of the Scribes, and shook them, sweat percolating on his brow and dripping down his temples, his cheeks red as roses. Roy threw book after damaged book at the lids of the Scribes' sarcophagi, his voice going hoarse as he shrieked blasphemies, droplets of tears and perspiration running down his face. When he eventually tired of damaging sacred property, he lumbered around the exterior of the cairn, panting and clutching his stomach, and flung his fists weakly at the walls. Blood beaded from the cuts he'd made on his knuckles, peppering the backs of his hands.

It was then, once Roy was beginning to lose momentum, that two spears of ruby light cut through the crypt. He and Percival halted in their ministrations, then twisted to the entryway. There stood a ghost, its eyes trained on Roy.

Roy watched, his feet fixed to the ground, as the shadow lifted a silhouetted hand. It curled its fingers into a fist, then slashed diagonally. Not an attack, Roy thought, but a gesture of some kind.

"Valusvar," Roy said. "Or Kharuan. Something about the swords..."

Percival boomed, "What is this, Roy? What the *fuck* is this?" The muscles of his throat stood on end, and his veins bulged like thick cords of rope. Then his face fell. "You told me about a... a shadow when we played the drinking game. This is it, isn't it?"

Roy nodded weakly.

"*Fuck*, I shouldn't have questioned it. What is it?"

"It's a ghost, Percival," Roy answered, dragging a long breath of cold, stale air into his lungs. The ghost made the same gesture as before, slashing out its transparent arm, and Roy added, "I think it wants the swords."

The ghost drifted closer, its feet not quite touching the ground. It rolled its head back, casting crimson light upon the coffins of the Protectorate, then dropped its brightening gaze to the swords. It was standing upon the edge of the dais now, each of its steps forward earning a step back from Percival and Roy. It rose higher into the air, remnants of darkness unfurling from the soles of its feet. It stretched outward like kneaded dough, its eyes taking on a spine-chilling liquid quality.

Roy monitored its ascension, a small, choked sound of fright escaping his lips.

Then came a voice, shrill and desperate, issuing from the general direction of the ghost and resounding throughout the chamber. *Please, please, please,* it hissed. *Help me, help me, help me.* Its pleas were abruptly cut off by a high, wavering scream.

Roy jumped, his heart climbing up his throat, and stumbled back into Percival, who clutched Roy by the nape of his neck, his harsh, ragged breaths bursting across the shell of Roy's ear. They stared, horrified, as the ghost started to crumble apart and fracture, breaking off into infinitesimal pieces of shadow. It curled its body inward, like a snake coiling to strike, then dove down and plummeted soundlessly into the sarcophagus at the heart of the chamber, the sarcophagus in which they'd found the swords.

Percival shouted, "Run! Run, *now!*"

But Roy could not move. He was locked in place, his eyes fixed on the central sarcophagus. He could feel the air shivering, then slowly realized why. The chorus of screams from before had thinned out and was now narrowing into one voice, an articulate and oddly aristocratic one. It sounded sharp and clear in Roy's mind.

Fret not, mortals. I mean you no harm and bear you no ill will.

Then a creature sat up from inside the sarcophagus, made from the bones of the Elder Scribe that had been buried within and outlined with shadow. Its strange eyes had dimmed but not died out.

Roy whispered, "Who are you?"

The ghost cocked its head with a strangely feline curiosity, as if in anticipation of their reactions. *I am Atticus Walestone, though in the latter half of my days, unbeknownst to my peers, I also went by Razkamun.*

Roy doubled back, reeling, and nearly knocked Percival over. He stared, uncomprehending. While he hadn't read much of Walestone's bibliography, as he wasn't particularly interested in the cosmos and the possibility of other worlds existing beyond his own, he had mentioned to Percival during their drinking game that some kind of amorphous magnetism had drawn him toward Razkamun's oeuvre. Perhaps he hadn't discerned any specific parallels between Walestone's and Razkamun's works, as the two scholars seemed to have engaged with entirely different fields of study, but Roy supposed Walestone had likely planned for this, considering the detestable criticisms Razkamun's papers had received. As Roy thought on it, he couldn't remember ever coming across a sketch of Razkamun, either, but this hadn't troubled him. Many old-world scholars had preferred to remain anonymous, terrified as they were of backlash.

"What?" Percival shouted. He spun to Roy. "We *argued* about Razkamun when we first got here, and now your addlebrained hero is going to kill us in these fucking tunnels."

But this wasn't his hero . . . and yet, it also was. Because he'd always admired Walestone, too—his eccentric interest in cosmology was unorthodox, sure, but also courageous—and knowing they were one and the same . . . It somehow clicked. And part of that was the fact that they had nothing to fear from this ghost.

As if sensing Roy's assent, Walestone leaned forward. *I heeded your summons, scholars—not to cause fright or alarm, but to deliver a warning. There is a great evil afoot, a tremble in the air.* As he said this, he stared raptly at the swords.

Roy wasn't sure what that look meant, but something more pressing nagged at him. "There are more of your kind, as we've seen in the library, but only you have thus far made yourself known. Why haven't any others?" Roy recalled, then, the unseen barrier that had prevented him and Percival from making out the whispers within the catacombs. They had heard voices, but only a few, and those only slightly, like they were indeed caught behind, or enclosed within, some sort of obstruction.

Although I have come to your world from my own, Walestone said, *others may be hesitant to do so.*

As though completely disregarding what Walestone had revealed, Percival demanded, "Release them from whatever cage contains them."

You argue it was I who captured those adrift souls. Walestone's red eyes flickered in a horrifying imitation of anger. *But how could that possibly be when I have withstood my own suffering?*

Roy assured Walestone, "We'll come to your aid and find a way to release you and your kind, if you might tell us what occurred. You can have peace. *Freedom.*"

My memories are a frail web, Walestone said, his elegant voice shaking with grief. *I have roamed too long a path to reflect and remember my end.*

Roy looked down at his feet, ashamed and slightly disappointed. He'd expected Walestone to impart some crucial piece of information after millennia of drifting through the afterlife. Perhaps he was still clinging to the echoes of his grief, though, something to feel so he did not lose his way.

"No memories?" Percival pressed, his face paling. "None?"

There have been . . . impressions, of late, Walestone admitted. *Screams. Cries. Pleas for mercy.*

Roy recalled what he'd heard the last time they'd been in the catacombs. *See what they made of your kind! Oh please, I say! I plead to the Above! Heed me! They butchered us and killed our young—*

Color washed back into Percival's face. "You've been looking at the swords this entire time!" he shouted. "Tell us! What are they?"

The bones stitching the ghost's form together had begun to shiver and clatter, though at Percival's shout, Walestone stilled. *Again, my memories are not as reliable as they once were. But I . . .* He squinted at Valusvar and Kharuan. *I believe those swords, if employed correctly, might be the cornerstone of our liberation. You both unsheathed them, yes?*

"Just one," Percival said. "Valusvar. When I lifted it, I accidentally pointed it at Roy, and he saw these . . . visions of his own death."

Yes, the visions, Walestone said with burgeoning recognition. *A method used by the wielder to incapacitate unsuspecting victims. But there is another power, scholars. Another . . .*

Roy was about to say something, but Walestone began to tremble, the bones holding his form collapsing to the base of the sarcophagus. Wind snagged on him like tearing cloth, and then he was gone.

21

THE FOLLOWING AFTERNOON, WHILE ROY AND PERcival had their heads buried in their work, still recuperating from the knowledge that Atticus Walestone—one of the Elder Scribes and, apparently, the secret identity of Razkamun—was haunting the Orphic Basilica, a series of piercingly loud knocks came from one of the lower floors.

Percival jerked upright, the side of his raised left hand stained with ink, and blinked at Roy with befuddlement.

The rapping knocks came again, louder and with heightening urgency.

Roy bolted to his feet, not noticing how sweaty he was until he tied his gown tighter around his waist. Dots of perspiration were beading on the backs of his hands and running down the nape of his neck.

Percival dropped his quill, which he'd been gripping tightly, then stood and rushed over to the balcony at the other side of the room. He peered over the railing, dragging one hand down his face and clenching the railing with the other.

A sickening but nameless premonition rising inside him, Roy joined Percival, too aware of the bare inches of distance between them.

Again, the rapping sounded, pounding and hammering with

increasing frequency, advancing closer like doom on swift wings, and it was only then that Roy realized it was coming from the double front doors. They were trembling in their frames, shaking from the force of the fists thudding against them.

Someone had come to the Orphic Basilica.

"The Governor," Percival stammered. "He and his Droves must have come for their third supply drop. They're a tad late, don't you think?"

"The storm has gotten worse since its last respite," Roy said. He'd suspected, *feared*, that this would happen when he'd looked out the window in the hallway leading to the Museum of the Elder Scribes. "It probably delayed their journey."

"By a week, though?" Percival asked, skeptical.

Roy gulped. Why else would the Governor have visited, though? Had he uncovered something that might delay or expediate their investigation? Had he possibly recruited another scholar to assist them? Then he recollected what the Governor had stated in his letter to the Dawnseves, which seemed like years ago. *This mission is of utmost importance,* he'd warned. *If any individual whose involvement I have not sanctioned were to become aware of this assignment—including the maids and butlers in your employ, who are not to spread word of Roy's task—or interfere with it, it would be considered a breach of the Law of Intervention...*

Roy asked now, "What do we do, Percival?"

Percival glowered. "Leave the one man legally allowed to kill us out in the snow, clearly." He shook his head and started toward the staircase on their right. "Honestly, Dawnseve, you'd think you would've grown some brains by now."

When they got to the first floor, Percival hastened toward the entryway and hauled open the door.

A blizzard of snow and gale-force wind whirled inside, and Roy raised an arm over his face, peering at the scene before him through the gaps between his fingers. Percival tightened his grip on the door handle, hissing out clouds of white breath between his teeth, but fortunately the door was more than heavy enough to stop from slamming open and striking him to the ground. He was standing just before the threshold now, and ahead of him, Roy spied a solitary figure upon the doorstep.

As he came forward, he saw it was a Citadel emissary. A scarlet-haired woman, in her late thirties if Roy was forced to guess, she was dressed in the same green felt cap and white military coat as had been worn by the mustachioed man who'd accompanied Matron Dawnseve. That was where the resemblances ended, though. She looked frightened, in contrast to her dreadfully stern counterpart, the lashes of her round brown eyes speckled with frost. She was holding something out to Percival. An envelope that had been folded two or three times over, Roy realized.

"Take it," the woman said, sharp and urgent. She thrust out the envelope to Percival, who fetched it from her trembling, black-gloved hand with a disbelieving expression. She stared at him a moment, then grasped his spare hand in both of hers. She looked from Percival to Roy, then back to Percival. "Tell not a soul I was here. Please, I beg of you." Her voice broke, and tears sprang to her eyes. "I *beg* of you, boys, for the sake of my wife and our son. Tell not a *soul!*"

Percival gawked at the woman, then down at their joined hands, speechless.

Uncertain what he was agreeing to, Roy stepped forward and intervened, reassuring the woman, "Not a soul and not a word. That I promise you."

The woman let go of Percival's hand with a cry of relief. "Oh, bless you. Bless you to the Above." She sniffled and glanced behind her, down at the foot of the steps. There, the horse she had ridden in on—equipped with winter riding gear—was stamping impatiently at the snowy ground. She looked back at them. "I'd best be off. It's quiet around here, but I'd wager it won't stay that way for long." She adjusted the cap atop her head, which had gone askew while talking with them, then started back down to her horse.

Still too bewildered to speak, Percival reached for the door. He stopped, though, as the woman suddenly turned around.

"The envelope!" she called up to them, pointing at it feverishly. "I'm afraid it's taken a bit of a trek in my satchel, so I'm dearly sorry if any of the message is smudged, but I hope her words will read all right." Then she jogged down the steps, tightening the straps attached to the sides of her felt cap, mounted her horse, and cantered off into the snow.

Seated at opposite ends of Roy's desk, which he had cleared of its clutter of manuscripts and inkwells and other research paraphernalia, Roy and Percival gawked at the envelope before them with breathless anticipation. The upper left corner was damp and leaving faint tracks on the table, the lower right creased from the indentations left behind by the Citadel emissary's thumb and forefinger.

Everything had fallen deathly quiet and still, as though the world were encased in amber. Roy waited for the library to recognize the letter and the advent of whatever development its arrival implied, for the wind to stir through his hair. But the air was so stale, so cold. He tried to steady his breathing and, when that did not work, to force himself to retrieve the envelope and open it. But he couldn't move.

"Who *was* that, darling?" Percival asked. He had not taken his eyes off the letter since he'd put it on Roy's desk.

Roy shook his head absently but somehow found the strength to reply, "She must have been sent by the Governor. Perhaps he's... he's preoccupied or—"

"She was *trembling*, Roy," Percival said, exasperated, "and you know damn well it wasn't from the cold. Did you see her eyes? There was fear there. True fear."

Roy scrambled for a rational explanation, but nothing sounded right in his head. "Maybe the Governor *did* assign her to some duty, but she disobeyed his orders." Something came to him. "She could be a scholar in hiding."

Percival shook his head this time, either disoriented or not completely convinced. "Who could this other woman she mentioned be, then?" He paused, ruminating. "'*I hope her words read all right*,' is what I think she said."

A confusion of speculations swirled through Roy's head, but as he observed the envelope again, he realized that when you came down to it, there was no point in guessing. This was to be his and Percival's first contact with the world outside the Orphic Basilica's walls, aside from the Governor and his Droves, in over two months. In this moment, it didn't matter who the sender of the letter was. It might as well be Dimestra or the emissary's wife or the Governor's seamstress.

What was important here was that this person could become their correspondent, a crystal ball Roy and Percival could use to inspect the goings-on of Northgard.

"I suppose there's only one way to find out," Roy said. He removed his hands, which were shaking with trepidation, from his lap, then picked up the envelope, tore open the flap, and removed the contents.

Inside of the envelope were four sheets of parchment. The first had a note on it, which began with *Read first*. But the next three were filled with delicate, slanted handwriting. He recognized the penmanship immediately. He had helped improve it, had looked over the shoulder of the writer every time, much to her constant annoyance, and pointed out even the smallest slipups.

Roy pressed the back of his hand over his mouth, stifling a sob. "Briar."

Percival, noticeably more intrigued, stood up from his wing-backed chair and dragged it over next to Roy, who shuffled aside and slid the letter over so Percival could better see it. "Your sister?"

Roy nodded.

Percival proceeded to read the letter, his eyes wide, as though hardly believing what he was seeing.

Read first:

Apologies if I gave either of you a fright.

I suppose I should introduce myself. I'm Tessa Ardwell, the professor for Introduction to Governorship at Rasileus Academy. But primarily, I'm a dedicated old-world enthusiast. Roy: when Briar got in contact with me through Irene, who you'll learn about in your sister's letter shortly, she told me about your investigation. I readily agreed to supply you with information pertinent to your cause.

Communication will be tricky, to say the least. Briar, Irene, and I have enlisted several scholars in hiding to assist us with gathering and reporting intel. I would have informed you sooner, but the storm has disrupted the schedule of all our plans. I ask you to forgive me.

Before you read on, a due reminder: Do not forget yourself nor your worth. This city is spiraling rapidly out of control, but not out of your control. That seems clear to me, now more than ever. You will learn this for yourself when you read Briar's letter.

I do not know when we will write to you next, but hopefully soon. It may be every second day or so. Until then, do not tarry. Keep your head down, your mind firm, and your distractions limited.

Tessa

His hands shaking, Roy moved on to Briar's letter. He looked at Percival, who appeared enraptured, and then read it aloud.

Roy,

I'm so sorry that it had to come to this. I know this is a terrible risk I'm taking, that the consequences are dire, but I wouldn't be writing to you if it wasn't important. Please forgive me.

I miss you horribly, Roy. I do hope you're not losing your mind, all alone in the library. It's dreadful here without you. Granted, it wasn't so great before, but now I have begun to feel trapped, like I've been buried alive. If it weren't for the maids and butlers roaming the manor like phantoms, I would probably start wondering if I'm in Hell. Maybe I am. There is nobody to talk to, aside from the correspondents whose details I found under the loose board beneath your bed. Sometimes I think about reading the books you've stowed away, but I suppose that would only make matters worse.

That brings me to why I'm writing to you. I cannot believe that I'm about to put these words on paper, that I'm about to set in stone what I could hardly comprehend with my own eyes, but I fear if I don't do it now, in this short window of time I have, it'll never get done.

The Matron, through the Governor's orders, has sent a Drove to guard me. But this doesn't feel like guarding, Roy. There is something deeply, unsettlingly wrong with this man.

Roy sat back, a feeling of unease settling over him, and clasped a hand over his pounding heart.

Petrified, he read on.

> *He's still here. Gregori, his name is. I can hear him now, walking around and mumbling to himself downstairs in the guest chamber. I stumbled into him last night, luckily without incident. I stared at him across the room, and it was like I could feel the things he'd seen, the things he'd done. I was so scared, Roy. All I wanted, all I want, is to come see you. I can't stand being in the same place as that horrid man. He's like a beast.*
>
> *I think it's safe to say the war did something to him. He stands out in the cold, unblinking. He stares at his reflection and talks to himself, and he uses different features, different accents and voices. These strange noises ... Sometimes I wake to sounds in the middle of the night—howls and yips, like a wolf. Other times, he'll trudge back and forth out in the snow, repeating to himself in this gravelly, slurred voice, "I passed the tests! I passed the tests!"*
>
> *Last night, I heard something scratching on the other side of the wall, like some creature was trying to crawl its way through and onto my bed. This obviously wasn't the first time he's acted strangely, so I was reluctant to see, but I mustered the courage eventually to visit his chambers again. There, I found him clawing at the walls. His hands were bloodied, his nails torn to shreds, and by the time I'd entered the room, he'd begun to gnaw on the plaster. His teeth were rotting, and his gums were bloody stubs.*
>
> *He hasn't laid a finger on me—not yet, I should say—but something makes me wonder if he would even register anything if he did. He could strike me, slap me, or do much worse, and I suspect he wouldn't remember any of it.*

"By the fucking Above," Percival whispered, pointing a trembling finger at the letter. "'I passed the tests!' Is that what the Radiant Droves have been doing to their soldiers? Experimenting on them?" He passed Roy a questioning look.

But Roy was speechless. He couldn't stop reading now. Something had seized him, a sort of morbid fascination.

> *It makes me think, too, of the Old Ones. I have heard from Irene Larifor—one of my dearest friends at Rasileus Academy, and whose parents are advisers for the Governor—that three of the Old Ones' five squadrons have relocated in front of the gates to the Iron Citadel. Why, I do not know. Irene speculated that it's an incoming attack, but I'm not so sure. These soldiers slaughtered their way through southern Northgard, yet apparently, they have made no move against the Droves' barracks. They're just standing there, motionless. It's plain bizarre.*
>
> *I hope Irene is safe, Roy. She and her family, despite their political leanings. Before the snowstorm, she and I would always meet at Rasileus's rose gardens before our lectures. She'd always bring me a morning treat from her local vendor, wearing this big, beautiful smile. Then, as word spread of the weather's worsening conditions, I told Irene we must write to one another. I couldn't fathom a day without knowing how she was faring, and now I cannot fathom a day without knowing if she is alive.*
>
> *I understand the perils I could face if it is discovered that Irene and I have been exchanging confidential military speculations via her parents' meetings with the Governor and the Matron's meetings with her captains here, but I'm out of options. To cover my tracks, Irene asked Tessa to convey this letter to you. Irene let Tessa borrow her mother's spare emissary uniform, and*

their family's horse, while her parents were at their lodgings in the Citadel. I'm sorry if her appearance alarmed you.

And I'm sorry, again, that I resorted to the worst scenario. Irene's parents are currently in the early stages of an extensive conference with the Governor, Mother, and his other associates. They'll be there for the next few weeks, so I hope you and I can trade letters relatively undetected. Tessa has even committed to riding to the Basilica every second day, which should be enough time for you to compose a reply—and, of course, Irene has been perfect as ever...

I know this is a little irrelevant to our cause, and that I may be wasting time by telling you this, but you're my brother, and it would feel wrong to keep this from you, especially since we have been apart for so long.

Something changed between Irene and me. Something beautiful and miraculous. I thought I was imagining things, that the cold winds had gotten to my head, but there was no mistaking the hearts she started drawing at the bottom of each page, or the way she talked about playing with my hair, holding my hand, tracing the scar on my thumb I got when I tumbled onto that frozen creek near Rasileus Academy. I'm scared of change, of how it can make you into someone you're not, but this one doesn't seem so bad.

Anyway, I hope this gets to you. I have done this all for you, Roy. I wish I could see you and hug you, but I suppose this will do for now.

Much love,
Briar

Roy had thought that, for the most part, he was doing a fine job containing his emotions, but when he reached the conclusion of Briar's letter, he lost his composure. He buried his head in his hands and burst into great, chest-racking tears. He sobbed so hard, so forcefully, that his temples were throbbing and his shoulders were convulsing. After a moment, Percival pulled Roy toward him, wordlessly cupping the back of his skull, and placed Roy's forehead on his shoulder. Roy leaned into Percival and wrapped his left arm around his waist.

Once the tears had dwindled to a trickle, Roy sat up, gently pushed Percival away, and kneaded his pounding temples with his fingertips. "I'm sorry," he said, his voice thick. "I didn't—"

"Don't be ridiculous," Percival said, softer than Roy had ever heard from him. He rubbed the back of his neck, his lips pursed.

"She's in danger, Percival," Roy whispered, running a hand down his face. "The Governor's going to find out about her sending this letter, and I'm not sure *what's* happened to Gregori, what experiments he's undergone, but..." A cold shiver went through him. "Oh, by the Above, what if he goes after her? Why would Dimestra send someone like this to guard Briar? What if—"

"I don't know about the Governor, nor about the Matron," Percival said with desperate reassurance, "but perhaps one of the maids or butlers will do something about Gregori." He didn't sound at all persuaded by this, though.

"What could they *do*?" Roy asked, a humorless laugh escaping him. He wiped away his tears. "I just hope Briar stays safe for the next few days, just until we can draft a response and deliver it to Tessa."

Percival seemed about to grab and squeeze Roy's hand, then stopped himself. "From the sound of it, Briar and her accomplices have concocted this plan rather meticulously. I would like to see the Governor get ahold of her and Irene's communications."

Roy mulled this over, nodding absently at first and then with increasing conviction. Briar *had* organized her machinations—

alongside her conspirators, Tessa and Irene—with an acute eye for detail. She had considered the conditions, chiefly relying on Irene's parents' lodgings, and arranged her plot around the most important variables.

Roy wished he had his sister's perception, which he was sure she must've inherited from their mother. More, he wished he could use the information Briar had provided and somehow twist it in his favor. He wished he could make his mission *here* something he could actually accomplish, make it so the Governor wasn't holding an ax above all their necks . . .

"What are we going to tell her?" Roy asked. "That we've found a sword? That we met the ghost of a philosopher? That the Old Ones have been adhering to the violent habits of their ancestors, who've been battling in wars the world over for generations? It's new information, sure, but it won't stop, or even put a temporary halt to, the war."

"You're saying we *don't* respond to Briar?"

Roy sighed. "I'm *saying* that it has been almost three months since we arrived. We have no clue when the Governor will return for his next check-in, and there are three more months until our deadline. I hate to say it, but maybe . . . maybe we need to figure out if we even have time for this."

"This is your sister we're talking about, darling," Percival said, a glum look coming over his face. "She's just as important as our research—maybe more so. You said yourself that you were doing this for the people of Northgard, and specifically for your sister, so you could see her. You must never forget that."

That decided Roy. He needed no more incentive.

"No, I mustn't," he answered Percival. He rummaged through the stack of books he'd deposited beside his desk, found his notebook, tore out several pages, and then wrote the following letter:

MAX FRANCIS

Briar,

There is nothing to forgive. I love you and I miss you. More than I can bear.

I'm afraid I have little to say, though I can assure you my sanity is thankfully intact. Prior to my initial meeting with the Governor, he assigned another scholar—Percival Atherton—for the task. We butted heads for a little while, which is understandable considering our clashing methodologies, but we have recently come to appreciate one another's company. I must admit, it's rather nice to not work alone for once.

While we have made progress on identifying the Old Ones and their objectives, we still have a great load of work ahead of us. I am as impressed with the number of books here as I am intimidated, though it's challenging to take in the view when my awe is so often eclipsed by dread.

What we have uncovered can be summarized in no more than a paragraph, but I shall state it here regardless:

We know the Old Ones currently based in Northgard are descendants of a very long bloodline, that they employ upon the battlefield military strategies unfamiliar to us, and that, millennia ago, they encroached onto Northgard but were banished by the Elder Scribes. More, Percival and I have found two swords, both interred in the sarcophagus of a Scribe. Allegedly, the Scribes used swords to banish the Old Ones from Northgard during that long-ago attack, though whether the swords we discovered, in this place of learning, are those in question is as yet unknown—and how to use such swords for this purpose eludes us.

I promised myself to keep this short and to the point, so I'll stop here, but please notify Tessa that Percival and I are eager to correspond with you whenever possible.

Too, I'm pleased to hear about you and Irene. Make sure to continue writing to her; it sounds like you both need the comfort. And please, if you can, lock your doors and stay as far from Gregori as possible.

Much love,
Roy

He blew out a long, quivering breath. "That will do. We'll wait for Tessa to return in the next couple days, give her this letter, and then wait again for Briar's following response." He sighed. "I'll admit it already feels irritating, having to wait out the interim periods, even if they *are* only a couple days."

"Then it's a good thing we're not just going to sit around and wait," Percival said. "As you said in your letter, there's more work to be done."

Roy put his quill into the inkpot on the corner of his desk, picked up the rest of the texts he'd put on the floor, and set them down in front of him. "Yes, there is."

"Then let us get to it."

Four days went by. On the second, they'd handed their response to Tessa, who then vanished into the snow as quickly as she'd appeared, like a wraith. Now, Roy was unfolding Briar's letter, Percival reading over his shoulder. Her script was erratic, as if she'd tried and failed to still her hand while writing.

Roy,

Gregori has gotten worse.
    So much worse.

I have done what you said and rarely leave my room, and when I do, it is only to run into the kitchens and rummage for food. Usually I come up empty-handed, but sometimes I return with a tureen of water and a handful of apples. It's not much, but it's all I can stomach.

You may ask why I have to fetch my own food. It's because he killed Maisie last week. Do you remember her, Roy? That poor old maid. She was supposed to reunite with her brother tonight. He'd been conscripted in the war and was released from service on account of an injury. I wonder where he is now, what he's thinking. I wonder if he knows that his sister is dead, that her spine was ripped out of her back, her flesh chewed through the wound.

"By the Scribes," Roy whispered, his stomach dropping. He looked over to Percival, whose face had turned several shades paler, then read on.

The manor smells like a slaughterhouse, and I dream of nothing but blood and Gregori's eyes. Those devil eyes. I have tried to ignore them. Him. Sometimes I can, when Tessa or Irene or Farrek (he's a new friend) leave their letters wedged in my windowsill, but the stench is so thick. What if it's so ingrained in me that I'll never escape it? Can that happen? What if the other maids have scrubbed the manor clean of blood, but my mind has not? I don't think so, though. I think that smell of death is real, and mine is next.

Mine or Northgard's.

Or both.

I'll attach what Farrek sent to me. He has been based in Rasileus, acting as our informant, for about a week now. It's better if you read from the source itself.

Tacked to this introductory section of Briar's letter was a two-page letter, scrawled in a bolder hand.

> *The breakdown of modern civilization is upon us, Briar. It was bound to happen, but I cannot imagine even the sagest analyst could have predicted it to happen so soon as this. Now that I've collected more intelligence, however, I'm shocked that this city has not yet fallen.*
>
> *As hard as it might be to believe—and trust me, I have had my own doubts—the Governor does make sure that every citizen of his city, on all tiers of the social hierarchy, is well fed. Northgard would almost certainly fall to complete ruin if this simple responsibility was not carried out. All things considered, the snowstorm especially, he has done a satisfactory job of maintaining the distribution of sustenance to the broader populace. All things considered, that is, except for one.*
>
> *Years ago, the Governor ordered the construction of a subterranean refuge, known among the aristocracy as the Burrow, beneath Rasileus Academy. This, I have learned, is regularly stocked with fresh fruits, vegetables, meats, and beverages brought from the kitchens in the Iron Citadel. Recently, as you well know, the Old Ones marched farther eastward to obstruct the Citadel's gates. This brought no discomfort to the Droves; the Burrow contains enough essentials to last the Governor's soldiers a lifetime. Possibly more.*
>
> *All this time, these soldiers have had something to fall back on, a last resort, a contingency plan if—when—all other plans are blown to Hell.*

"I'm not liking where this is headed," Percival said, his voice thin. He looked as gray as the room in the museum had after being leached of color by the sword.

Speechless, Roy continued reading Farrek's account.

Rumors began to stir of an arrangement made for the lower classes. A sled loaded with cargo—a fraction of the provisions delivered to the Burrow—would be shipped weekly to the communal shelters situated at the northern outskirts of Rasileus. These sleds would make the same journey: out from the front gates of the Academy, then through the valley nearby and to the shelters based on the other side, ending at Rasileus's northern border.

Unfortunately, the storm rendered this area nigh impassable. Snow fell in and blocked up the valley, building twice as a man is tall. The Governor refused civilians' pleas to invest in horse-drawn snowplows, as the only two available were at the time being used to clear the courtyard of the Iron Citadel to extend the Droves' range of mobility, in case the Old Ones stationed at the gates pressed farther inward. The drivers made efforts to clear the snow themselves, with what equipment they had at their disposal, but were unsuccessful and died in the attempt.

As you can imagine, the circumstances grew very drastic, very quickly. None of the rumored caches of food reached the communal shelters. The civilians posted there mourned the loss of the valuables. For it was not only the food they were mourning but the lives of their mothers and fathers, their children and siblings, their lovers, themselves. They'd been waiting two weeks for a delivery, Briar, and there was nothing remaining of their last save for chicken broth, stale tea biscuits, and plum jam.

Roy knew what was coming. He could feel it winding through his chest, coiling tighter and tighter. He turned to the penultimate page of Briar's letter, sweat trickling down into the notch between his shoulder blades.

Once word of the snowbank got to the communal shelters—sighted by a team of five scouts, only two of whom returned, the others likely lost to the cold—panic set in and broke out. The civilians' meager supply of biscuits and jam and broth was raided and scoured clean. Not a crumb left. Those who did not participate in the looting either did not eat and were later discovered dead of starvation and frostbite... or else found other ways to survive.

These once peaceable folk picked up their rakes, pickaxes, and shovels and hunted down their own. When the doing was done, the town was as filled with blood as it was with snow. The survivors of the massacre celebrated their triumph by feasting on their winnings, the food they'd stolen from their neighbors, but neglected to consider just how long this half-spoiled food would last them. Not very, it turned out.

The last several lines were written in a jagged hand, as though, like Briar, Farrek had been trembling while writing.

Tell me, Briar, and truly think about this one:

How precious is this life to you? How important? We live and die to serve a system that holds in its heart no love for people like us. We read and learn and educate, but our knowledge is suspended on a string, and that string can be cut at any moment and for any reason.

Would it be melodramatic to say I heard the sound that was made when the string poised over Rasileus was severed? I <u>felt</u> it, too. Above, I swear I did. The cries, the gurgling, the screams of confusion and disbelief... The <u>screams</u>! What harrowing measures we must endure to forsake our humanity and eat those who once ate with us. Mothers filling their bawling children's stomachs with tongues and intestines. Lovers begging one another

> to amputate a leg, an arm, <u>something</u> to stave off the crippling hunger.
>
> Questions hound me. Is it better knowing that the massacre preceded the cannibalism? Can this tableau of despair be justified by the hopelessness of the underfed and the impoverished? Or am I the fool for bringing morality into a scene where there is none?
>
> I only discovered what I have told you because the Governor eventually sent out a handful of his Droves to plow the road—only a few hours after the massacre, mind you. Why he chose to clear the pass at all is still up for debate. I attempted to inspect the shelters in search of any scholars I recognized, but with no success. In fact, it seemed to me that there weren't nearly as many corpses as the size of the shelters indicated, though I can't be sure. Probably they were cannibalized. Still, it keeps gnawing at me—that the Governor only responded to the outcry once the bodies had finished piling up ... and yet when I arrived at the scene, once his sled was out of sight, most of the bodies were gone.
>
> Forgive me. I am chasing shadows at this point. I know my end will soon come, because while I've taken up accommodations in the beating heart of Northgard, other regions of the city will no doubt be drawn against the carnage that befell Rasileus. A matter of hope no longer; it is only a matter of time.

Underneath this was the conclusion of Briar's letter.

> What is this all for, Roy, if our fate is sealed? Why fight, why defy, when the path is paved with unknowns and leads only to death? How precious is this life? How important is it to keep?

Roy gawked at the letter for a long while, silent. A chill went straight through the middle of his heart at Briar's words, so haunting and bleak, so unlike his sweet-tempered sister. But it wasn't her unfamiliar demeanor alone that troubled him. It was how she'd described Gregori. His eyes, specifically.

Those *devil* eyes.

"Percival," Roy said, his ears ringing, "you said you've seen the Old Ones before, that they march as one unit, but have you ... have you ever seen them *unarmored*?"

Recognition flashed across Percival's face. "Devil eyes."

"'He stares at his reflection and talks to himself, and he uses different features, different accents and voices. These strange noises ...'" Roy said, gripping the letter in his hand. "There might be some discrepancies to this theory that I'm glossing over, of course, but those soldiers ... They're us, Percival. Humans. But altered in some inexplicable way."

Percival sat back, fear plain upon his face. "The Old Ones. *The Old Ones*. Roy, Northgard gave them that name because of the outdated design of their armor." He let out a sharp, hysterical laugh. "But they truly are old. Which means we were fucking *wrong*. They aren't the progeny of a long-standing bloodline. They aren't their *descendants*. They're the same legion as all the stories we've read, sustained by some kind of dark, macabre magic. This city is at war with an enemy as ancient as, or maybe even predating, the Age of Scribes."

I can't stand being in the same place as that horrid man, Briar had written in her letter. *He's like a beast.*

On his journey to the Orphic Basilica nearly three months ago, Roy had watched, appalled, as a Drove cracked open the skull of a young boy who'd shoved ahead of the line waiting for food at a communal shelter. But before then, the Drove had looked over her shoulder as the sled had jolted into motion. Roy had at the time thought her eyes were bloodshot, though the snow had been falling thick, obscuring his view, and he had been weary, cold, and preoccupied. It occurred to him now that her eyes could very well have been red—the same burning light as that which streamed forth from the ghosts' eyes.

"'*Burning light*,'" Roy said, and an apt, uncanny portmanteau crossed his mind. "Blight."

Percival gaped. "Charles Patiny's poem. '. . . whose eyes of burning light do glow / upon their prey's final breath.'"

"The Old Ones didn't cause Gregori or any of his comrades psychological harm; they . . . they *Blighted* him," Roy said. "They killed him, then somehow brought him back and made him into one of their own. All those traumatized Radiant Droves on the front lines . . . Percival, they're all turning into the Old Ones."

22

THEY SAT STARING AT ONE ANOTHER FOR AN INTERminable length of time, their eyes nearly bulging out of their sockets as they took in the magnitude of their discovery. Then, all at once, it clicked into place.

They blurted out their conclusions simultaneously:

"The Governor—"

"The Old Ones—"

"You start," Roy insisted.

"No, go on, darling," Percival said. His eyes widened. "The *implications*, Roy—"

Roy nodded enthusiastically. "I know, I know. All right, one moment. Let me get my thoughts into some sort of order."

But where to start? There was a heap of questions unanswered, a profusion of theories unconfirmed. Foremost, though: what kind of affliction was the Blight? Was it a disease? A result of prolonged exposure to trauma? Some sort of magic (which, despite what he'd experienced for close to three months, Roy was still loath to acknowledge, since "magic" was what small minds pointed to when they couldn't find the real cause)?

Roy stood up and paced in front of Percival to keep his mind working, all the while crossing his arms to stop them from trembling. Finally, he started with what he truly knew:

"I have seen one of the Blighted Droves before."

"Yes?" Percival said, excitement and fear warring with each other in his voice.

"Yes. When I was escorted to the Basilica. At the time I thought her eyes were bloodshot, but in hindsight . . . it's completely possible she could have been Blighted. She had this crazed way about her, like . . . like she'd lost her mind." *Lost it?* he thought. *Or had it stolen from her?* "I think I dismissed it because the Droves have always loved violence and madness. It makes them feel bigger. Superior. Gabriel felt this way, too."

"Meaning?"

"Meaning that this isn't something new to them."

"And yet perhaps this is something more," Percival said. He pondered for a minute. "Perhaps the Old Ones see their own advantage in that sort of attitude, so they target people like Gregori—like the Drove you saw on the streets—those who voluntarily, *eagerly*, fall in line with the Radiant Droves' ethos. They're young. They're untested. They believe that they are the new and improved order, soaring on the coattails of the grizzled and experienced, if only so they can eventually surpass the veterans. Wouldn't the Old Ones target them? Such recklessness—and such disregard for innovation—would make for perfect soldiers."

Something about what Percival said there made Roy pause. Not so much *what* the Old Ones were doing, but who they were doing it *to*. And yet, paradoxically, exactly what they were doing.

The Old Ones kill, Roy thought. *That's what they do. They don't discriminate, and they don't hesitate. They attack, and they conquer.*

They are, in fact, the perfect soldiers.

Roy's eyes widened. "Percival, you're right. Recklessness *does* make for good soldiers, and that's *exactly* where the Governor comes in: the unarmored, Blighted Droves. And that's what makes them his perfect soldiers." As soon as he uttered this realization, another struck him.

Dimestra had said something to the Governor before his first meeting with Roy. *I considered it my responsibility to administer all aspects of my rule as both a Matron and a commander of Drove squadrons and, as such, would have thought my presence for this discussion necessary.*

"The Matron," Roy said. "She told me *months* ago that she'd supplied him with more soldiers and, in exchange for her contribution, she requested the security of the aristocracy. But she never knew the truth—not about the Old Ones, and therefore not about precisely who she'd ordered to watch over Briar."

Percival rested his forearms on the desk, a crease between his brows. "Wait a moment. 'His perfect soldiers'? What do you mean? *Whose* soldiers?"

"By the Scribes! Who else, Percival?"

"The Governor?"

"Exactly! He benefits from this war, and the undead creatures it's made of his soldiers—some of which were once under the Matron's command—because he has them under his *thrall*," Roy explained, a myriad of interlinked realizations whipping through his head. "All of them. I don't know if it's the oaths they take or some natural affinity to him as their leader, since he basically stole them from the Radiant Droves' leadership, but for whatever reason, the Blight isn't swelling the ranks of the Old Ones. It is, however, expanding his own personal death squad. Which in turn means he doesn't *need* to feed the lower class. He doesn't *need* their support. He doesn't *need* what they could provide, because none of it aids him. The storm winds will keep on blowing, the people will keep on eating each other, and he will *still* have his muskets, his Burrow, and his Droves, these glassy-eyed resurrected soldiers. And probably more and more of them, it appears, as the bodies pile up. I'm sure the only reason he cares about the cannibalism—the only reason he eventually reopened the pass—is because he was worried he'd be losing out on more soldiers for his command. Remember what Farrek said about there being a shortage of bodies after the massacre? The Governor must've carted them away and used them. He's completely content with all this, and not only with these cogs churning, but two others."

"*Us*," Percival whispered.

"He has us here, beavering away at this mystery," Roy said. "So that when he *does* have a big enough force of resurrected Droves, he can banish the rival army that's laying siege to us."

"Which he must believe will happen in roughly three months," Percival surmised.

Roy nodded. "At which point, the moment we deliver the key to the shackles which are the Old Ones, we are through."

"And should we not," Percival added, "then he picks two more of us from those still hidden."

"Until he has no use for scholars anymore—and an army that he is no longer beholden to the Iron Citadel for, to hunt us down." Roy could almost see it: hundreds of thousands of red-eyed conquerors, hunting down those whose only interest was to find and share the truth; the darkness of the Old Ones' armor replaced with the darkness of the Governor's iron rule.

"These are our people, Percival. Or, at least, they *should* be our people. We can't let this happen. Our time here has shown me just how much we can accomplish if we're not hidden away in warrens and immolated bookshops, hoping for a bit of correspondence that will bolster or refute our theories. The Old Ones are proof of how unthinking brutes are the antithesis of an enlightened society. That's what the Governor is looking to create, only under his terms.

"We need to offer him something that he *cannot* refuse, then. And in return ... we will make him guarantee our people's safety, that those who have survived will be *permanently* exempt from the hand they've been dealt. That scholarship *will* live, so that the next time something like the Old Ones approaches our island, there will be those with the proper tools to stop them."

"And how do you propose to do that?" Percival asked. "Negotiate with him? When are we supposed to do that—when our six months are up?"

"Yes. We withhold what we discover until he agrees."

"And if we don't discover anything?"

"Then we're sealed for death anyway, no?" Roy said matter-of-factly.

Percival was silent at that, and they looked at each other for a moment, thoughtful.

Then Percival said, "We must keep what we know about the Blighted quiet, then, yes?"

"For certain. That might be our only source of leverage besides what we find to fight and hopefully remove the Old Ones. I'm not sure we can trust him to honor his word without having the threat of exposure in our pockets." When he saw the incredulity on Percival's face, Roy added, "Look, I'm not suggesting that the Governor is our ally or in any way honorable. But he's the one in power, so what choices do we have? Let's see."

Roy ticked off a finger with each point:

"One: We give him nothing. We die. The other scholars die. Briar and the rest of Northgard dies, at either his hands or the Old Ones'.

"Two: we give him everything we know, including what we've learned about the Old Ones, and he takes that information to further his own goals. You and I probably die. The scholars probably die. Northgard is under his authoritarian thumb while the people are under the undead boots of his Blighted.

"Three: we at least *try* to find a better deal for us. For the scholars. And for Northgard." He lowered his hand and looked up. "Percival, I don't think there is really a choice at all."

After a moment, Percival observed, "You have given this a lot of thought."

Roy shrugged. "We've both had the pleasure of meeting him. I've just been looking at every choice we could make since then."

"And you think when he is given a choice, he'll be amenable?" Percival asked, raising an eyebrow.

Roy frowned. "Well, we know he'll do anything to make this difficult."

"So what more can he threaten us with?"

Roy instantly comprehended what Percival was intimating. "You mean, when he counters, what else do we have to give him?"

"What else *beyond* exposing his army of Blighted Droves. Because, while damaging, it's not exactly something we can *prove*. It needs to be something tangible."

"Right. It needs to be a sacrifice. For us. Something that will appease the Governor and his hard-liners, while convincing him that he still needs our intellect. And not just you and I, but *all* the scholars."

"You talk about the scholars like they aren't already on the verge of extinction. How can we save something that's almost dead?"

"Because they aren't all dead—not yet. A community is a people, not a building." Roy sighed. "And more and more, I'm convinced we'll need them at the end of this investigation. For the aftermath, so that Northgard can have a future."

"Fine, I'm convinced it's worthwhile. But it still begs the question—"

"What would both appeal to him *and* keep the remaining academics in Northgard protected?" Roy finished, his heart thrumming at the pensive look on Percival's face, at how he looked around at the library at the same time as Roy.

Somehow, their thoughts had aligned. That they were even *considering* something so horrific, so profane, stunned Roy.

Not a building...

It was Percival who said it. "We'll find a way to bring the Basilica down. Our community, or whoever among them has escaped persecution, might—*will*—shun us." His eyes went hazy, as though he was dredging up some lost memory. Roy wondered if he was thinking of his fallen friend, the friend whose death had somehow led Percival here. "But at least they'll live on."

A maelstrom of stifled wails and whispers uncoiled from the rafters, springing back and forth.

I'm sorry, Roy thought, his throat thick with tears, but he couldn't conceive of any other way to help the Governor see Northgard's situation from the eyes of the old world. The souls imprisoned in the Basilica might not live on, if this was what living after death was, but Roy longed to see Northgard free of disorder. Perhaps then, he could find a place for himself—he might at least have the right to argue his case to the other scholars— but now, the dream of belonging seemed worlds away. Instead, he could only see the nightmare of what the decimation of the Orphic Basilica would render and how it would mark him as a traitor, a heretic.

Better it be my nightmare than a whole country's.

At least, that was what he needed to tell himself in this moment.

As though in the same predicament, Percival looked deeply into Roy's eyes, asking him something.

Not a word needed to be said. Roy heard the question clearly: *Do you want the library to live or Northgard?*

Or Briar?

The answer was simple. A community was its people, and people were always the answer. If he had a chance to save as many as he could at the cost of these stones, these spirits, these books, and all the mysteries waiting to be solved within them, then he would take it.

Now Roy only had to wait for that very opportunity.

I T WAS A WEEK LATER—ON THE FIRST WEEK OF THEIR THIRD month in the Orphic Basilica, a fortnight later than they'd expected their next delivery of supplies to appear—that a commotion came from below.

Roy trudged to the balcony, his head spinning from the excessive amount of cramming he'd accomplished in the past few hours. There, he looked down and immediately picked out the source of the ruckus.

A churning, frantic crowd of ghosts was assembled before the front entrance on the first floor. They were shoving against the double doors, which jostled and jumped in their frames, and piling atop one another like shadows crawling up the walls. Screams and groans sounded through the library, echoing. The ghosts wandering the upper floors floated toward the scene, drawn to the uproar.

Far beneath the clamor and the droning moans, Roy made out a rhythmic pounding. It grew louder and louder, more distinct by the second. He thought the ghosts were rattling the doors, that they were forbidding Roy and Percival from leaving, for some reason, and so it didn't occur to Roy until then that someone was outside.

Roy remembered the first time he'd heard that sound, thinking it was the Governor and instead finding Tessa at the library's threshold. He didn't think that luck would be on his side now.

Roy and Percival left the fifth floor and strode down to the first, each of their footsteps loud as a judge's gavel. They couldn't stall, couldn't even demonstrate their paltry strength; anything less than absolute submission would be misconstrued by the Governor as an act of treason, a breaching of the rules he'd laid before Roy's feet over three months ago.

No, Roy thought. *We have a chance.*

It was slim at best, but they had discussed at length what they would say to the Governor. That didn't stop him from feeling sick in the stomach, though.

Percival rushed up to the heaving multitude of ghosts swarming before the front doors and flapped his arms. "Go! *Leave!*" he yelled. "You're not helping us! If the Governor is out there, then we need to answer him!"

Some moved, as if startled by his approach, but they glided right back, hissing and groaning at him. Two or three of the ghosts merged together, fusing, and created a looming shield of translucent darkness, which solidified the closer Percival got to the door.

They're not intimidated by us, Roy thought. *They saw the minimal damage we did in the crypt, and so they don't fear we can do anything more to them.*

What are they afraid of, then?

"If these are ghosts of scholars," he mused, wandering around and scanning the hall until his eyes alighted on something he might use, "and they linger in the limbo of this library, then the most precious thing to them would be . . . the books." He strode toward a wall with purpose. "And what do books hate?"

He pulled a torch out of its sconce.

"Fire."

He turned back to the front doors, tightened his grip on the torch and then pitched it head-over-end at the ghosts.

The effect was immediate. They spread outward, dodging the unlit torch and uttering shrill, horrified screams. About twenty or thirty of the ghosts stared at him for a moment, red eyes brightening with panic and disorientation, then swirled through the air and retreated to the floors from which they'd come. Others zipped back and forth like streaks of ink, painting tracks of darkness across the carpet and trailing ribbons of crimson light. Then they scurried off, joining their companions in hibernation.

Percival watched the exodus, in turns fascinated and ashamed. "They remember," he whispered. "They remember what happened here."

"Yes," Roy said. "But what was once war may bring peace. Or war again."

Gulping, Percival reached forward and pulled open the door, letting in a gale of cold, howling wind.

Two hulking figures dressed in verdant felt caps and white-furred coats stamped through the doors, large black batons hung on their belts. They wore fingerless white gloves and black boots. Roy was no fool, though; now that he knew the truth, he could see past these mundane details, could recognize the peculiarity that had eluded him on his ride to the Orphic Basilica: those effulgent red eyes.

These were the Governor's guards, these inchoate versions of the Old Ones, compliant and brought back from death for a higher duty.

The Governor strode in behind his guards, garbed in his snow-freckled cream coat. His rheumy green eyes landed on Roy. He slicked his hair back, laying the unkempt white wisps flat against his scalp. He was much shorter and podgier than the men who accompanied him, though despite his harmless appearance, the predaceous glint in his eyes rooted Roy in place. Once the Governor came to a halt before his guards, they paced forward to flank him. Then he grumbled to Roy and Percival, "Follow me."

"There's something beautiful about this building," said the Governor.

Roy sat before him, Percival on his right. A large desk separated them from the Governor, whose guards surveyed them expressionlessly.

The room where they'd gathered, situated on the seventh floor, was strangely bereft of bookshelves. Diaphanous drapes hung over the great window behind the Governor. Through the narrow gap between them, Roy saw that high above Northgard, which was scattered with freckles of firelight and mostly buried in snow, the crescent moon glimmered like a luminous hook.

"But you know I am not here for splendor," the Governor finished.

Without being asked, Percival advised the Governor on what they'd found since their most recent progress report.

Roy felt himself shriveling, and his integrity dwindling, more and more with every word that came out of Percival's mouth. This was a betrayal of the Orphic Basilica's desire for honor, a desire which, while unspoken, was clear in every interaction he and Percival had had with the library. Both the Orphic Basilica and the Elder Scribes would welcome open discussions and exchanges of knowledge, but that the information currently being shared was designed not to further the advancement of knowledge and instead to *subjugate*...

Roy couldn't quell his guilt, but he reminded himself that this was the plan they'd made.

This was what it had to come down to.

When Percival finished his report of their findings, from which he omitted their awareness of the Governor's army of Blighted Droves, along with his plans to enlarge and thereby augment this resurrected military unit, he said, "Although we haven't uncovered who the Old Ones are or where they're from, we've identified that these soldiers are forces of nature. They are more akin to a plague than an army, and so must be treated as such."

"Splendid," the Governor said. "But as you've said, you haven't reached the truth of who these soldiers are, what they actually want."

"No," Roy said, fighting to maintain his calm. He and Percival were relatively certain they had the solution to pushing back the Old Ones from Northgard. But panic still fastened its hold around Roy's heart. He feared that, at any moment, they might be asked a question they would have to lie about, and Roy didn't want to imagine what might happen should the Governor ferret out their understanding of his exploits. "But we still have three months. We're close."

"As is our defeat," the Governor said, ignoring Roy's mention of their deadline. "I need answers, but since you seem to be if not at a loss for them, then at least struggling to uncover the complete identity of our adversaries, I believe some technicalities must be addressed, and some amendments must be made."

"What were you hoping to discuss?" Percival asked, cautious.

"Amendments to what?" Roy asked at the same time.

The Governor rested his chin upon his clasped hands. "I would like to make an official modification to the Law of Intervention."

Roy stiffened. "*What?* What modification?"

"The Old Ones are gaining on us," the Governor said. "They've enforced their ranks around the Citadel. No attacks have yet been launched, but the long weeks of tension, made worse by the snowstorm, indicate it's imminent.

"Moreover, small changes in the administration of the city"—Roy assumed this was Northgard's brutal treatment of Rasileus's lower-class citizens, deprived of food and forced to cannibalism, which was decidedly a very large change—"have resulted in outbreaks and acts of violent resistance from the working population. I am often hesitant when it comes to alliances, but I love this city. I would live in regret for all my days if I knew there was something I could've done and had refused to do it. As such, I have needed to repay the debts of a few Manors and their Masters and Matrons. Your mother, Roy, is among them."

"Debts?" Percival asked.

"Past liabilities," the Governor explained. "Broken peace negotiations. Failed attempts at allegiance. Some treaties have an expiration date, you see, but Matron Dimestra and I have struck a new deal befitting our positions."

Roy did not like the sound of that; the deal the Governor had already struck with the Matron was bad enough—worse, given that it had transferred loyalty of her Droves to the Governor and granted him the resources to build his revenant army. But Roy was unclear what any of this had to do with his and Percival's mission.

The Governor provided immediate clarity.

"Something similar has crossed my mind regarding your assignment."

"We, too, wish to discuss our terms," Roy said, his breath shaking, and then tried to assure the Governor. "And I want to be clear that Percival and I have guaranteed there's no power imbalance or unjust consequences tied to our proposal."

The Governor beamed; his flabby cheeks indented by dimples. "Ah, have you? Well, do tell me, then! I would be *delighted* to hear what you've planned."

Roy suppressed a grimace at the mockery in his tone. And although this had been his idea, it dawned on him just how grievously this discussion could go wrong. The Governor could sic his guards on the two of them and have their heads removed from their shoulders. He could drag them out of the library by their ears and send them to be tried, tortured, and then publicly executed. The possibilities unfurled in Roy's mind in a dark, ghastly exhibition, not unlike Valusvar's visions.

The Governor raised a brow. "Well?"

Roy cleared his throat, then declared, "In return for the answers you seek, you would promise us the collective safety of Northgard, *not* excluding the remaining survivors of our community."

"Oh, is that all? What, pray tell, would I get in return for upending years of established policy?"

With another calming breath—and a nod from Percival—Roy said, "We would burn the Basilica to the ground upon the completion of our assignment."

The Governor uttered a croaky laugh. "Well, boys. I'll admit that this was not what I expected. Too, I admire your tenacity. But I have dispatched my men many a time to immolate these ancient grounds. What makes you believe you're capable of accomplishing what we could not?"

Roy battled the temptation to place his hand on Percival's leg, which had begun bouncing in agitation, then said, "While Northgard is generally unsympathetic toward, and disbelieving of, old-world mysticism, the Orphic Basilica is an unmistakably arcane landmark. I was once skeptical myself, but on multiple occasions, I have encountered the uncanny."

The Governor cocked his head, awaiting an explanation.

"This library has openly communicated with us," Roy said. "It has provided us food and beverages, sometimes upon request. I realize you've tried your hand at leveling the Basilica, but neither of us has been rejected by the library, like you and your Droves were."

The Drove standing rigidly on the left of the Governor swiveled his head and assessed Roy, his crimson eyes shimmering with unnerving intelligence. Roy attempted to make out, beneath that infernal glow, the light of vitality. But the red light seemed flat and lifeless, as though some unholy sorcery had excised the soul. Was this what Briar had seen in Gregori? Roy shuddered to think of it.

Something else struck him, too. Neither of the Droves seemed at all affected by the library now. He had no sound theories at this moment for why that may be, but this ephemeral idea—that it was as if the Orphic Basilica was anxious to see the fallout of the impending interrogation and so had somehow immunized the two men—was one he could not shake.

Roy lowered his voice and continued, "We should be the ones to wield the torch against the library, however it can be done. We'll secure further rapport with the Basilica—"

"Something we've already been establishing," Percival interjected.

"—and then burn it all down, but"—Roy raised a hand—"we will not spark a single ember without being ensured of our dying community's well-being."

Almost as soon as Roy had finished speaking, the Governor slapped the desk. "Done! A fine deal, Roy Dawnseve."

Percival's jaw dropped.

"A... A fine deal?" Roy asked.

The Governor laughed. "Why, by all means! The library is as beautiful as it is a large, unwieldy nuisance. Without it lingering near our city like an unwanted pimple, our industries could expand their resources and hubs of power over this valuable land. Once the Old Ones are finally bested, revenue will soar and Northgard's military influence will reach the southern islands of the Hasdan Isles. Imagine the *solidarity*. What a beautiful prospect! Oh yes, burn this library down!"

It wasn't so much the Governor's words but his enthusiasm that almost destroyed Roy. He felt trapped inside himself, confined in his own skin, unable to look away from the egregious mistake he'd made. Because the Governor had been manipulating the deprived citizens of Northgard for longer than Roy could fathom. So how could Roy have convinced himself the Governor wouldn't pluck some permanent advantage from their offer? And yet...

Yes, his tyrannical government would persist, but so would Briar, Percival, Roy, and the rest of the scholars. Furthermore, if he was being honest, there would certainly be *some* economic benefit to the whole city if the Governor's dream came to fruition.

But even as he tried to feel relieved—he *had* mostly concocted this deal to save the academic community—Roy knew that he had also somehow consolidated even more power into the hands of the Governor, and that Northgard would be held captive in its own walls, just with a less visible threat.

Not to mention what he'd said about the southern islands.

"Solidarity?" Percival echoed, homing in on that latter point. "You're talking about unification."

"Long ago, the islands *were* united," the Governor said. "They lived under one name, Northgard, since the landmass first rose from the sea. As time passed, though, rifting tectonic plates broke the supercontinent and fractured the southern tip of Northgard into several islands. The rift valley, that little slip of sea between Northgard and our southern neighbors, divided us." He smiled. "Now, I may not be able to shove two lands together, but I at least want to do my part and join our forces once again."

"Is that unification . . . or subjugation?" Percival asked, and Roy felt a slight catch in his breath.

The Governor only smiled. "If it is ultimately to their benefit, which word seems more appropriate?"

They all sat there with that lingering in the air before the Governor cleared his throat.

"But first we must rid ourselves of the Old Ones," he said. "It's clear their story is steeped in evil, and like most fanciful stories, they must be stamped out. I want them banished, never to walk this land or any other again." The Governor tugged on his collar, and Roy caught a small glimpse of the necklace encircling his throat. His eyes had happened upon it during their first meeting, and he could've sworn it had been onyx, but perhaps the dim light had muddled his vision, confusing him. Because now it almost certainly looked duller, muted, not quite as lustrous as before. The Governor drew it out and fiddled with it unconsciously.

"Have you always had that necklace?" Roy asked.

"Only since my wife passed," the Governor said, a slight flush on his cheeks. He tucked the necklace back beneath his collar. "She gifted it to me before she . . . she left us. I wear it to honor her vision of unity."

Dimestra had told Roy something of the Governor's late wife. Again, he cast his mind back to the ride to the Orphic Basilica. *The Governor has been . . . absent since his wife passed some few years ago. Her death has taken a mercilessly heavy toll on his health.*

"You're doing this for her," Percival said suddenly, "even beyond her death."

If the Governor seemed shocked by this conclusion, he didn't let it show. "We shared our sentiments about Northgard. She ... She ..." The Governor shook his head, his lips curved into a brittle, trembling smile. "She would want me to do what's best for Northgard. You know, I should really thank you both. You've arranged the perfect groundwork for a swift political reconfiguration. This has been long in coming." He rose to his feet with a groan. "And with that in mind, I have duties to attend. I apologize for the brief meeting."

Roy and Percival followed behind him and his guards on their descent to the first floor. During the walk there, the two Droves—whom Roy had previously believed insusceptible to the migraines and skittishness to which the Matron and the Governor's first entourage of Droves had fallen prey to—were pestered by ghosts. They swirled over their heads and around their arms and through their legs, screeching. They shrieked in various degrees of agony, from promises to what sounded like profanities.

One ghost made a sly grab for the baton of the guard on the Governor's left, but he managed to bat it aside before he could be divested of his weapon.

Amazed, the Governor looked around, marveling at the spectacle that his appearance had produced. A small smile touched his lips.

Roy did not want to wonder what was on his mind, but the thought came to him of its own volition: The Orphic Basilica, engulfed in flames. The ghosts, entombed in a perpetually burning graveyard. He wondered if they would die with the library, or if they would be stuck in purgatory, some excruciating state of limbo from which they would witness the goings-on of the world beyond but never again roam it.

Once they were on the first floor, the five of them gathered near the entryway in a loose semicircle, the Governor slowly turned, his blank-faced guards doing the same. "You know, I'm rather glad you're still here," he said. "There's one last thing which I would like for us to tackle before my departure tonight." He brusquely plunged a hand into a pocket of his trousers and pulled out a pile of soggy papers, which he threw at Roy's feet. They made a wet slap, splattering water across Roy's boots. "My guards spotted a dead horse and its rider, a young woman—both fallen to frostbite and hypothermia—on the side of the road on our journey here. These papers were in her pocket. I assume she'd been on her way to the library."

Frozen, Roy looked down at the crumpled, damp papers, but dared not touch them. He knew what they were.

"Pick them up," the Governor demanded, his voice monotone. "Read them."

Roy picked them up. There was nothing else to do, no way of escape. He wished the ghosts would wreak havoc upon the Governor and his guards, that they would drive them beyond the brink of madness, that they would steal into their minds and memories and crush every thought they'd ever had.

Instead, Roy unfolded the papers. There were four sheets of parchment. They were soggy, but the writing was legible.

In essence, the letter—penned by Irene—detailed the urgency of Briar's mission, which was to inform Roy what had transpired during the time they'd been separated, as well as to relate the ever-shifting relations of Governorship and the Radiant Droves' barbarous acts of harassment inflicted upon the middle class, the lower class, and the academic community. Some scholars were scarred and flogged. Others were stripped naked and forced to survive the worsening climes.

At the end of the missive, Roy was petrified to find a blueprint of the Burrow, which Irene claimed Farrek had stolen from Drove's military coat.

Everything was in this letter. *Almost* everything, anyway, but Roy didn't believe that the Governor was foolish enough to think Irene, Briar, Tessa, and Farrek—and whoever else Briar had recruited into her secret circle of conspirators—were not aware of what had taken place in Rasileus. If word got out, Northgard would spiral deeper into despair and desperation, exacerbated by the Old Ones' continuing assault, and the Governor would have to pick up the pieces.

Word hadn't gotten out, though. It was in Roy's hands. And before him was the despot who had proven he had no compunction leaning into the darkness if it meant keeping just a bit more control.

Just like he'd done fifteen years ago when he'd ordered all those bookshops and libraries burned.

The Governor met Roy's horrified stare. His skin was limp like melted wax, but there was something thrashing and alive in his green eyes.

"Roy," Percival whispered, looking wide-eyed at him. "Roy, what—"

"I was fortunate to make sense of it," the Governor said. "I guess I should thank your sister's friend. Had it not been for Tessa, I might have been oblivious to Irene Larifor leaking military secrets. Her mother and father have demonstrated their unswerving loyalty and devotion to my cause, so I should think that they will be pleased to attend their traitorous daughter's public execution tomorrow. And your sister..." He smiled. "Well, Briar Dawnseve might have escaped my notice, too, had Tessa been a little more careful not to reveal telltale information. Therefore,

Briar will be joining her friend—or lover, I suppose, according to the nature of some of their letters—on the execution block. A final reunion, at long last."

Roy had thought he'd sorted carefully through the outcome of Briar's treachery, that his and Percival's deal with the Governor had circumvented the safety not only of his country but of his sister. But as dread crawled through his bones, Roy began to doubt everything that he'd worked for, everything that he'd given up.

"Please," Roy murmured, then said aloud, "My sister is an asset, a second heir. Briar's . . . She's exempted from the Law of—"

"*Nobody is exempted from justice*," the Governor snapped, apoplectic. Spittle flew from his lips and struck the carpet at Roy's feet. "Law is undeniable; it is the answer." He pointed a shaking finger at Roy, gave him a vicious, spiteful smile. "Your sister did me wrong, boy. She aimed to ruin *me* and *mine*."

Mine.

He means the city. Its people. Northgard.

He truly believes they belong to him, and him alone.

The ghosts had vanished without a trace since the Governor and his entourage had stopped in their tracks before the Orphic Basilica's entryway. The library was silent but for the occasional raucous blast of thunder or lightning, and no loitering entities monitored the bookshelves.

Now they returned, peering out with their iridescent crimson eyes through the risers of the iron staircases and uttering low, aghast moans. Books and scrolls started shuddering and toppling from the shelves again, filling near and distant pockets of the library with booming cracks and thumps, repeated and amplified by a persistent echo.

But it was all faint and other to Roy, so painfully far away.

He was rooted in place, his mind spinning around the Governor's words. *Nobody is exempted from justice.*

Roy sprang forward, overcome with uncontrollable rage. He took no more than three steps before one of the guards lunged and tackled him to the ground. Roy uttered a nearly soundless gasp, the air whooshing out of his lungs. He reached up, attempting and failing to claw at the guard's face, when the guard suddenly wound his hand around Roy's long hair and pulled hard.

A bolt of agony shot through his scalp and spread across his skull. His head felt like it was catching flame. He screamed, tears streaming down his face. He couldn't think clearly through the pain, couldn't wrap his mind around what had occurred, what the Governor had said, what he meant—

Above him, the guard yanking at his hair shouted and went flying off Roy, skidding across the carpet.

Roy scrambled to his feet; his hair tangled across his tear-streaked face. He brushed it back with a quivering hand, clearing his vision, then glanced to his right, where the guard had disappeared. He was squirming on the ground, digging the heels of his boots into the carpet and leaving smears of muddy snow.

A horde of ghosts, maybe four or five, was upon him. They pulled at his arms, his legs, his skull. They shrieked in his face, babbled in his ears. His eyes rolled up into the back of his head. He raked his fingernails down his cheeks, drawing shallow trenches that slowly filled with blood.

The second guard marched forward, then reached in through the cloud of ghosts surrounding his companion and pulled him out by the collar of his coat. The incapacitated guard staggered to his feet, and after a moment, the ghosts slinked farther back into the gloomy alcoves and reading rooms on the first floor.

Percival looked frantically from the dazed guard to Roy,

then finally landed his gaze on the Governor, his arms hanging motionless by his sides.

The Drove returned to his station, mumbling incoherently underneath his breath and feverishly shaking his head.

"Please," Roy whispered, his skull throbbing. "Just grant my sister mercy."

"I'm afraid I cannot do that, Roy," the Governor said. Somewhere past the ringing in his ears, Roy heard the Governor say: "You both have three *weeks* to stop the Old Ones and to tear this *blasphemous* building down. I trust you know the consequences you will be subjected to, should you not meet this new deadline. But at least you *have* those three weeks. As your sister and Irene can attest, justice in Northgard is usually much swifter." Then, with a pat on Roy's face that was abnormally paternal, the Governor smiled and said, "Consider it a demonstration of my generosity."

Then he twisted on his heel. One of the guards hauled open the door, letting the Governor depart first, accompanied by his companion, and then himself after. The door banged shut.

Roy fell to his knees and screamed.

THE OLD ONES

Part Three

24

ROY WENT MAD WITH GRIEF.

He did not eat. He hardly drank, and the little that he *did* drink, he couldn't tell whether it was water or whiskey, so clouded were his senses. He was a stranger to himself, a dead man walking, a wayward soul floating on the outside of its vessel. At one point, he wondered if he was breathing in this gray hellscape or if he was merely clinging to reality by his diminishing will to survive. But he could not move on, nor accept what had happened, and so he would hurt himself. He would push himself to his limits.

On the first three nights of his psychological decline, he began to skip sleep. He didn't need it, he decided. It was a burden, a necessary sacrifice. He'd worked himself to the bone before, gone a day or two without rest, but now there was no respite. If he gave himself a break, even for a moment, his mind would start to drift and splinter, and the memories would burst through, shattering the mental dam he'd subconsciously forged after the Governor had left, after Roy had crumpled to his knees and screamed.

On the fourth night, Roy threw himself back into his studies, disregarding Percival's protests and implorations, not at all aware of what he was reading. He picked up books at random, his vision glazed and dim, the words swirling and blurring in the air before him. He walked into walls and bookshelves. He stumbled past paintings that stared at him and statues that seemed to follow his movements. He plunged in and out of consciousness. He would be torpidly wandering to his chamber, then blink and find himself in a reading room on the third floor, entirely oblivious as to how he had gotten there.

On the fifth night, his awareness had so deteriorated that he could not multitask, something which had once cost him minimal effort. He could not concentrate on what he was absorbing, but he still forced himself to absorb it regardless. He read three books a night, four sometimes. He understood none of it, hoping that his subconscious would pick up on what the rest of his grief-addled mind could not. When the day drew to a close, he ate a small portion of the Orphic Basilica's provisions, which had strangely decreased since, but it took him two attempts to consume the food without vomiting. Then, as midnight came around, the Governor briefly visited the library, attended by his Droves, and personally handed Roy an official proclamation of Briar's execution—complete with Dawnseve Manor's emblem of a bloody eye set within a rising sun. He also gave Roy Briar's beloved talisman, the carving of the two-faced woman she'd always kept on her person, even in her crib. Then, once the Droves slammed the doors shut behind themselves and the Governor, Roy threw up all the food he'd forced down. He didn't deserve the momentary strength it had afforded him anyway.

On the sixth night and onward, as the veil between sanity and madness thinned and threatened to fall, he started hearing voices and seeing faces that were not there. Initially, these hallucinations were more distracting than damaging. He saw a woman in a white gossamer dress, her arms covered in gashes and lacerations, thick, dark blood pouring from her empty eye sockets. Another time, he heard someone weeping, then looked over his shoulder and saw a man bent over his decapitated daughter, cradling her to his chest. Only hours after, a wind curled around Roy's neck and swept to his left, and he glanced there to find another man, who had an unnervingly wide grin on his face as he slipped his head into a noose.

The visions became more vivid, more complex... but infinitely more difficult for his mind to explicate. He saw a stampede of slender, pallid beasts loping between bookshelves, wailing infants swaddled in loincloths held to their waists. He saw a woman with great, bloodied shears cutting off chunks of her body—her arm, her eye, her cheek—and throwing them over the balcony, laughing hysterically. He saw, or *thought* he saw, Percival lurking within the shadows of a bookshelf. Then Percival stepped out into the moonlight, and Roy could not entirely grasp the creature that shambled toward him on four crooked stumps: his and Percival's bodies hacked and spliced together, a horrific, anatomically crude grotesquerie.

On the ninth night—or maybe it was the tenth—Roy's mind, softened by sleep deprivation, began the process of recollection. Then it ricocheted against the mental shield he'd constructed. All he could rely on was the time before that moment of reckoning, before the Governor and the Orphic Basilica had come into his life. He remembered racing alongside Briar through Dawnseve Manor's garden house. He remembered when they would sip lemonade from carafes and pretend they were attending a royal luncheon. How had he forgotten such bright and pivotal moments of his life?

But these recollections didn't last long.

His hallucinations continued, becoming progressively realistic. But over time, they shifted from unnatural, unfamiliar horrors to people he knew, both those who he loved and those who'd done him wrong.

He saw Briar in a hallway, her face pale as milk and pockmarked with punctures, from which blood flowed. It flooded her face. It dripped off her chin. It pooled at her feet until she was standing in a widening crimson river.

He saw Matron Dimestra in the Observatory, standing in front of the piano and pointing a musket at his face. He stared into the black mouth of the barrel. She pulled the trigger. Smoke issued out of the barrel, engulfing Roy, who had his arm raised as if that might somehow thwart his death. But no projectile came whistling toward his head.

And despite Roy's wavering certainty that admitting his trauma to Percival would evict his brother from his mind, he saw Gabriel again and again. He was in every corner, near every bookshelf, and on every floor of the library. He was a specter, the mastermind pulling the strings behind the rest of Roy's hallucinations.

Somewhere in the farthest corners of his mind, Roy knew that this was the Orphic Basilica's otherworldly inhabitants tugging on and uprooting his memories, forcing him to relive his deepest agonies, as had happened to the Droves when they had embarked on their own investigation prior to Roy and Percival's. A part of him was saddened by this idea—that the Orphic Basilica could not presently recognize him as a scholar, that his indisposition had made it so that his trauma exclusively constituted his identity, that, with his mental defenses lowered, he was completely unarmed... and the Basilica could no longer support or protect him. He asked it for more whiskey, having imbibed the last of what Percival had left out in a reading room one night, but the library ignored his request. So instead, Roy stumbled around from the first floor to the seventh, sobbing with Briar's carving clutched in his hands, and frantically searched for a drink. Whether it was wine or whiskey or cider, he did not care. He just needed something that would drown him, something that would pull him deeper into his misery.

Aside from his insobriety, Roy found that the longer he went without sleep, the more time he had to stew on his hopelessness, and therefore, the more grief he was inadvertently feeding to the ghosts. This went on for long enough that, in his regressed state, he became just as detached from scholarship as the Droves. Within days, it was almost impossible for Roy to distinguish between reality and recollection.

So for what seemed like the first time, but what his shattered subconscious dimly knew was not, he bore the full impact of Gabriel's anger. He was beaten. He was kicked. He was told he was nothing, a purposeless waste of existence. He had his scars whipped. He had his eyes removed with the poker, again and again, until he grew too scared to blink, too scared that it might be the last time. After a while of this torture, Roy could not remember the shape of his own face, nor when he had looked into the mirror and seen a man, not some detestable wretch masquerading as a man.

But again, he couldn't bring himself to care. It did not matter anymore. Nothing did. He'd tried everything he could to save Northgard and its depleting academic community, and all of it had amounted to nothing. He had put the assignment before every other component of his life, including Percival. He had unmasked the Old Ones, but he still hadn't figured out how to defeat them. And now he had less than two weeks to do it.

I killed her, Roy thought at some time during the cycle of days following Briar's death. *She's dead, executed. I killed my sister. The Governor may have been the weapon, but I was the one who handed him the right to do it. If not for me, she might still be alive.*

A brother was meant to be trusted, meant to be a protector, but he hadn't given her that. He was a traitor, a murderer, a disobedient dog in need of being put down. But there was no one around to do the deed, to finish what he had once, in Dawnseve Manor, been determined to start.

Maybe this was his sign. Maybe he ought to complete what Gabriel hadn't had the gall to do. Roy had been enticed by the prospect of suicide on several instances, although he'd never devoted himself to the task.

Now he could hardly quell the urge. He visualized the myriad ways he could accomplish it and fixed them in his mind. He could climb over the railing on the seventh floor and jump, his body shattering on impact. He could drink himself to a stupor, then to death. He could throw himself into one of the fireplaces and burn to a crisp, filling the library with the stench of his seared flesh. But these attempts would necessitate effort, resolve, and strong cognitive functioning, and of these three Roy had none.

He *wanted* to do something. He wanted to stand up and remember what he was fighting for. But the thought of putting quill to parchment, of cohering the interconnected workings of the mystery into an answer, exhausted him. He was *tired*, so damn tired. And he didn't know if that was for better or for worse.

Sometime during his grieving, the Orphic Basilica began to teem with the sorrowing moans of the dead, increased twofold by the storm's strengthening wails. Books rattled upon their shelves. Loose sheets of paper spilled out over balcony railings and glided through the library, stirred about by the passing of anguished ghosts. Some of these creatures did not move, though, instead choosing to hover in multitudes in front of snow-glazed windows. The maroon and crimson light of their eyes cast an infernal glow over the floorboards, illuminating brighter with every ghost that seeped out of the shadows. Only once the sun fell and the moon rose to take its place did Roy come to understand what was happening, what had ushered the ghosts out of hiding. *Why else would they be behaving this way?* Roy asked himself. *What else would disturb and induce fear in a ghost other than grief, than death?* A large part of it could be the war, he reasoned, but these creatures had been imprisoned within the library for who knew how long. They hadn't been pushed to their turbulent state of mind by the battle raging in the city, but by their own personal turmoil, their demons. Roy had spoken his own; he'd shared it with Percival loud and clear. The ghosts had no doubt overheard his story.

Percival, Roy thought, horror creeping through him. Percival had been quiet, inattentive, as of late. Roy hadn't seen much of this taciturnity, as he'd been much too enshrouded in his own despondency, but these discomforts did not happen immediately, as Roy well knew. They accumulated over time, swelling and broadening, and Roy was frightened—why understate things? He'd already slept next to the bastard—he was *petrified* of what exactly would transpire if Percival didn't say something. What visions and horrors would Percival see if he didn't tell Roy what had happened to him, what had bitten and gnashed through his brilliant, beautiful mind all this time? All this *damn* time, he'd been outracing the shadow bound to his feet like manacles and he'd been too afraid to tell Roy the full of it.

Roy entertained the theory, however briefly, that maybe it wasn't Percival's silence that had caused this supernatural disturbance. Maybe it was Briar's death, and all the memories it had dredged up within Roy. But one night, when the hallucinations started to come few and far between, something occurred that proved to him that this was not, in fact, the case.

Roy was at the head of the staircase that spiraled down to the second floor when, far down below, a very human scream filled the library. The books and the windows shuddered and rocked.

"*Percival!*" Roy cried out. Nauseous with fear, he raced to the balcony, gripped the railing, and looked down.

Initially he could not quite comprehend what he was seeing. Then it came to him.

Percival was kneeling near the foot of the staircase leading up to the second floor, sitting on the heels of his boots. He had his hands clamped tight over his eyes, the skin underneath the right gouged and dripping blood, which wandered down his face like a tear. He bellowed, a long, anguished roar, shaking his head back and forth. Roy saw all this faintly, though, as if through fog-smeared binoculars; for Percival was enveloped in a seething, red-eyed shadow. A ghost.

It was wearing Percival like a black shawl, its eyes jutting two inches or so above his head and bearing witness to the gradual deterioration of his senses. He scrabbled at the ghost, the palm of his right hand streaked with the blood he'd drawn, but his curled fingers passed straight through it.

"*I didn't mean to!*" Percival screamed. He scrambled up to his knees, then fell, thrashing and writhing, lashing out at the ghost. It hovered about his head as if pinned into place there. "*I didn't think they'd come for us! I didn't know!*" He crawled across the floor, his eyes squeezed tightly shut, the drooping purple bags underneath them wrinkled and wet with tears. "*I thought it would just be him, I swear it!*"

Roy bolted down the stairs he'd been standing near, then down those that would bring him to the first floor. Once he was there, he rushed over to Percival, his heart slamming against his ribs—*Hard enough to shatter them*, Roy thought distantly—and then wrapped his arms around Percival's chest, dragging himself into the shadow of the ghost.

Inside it, a string of images appeared before him, similar to those generated by Valusvar's premonitory abilities but darker, opaque. The blurry shape of a building—a manor, he realized; the design was similar to Dawnseve Manor's—emerged from the gloom, dressed in skeins of roiling smoke. No, *flames*. He was looking at a house fire, but through the dark, spectral lens of the ghost holding Percival hostage.

"Don't look!" Percival shouted. He attempted to shove Roy away, but Roy held on, banding his arms tighter around Percival. Their heaving breaths shuddered out before them but did not disturb or twist the ghost's humanoid form. Percival thrashed again, trying to pull himself out of Roy's tightening clutch. "Don't look, Roy!"

Panic and helplessness seized Roy. He could feel himself fading, his ideas for a possible escape route rapidly fleeing him. The ghost had to be affecting his mind, too, playing with his memories and fears, his delusions and concerns. But as its influence took hold of him, diminishing logic and reason, he remembered, as though from some great distance but still there nevertheless, *why* this ghost and its kind had rallied their forces, why they had been so drawn to the scholars effectively trapped in the Orphic Basilica with them. He remembered, and it smoothed out the tension in his shoulders, alleviating the secondhand dread he felt for Percival.

"This is all behind you, Percival," Roy whispered. He laid his arm diagonally across Percival's chest, wiped away the sweat from his brow, brushed back the clusters of hair that had fallen over his forehead and into his eyes. Percival shivered in Roy's hold, crying. "This is in the past. It'll still hurt you. It'll still work its way deeper into your mind. It'll steal from you your energy when you most need it. It'll leave you blind sometimes. It'll leave you in the dark." He kissed Percival's forehead, tears welling in his eyes. "But I won't," he vowed. "I won't."

Percival was quiet for a while. Then he whispered, "I failed them, darling." He sobbed. "I failed them. I failed *Owen*."

Owen? Roy thought. *Is this the friend he lost?*

The ghost was still loitering about Percival, captivated by the passion of his grief and the vividity of his recollections, but it kept looking back from him to Roy. Roy had thought these ghosts were benign, that their private histories had given them a comprehensive grasp of the histories of the library's two living inhabitants, but something Walestone had said had slipped by him, a piece of information Roy had thought small and meaningless until now, as Percival fell prey to his grief.

My memories are a frail web. I have roamed too long a path to reflect and remember my end.

Had the same fate befallen the rest of the ghosts? Roy wondered. Had they forgotten who they'd been, the core of their identities, their codes of morality and their ability to feel respect or compassion for humans? Had time done this, diluted—and eventually disintegrated—their spectrum of emotions? Or had the Blight?

"Don't give in to it, Percival," Roy whispered, again kissing Percival's forehead, where underneath, his deepest scar was feeding on him, glutting itself on his sorrow. "Don't give it what it wants."

Percival shook his head, an expression of weary consternation forming across his features. After a moment, though, he curled his fingers around Roy's arm, the one clutching Percival's chest, and slackened, sagging to the ground, letting go of the tension he'd been holding desperately on to. He opened his eyes, and Roy was relieved to see they were clear—lined with tears, yes, but bereft of shadows. The ghost, apparently tired of maintaining its grip on him, soared upward and out of sight, blending into the darkness engendered by its companions.

After a silent while, Percival said, "I've kept you in the dark long enough, darling. I thought that I could run from my past simply because you revealed yours, because I was too horrified to reciprocate."

Roy murmured, "I'm sorry."

Percival sat up, clutching Roy's forearm. "No. This is on me. And you're right; I won't give my pain what it wants. I won't give in." He sighed. "I've been a fool to think for so long that I could."

"I don't want to pressure you," Roy said, "but . . . but the ghosts—"

"I know," Percival said. "They want us to share our burdens and our torments, the things that have weighed on our minds since coming here. Before then. Perhaps it's some . . . cruel perversion of the wind's guidance."

Indeed, some of the ghosts that had amassed around Percival while he had been thrashing helplessly on the ground were drawing back now, as though in slow realization, as though to say, *This is the path, the next stepping stone.*

"Should we go somewhere more comfortable?" Roy asked.

Percival proffered his hand to Roy, who took it. "No, just on the steps here. I don't want to stall another moment."

They sat on the first few risers of the grand staircase, their knees brushing. The ghosts observed expectantly from the shadows.

"Where should I start?" Percival asked, wringing his hands.

Roy hesitated. "Who's Owen?"

An empty, dismal smile touched Percival's lips. "I guess that's as good a place as any. Owen was my partner. He and I met five years ago through one of my correspondents, but I'm sure that's not an unheard-of story. It's how most romances between scholars develop these days, isn't it?" His smile faded. "We were both twenty. I thought I fell in love at first glance, although in hindsight, it was probably that initial phase of enchantment. He . . . Oh, Dawnseve, he was perfect."

Roy waited to feel jealous, or resentful, but there was only this ineffable dread coiled up tight in his stomach.

"We spent every available space of time together," Percival continued, "no matter whether it was two minutes or two hours. I read him poetry, some penned by his favorite poets but most by me, and by the time I was through the third or fourth poem, he would fall asleep in my arms. But I didn't mind. That only gave me the chance to look at him, to commit his face to memory. Somehow, I noticed something new about him whenever I did this. A scar. A birthmark. His freckles. It was like he had a million facets to him, and I was honored to bear witness to them, to keep them, to remember them."

Percival hung his head. "My family never knew about Owen. My brother and sister—Edgar and Louise—could tell something was different about me, but they never addressed the change. My parents were teachers at Rasileus Academy, which is always understaffed, and so they were rarely home to see."

"You didn't trust Edgar or Louise?" Roy asked.

"No, not with that information," Percival said. "I had a . . . difficult, maddening sort of love for those two. They were both zealous Drove sympathizers and would have alerted one of the baton-swinging brutes if they discovered I was trading forbidden texts with Owen, but some part of me couldn't abandon the memories I'd shared with them. Anyway, they never suspected my transgressions, and I thought, imprudently, that I could live in peace with that. But maybe I was wrong. Maybe there *was* some slim possibility—so slim I hadn't seen it at the time, yes, but there nonetheless—that they could have tolerated my scholarship, if they had ever learned of it."

Roy thought of the fire he'd faintly seen through the dark form of the ghost that had accosted Percival. "Did they? Did they find out?"

"Not as far as I know," Percival said. "I was seldom at our family manor, though. I weaved this illusion among my parents and siblings that I'd formed a study group with my classmates at Rasileus Academy, but in truth, Owen had begun introducing me to scholars he'd met through his correspondences. I hadn't realized there were so many of us. Before then, I had only fallen in with a few like-minded academics—those who had survived the Governor's purge—but to think that the survivors numbered in the hundreds was . . . It was inconceivable. In retrospect, I shouldn't have combed so deeply through the network. I was much too curious, and as I reflect on what occurred soon after Owen showed me all of his colleagues, I think it was my curiosity that led me astray."

Percival released a long, steadying breath. "Four months ago, I embarked on a rather arduous research project. I was in desperate search—if only out of personal desire—for a book on the Themelian Spires, a stealthily hidden mountain range near the Timeless Gap. Allegedly, it was there that Tobias Enghall and Nemene Aftford initially devised the concept of the Orphic Basilica."

"The first two Elder Scribes," Roy said, awestruck.

"Indeed," Percival said, his expression crestfallen. "Owen selected his contacts meticulously. He was wary, and not without good reason. Have you ever been to the Western Ranges, Roy?"

Roy slowly shook his head, unsettled by the dismay in Percival's voice. "I've barely seen half of this city, much less anywhere else."

"The Radiant Droves stationed in the Western Ranges take drastically worse measures to unmasking and torturing suspected scholars than those in Northgard," Percival said. "They skin them alive. They whip their exposed wounds. They brand them. They treat them with absolute, unremitting disrespect. I haven't a clue who rules the soldiers over in the Ranges, but from what Owen told me, I bet they'd *sneer* at the Governor's decision to make use of us. Owen was strict about who he kept in contact with for this very reason. Because he'd seen the worst of this world, had lived alongside them, and he could differentiate between a scholar and a spy. *'The differences are easy to spot,'* he told me once, *'so long as you have the eye to spot them.'*

"And I didn't. I was *adamant* on locating that damn book, darling. You know how it is. Once we've set our minds on something, we become relentless in our pursuit, tangled in the chase." Percival kneaded his throat, as though it were hard to speak. "None of Owen's allies knew where the book was, but one—a young woman, new to the network—had heard of an archaeologist who was allegedly planning a trek to the Themelian Spires to do an excavation of the region. Naturally, I told Owen. He'd always admired my dedication. It was one of the things, he'd said plenty of times before then, he loved most about me. But his reaction was . . . Roy, I had never seen him so *mad*. Embittered. He claimed I'd gone insane, that he had fled to this city for a life of obscurity, that I was taking it all away from him, exposing him. I promised him that I would take the necessary precautions to guarantee his protection, to *ensure* his life here was just the beginning."

Percival clenched his teeth, tears slithering down his cheeks. "I was so *stupid*, Roy. So fucking stupid. I should've listened to him. I should've sworn I wouldn't meet anyone outside the inner circle he'd made within the network. I should've realized the new recruit and her companions weren't meant to be trusted, that some of them *were* underhandedly doing the Governor's bidding, but instead, I unwittingly threw my entire inner circle to the wolves."

Roy took Percival's quivering hand in his own. "Percival..."

"There were ten of us," Percival choked out, his cheeks turning red. "Not many, but... but more than I could've ever imagined existing five years ago. By the Scribes, I thought I was alone, but I guess I didn't know what alone felt like until that..." He sobbed. "Until that *fucking* day. One day, darling, and it all went to Hell. I still remember it as vividly as if it happened yesterday. A week after I came back from the Western Ranges, I was leaving a morning lecture at Rasileus Academy, where I still attended classes, mainly to keep up pretenses, when I smelled smoke on the wind. I remember thinking that a second purge had begun, that the Governor had invented some way to permanently root us scholars out. But at least then, I would have gone into the dark with Owen. I wouldn't have had to be alone." He paused. "Darling, do you... do you know the bookmark penalty?"

"I do," Roy said. He remembered seeing it for the first time... and shuddered. That line of frost-coated corpses, opened books nailed haphazardly to their faces.

Percival nodded, his eyes bleary. "I saw the bodies before the fire. The Droves bookmarked them. All nine of them. They spread them out like... like breadcrumbs, leading me to the flames. Owen was at the very end." He cried silently, his shoulders shuddering. "The Governor's agent must have learned about our relationship somehow. Or maybe they'd discovered the truth long ago and were just drawing out the punishment, making sure I never forgot the price of my failure.

"And I never did. I still see those nine bodies every day, every night. But none more so than Owen. I'll never forget how they placed the book beneath his eyes so I could see the fear in them, the *horror*." Percival's voice cracked. "Then—Then I saw the smoke. By the Scribes, I can still smell it, Roy. Burnt, charred flesh."

A silence hung between them, strangely bereft of the moans of passing ghosts.

"They killed my family," Percival whispered. "The Droves rounded them up in Atherton Manor—Edgar, Louise, my parents, and all the butlers and maids—and pointed muskets at their heads while the windows were boarded up. All escape routes blocked. Then the Droves went out through the front doors and boarded those up, too. Everyone inside was banging and pounding on the doors, begging to be spared. '*We didn't do anything,*' they said. '*Our hands are clean. We didn't do anything.*' But the Droves weren't punishing *them*. This was my penalty... but it wasn't over then."

Roy clutched Percival's hand tighter. "How do you know about this? Didn't the fire start before you arrived?"

Somehow, through a great summoning of willpower, Percival wiped away his tears, stopped crying, and said, "The Governor came by a while later. I was hauled into his carriage, and he explained to me, in no uncertain terms, that, if I wanted to continue my studies, if I wanted to insinuate myself deeper into the underground network, that was all well and good. But he knew my name, and I knew what he was capable of. I would only be digging myself and others deeper graves if I didn't hang my head and admit defeat. So I did, and guess where I ended up?"

A cold sliver of understanding went through Roy. Earlier on in their investigation, Percival had indicated some sort of warning he'd been given. *I didn't say that. I'm just saying the deal—or threat, I should say—the Governor and I made is not the same as yours. Moreover, I don't entirely buy the premise.*

"I'm sorry," Percival said. "I'm sorry it took me so damn long to tell you, to gather the strength."

"What have you to apologize for?" Roy said, wrapping his arm around Percival's waist. "There was no rush."

"But there was," Percival said. "I was holding us back, impeding our progress. If I had only just spoken up . . ." He sniffed. "I've seen them around the library, darling. Owen and his compatriots. For a long time, I thought they were hallucinations, that my grief was so fresh and unprocessed that I had conjured them as these shadows. I don't think it was until we saw Walestone in the catacombs that I reckoned with the truth. I've tried my hardest to speak with them, but nothing has ever gotten through. I assumed this was the barrier's doing, but after you told me what Gabriel had done to you, I saw that maybe I ought to do the same."

Roy muttered, "I feel horrible. I've stolen the feelings you had for Owen. I'm using them as my own—"

"By the Scribes, I knew it would come to this," Percival said underneath his breath, as though to himself, and then clasped Roy's cheek in his hand. "Darling, I assure you, I'm still coming to grips with what happened and what it means for you and me, but I *forbid* you from assuming that my feelings for you are untrue. I used to believe those feelings would discount the strength of what I felt for Owen, but I'm not so convinced anymore."

"If you still need time to sort this out in your head, then you don't need my permission for that," Roy said, then kissed Percival's cheek. "But I'm honored you told me this, and I'm sorry if I ever made you feel like you couldn't."

Percival smiled, tears glistening anew in his eyes. "Thank you. That means more than you know."

Roy brushed back an errant curl of Percival's hair. "I know we've been a little distant lately, but let me amend that, Percival. Let me hold you tonight."

Percival drew back, his eyes widening in concern. "Darling, you know I would, but you need your space—"

"Tonight," Roy said, his voice firm with certainty, "I need you."

Percival gently held Roy's chin, then kissed him. And for one blessed moment, Roy sensed something within him deeper than admiration, a mystifying blend of confusion and pride and...

Love? Roy thought. Is that what this is? Is that what Ridell Entuon meant by "our befuddling alchemy of sympathy and empathy, of sounds unheard and surfaces unfelt"? Is that what Lucia Maydew, seconds before dying, foresaw "in the crimson clouds of my reverie"?

Percival rose to his feet, taking Roy by the hand, and up they went to Roy's bedchamber. No ghosts followed them.

25

ROY WOKE UP A FEW HOURS LATER, GROGGY BUT content.

Percival was sleeping beside him, rolled over on his side with one leg draped protectively over Roy's. He snored quietly, his face soft in repose.

A solemn breeze curled around Roy's head, ruffling his sweat-matted hair. It had followed him since Briar's death, that breeze. A silent pursuer. It had caressed the line of his jaw and the breadth of his shoulders. It had danced and frolicked around him as he hunched over ancient texts, Briar's carving standing vigil by his side. He had fumbled, at first, to place his finger on the entity, but now that his fog of grief had cleared—or at least somewhat, Percival's story a somber reminder that he wasn't alone; the young man's body next to his a more hopeful one—Roy remembered that this wind had accompanied him when the Governor had admitted to Briar's and Irene's imminent execution.

Now it wove through Roy's tunic, which clung to his sweaty skin. It wound through his hair, playful and maternal but somehow reluctant, as though afraid to cross some line, to betray his trust.

Roy stiffened at that thought, then glanced fleetingly at Percival, nervous that he might have woken him. There was a suspicion swirling through his head, traipsing at the borders of his mind, but he could do nothing beyond giving it due thought, at least not while he was in Percival's company, asleep or no.

Although I have come to your world from my own, Atticus Walestone had told them when they'd journeyed to the Elder Scribes' burial vault, *others may be hesitant to do so.*

Roy had cleaved to this ominous intelligence, though he'd been uncertain as to why. But if the suspicion that had roused him from his slumber held even a grain of truth, then he had to take this leap in the dark.

Roy rose from his bed, passing a fleeting glance to the two-faced carving on his bedside table, then donned his trousers and boots, watching Percival as he did so. He trod silently out of his room, leaving the door slightly ajar to prevent it from snicking shut or the hinges from creaking. He came to the end of the hallway, steering clear of groaning ghosts, then took a torch from the nearest wall.

He scouted the floorboards to the left of the carpet runner, found what he was looking for, and pressed his foot into the wooden entryway to the underground crypts. Once he had rallied his nerves, he descended into the darkness.

It encased him, consumed him. He went farther and farther down, each step tightening the clamp around his skull.

Fifty steps, seventy steps, a hundred...

He saw faces in the blackness, imprinted on the slick cobblestone walls. They stared at him as he made his way down, bloodshot eyes bulging out of inhumanly wide sockets. They cursed him. They reprimanded him. They spat at him, though when he swiped the back of his hand across the places where he thought the spit had landed, his skin was faintly moist from the damp, but mostly dry.

He could still not yet comprehend the bizarre nature of the library, especially its tunnel network, but he pushed onward, suppressing the unease swirling in the pit of his stomach. He endured it. For Briar, he persevered. His denial had brought him in here. Now his acceptance would bring him out.

When he arrived at the catacombs, Roy held the torch aloft. Firelight flickered across the rounded walls, dappling the coffins of the Protectorate with a rosy glow.

A peculiar sense of confidence came over Roy. He was unsure whether it was the sight of the sarcophagi and the bodies of his idols within them or the reminder of what existed under the Orphic Basilica, but he felt like he belonged here. Had this been a test, engineered by the elemental entity that had been shadowing him over the past week or so? He didn't know, but what had risen him from bed, and out of his grief, recurred to him now. And instantly, he felt restored.

"Hear me!" Roy called out. He raised the torch, his heart pounding against his ribs. "Hear me, I said! Hear me! I will the dead to hear my summons!"

Cold air and mist swished about his feet. The crypt remained silent but for the dwindling echoes of his voice.

Again, Roy screamed, "I will the dead to hear my summons!" He thrust the torch out, and the flame swayed back, then hovered upright. "Come forth! Come to the light!"

Whispers sounded from afar; they were formless, unintelligible voices, hissing like the sigh of wind through bare branches. They seemed to come from a place deeper than the crypt. Roy thought of a severed bond, the link between the library and the supernatural world from which the ghosts had come. Perhaps if he put them under pressure and brought them to the surface of *this* world, he could give them shape, but there was only one spirit with whom he wished to commune.

"Hear me, for I will not break this vow!" Roy exclaimed. "I promise to take your pain! I will bear your agony! I just ask of you . . . May I see her?"

As if in confusion, the voices quieted, then disappeared.

Roy choked on a sob, tears obscuring his vision, but the breeze brushed them away, bestowing upon him a newfound sense of clarity.

Unseen spectral heads seemed to lift in recognition of his torment. Roy could feel their unrest, like a sailor reading patterns in the sky: a black storm of agony, trepidation, terror, and fragmented empathy.

"You know this pain!" Roy screamed. "You know it! You've carried it for years or centuries or longer, how long I do not know, but I cannot *stand* it!" His hand shook, and the torch in his grasp flung crooked shadows across the coffins. "I don't know how to live, how to move on!"

Voices rose from beneath him, ascending in pitch and volume, until he was surrounded by a whirling pillar of the dead. A din of shrieks, howls, and wails spoke of their misery, of their thousands of lives eradicated by tragedy and heartache. They pulled and tugged at Roy's heartstrings, pouring their anguish into his own.

"*Please!*" Roy shouted. "How do I move on? *Why* should I move on? There is no point to this life if the end is just silence—"

Something shifted behind him, disturbing the stale air at his back. Sweat beaded on his palms, prickling his skin. He turned on his heel, his breathing rapid and coarse, and then pushed the torch out before him, squinting to discern the newcomer.

A ghost lingered at the yawning mouth of the tunnel, its blazing ruby eyes contrasting sharply with the orange torchlight. By this dual illumination, Roy discerned the slightest of features, the barest indication of its humanoid structure: the crook of an armpit, the line of a jaw.

It was Walestone.

I may not be whom you seek, Walestone said, *though I offer you my condolences for your loss.* His sibilant voice meandered around the chamber and rebounded off the stone walls and the wooden coffins.

"Bring her back," Roy demanded, his voice dry and cracking. "Bring her back to me, not as an Old One, not Blighted, but as the sister I know. I will the dead to heed my directives."

Walestone shook his head, slowly and with great solemnity. *Even if I could exercise such powers, that sort of sorcery has been forbidden for thousands of years and was only recently discovered to be impossible. The repercussions are ... troubling.*

"Resurrection. It was once accessible, then. It was once used to breathe life back into the dead, to restore not just the animus"—he was thinking of the Blighted as he queried this—"but the actual humanity within them?"

You misheard me. You think without regard for consequences. Given the state you are in, I do not condemn you for this lack of judgment, and so I warn you again: These powers have, over time, been rendered inoperable.

"Would you return if you could?" Roy asked. "To the world of the living?"

Walestone drifted around the sarcophagi of the Elder Scribes, his amorphous, fuzzy hands clasped delicately over his middle, then answered contemplatively, *How many years or eons I have walked among the dead, I know not. My soul is immersed so deeply in the world I now inhabit that if I were to march through the gates of reality, I would not even vaguely resemble who I had once been.*

Roy contemplated this. "You're saying the soul of a person undergoes some ... some *change* in the interim between death and whatever comes after?"

In many ways, yes, Walestone confirmed. *Humans are brimming with contradictions. Your kind dread the end and what it comprises, but you also long to be rid of the anxiety, the anticipation, to bear witness to the other side of the horizon. Similarly, when a soul passes into the afterlife, there is resistance. Some cling to reality tighter than others, to linger, to say one last farewell, but all, in the end, come to a state of acceptance. A place of weightlessness. A period of blessed absence.*

"And that is where her soul resides?" Roy asked, hope rising inside him. "A neutral zone? A sanctuary?"

Walestone recoiled. *Your... your sister.*

Roy swallowed at Walestone's unexpected reaction. "I tried to summon her, but you came to my aid instead. Could you not find her? Was she not in this purgatory that you've mentioned?"

Walestone held up a hand. *You do not quite understand.*

"There is a barrier," Roy said, unease moving through him, along with an eerie, murky premonition. "A wall of some sort, dividing the ghosts confined within the Orphic Basilica from your world. Is my sister suspended in that barrier? Is she stuck?" He had a possibly mad urge to scream for Briar, to cast her down from her prison, to anchor her back to Northgard, but he stilled himself. "Why did you come to me?" he asked. He sounded childish, although he was running out of options, out of patience. "Why are *you* here, and not her?"

I cannot bring your sister back, Roy, Walestone said in an apologetic tone. *I sincerely wish that I could, but even if it were possible, the repercussions of resurrection are perilous and irrevocable. The Old Ones would seem a minor obstacle compared to the danger that would emerge from such a spell.* He paused. *But I can show you how to free Briar Dawnseve from purgatory. Your sister could have peace, Roy.* A hint of sadness came into his voice, but Roy couldn't puzzle out why.

Then a troubling notion stole into his mind. "She might be

erased from existence completely, right?" he asked. "Her peace might not come in the form of an afterlife, but rather no life at all."

That is a risk you will have to consider, yes, Walestone affirmed, then, with surprising diffidence, he asked, *Would you like to see how it can be done, Roy? Would you like to see how to release the ghosts?*

Roy didn't need as long as he would've thought he might to come up with an answer. He'd heard the ghosts' anguished screams, their despairing cries and pleas, and he couldn't bear the thought of Briar—his polite, sweet-hearted sister—enduring such agony. She'd already gone through unimaginable distress, having been harassed by Gregori, a Blighted Drove, and then executed for the Governor's entertainment. Roy couldn't fathom the world of pain she would be in if she continued living out her days trapped in purgatory.

"I would," Roy said to Walestone. "Show me."

Walestone nodded. *Steel yourself, mortal. This may cause you some discomfort.*

Not a second after Walestone spoke did a crackling bolt of darkness erupt out of his hand, split into two tenebrous prongs, and puncture Roy's chest.

Roy keeled over, grasping at his chest. He was filled with pain, like a thousand rivers of flame were chasing through his veins. He clawed at his heart. He tried to rip through his tunic and wrench the dark bolt of energy out through brute force. He tried to scream it out, to expel the magic with sheer defiance, but it had already wound its way inside him, coiling in his gut like a serpent.

He crumpled to his knees, and the pain came again, slamming into the back of his skull with a sickening crack. He doubled forward, on all fours now. A viscous rope of bile hung from his agape mouth, swinging. He went to wipe it away, then tumbled face first to the ground.

A gossamer veil of darkness closed in over his vision, and in Roy's mind, Walestone said, *I will see you shortly, Roy Dawnseve. I cannot do this without you.*

THE ORPHIC BASILICA
TWO THOUSAND YEARS AGO

ATTICUS WALESTONE HAD NOT SEEN DAYLIGHT IN two months. After his recent breakthrough with purgatory, he suspected it might be another two before he saw it again.

He stood over the untidy but calculatedly placed clutter of unrolled scrolls, documents, sketches—some of which were discarded ideas for a future collection of short philosophical essays by his pseudonym, Razkamun—and stacks upon stacks of books before him. Then he leaned against his desk, his hands thrust into the inner pockets of his voluminous brown robe, and deliberated.

Either by some divine stroke of fate or simply by a long period of isolation and concentration, Atticus had finally, albeit temporarily, made contact with a ghost trapped in purgatory.

And he'd only had to rip open the sutured wounds of his past to do it.

Well, that was not strictly true. He had first been met by the initially daunting task of looking through the oldest, most esoteric books within the Orphic Basilica for theories and reported sightings of thanatological energy. That had taken the better half of his first month cooped up in his office.

Then, he'd painstakingly interviewed select members of the Protectorate, who would be charged with the responsibility of trekking across Northgard, some even voyaging beyond the Hasdan Isles, in pursuit of the places Atticus had excavated throughout his indefatigable investigation. The Protectorate had originally protested Atticus's decision, claiming that they were librarians, not globe-trotters. Although after a brief but impassioned meeting, Atticus had convinced them of the prospective expedition's contribution to his studies.

"And if you ever doubt the mission ahead of you," he had told them during the meeting, "remind yourselves of what we're fighting against, but most importantly, what we're fighting *for*."

The Protectorate had collectively bristled at the implicit mention of the enemy, but they remained steadfast. They would not be cowed by the unknown. Every question had its answer. Every problem had its solution.

Atticus repeated this counsel to himself, whispering it under his breath.

"Master Walestone."

Atticus started, barely catching himself from scraping his boots across the documents directly in front of him. He placed a hand over his thundering heart, then looked up at the doorway. "Gods Above, Maude. You gave me a fright." He stilled, unnerved by the dismay on her typically cheerful face. His stomach twisted. "*No—*"

"They're here, Master Walestone," Maude said. "Mistress Aftford spotted them first, cresting the western foothills. We have ten minutes."

Atticus's heart sank for Nemene, his fellow Scribe and his old friend. She had been plagued by nightmares of the enemy for years now. He couldn't fathom how she must be faring.

A sudden sense of urgency, a need for action, seized him.

Atticus pushed himself off his desk and trod over his meticulously laid out research, strangely indifferent toward the damage left in his wake. Then he walked to the cabinet on his left, opened it, and pulled down Holyborn, one of the three black-scabbarded swords mounted within. His expedition teams had unearthed the other two, Valusvar and Kharuan. Atticus then closed the cabinet and strode toward the door.

Maude stared with openmouthed astonishment. He'd gotten a good read on his only student throughout the years he'd been teaching her. She admired his mindfulness and calm attentiveness as much as how unwaveringly he cleaved to the ancient code of nonviolence. And while she'd known these unduly powerful weapons existed, it was common knowledge that they'd always been a last resort.

We academics are dauntless in the face of every battle, Atticus's own tutor, the retired Tarnan Eldreave, had once told him. *Every battle, that is, except for the one which is fought with fists and swords.*

Until now.

Atticus placed a trembling hand on the doorknob, his entire body numb with dread. He had already expected, from the moment Maude had informed him of the enemy's arrival, that the sight beyond his office would break him. But nothing could have possibly prepared him for what he next saw.

Ten years ago, when he had been instated as an Elder Scribe, Atticus had specifically selected an office on the seventh floor, having taken a liking to its collection throughout his apprenticeship with Master Eldreave. There was something intimate, something heartening, about the topmost archive. The zenith of the arts. The summit of all knowledge.

But as he looked down from the balcony outside his office now, Atticus could not help but wince at the young, naive man he'd once been. Great heights did not mean great wisdom. All it meant was you had a better view of the madness beneath your feet.

Brilliant streaks of sunshine spilled through the skylight, flooding the Orphic Basilica in an ethereal, incandescent glow. But that only made the pandemonium unfolding below all the more evident. Scholars, professors, and librarians hastened toward the nearest reading rooms and study nooks, either scampering for safety or ascending from one floor and up to the next, borne aloft on glimmering alchemical runes pried from the pages of mystics' spellbooks and forbidden grimoires. Tourists scurried aimlessly through the commotion, their tear-laced eyes darting back and forth with confused trepidation. Two men sprinted toward the stairs leading down to the second floor, one of them clinging to the other and the second carrying their son in the crook of his arm.

A pair of airborne scholars, whom Atticus recognized as Nemene's apprentices, floated toward the skylight, casting intermittent runes at their feet to propel their ascension. Once the two made it to the base of the skylight, they peered through the window, scuttling around the edges, until one of them flung out their arm and pointed to the west. The other drifted over to their companion, their face paling with fear.

Maude came to stand beside Atticus, and after a moment, she whispered, "This is it, isn't it?"

He wanted so badly to give her hope, to assuage the worries no doubt gnawing at her mind. But what could he say? Maude was no stranger to the nature of academia. They were, or had at least sworn among themselves to be, the peacekeepers of the realm. They were not to fight, not to swing swords and spill blood.

But none of them had been oblivious to the doom marching their way. They had heard whispers of the red-eyed, black-armored devils long ago, but it had only been once Atticus's chosen candidates had returned from their research expedition, bearing portentous reports of the enemy's whereabouts, that the academic community had begun to feel true fear, to count down their precious few days.

Before the Reaper could bring down its scythe, though, Atticus had work to do.

"Yes, this is the end," Atticus said, then clapped a hand down onto Maude's shoulder, the other clutching Holyborn. "I have heard stories of these creatures, Maude. Patiny even warned me in this damn poem he wrote, and yet I dismissed it as folly. Their gaze incites madness. It lingers like a sickness, like a disease."

Maude cried, tracks of gleaming tears swiveling down her cheeks. "Master Walestone, what—"

"I know I have been reticent throughout your apprenticeship, though I promise you, child, this was not without reason." Atticus spoke with haste, his heart thundering. "I vowed to keep secret what Eldreave passed on to me, and so I shall, but there is one thing I ask of you. One duty. It will be the hardest thing you will ever do. But do it, and our kind might yet be saved, our knowledge conserved."

"What is it?" Maude asked, a quaver in her voice.

Atticus looked her hard in the eyes. "I want you to find as many scholars as you can, Maude, and then I want you to *run*. Run as fast and far as you can. I need the Protectorate and a few other scholars here to fulfill the obligation I was given, but the rest of you . . ." He held back tears. "Once the Protectorate has engaged the shield, and once I've opened the doors to the catacombs, run straight out the front doors. Lay low and take shelter until the day is done, however it plays out. Make art—books and poems, paintings and sculptures. Our history mustn't fade. If we fall today, all will be lost. Thousands of years of painstakingly acquired information, gone. I will not, *cannot*, see that transpire."

Maude stared at Atticus with a petrifying intensity. She stood stock-still with fear, as if rooted in place by the magnitude of the task set before her.

"Please, Maude," Atticus implored. "If I could have asked you sooner, I would have, but I have sworn my promise. And now the day has come."

It took some moments for Maude to recompose herself, but when she did, she nodded with an eerily calm confidence.

No, Atticus reflected, *that is not confidence. That's resignation.*

She had known, for years now, the potential price of admittance within the Orphic Basilica. She had likely faced the same, or similar, abuse as that which Atticus had battled for most of his life. He hadn't been privy to the details of his only student's history and background, for he believed such a breach of privacy to be a transgression of the highest order, a trespassing of the boundary between the domestic and academic roads of life.

But now, as they stood within the shadow of the apocalypse, regret swirled in his stomach. He should have talked to her. He should have made a conscious effort, or *pretended*, at the very least, to sympathize with her suffering, to show her that he was as much her friend as he was her professor.

So many mistakes made, and yet, so little time to make amends.

"All right, Master Walestone," Maude said, swallowing. "You can lay your faith in me."

"Thank you, child. Now go," Atticus said with insistent

demand, pressing Maude lightly between her shoulders. "*Go*, Maude, and farewell. If all goes right, we shall meet again."

Then Atticus stepped up onto the balcony railing, Holyborn in hand, and vaulted off. He closed his eyes briefly, relishing the sensation of weightlessness, of gravity challenged, and opened them. He drew in a deep breath, willing the magic stirring dormant within his veins to surface.

Calligraphic runes spiraled out of his fingertips, summoned from the indexes of memorized grimoires. A sheen of prismatic light momentarily encircled his body and then dissipated. He brought his hands down to his sides, redirecting his trajectory, and as the runes obediently followed the movement, he made his descent.

Atticus landed on the first floor.

The scholars running amok around him hastily retreated, then, recognizing who had joined the turmoil, drifted back into Atticus's orbit as if entranced. He knew he could not save them, despite the efforts he would soon make to preserve their blessed sanctuary, but he seared into his memory the tentative hope shining through the masks of grave certainty set over their faces.

"Master Walestone!" they cried. "Master Walestone!"

Atticus recoiled, his knees threatening to buckle at the relief in their voices. Frantically, he dispelled the levitation rune and supplanted it with an amplification rune. He shouted, "To me, Protectorate! To me!"

Perhaps thirty paces ahead, the looming double doors to the Orphic Basilica boomed and rattled, straining at their hinges. A glint of sunlight peeked through, then vanished like a torch snuffed out by wicked winds.

"To me, Protectorate!" he shouted again, raising his voice over the commotion. "To me, to me!"

He made the summons again and again until, at last, ten or fifteen archivists dressed in flowing white robes shouldered through the throng and then stood before Atticus, their chests puffed out in feigned defiance. They were playing at soldiers, Atticus thought, the last duty any one of them had ever believed they would take up.

This damned city has ruined us. And they had no more time to appraise their losses, no more chances to rebuild themselves into the civilization they'd been striving day after day to become . . . but for this.

"Raise the barricade!" Atticus ordered.

As one, the gathered members of the Protectorate turned on their heels and assembled themselves into a rectangular formation, mirroring the structure of the double doors. Scholars gave them a wide berth, shuffling from foot to foot, and then rocked back as the Protectorate uttered a sequence of convoluted incantations and lunged forth, thrusting their upraised palms toward the doors.

A horizontal, milky shield of protection sputtered into existence, raining sparks down on the Protectorate. They gritted their teeth, laboring beneath the accumulation of invoked runes, then shoved the shield forward. It sprang ahead, although before it could coat the entrance and lock into place, the doors burst inward with a resonant crack.

Atticus turned and ran. But he couldn't stop himself from looking over his shoulder.

The enemy streamed through, their eyes red as murder and their boots black as sin. They seized scholars by the backs of their necks and shattered their skulls with black-gauntleted fists. They pursued those who had fallen, then brought their boots down on their backs, splintering their spines into bloody shards. They wrestled children out of their mothers' and fathers' arms so they could watch as they dashed their skulls across the walls.

One of the soldiers stilled above the corpse of a boy it had slain, then abruptly lifted its head. Its shoulders rose and fell with increasing regularity. Steam furled out from the narrow slits over its nostrils.

Can it smell something? Atticus thought, his mind racing for an explanation. He seethed. He wanted to scream at the frustrating shortage of information he had on these unfathomable beings. He should have dedicated more time to the coming evil instead of to the evolving design of purgatory and the cosmos. Eldreave had always reprimanded him for his dreaminess.

There's nothing to do about it now, I suppose.

No, he could still take initiative. He could still honor his master, and salvage the prized possession of his people, in one fell swoop. He had his doubts, of course. This endeavor could very likely be the undoing of intellectualism. It could reverse, and consequently erase, every thesis written and every poem drafted. It could topple the foundations of scholarship once and for all.

But as bleak as these recent days had become, Atticus was an optimist. He had endured years of adversity and prejudice, had survived his uncle's fists and his aunt's repulsed scowls, had crawled from the trenches of Hell and ended up in the arms of his parents, who'd finally, after casting him out on the streets, accepted him for what he loved. Even through those dark, unforgiving tunnels, even now, he could see the light.

Atticus snapped back to attention. "The catacombs!" he roared. He raced to the left, where inserted in the redwood floorboards was the slightly declined platform which, when activated, opened a passageway to the subterranean level of the Orphic Basilica. He had used it on few occasions, mostly to appraise the tombs of long-departed academics—constructed from earth and crumbled cobblestone by the nameless wind drifting about the library—but he'd never thought he would have to employ it in an invasion. "Get to the catacombs! Go! *Go!*"

Much of the crowd had scattered, either pursued or slaughtered by the enemy soldiers, but those who heard Atticus's command frantically obeyed. As the platform rippled outward, revealing a cobblestone stairway leading into an impenetrably dark abyss, the scholars who had heard the cry poured in.

Hundreds upon hundreds of scholars hurried into the darkness. A little way down, someone summoned a ball of flame. It rose and dipped, setting a burnished orange hue across the sea of churning bodies jostling past one another in the narrow enclosure.

As the scholars fled into the darkness, Atticus cast about, his concern for Maude morphing into panic. Gods Above, had she fallen? Had the red-eyed devils crushed her spine, too, mutilated her as they were now doing to hundreds of others? Had—

Then he saw her. She was ushering a throng of scholars—some of whom he recognized as friends he'd glimpsed her researching alongside over the years—out of the Basilica's front doors. They'd covertly slipped around the western border of the shield of protection, which was deteriorating with speed under the enemy's bludgeoning blows.

Just beyond the shield, Maude raised a hand to Atticus, tears welling in her eyes. He returned the gesture, his smile quivering. Then she rushed out of the Orphic Basilica, and by the way events were unfolding, he had a feeling it would be the last he saw of her, though he hoped it were not so.

Atticus stood at the entrance to the catacombs, contemplating, mulling over the past. Even after receiving intelligence reports of the enemy's location, he had not allowed himself a moment to do this, to reflect on his scholastic accomplishments, to ruminate on the allies he'd made and the rivals he'd agitated. He had been grounded in the present, locked in his office, too stubborn to look up and watch as the world shifted on its axis, catapulted from an age of enlightenment into an age of materialism.

Had he had the chance, though, he would not change a thing. He had torn up the roots of existence and unearthed the secrets buried thereunder. A world hidden in their own, inhabited by the souls of the departed. A gateway within the subconscious, obscured from view by a fog of pain and torment.

And what if Eldreave's grand plan does not work? a cynical voice sneered in his mind. *What if you were wrong? What if, in doing this, you're erasing from history the archives you and your people, your friends, vowed to protect?*

I am strong, I am resilient, Atticus told the pessimistic voice that had been taunting him since Eldreave had passed the duty down. *I will persevere.*

The voice laughed at him. *You are weak, and the people you lead doubly so. Your supporters can barely secure a rudimentary protection rune. What has you so convinced that you will succeed?*

That gave Atticus pause. In truth, he was not completely persuaded that Eldreave's plan *would* work. For one thing, it hadn't been done before. For another, it was, at best, a slapdash escape route, a dull-witted soldier's getaway. But he was no soldier, and neither was his Protectorate. He hadn't expected their flimsy protection rune to impede the enemy. He was honestly surprised their combined spellwork had manifested into some semblance of fortification, however ineffective it had been. He hadn't needed them to *stop* the enemy.

He had just needed to buy more time, to get as many scholars as possible—no matter their proficiency in magic—into the catacombs.

Atticus grasped the nearest Protectorate member by the shoulder. "Don't let anyone follow me down there," he hastily ordered the woman. "I don't care for their rank, their name, their age. If even one of these red-eyed bastards slips in—"

The woman offered him a curt nod. "Understood." She turned her back on him and then yelled out the command she'd been given to her affiliates, who, without question, fanned out around the stairway and pressed inward.

An awful mix of terror and finality settled like lead in Atticus's stomach. He could not regret his choices now. He could not dither, could not back down or bow. He could only see to the end of his promise, even if it meant not living to witness the fallout.

Squaring his shoulders against the cries of grief sounding from behind the Protectorate's barricade, Atticus hurried down the stairway. He felt the grinding of old stone under his feet, heard a dry and hoarse breeze whistle about him. Then the floorboards that had once concealed the entryway again rippled closed, enveloping him in a darkness thicker than any he had ever known.

The blackness was suffocating, stifling. He stumbled down the first few stairs clumsily with his hands stretched out on either side, only for the walls to disappear and then reappear with wearisome irregularity. He envied the fire-wielding scholar he'd seen moments before. Historians had compiled theories as to why some mystics were more attuned to the elements than others, some claiming that it was a product of their birthplace or lineage, but none had found an answer.

Atticus shoved aside that mystery. It only reminded him of the hundred, the *thousand*, others he hadn't the time to unravel. Why could he levitate on runes but not manipulate the wind? What other mystical shortcuts could have he created? What did the enemy want? Why had they come for the Orphic Basilica?

The question was irrelevant. They had breached sacred grounds. They had made possible the eradication of millions of books, the expurgation of uncounted years of knowledge passed down from smooth and calloused hands alike and by word of mouth. They had launched upon the scholars first, though, not the books. And although Atticus knew it was immoral of him to think it, he could not quell the relief that swelled within him at the thought of those people as the intended target.

Hate me, scorn me, Atticus thought at them, the dying and the dead, *but without books, without stories, we will be stranded, forgotten in a world unknown.* He was comforted by the reminder that, at least, Maude was following through on her promise to keep the heart of the academic community beating.

After what seemed like hours of hurtling down the stairs, puzzled by the dizzying configuration of the library's subterranean tunnel network, Atticus spotted the scholars at the foot of the staircase, beyond which stretched a corridor built of ancient but well-preserved cobblestone. He counted the throng at perhaps two or three hundred people, excluding some stragglers jammed into the narrow exit of the corridor at the back. It was not an impressive number by any means, certainly not enough to prevent a siege, but Atticus was relying as much on numbers as on the durability of the glamour rune that would be imbued into the catacombs... and, of course, Holyborn.

Atticus remembered his terror when, during the second year of his apprenticeship, Master Eldreave had let him in on the secret of the sword's abilities. Atticus had nearly sprinted out of Eldreave's office and told his friends, but Eldreave had clutched his arms, holding Atticus in place.

"Master," Atticus had whimpered, a hot dagger of pain slicing up his arms. "You're hurting me."

Eldreave lowered his brows. "Speak a word of this to anyone, and I will permanently revoke your right to study here. I will send you and your family on a carriage and out of this city, off this continent, until you have drawn your last breath. I will make your life a living Hell, and I assure you, Atticus Walestone, I am a man bound to his promises." He tightened his grip. "This one specifically."

Once Eldreave at last let go, Atticus staggered away, rubbing the feeling back into his arms. "Why are you telling me this, then? If you cannot trust me with something as big, as . . . *important*, as this, then why—"

"I am not imparting this information out of trust," Eldreave interjected. He sounded offended, as if astounded that Atticus had even suggested his possible reliability. "This is a matter of obligation. Our field of work is purely confidential—student and professor, tutor and scholar—as decreed by the greats of thanatology, dating as far back as Edmond Azren, the first to brave purgatory."

Atticus frowned, puzzled. That was the first time he'd heard of purgatory.

"Don't fret about that, though. You won't be learning psychothanatological immersion for a little while yet," Eldreave said, then returned to the topic at hand. "I am telling you this, Walestone, because I want you to be prepared."

"For what?" Atticus asked, swallowing the knot in his throat. "What are you asking me to do?"

Eldreave opened a drawer in his desk, then riffled through the disarrayed books and documents inside and procured a sheet of parchment. He snapped the drawer shut. "Oh, this isn't a request, child. I am giving you a directive." He ran a hand over the parchment and slid it across the desk.

Atticus had picked up the sheet of parchment, turned it around, and held it out for his own inspection. Scrawled across the parchment in swooping penmanship had been a rune about half the size of Atticus's hand—an incredibly complicated design, sketched with unfathomable precision.

He had come across hundreds of runes throughout his apprenticeship. He'd learned that any mystic could draw and invoke a rune but that only elemental mystics could summon their core magic, as these were inborn, rather than granted from runes.

But the rune before him ... He hadn't been able to repress the shudder of bone-rattling fear that came over him. The longer he'd looked at it, the less sense he'd made of it. It almost seemed alien, profane.

"When the time comes," Eldreave said, "when evil draws near, you will invoke the glamour rune, and in doing so, fortify the Orphic Basilica. You will require hundreds of our students for this invocation." He stood, then walked toward the cabinet on his left and opened it. Mounted on the back was a black-scabbarded sword. He nodded to it, then closed the cabinet. "That is Holyborn, a sword of unmatched power. Though its origins are unknown, my colleagues and I have unsheathed it several times, and in each instance, we briefly saw purgatory."

"And you want me to ... wield Holyborn?"

"When the time presents itself," Eldreave had repeated, then elaborated, "Unsheathe the sword, grasp the hilt, and then drive the blade into the ground at your feet. The doors to purgatory will open and, thereupon, free the ghosts within."

"Has this been done before?"

"No," Eldreave had said, "and let us hope it remains that way."

Atticus snapped back to the present, pulling himself from his memories.

If not for Eldreave, Atticus would have spent his entire life ignorant. He would have combed deeper into the lore of purgatory, yes, but he never would have imagined that a microcosm of the spirit realm had been festering in the Orphic Basilica all along, suspended for millennia and, if not for the sword's unspeakable abilities, inaccessible. And he most definitely would not have known of the caretakers preceding him, for they had moved on, not into purgatory, where they would be forever tormented by the misery and madness inflicted upon them by the red-eyed devils ... but into the Above.

Atticus looked out over the crowd of scholars staring at him expectantly. *Is that where they think I'm taking them? To paradise?* he thought. *I'm sorry to disappoint you, my friends, but the only way out of this madness is long and hot and paved with bones.*

He closed his eyes and called into his mind the glamour rune, that convoluted symbol he'd had memorized since Eldreave showed him all those years ago. Then he sketched it into the stale, noxious air before him, cupped his hand over it, and pressed it into the cobblestone wall.

The rune glowed a brilliant cerulean, pulsing like the heartbeat of some mythic sea creature. Atticus recoiled instinctively from the glaring blue light. It flared brighter, as though in response to his reaction, and sent a wave of azure illumination across the perplexed crowd behind him.

See past the source, the memory of Eldreave's voice came into his mind. *See the result, the potential.*

Atticus drew in a deep breath, suppressing the violent urge to cough out the dust that seemed to have gotten caught in his lungs, and thrust Holyborn—still scabbarded—through the loop in his belt. Then he planted his hands on the glamour rune, spreading one hand to the left and the other to the right, extending the range of the rune inch by inch until it spanned the entire wall.

He suddenly doubled over, clutching his knees, struck by a tremendous surge of nausea and fatigue. His mind was foggy.

His vision was swimming. He saw two, and gradually three, of the runelight-coated wall. The ground was shaking beneath his feet. Had the sheer force of the rune ripped out chunks of stone from underneath him? But it was a *glamour* rune, Atticus thought. Not a—

"They're coming down the stairs!"

The scream cut through the cloud of panic that had immobilized the crowd, and a frenzy of movement broke out. Scholars shoved and elbowed past one another, determined to get to the corridor at the back of the chamber. Beams of sinister crimson light issued from Atticus's left, glancing across the walls, accompanied by the sound of metal-plated boots grinding and crashing against stone.

"*Halt!*" Atticus bellowed.

The order boomed through the tunnel network. Dust and stone tumbled down from the ceiling, raining upon those who either had yet to flee the chamber or had decided to stay and heed Atticus's instructions. The departed scholars returned, coming to their senses, realizing that there was no use running from the man who'd initiated their retreat to begin with.

Once silence had fallen over the crowd, Atticus said, in the sharpest, sternest tone that he could manage, "Do as I say, and the research you've done, the projects you've worked on, and the books you've read will not amount to nothing. Do as I say, and the future of our society—and thus all of humanity—may yet live on."

Atticus was not certain whether it was because he had convinced the masses, or because they simply wanted something to do with themselves before they died, but the scholars rallied to his cause, drawing up to the rune fixed onto the wall.

He darted a quick glance over his shoulder. He hadn't estimated how long it had taken him to reach this chamber, but he was hoping at least half an hour.

He hurried down the line of scholars, advising them on the conformation of the glamour rune, the exact length of its whorls and curves, the thickness of the singular straight line that carved through the middle. Some of their initial attempts were clumsy, though those who had already sketched the rune counseled them, gesturing at the places that required improvement. The shorter scholars wiggled between the taller, who shuffled aside to make room, and then copied their neighbors.

Atticus went back to his own position, then gave the command. *"Push!"*

The scholars obeyed. They shoved forward, embedding each of their glamour runes into the wall. The blue light intensified, merging with the glow of Atticus's rune, just as dazzling as moments before.

He drew another, then piled it atop the last, enhancing it. A horrendously potent burst of energy coursed up his arms, thrumming through his muscles. He could nearly *feel* the power of the runes cast long before his time, even centuries before Eldreave's, tracing the course of history all the way back to Edmond Azren.

No, Atticus could not just feel their magic, the rune taught to them by their professors, but the souls of the ghosts themselves. They thrashed and flailed at the barriers of his mind. They wept. They screamed. They recounted the chronicles of their disquiet. They told Atticus again and again, until he thought their voices might bleed into his skull and drive him insane, the torture they had faced, the agony they had seen throughout the thousands upon thousands of years they'd been entombed.

He drew back, satisfied with the added force of the rune.

Recalling Eldreave's instructions, Atticus unsheathed Holyborn, which was humming shrilly in his ears, and was promptly assailed by a destructive wave of power. He hefted the sword in his hands, grimacing at the weight. Around him, scholars screamed, recoiling from Holyborn, their eyes rolling into the backs of their heads. A young man crumpled to his knees and wailed, clutching the sides of his head. Blood gushed out of his nostrils.

Unsheathe the sword, grasp the hilt, and then drive the blade into the ground at your feet. The doors to purgatory will open and, thereupon, free the ghosts within.

Atticus wrapped his hands around the hilt, his knuckles whitening and his face alight with silver radiance. He slammed the blade down through the stone before him. When it met resistance, he held Holyborn high, groaning, and swung down once more. Nothing happened for a few moments.

Then reality dissolved around him. Holyborn evaporated, turning into black and silver flakes of ash that spiraled into the air. The scholars—those who'd managed to find room at the walls to invoke the glamour rune—disappeared.

Faintly, Atticus made out a tenebrous maelstrom of creatures, of *ghosts*, whirling out of the catacomb walls. They flooded through the chamber glowing with runelight, then through the arteries of the tunnel network. A roaring, shrieking amalgam of shadow and flaring ruby eyes. They nipped at the heels of the black-armored soldiers. They whipped around them and raked their dark, nebulous nails down their great gauntlets. Some of the ghosts were crushed against the walls, as though by crossing between one world and the next, they'd gained some degree of corporeality. But most of them rampaged through the soldiers, who started to turn heel, absconding.

Meanwhile, the world continued to dissolve.

Why aren't we out? Atticus thought.

A landscape materialized around him. Ten fortresses made of glimmering white stone, their dim peaks disappearing into the hazy sky above. And a river of molten lava.

The ghosts that had once been drowning in the river were gone, released from purgatory by Holyborn... but the scholars of the Orphic Basilica, Atticus included, had not returned to the material world.

Through some rapidly diminishing connection to reality, Atticus felt Holyborn shatter in his hands. A sound, as of crackling metal, came from afar.

Then the gates to reality slammed closed.

27

ROY WAS THROWN OUT OF THE VISION—*THE MEMORY*, he reflected with astoundment and disorientation—and tottered backward, as though he had been shoved in the chest by a pair of phantom hands.

He couldn't explain how, but when he'd been inside that memory, he had sensed and felt the world around him as crisply as he could now. He had seen *through* Walestone's eyes and experienced with surreal clarity the unrestrained magic of the Orphic Basilica, the urgency of the ancient scholars' retreat . . . and the revelation of the Elder Scribes' sorcery.

Roy blanched. For all he knew, Walestone could be lying, could have woven an illusion within his mind. But what purpose would lying serve?

No, Roy had to face the facts. His idols hadn't only been scholars, shoulders hunched from the arduous, though rewarding, burden of their studies. The Elder Scribes had been an order of mystics bearing a repository of arcane knowledge. They had chosen to use their abilities for these academic pursuits rather than the encroaching advent of continual warfare, and with that one goal in mind—to unravel the well-buried secrets of history—they had fallen, brought to their knees by the Old Ones and Walestone's failed mission.

Roy lifted his gaze now to Walestone, who still had a humanoid quality about his appearance—all but for his nebulous, shadowy form and glistening red eyes. "But you didn't fail, did you?" Roy said. "You just didn't know Holyborn alone wouldn't open the doors, free the ghosts, *and* let you back out because it hadn't been *done* before. Eldreave wasn't aware of this, either, nor were any of the caretakers preceding him."

Although Walestone bore no facial features with which to make an expression, in the ghost's brief silence, Roy could somehow pick up on a sense of melancholy. *The answer was right beneath our noses*, Walestone said. *I had cached in my study two swords of Holyborn's like, as you saw. Gods Above, I was a fool. A disgrace to my honorable, esteemed people. If only I'd known—*

"But you didn't," Roy interrupted Walestone, and surrounding him, there came the dispirited, disembodied groanings and murmurings of the dead. He could hear them strongly now, as though they were pressing against the boundaries containing them, longing to be set free, to be at long last liberated from the wasteland Roy had momentarily seen in Walestone's memory. "You *didn't* know, and moreover, the longer that you've been trapped, the harder it is to remember. Right?"

It has been . . . many years, Walestone whispered. Roy had to strain his ears to decipher the deceased Elder Scribe's words over the commotion of the ghosts. *My impressions of the past, of my demise, only grew substantial once I saw those unworldly swords in yours and your colleague's hands.*

"Valusvar and Kharuan," Roy said. "But the last I saw of them in that memory, they appeared to be in your study. How did they come to be in your sarcophagus? And how were the shattered pieces of Holyborn brought aboveground?" The answer to these questions came the moment that he'd voiced them. "The library. It protected you, *all* of you. By entombing the swords, it kept them out of the Old Ones' hands, should they invade again."

And out of the Governors' and the Droves', those before your time, Walestone said. *It carved out of this chamber—shortly after the Old Ones' incursion, I presume—the sarcophagi for my fellow Scribes and our Protectorate. There were some tombs made for our apprentices, though the amount is much smaller than how many scholars came down here to assist me in invoking the glamor rune. Perhaps they were so severely dismembered that the library could not recognize which parts belonged to which body . . . but this is all moot to the larger issue.* He leveled his gaze to Roy. *Do you see what must be done, Roy Dawnseve? Do you see how these souls can finally be freed?*

Roy ruminated. He knew how to put things to right, how to undo what had been done, but he was also acutely aware, again, of the frightening probability that Briar might be erased from existence. But as Walestone had proclaimed earlier, that was the risk that Roy would have to take to release these ghosts from their cage, to let them have their peace and return to them their diminishing memories.

"I see," Roy said. He felt the weight of purpose mounting on his shoulders, but it was not a burden.

Thank you, mortal, Walestone said with audible relief. *If all goes to plan, I shall see the both of you on the other side of the barrier.* Then the Elder Scribe disappeared, as though he'd slipped into some unseen fold of reality.

Roy didn't waste a single moment. He whirled around, the glow of the torch in his hand close to winking out. The ghosts shrieked with what sounded like triumphant satisfaction, and as Roy rushed back through the tunnel network, the torch swiftly brightened, like the library was lighting his way.

When Roy emerged from the depths of the tunnel network, Percival was standing over the entryway to the catacombs, his hair askew and mussed from sleep, his eyes ringed with deep purple shadows.

"By the Scribes, you *were* down there," Percival exclaimed, extending a hand, which Roy eagerly accepted. "Darling, you're *shaking*. What happened?"

His mouth drawn into a dismayed grimace, Roy hastily ran his fingers through his hair, clearing out the cobwebs and dirt, then started as the passageway to the catacombs rippled closed behind him. "How did you know where I was?"

"That wind woke me up," Percival said as he looked over Roy, probably for any visible signs of injury. "It must've slipped under the door and into our chamber. I followed it down here, to the first floor, then I saw one of the torches missing from the walls and figured you'd gone down to visit Walestone for a little chat." He said this with half-hearted mirth, but his tone quickly turned somber as he regarded Roy's expression. "Darling, goodness, you really seem on edge—"

Roy grabbed Percival's shoulder with one hand, the torch still clutched in the other. "Percival," he said, a small smile on his lips, "I know how to banish the Old Ones."

Percival gawped, aghast. "How—What do you—"

Roy kissed Percival's forehead. "We have to free the ghosts."

Once Roy had gotten his bearings, still a little unsettled by the confronting barbarity of the things he'd seen in Walestone's recollection, he related to Percival what he'd witnessed piece by piece, making sure not to skip out on any of the details.

Roy told him about Holyborn. How, when Walestone had used it, it had shattered into shards of black metal, which the Orphic Basilica had kept for two millennia in a box in the hopes that someone—someone, perhaps, from the group of scholars

Walestone had insisted that his apprentice Maude Chasile lead so they could keep the academic community alive—might bring their society of enlightenment back to its former glory. He told Percival how, since nobody had ever opened the doors to purgatory from *within* before, the process hadn't been recorded.

Finally, Roy finished with the other piece of information he'd been considering. The Orphic Basilica stood on *one* incredibly powerful source of thanatological energy. It was not the only one, and, as corroborated by the broad range of historical accounts he had read, the Hasdan Isles was not the only continent that had been targeted and invaded by the Old Ones. Therefore, Roy was sure there were other wellsprings of this power like the Orphic Basilica, twisting across the world.

Purgatory contained exclusively the ghosts of those slain by the Old Ones, but this race of red-eyed creatures had likely exterminated millions of humans, and Roy and Percival had already determined that they killed indiscriminately, unlike the Radiant Droves. Once freed, the ghosts would significantly outstrip the Old Ones in number.

"I think we need a second sword," Roy said, slotting the torch back into the sconce from which he'd taken it. "You left Valusvar in the Observatory, yes?"

When he turned back around, Percival was gesticulating wildly. "Darling, this is *absurd*. I mean, I completely agree on the number of ghosts, but as for the swords, you hardly lasted a minute under the influence of Valusvar's visions. How do you think we're going to open the doors to *another world* with two of those cursed weapons?"

"I know how it's going to go because I saw the reverse happen," Roy explained. "Just as I said: Walestone went exactly by Eldreave's instructions, and Holyborn unlocked the gateway to purgatory, like a key into a door . . . but neither he nor Eldreave nor the caretakers before them thought to use a second sword."

"I see the logic, I just . . . I don't want to see you in that position again," Percival said. "What if using one of those swords as a sort of key brings about some worse sort of power than when I pointed Valusvar in your direction?" Then he imploringly blurted out, as if he was begging for Roy to find another way: "What about Briar? What about Owen? What if being freed means being wiped out of existence? No afterlives, no second chances—"

"Percival, I've considered the repercussions, trust me, but these souls have been imprisoned for over two thousand years," Roy said, his eyes brimming with tears. "They need to be let go."

Percival wandered away from Roy and pivoted in a slow circle, his eyes sweeping around the library with solemn reverence. Then he stopped, the wind threading about his shoulders and through his unruly hair. "They've suffered long enough," he said. "All right, let's do it. I'll go get the swords."

Roy almost expected the wind to retrieve Valusvar and Kharuan itself, to place the black-scabbarded weapons neatly into his and Percival's hands like a squire equipping knights for a battle. Instead, it loitered around the first floor with fretful anticipation. Perhaps it was unsure of the outcome. Perhaps it simply wanted them to fulfill Walestone's failed duty, from start to finish, on their own.

When Percival reappeared, carrying both of the swords in his arms, the ghosts began shrilling in earnest. They exploded out of bookshelves and study halls, reading rooms and bedchambers, the foundations of the library—and the twisting tunnels thereunder—shaking from the tumult.

As Percival quickly thrust Kharuan into Roy's hands, Roy shivered at the droning hum that sounded in his ears. He closed both hands around the scabbard, which was exuding thin tendrils of silver luminescence like moonlight sliding through parted curtains. It had been a while since he'd carried the sword, and so as he lifted it, his shock at its weight was quickly renewed. He couldn't imagine how Percival had carted both in his arms.

Although Percival was struggling now, too. He clasped the hilt, the blade pointed down, and was about to reach up and pull off the scabbard when he paused, likely remembering that he had to rotate it. "We'll open the gateway with Valusvar," he said, panting, "and get out and close it with Kharuan. If we can even *lift* the fucking things, that is. Damn, they're heavy. Did Walestone truly plunge Holyborn through stone?"

Roy shrugged, then grimaced at the tension strung throughout his shoulders. "That's what I saw."

"Do we both need to be *touching* Valusvar when I do this?" Percival asked.

"I don't think so. When it happened for Walestone, the world seemed to crumble around him, then brought him to the other side."

Percival looked daunted and stunned, as if he had only just now comprehended the magnitude of what lay ahead of them, then nodded resolutely. He closed his left hand around the hilt and his right around the scabbard, twisted, and then tugged. It didn't come free at first, at which his face reddened, but on his second attempt he gave the scabbard a quick jiggle and it slid off. He flung aside the scabbard, which clattered across the floorboards.

"Now drive the blade through the ground at your feet," Roy said, echoing Eldreave's instructions.

Apprehension skittered across Percival's face, but then he looked up at the ghosts amassing overhead like a murder of crows, his handsome features awash with the shadows of the library, the red glow of the ghosts and the radiant silver light of the sword. "For you," he whispered, and when he plunged Valusvar toward the ground, the wind—which had been hovering companionably about them—abruptly reared up over his head and bore down onto the hilt of the sword with incredible force, thrusting the blade into the carpet and the redwood underneath.

The floorboards splintered, sending chips of wood spraying in every direction. The persistent humming that rippled out of Valusvar increased in pitch and volume, turning into a livid, distorted scream. A shock wave of wind and light blasted out of the blade, which had brightened significantly, painting Roy's and Percival's faces in a silver glare.

Percival reinforced his grip on Valusvar's hilt, his eyes sparkling with amazement. Another shock wave erupted out of the sword—weaker than the first but still formidable—and Percival frantically reached out for Roy's left hand, the right clutching Kharuan, and pressed it atop the hilt with his own.

Around them, the world had begun to disintegrate. The walls peeled back in scrolls of gray ashes. The bookshelves crumbled apart and were then blown away on a strong breeze. The thunder rumbling beyond the walls became distant, then quieted completely. And just before the silence could take over, Valusvar shattered, fragmenting into scintillating shards, the silver luminescence gradually subduing and reverting to the dull black metal—the same, Roy reflected distantly, as the Governor's necklace.

A thick darkness suddenly consumed Roy's vision, and immediately after, he and Percival were surrounded by a chorus of screams.

It was like nothing that Roy had ever heard before, an infernal cacophony of misery. It went on and on, beating him, demoralizing him. He felt defeated, crushed beneath the weight of a thousand wounds, like someone had taken a cudgel to his soul—

The darkness disappeared, replaced by a searing white light that nearly blinded him. He grimaced, raising a hand to shield his eyes. Then, slowly, he lowered it in utter disbelief as an alien landscape materialized into existence.

The scene developed with dexterous calculation, as though some invisible painter was rapidly finishing the backdrop of a painting. Rivers of molten lava appeared, snaking across cracked gray earth and overlapping, creating intercrossing tributaries whose spindly branches streamed out in every which direction, far into the mist-wreathed horizon. These rivers were overflowing with an unfathomable number of ghosts—millions, easily. All struggled to keep afloat, their heads craned back, their mouths contorted into unnaturally elongated chasms that ejected tormented screams.

As soon as the rivers appeared, another geographical feature emerged, encircling the interconnected tributaries. Ten fortresses protruded from the fractured earth, each forged from an ethereal, smooth white crystal. Once erected, they stood at least seventy feet tall, their peaks indistinct and fuzzy high above, like the beaks of phantom birds. They cast no shadow upon the rivers.

Roy stared, equally amazed and petrified. "Purgatory." He could hear his own voice, could feel his mouth working and his heart pumping. He had a body here, and with a body, he could still return to his home world.

Percival stepped up beside him, gawking at the fortresses and the rivers with incredulity. "We made it."

Ahead of them, Atticus Walestone materialized, levitating before them. His features—vaguely human and enshrouded in shadow, as always—were arranged into a look of placid, unaffected calm. When he spoke, though, there was a tone of pensive gratitude in his voice. *So you have, mortals, and for this I thank you. Finally, after two thousand years, my people will know the peace for which they have been desperate. No longer will they languish. No longer will they wallow, trapped in a place where memories die, where their accomplishments and their hardships are pale compared to their pain.*

Percival, who had recovered from his disbelief and was now watching Walestone with melancholy, said, "No one should have to suffer like this. I'm sorry you had to wait so long, that the answer was not discovered sooner."

As am I, Walestone said, *but the deed is done. You unlocked the gateway.* He glanced at Kharuan, still clutched in Roy's hand. *You have your way out, and now these millions of souls will get the revenge they rightfully deserve, that which they have gone without ever since that fateful day.*

"Millions," Roy muttered. He hadn't come to even a rough estimate of the amount of souls trapped within purgatory when he'd considered the idea of multiple power sources of thanatological energy, but *millions?* He turned to Percival, who seemed dumbfounded. "That's it. That's the advantage we were banking on."

"Will it be enough?" Percival asked Walestone. "It must be. The Old Ones have been indulging in wholescale murder across the world for thousands of years. If all those ghosts are contained *here*, then . . ."

Walestone hung his head, though it was not with shame. To Roy, he almost appeared rancorous at the prospect of the violent fallout of the ghosts' liberation, his red eyes shining with perverse glee. *It will be enough.* More *than enough. A great many of the souls pooled here were at the siege of the Orphic Basilica, though all sources of thanatological energy, including the one beneath the library, lead directly here.*

Roy could hardly envisage the magnitude of this ultimate deliverance. He had not educated himself as strongly in geography as philosophy, but he knew the archipelago of the Hasdan Isles was a speck on the map. A single continent in a world full of them. By the Scribes, the quantity of the weaponized ghosts—and thus the scale of destruction soon to be exacted—would be catastrophic.

He thought of Briar, then, how frightened she'd sounded in her letters. All she'd wanted was to help her brother and the girl she liked—might have even *loved*, if the way that she had spoken about Irene was anything to go by—and because of this, because she had seen faith in a world of endless evils, she had been put to death.

Roy tried to search for Briar now, but it was impossible to do so when she was within the milling crush of ghosts.

"Briar," he whispered, "if you can see me, if you can hear me . . ." His vision blurred with tears. "Know that I'm proud of you, that you did all you could, and without you, we wouldn't be where we are."

He got no reply, but he held out hope.

Walestone raised his arms and spread them wide, gazing out over at the multitudes of ghosts, who were roiling and writhing with pent-up agitation. He bellowed at them, his voice somehow amplified and causing ripples across the rivers, *The doors have been flung open! Your fury may now be spent! Fly free, my friends!* As the ghosts stirred, staring skyward, he hissed, *Make it hurt.*

An earsplitting crash sounded from above the clouds, which parted to reveal a broadening fissure in a shape loosely reminiscent of a lightning bolt. As it extended, like a scar being pulled at the edges, Roy made out the skylight of the Orphic Basilica, through which amassed thunderclouds tossed and boiled with preternatural quickness. From what he could see, this tear in the sky seemed to be directly above where Percival had plunged Valusvar through the floorboards.

"Back! Back!" Roy screamed, scrambling away from the intersecting rivers, hauling Percival along with him.

Percival complied, twisting and burying his head into Roy's shoulder.

Then chaos took the reins.

The ghosts poured out of purgatory, drawn by some gravitational force created by the rip between worlds, then shot through the fissure in the clouds and surged out into the Orphic Basilica.

They rushed out of the hole in the floorboards—left behind by Valusvar, which had exploded into shattered pieces that lay strewn about the carpet—as a roaring black cloud, the mass flickering and fluttering with the ruby glow that blazed out of their eyes like furnaces of Hell's light. They screamed with untrammeled fury and passion and their ravenous hunger for retribution, the sound ringing and echoing throughout the library. Some of them zipped back and forth and up and down, their sense of direction warped after millennia kept in captivity. They bounced and ricocheted off the walls. They clashed into one another, seeing faces they could hardly remember, all of them frozen in the moments before their deaths—big, shaggy beards speckled with brains; gore-drenched snarls of hair; jaws and noses smashed to pieces. Some faces were more familiar to one ghost than the next. Some thought they saw a sibling or a parent or a lover but couldn't tell for sure. Their memories had been twisted horribly out of shape, the meanings lost, the details watered down by time and torture.

Quite a few of the ghosts were not as eager to leave the Orphic Basilica as the others were. A couple drifted about, either despondent or panicked by their sudden evacuation, like confused children being towed out of their bedrooms by their parents during a house fire. Then they looked up, noticed the seething mass above them, and joined their companions, as though it had slipped past their fractured minds that they'd been let free.

After a few moments of wheeling around one another, forming a turbulent cyclone of deepest black and glistening red, the ghosts coursed through the skylight. The thick pane of glass smashed, and the blustering breeze and the wind-driven snow snuck in and added to the disorder brought about by the release of thanatological energy, tearing through the library and ripping books and scrolls from their shelves. The spinning typhoon of ghosts resumed their ascent, heedless of the obliteration they were causing. It was the last thing on their minds.

The first? Revenge.

They sped through the congregation of grumbling thunderclouds like a massive black spear, cackling and snarling and screeching. The crimson light of their eyes blurred together and whipped across the storm-darkened sky like comet trails. A great shadow spread across the snow-caked earth below in their passing, accompanied by a violent streak of red light. They soared past the Orphic Basilica, whose foundations were now quavering from the aftershock of the opened gateway to purgatory; past the outskirts of the library; and then they made for the grid of streets beyond.

There, ahead of the decimated town of Rasileus, the ghosts found a boiling cauldron of madness. There were throngs of humans huddled around the carcasses of their own, their hands and mouths covered in half-frozen blood and entrails. There were humans in big white coats and green felt caps, wreaking havoc across the streets with their instruments of war. Some of these weapons the ghosts could not comprehend, having come from an earlier age, but they understood what they saw—superiors beating inferiors, gore spraying through the frigid air in gruesome stripes. Indeed, they understood this fight, though it was not their own. They had another score to settle.

Past the villages and towns, all beset by those fearsome human soldiers, were the Old Ones. They stood nine to ten feet tall, their bodies completely sheathed in suits of black metal armor, red light streaming from their eyes. Families nestled together, soon separated by the Old Ones' prying claws. They destroyed them all, scattering blood and bodies and detached appendages through the crowds in the jam-packed streets. The massacre filled the air with a sort of animalistic malice, fueling the Old Ones. Carnage was their feast, death their ambrosia.

Though the ghosts could not exactly recall their ends, they remembered the confusion, the turmoil, the rage. They remembered the seemingly endless years of anguish, the long stretches of time where all they could do was forget, where their memories lay just out of reach. No, they did not remember the details of their fate . . .

But they knew the culprit.

The legion of ghosts—millions upon millions of them, all killed by the Old Ones, all victims of the Blight—dove headlong into Rasileus. Not all the ghosts lingered in Northgard, though. Some had to get their long-overdue revenge on continents beyond the Hasdan Isles, in kingdoms and empires and territories that were unfamiliar to other ghosts. But before they did, they offered their assistance in Rasileus. They gathered in twos and threes, shot through the howling winds, and swooped around the Old Ones' ankles, sending them crashing to the ground. They wriggled into the eye slits of the soldiers' helmets, slid through the membrane-thin gaps around their eyeballs, and then into their brains, flooding them with hallucinations and suicidal compulsions. The Old Ones convulsed and writhed, snapping their legs and arms out in a strange death-dance until, eventually, their bodies went still and their gleaming eyes winked out.

Although, as the ghosts of distant lands soared off, spurred onward by the wind, those who remained in Northgard realized that some of the Old Ones were not so easy to defeat. After all, they *had* spent innumerable years subjugating the known world, across lands near and far, and so some of the ghosts' attacks they anticipated. Their bulky black armor made them unsteady on their feet, hindering their ability to move with grace, but they had adapted to this. They swung their fists through the ghosts, slashing them into ribbons of shadow. The ghosts cried out in pain and horror, assaulted by memories of the Old Ones' first incursion. The soldiers took quick advantage of the ghosts' incapacitation. They clamped gauntleted hands on either side of their nebulous heads and squeezed. The ghosts' eyes brightened like lanterns, then burst, and the rest of their forms followed, evaporating upward like smoke from a smokestack.

A collective wave of terrified astonishment rippled through the supernatural legion. Screams and wails came from those who had witnessed the tragedy. Those fortunate to have missed it were soon subjected to the same fate. The Old Ones clambered through the crush and gripped the ghosts' heads, forcing them into submission. Some of their features cleared, revealing agape mouths and scorched eyes. They were agonized, confused.

None of them knew where they might go next, if defeated by an Old One in this form. Even if they wanted to fly back into purgatory, that cursed prison, the scholars—the mortals and Atticus Walestone both—had already determined that they would close the doors. They had no way back.

So where next? thought the ghosts.

The question followed them like some insistent specter as they fought on, as they barreled through the soldiers who had conquered their people, as they felled the Old Ones like collapsing bridges.

Where next? they wondered. *Where do you go once you've been through Hell and back? Where do you go when there is nowhere else to go?*

The ghosts kept moving.

The Old Ones kept falling.

Roy looked up at the spinning tempest of ghosts, cradling Percival close to his side, and marveled at the spectacle. It was strangely beautiful. He couldn't believe he had once been afraid of these creatures. How? How had he feared his own people? As he watched them depart, the rivers now more flame than souls, he felt the stirrings of an emotion he'd thought he would never feel—self-acceptance. It scared him, yes, though maybe this fear was good, something he could grow from.

Once the last of the ghosts had left, the clouds smeared lackadaisically across the sky—still foggy, like an unfinished painting—grumbled and groaned, and the gash between the two worlds slowly slid closed. A seam lingered there for a moment, like the fading impression of a scar, then disappeared.

A long silence descended.

Roy regarded Walestone askance, wondering what must be on his mind, but he couldn't make out the expression on the Elder Scribe's ill-defined face.

Still, Walestone admitted, *I do not know what to feel, how to process this development. You would expect me to be content, and I suppose I am, but . . . there is a part of me, however small, that knows my people* must still carry the demons which haunt them. He sighed. *Must the past always leave its mark?*

"If it did not," Percival said, pulling himself from Roy's hold, though only to squeeze his hand, "we would not grow."

Roy smiled and squeezed back, then said to Walestone, "If all else is lost to memory, then at least your friends and followers will remember your perseverance. You tried. And we're here to chronicle it. So that the memory at least has a chance to be visited time and again."

But I did not succeed, Walestone said. *There is nothing to chronicle.*

"How can you say that?" Percival pointed to the clouds. "This is as much your achievement as it is ours. We gave them an out, but we wouldn't have known what to do had you not shown Roy your memory, your own demons, and that takes bravery."

Walestone considered that. *I suppose I have gotten so mired in my failure that I neglected to give myself credit for my accomplishments. Though that is the way of most academics, it seems. I know you both must share the sentiment.*

Percival shrugged. "And then some."

Walestone spared another glance at the clouds, which continued to twist and roil with displeasure, the sounds now overtaking the crackling of flames and the spitting of embers. He looked back at Roy and Percival with urgency, though he appeared less anxious, the crinkle between his vaguely visible brows gone, at least partially assuaged by the scholars' reassurances. *It is time for you to leave*, he told them. *I know not the consequences of opening the door to this place from inside out, but the power invested in those swords is volatile, so I would take caution.*

"Will you go with them?" Percival asked Walestone. "Your friends? When we open the doors, will you fight?"

No, my fight is over, Walestone answered, then gestured emphatically to Kharuan. *Go back, mortals. I do not know if there's a next road I might take or if this is my last, but either way, I am eager to find out.*

Roy was happy for the Elder Scribe, and yet there was a profound sense of loss in knowing this potential fount of knowledge was moving on. He knew it was Walestone's choice, and he respected it, but it took all Roy's strength to hold himself back from asking Walestone the litany of questions that troubled him: Where had the Blight come from? Was there truly no cure or had Walestone merely not found it? Were the Old Ones' plans of conquest central to Roy's world? Or had Walestone discovered, through his research, the existence of other worlds? Were these in peril, too, threatened by this incomprehensible army?

But even if he had the time to ask these questions, he knew they were not his and Percival's to examine. They'd identified the Old Ones, those who had originally invaded and stormed Northgard. They knew that, if they were to tear off their masks, they would find the faces of mortals who should be dead, whose lives had been extended against their will like the Governor's—and Dimestra's—Droves. And in figuring this out, they had banished them from their home *and* saved the scholars, bonuses they would not take lightly.

At last, Roy took up Kharuan in both his hands, the muscles in his forearms straining at the weight. When he had finally found a good hold and repositioned the sword so that the blade pointed downward, he located a wide fissure in the fractured earth and plunged it deep, Percival standing prepared next to him.

The fuzzy landscape evaporated around them, and before Roy could figure out whether their plan would work, everything went dark.

28

WHEN THEY REAPPEARED IN THE ORPHIC BAsilica, Roy immediately became aware of the tremors coursing beneath his feet.

He stood braced in the same position as when he and Percival had crossed from purgatory to the material world, but he was no longer grasping Kharuan in his white-knuckled hands. The sword had exploded into glittering smithereens, scattered around the redwood floorboards alongside the remains of Valusvar. The shuddering vibrations continued, pitching Roy into Percival, who staggered to the side and almost tripped over his own feet. But Roy hauled him upright, clutching him by the sleeve of his tunic, gazing around with increasing fascination and incredulity.

A torrent of snow blew violently down through the shattered skylight, whipping and stirring past bookshelves and sculptures. The tremors intensified, rumbling and trembling through the foundations of the library. Rolling ladders skidded back and forth, producing a terrible screech that grated against Roy's ears. The wind whistled and howled and ripped a sculpture off its plinth, then hurled it against the staircase with dreadful strength. Splinters and chips of wood cracked off the risers and spiraled through the air, nearly slashing across Percival's cheek.

Roy cried out and wrapped his arm around Percival, tenderly cupping the back of his head. He pressed down, lowering them both to the carpet, which was sprinkled with glass and metal.

He did not know how—perhaps because of the gaping hole in the floor to his left, from which the ghosts had evacuated—but he could *feel* the erosion of this ancient, long-believed-invincible building underneath him: the grinding of cobblestone, the crumbling of mortar, the eerily human groaning of its skeletal framework . . . and the prolonged booms and echoes of the release of thanatological energy. Intermittent pulsations of silver light, much stronger and more vibrant than what had emitted from either of the swords, erupted from the chasm that tunneled deep down into the catacombs. Paroxysms of dust and dirt shot out of the blackness. A brown mist of earth rained down on Roy and Percival, their heads still covered, their bodies still hunched and curled around one another.

They began coughing, and Roy was instantly filled with alarm. He remembered when, during their initial foray into the catacombs, he'd coughed and hacked and then been assailed by a series of disturbing visions. He waited, dread curdling his blood, but nothing happened. The visions seemed to have gone with the dead.

Now new visions assaulted him: premonitions of himself and Percival being crushed to death, pummeled by books and sculptures and stones. Because the waves of destruction went on, and those reverberations and lights coming from the catacombs did not seem to be ceasing anytime soon. One did not need to be a seer to know how easily that timeline could become their reality.

A plangent *crack* sounded from their left, like a stack of wood dropped from the precipice of a towering cliff. The doors to the Orphic Basilica had swung wide open, one of them hanging askew, the hinges torn free by the force of the wind. A bestial howl blasted out of the entryway, as if from the maw of some prehistoric leviathan, and began dragging Roy and Percival by the heels of their boots.

"The wind!" Roy shouted in Percival's ear, clutching him tightly. His teeth were chattering, and his extremities were growing number by the minute, but there was a wild grin on his face.

Percival trudged toward the entryway, the intact door of which was slowly coming loose from its hinges. He looked pale as an apparition, a path of half-frozen tears imprinted onto his cheeks.

"Come on," Roy yelled, tugging on Percival's sleeve.

Percival, who seemed unusually reticent, at last pulled himself out of his thoughts and came back to his senses. He grabbed Roy's hand, his grip firm.

They tried briskly walking toward the entryway first, though the wind of the Orphic Basilica and the wind of the snowstorm contested for control, battering Roy and Percival from side to side. The biting chill rushed into them with an almost sentient fury, as though eager to take them off their feet. But the other wind, that which had followed and assisted them throughout their investigation, set them back to standing. It even protected them from the cyclone of debris whooshing through the library behind them. A book flew toward them and nearly struck Roy over the head, but the wind soared off with it, leaving them briefly exposed, then returned just before a hail of ice and snow could attack them.

After what felt like an eternity of pushing back a wall of raging winds, they eventually made it past the threshold and out of the Orphic Basilica. As they did, a plaintive cry—high and angelic—issued from the wind, like a mournful farewell. Then it rushed forward, sending Roy and Percival wheeling through the air, far beyond the range of danger.

For a few dizzying moments, Roy rolled through the snow. It got into his mouth, his nostrils, and his hair. Then, shuddering against the cold, he rose to his knees and watched the library he had come to love buckle under the pressure of the swords' expended abilities, crumble, and fall.

The roof caved in from the broken skylight. The impossibly large steeple, which jutted toward the clouds like an upthrust spear, listed forward with exquisite slowness then crashed down onto and split the gable of the seventh floor in half. A rumble went through the ground, deeper than Roy had felt moments before, and drove the steeple farther into the wrecked front of the building. The left and right facades toppled inward and slammed into the steeple with colossal force, crushing it, driving it farther into the widening, cavernous hole in the rooftop. The steeple tipped, slanted, then drilled through the seventh, sixth, and fifth floors, destroying the Observatory and the sitting and reading rooms where Roy and Percival had sat when they had started collaborating. Several of the curtains had been ripped away and torn apart by the storm, Roy noticed, showing dark chambers littered with damaged texts. A cobweb of cracks slithered down one of the limestone pillars that had held up the front vestibule, and when the steeple plunged down into the fourth floor, the pillar collapsed entirely. It leaned to the right, then collided into its counterpart, and the vestibule crumpled right after. The overhang bowed forward, fell, and crushed the platform at the head of the front staircase. The birdbaths resting on either side of the absent doors tumbled, too, crushed by the overhang. Once all four facades had plummeted, the rest of the Orphic Basilica's downfall happened rather quickly. The storm wind gave a tremendous gust, and it all sank in and blew over.

As the breeze lessened, a haunting silence swept in around Roy. He stared unblinkingly at the rubble, his gut leaden with dismay and awe. The detritus of the library, a millennia-old accrual of countless outlawed tomes and scrolls, lay in heaps and piles. It looked so mundane, so bereft of the magic that had kept all those pages bound and unharmed for untold years. He could hardly believe it.

"Percival..." Roy whispered, his voice shaky with disbelief. "What have we done? What... What did we just do?"

"What we set out to do," Percival said, standing and brushing snow off his knees. "And more." He sounded put together, like he had everything in control, but Roy knew Percival, knew that his inattentive expression was from sadness, not exhaustion. Despite this, he explained, "This was always the plan. We meant to do this when we decided what the Governor would get out of the bargain. Maybe we hoped it wouldn't come to this, but what happened is actually *convenient*, Roy."

"How can you say that?"

"Well, we hadn't actually gotten around to how we'd tear it down, now, did we?"

Roy nodded with numb acknowledgment, and yet the sight of the Orphic Basilica stripped down to its bare bones flooded his heart with such despair that he could not help but turn his back on the damage. He clapped a hand over his mouth, tears running down his face and slowly freezing there.

"I know, darling," Percival murmured, embracing Roy for a while, running the palm of his hand down his back, and then pulling gently away. "I know. But perhaps it's for the best. Just think: If we hadn't done what we did, if we hadn't taken it down, the doors to purgatory might have stood open for years until someone else with one of those swords came around. And who knows how long that might have taken?"

"I know. I *know*." And Roy did. But... "All those books, the Observatory... Briar's carving..."

Percival brushed a knot of windswept hair back from Roy's face. "I know," he repeated, "but we'll have time to grieve later."

"Why? Where are we going?"

"I'm not quite sure," Percival said, looking around, "but all I'm concerned with right now is getting out of the cold."

They stood there shivering for a moment—bunched closely together, aimless and confused—then slogged to the left down the slight mound of snow on which the library, lying in ruins behind them, had once been erected. Percival led the way, despite evidently having as little an understanding of where they were going as Roy. There hadn't been any inns or villages on the journey to the Orphic Basilica where they could ask for shelter, from what he could remember, but that had been almost three months ago, and his mind had not been as strong since Briar's murder.

They walked onward, their boots leaving deep prints in the snow. Minutes trudged by, then became an hour. The landscape before them, whose contours and lights had once been hard to define, resolved out of the thick white haze. The outskirts of Rasileus were still quite far in the distance, but whereas months ago Roy would not have been able to make heads nor tails of it in this weather, now the numerous dwellings of Rasileus were clear. And as their slow trek resumed, he saw why.

Across the sky, from the isolated patch of snow-packed land solely inhabited by the destructed Orphic Basilica, all the way out to the heart of Rasileus and far beyond, the clouds were thinning—and with amazing speed, too, Roy noted. The large gray masses drifted away, taking with them the darkness that had cloaked the sky.

A brilliant beam of sunlight, the first which Roy had seen in over three years, sifted through a break in the clouds and illuminated the city in an aureate glow. Roy had opened a bridge between worlds with a sword of unknown origins, and he still thought that moment paled starkly in comparison to this breathtaking view.

The chill that had stubbornly clung to the breeze disappeared. There was no menacing bite to the wind, no cold that snuck under the layers of his clothing and seeped into his bones. Instead, a relieving and much-welcomed warmth hovered in the air. The snow on his clothes and hair began to melt, and a delightful thin film of sweat gathered on his palms. He brought his hands, clammy from the growing heat, out before him and tipped his head back. Then he grinned at the golden sunlight.

For years, rumors and theories about the beginnings of the snowstorm had floated around the city. Once, Briar had tattled to Roy that one of her professors at Rasileus Academy thought the unusually long season had somehow spawned from the fumes that emitted from the Governor's up-and-coming military inventions. A sign not of foreboding and misfortune, but of success and modernity.

Roy still wasn't sure on what side of the argument he fell. Science or mysticism? Coincidence or miracle? All he knew was that once the Old Ones had been unmasked, and the ghosts freed, the storm had gone from blizzard to breeze, and now, to breath.

A little while later, Roy and Percival were traversing a small valley covered in still-melting snow when they spotted a sled, drawn by two horses, gliding steadily toward them out of the white haze.

Once it drifted up to them, the sled came to an abrupt halt on Percival's side. A Drove was gripping the reins in her black-gloved hands, a harsh scrutiny settling across her freckled face as she considered Roy and Percival. Roy searched for a hint of the Blight's red glint in her hazel eyes, but there was nothing there.

They're gone, he thought. *All the Old Ones. And all of the Governor's undead.*

The Drove assessed them a moment longer, squinting, then sat back. "Hop in," she ordered. "He's waiting for you."

Rasileus and the streets beyond were in a shambles.

Gray mushrooms of smoke billowed out from the remnants of flattened, burnt, and destructed tenements. The roads were carpeted with blood and scattered with the corpses of the Old Ones and the undead, unarmored Droves—whose ruby eyes had now returned to their normal, albeit lifeless, gaze—and the countless civilians whom they had slaughtered. Entrails littered the road down which their sled passed, and at one point, the driver had to bellow out of the window for someone to clean the mess.

It was at this instance, when he distinctly heard the squelching of guts being shoveled and dragged across cobblestone, that Roy looked away and had to concentrate on his breathing. Percival placed a hand on the small of his back, although he appeared equally horrified by the massacre, his face pale and his lips pursed with disgust as though he was trying his hardest not to vomit.

They sat the rest of the way to their destination in tense silence.

When the sled stopped about an hour later, at the tail end of which Roy had fallen into a pleasurable light doze, the Drove sitting opposite the two of them opened the door, then took Roy by the arm and pulled him none too gently out into the dazzling sunlight. He was still unaccustomed to, and rather startled by, the unforeseen change of weather, so he blinked several times, letting his vision settle.

Percival pulled himself out of the bruising grip of the Drove, who had deposited him beside Roy, and grumbled, "Careful."

Roy inspected his surroundings. They had been brought past the wrought-iron gates of the Governor's manor—a large and rambling estate laden with snow, squares of golden lamplight shining from its many windows—and into a courtyard encircled by imposing white limestone walls. The sled stopped in front of an ascending staircase that led to a pair of teak doors. They hung open, manned by two Droves, revealing a cramped office whose only furnishings comprised of a cabinet stocked with unrecognizable curiosities and a tidy desk. Sitting behind this desk, his skeletal, liver-spotted hands folded before him, was the Governor.

"Fuck," said Percival, taking a step back and giving a panicked, sidelong look to Roy. "Darling, I'm not so sure about this."

Roy understood his consternation. But just as Percival had convinced him that the loss of the library was ultimately for the good, so now he felt it his job to do the same for Percival.

"Why?" Roy asked. "As you reminded me, we did everything he asked for."

"But I also said, 'and more.' And that 'more' stripped away a large part of his power."

"You're right, then—without his Blighted, his plans went up in smoke. He has nothing left to gain from us. And it's not like he has any additional tricks up his sleeve."

"How do you know that?"

"Because we know his goal," Roy answered with ringing certainty, "and without the Blighted, there's little he can threaten us with that would keep us from sharing his vision for Northgard." Though even as he said this, Roy acknowledged that he *was* curious as to how this discussion, whatever it was that the Governor wished to discuss, would proceed.

We'll find out soon enough.

They entered the little office, Roy first and Percival following cautiously. The Droves posted outside closed the doors shut behind them and enclosed them in the dark space, which was illuminated solely by a dim lamp placed on the corner of the desk.

The Governor regarded them in an uneasy silence. His complexion had been ghastly three and a half months ago, but it seemed markedly unhealthy now, like something within that short period had accelerated the process. His sagging skin had a troubling quality. It was jaundiced in some places and cadaverous in others. The gaudiness of his bloodshot eyes—*truly* bloodshot, Roy realized, not infected with the Blight—were appalling in the subdued lighting.

"You did it," the Governor said, his voice croaky and dry. "You tore the damn thing down." Before either of them could think of a response, he asked, "What about the Law? Did you amend it?" He coughed into the side of his fist, dappling it with mucus and blood. When he repeated his question, his eyes were wide and shining with desperation. "Well, out with it, boys. Did you?"

Roy had been turning over the words spinning through his head, working out how to construct them into an answer, a reasonable justification for their failure to keep up their end of the bargain, but it was Percival who said, "No, we didn't. Although in all fairness, we had not anticipated the Orphic Basilica being destroyed so soon, you see. However, without any of the other scholars currently lying low in Northgard to assist us, we fear that we'll never be able to help you expand the Law, to spread the city's political influence over its neighboring nations. In a way, we *did* fulfill our part of the deal, not to mention that our releasing the ghosts effectively destroyed the Old Ones, so I believe that should compensate for not having expanded the Law of Intervention yet."

All the flimsy arguments Roy had been assembling in his head vanished once he heard Percival's. They were all good points, and moreover, they were *indisputable*, made evident by the efforts the Governor had already acknowledged they'd gone to. Percival was demonstrating, right in front of the Governor's eyes, what Roy had told him moments ago: *He has nothing left to gain from us.*

So now the Governor studied them with heightened suspicion and indecision, his squinted, bleary eyes deepening the wrinkles around them, as though on the hunt for something written between the lines—something which only a continued examination would reveal. He opened his mouth, and Roy flinched, preparing himself for an interrogation or a beating or worse. He grasped Percival's forearm.

Then the Governor stumbled to his feet, his face blanching with shock and his attention fastening on the left corner of the office. A faint and familiar silver light illuminated his age-weathered features.

Roy followed the Governor's gaze to the left corner, twisting in his seat with his fingers still clamped protectively around Percival's arm, and let out a hoarse gasp.

The ghost of a stunningly beautiful middle-aged woman drifted noiselessly in the shadows. Though her passing had reduced her physicality to a murky humanoid shape, when she cupped her hands and placed them over her face—as Roy had seen a ghost do in the Orphic Basilica—her features, and the circumstances of her death, gradually grew clear. A ragged hole went through her left cheek and exited out of the top of the right column of her neck. Her full lips were curved into a shaky, crestfallen smile. She raised one hand, covered in a fingerless glove, toward the Governor. Then she curled it into a fist and pressed it over her heart.

The Governor planted his hands against the desk and leaned forward, his face marked with a look of grave sadness ... and fascination. He looked utterly spellbound.

Silent, the woman stared at him with increasing studiousness. She tilted her head, and though Roy attempted to make sense of what seemed an innocuous gesture, he couldn't quite interpret it. There was some sort of unspoken conversation taking place here, but the nuances were so intimate that Roy sensed he wouldn't be able to plumb any deeper for answers if he tried.

Yet still, something struck him as odd—a bizarre incongruity. Several months earlier, when Roy had inquired to Dimestra as to the reason behind the Governor's absence, why Roy hadn't once in his life met the man who was dictating his immediate future, Dimestra had answered, *The Governor has been ... absent since his wife passed some few years ago.* But as he took the recency of the tragedy into account, alongside the obvious youthfulness of the woman before him, Roy couldn't help but wonder whether Dimestra had gotten the story wrong.

Had the Governor really married a woman easily fifty years his junior? As far as Roy knew, in Northgard, it was uncommon but not unheard-of. Even so, he couldn't quite quash his suspicions. It was then that two details came before his mind's eye, instantly ruling out the possibility that the Governor's and Cordelia's marriage was simply an unorthodox union—the black metal necklace and Atticus Walestone's puzzling allusion to resurrection.

Even if I could exercise such powers, that sort of sorcery has been forbidden for thousands of years and was only recently discovered to be impossible. The repercussions are ... troubling.

Before Roy could continue ruminating on his speculations,

the ghost of the woman redirected her attention to Roy and Percival, though with decidedly less interest. She looked back to the Governor, the ruby light in her eyes quickly diminishing and petering out. Then she pivoted, and as she turned, she vanished.

"Come back!" the Governor shouted at the empty corner, his voice gruff but filled with sorrow, his eyes scanning the semidarkness with despairing hopefulness. "Cordelia! My dear Cordelia, please! Come back!"

There was no answer. The shadows had already filled in the space the woman, whom Roy could only assume had been the Governor's deceased wife, had once occupied.

The Governor kept his eyes trained on the gloom nevertheless, his gaunt and fragile hands crumpling the documents beneath them. He raised one of them, though, and absently toyed with the black metal necklace around his throat. It felt to Roy like minutes had passed before the Governor finally addressed him and Percival, but the dejection was gone from his face. He glared, his brows lowered and his wilting skin covered in a slimy veneer of sweat. Death had its sure grip on him, but he was holding on.

He's going to lash out, thought Roy, panic spreading hot and eager within him. *We've fulfilled our duties, honored our—his—commitments, and now he's going to pull out of the deal. He'll take everything out on us. His frustration, his resentment, his fury and grief and sadness.*

Roy was so confident his fears would come true, that he and Percival would not be dismissed until they'd been castigated, that he was stunned when the Governor's expression softened. He took a few seconds to avert his gaze and compose himself, and when he set his eyes back on them, he was wearing a shrewd half smile. "Here is what I will do," he said. "I will allow the scholars to safely come out of hiding, those who have survived the Old Ones' invasion and the ghosts' subsequent attack, but with the added stipulation that they all help change the Law of Intervention and expand Northgard's influence. I will give them a year to do this. No sooner, no later. What do you say?"

Percival said, "That's not our deal—"

"And you did not fulfill yours," the Governor interrupted. "Not to the letter, as you admitted. So, as before, an amendment."

Doubt snuck into Roy's gut. He felt inclined to protest, to slam his fists against the desk in defiance, because he knew how treacherous this was. He knew from experience. He had been deceived by this man before, and so the consequences of agreeing to the Governor's new conditions couldn't be clearer.

Then Percival took Roy's hand underneath the desk, which sent a reassuring, pleasing warmth though Roy. "We say yes," said Percival. "You have our approval." He interlaced their fingers and stood, pulling Roy up with him and tugging him toward the door. He turned the knob and they both stepped out with haste, afraid that the Governor would change his mind.

29

PERCIVAL PULLED ROY ASIDE TO UNDERNEATH AN arch in the courtyard—out of earshot from the Radiant Droves milling about in confusion and agitation, likely dumbfounded by the defeat of the Old Ones and the supernatural entities which had ground the interminable conflict to a halt. Then he blurted out to Roy, "Please tell me you saw what I saw."

"That was his *wife*," Roy exclaimed, then belatedly remembered where he was and who was around him and lowered his voice. "Dimestra told me that she died three or so years ago, right around the time the Old Ones launched their second invasion..."

He couldn't purge from his mind the disconcerting image of the Governor's frailty—his hazy eyes, his liver-spotted hands, the concerning prominence of his veins. Even upon first appearance, Roy had noted these physical disadvantages but dismissed them as the inevitable side effects of old age. Though the longer he chewed on it, on the direction his thoughts had taken when he'd seen Cordelia, Roy found himself returning to Atticus Walestone's offhand comment... And so he told Percival, who reacted suitably.

"Fuck," Percival muttered, running a hand over his stubbled jaw. "So you think the Governor attempted to bring Cordelia back, and it . . . backfired?" He looked furtively around, but the closest Droves were on the other side of the courtyard and deeply engaged in a heated argument. He frowned at Roy, shaking his head. "But that would imply he'd been researching thanatology. Wouldn't he be disparaged for such hypocrisy?"

"He would," Roy said, nodding and folding his arms, "which is why, I believe, he laid low. According to Dimestra, the Governor essentially isolated himself here"—he pointed his chin around them, indicating the manor—"after Cordelia died. My thinking is that he hid away in that office there and stocked up on volumes on dark magic. Necromancy and the like. Maybe he trusted some of his agents with this information and had them retrieve these texts from the libraries and bookshops he destructed."

"By the Scribes, I *knew* there was something about him—his skin, his eyes. They seem cloudy but comparably more aware, more *intelligent*, than a man of his age," Percival said, then amended, "His *apparent* age. He must be . . . what, close to Cordelia when she passed? In his forties or thereabouts?"

Roy shuddered. "This botched attempt at dark magic must've come with a price. It took something from him. It stole from him his strength, his vitality, and made him this defenseless husk of a man, as helpless as the scholars whom he so detests. And then he went on the hunt for answers, a pursuit of knowledge he, in hindsight, shouldn't have dared disturb." He paused, his brows drawn together. "Though, as terrifying as it is to consider, I'm not so sure that his accelerated aging is the only one of these 'repercussions' of the Governor's attempt at resurrection that Walestone mentioned. Percival, everything we're discussing seemed to have occurred three years ago. Cordelia's death, the Governor's search for a resurrection spell, the Old Ones' encroachment . . . but also the storm."

Percival looked taken aback. "The storm?"

"Well, haven't you ever wondered why snow hasn't stopped falling for three years?" asked Roy. "Why the clouds never seemed to go away?"

"Sure, but I didn't attribute it to magic."

Roy glanced sidelong at the sunlight spilling in through the courtyard, at the brightening cerulean sky past the towering limestone walls. "I think—no, I'm *convinced*—whatever spell or rune the Governor invoked led to this convergence of devastating powers. He sought and exploited knowledge from a spellbook, almost insane with grief from Cordelia's passing, and it brought on the storm. Walestone even suggested that such sorcery hasn't been practiced since, maybe because the Governor stored the spellbook away after the storm came on, after the Old Ones besieged Northgard—drawn here, perhaps, by the Governor's failed attempt at resurrection."

Percival pressed a hand over his mouth, his eyes wide. "And then the Radiant Droves started to go mad. Then their eyes started glowing red."

Could love really have been the cause of all this chaos? Roy wondered. He didn't see why not. History was rife with stories of lovers crossing moral boundary lines, committing acts of depravity, things they would have never imagined doing before meeting their paramours. He didn't find it difficult to believe at all, then, that the Governor had repeatedly experimented with occult magic just to see his wife again, to clasp her cheek and kiss her brow; that he had pushed the limitations of mortality until they bent and snapped; that he'd only stopped when he realized his body was deteriorating exponentially. And what would be the point in raising his beloved from beyond the grave if he wasn't there to see her?

As though pondering this same question, Percival asked, "Is

that why he hired us to investigate the Orphic Basilica? To find a way to resurrect his wife?"

"No," Roy said. "I think he discovered, probably at some point during his search for a resurrection spell, that Cordelia was gone. Perhaps he saw a ghost on his first visit to the library, the day we arrived, and concluded that his investigation had always been ineffectual. But he was haunted by her, ashamed of his physical limitations, so he began to wear the necklace—which Cordelia herself had gifted to him before her death—to hide from her and spare himself the guilt. It'll always live with him, sure, but to *see* her..."

Percival nodded. "Quite another thing entirely. Why didn't the necklace work in the office?"

"I don't think it would work anywhere now. With the doors to purgatory closed, it's useless. Just a hunk of metal. When the Basilica crumbled, so too did the rune Walestone invoked all those years ago."

"She's free to go home now," Percival said with a small smile. "They all are."

"But *we're* still fighting," Roy snapped. "To survive, to be seen, to be acknowledged as more than just containers of knowledge to be emptied and exploited."

Percival shook his head. "What are you going on about, darling?"

"The deal, Percival. This new one. That man used us for nearly *four months* because he didn't know how to clean the mess he'd made. What were you *thinking* giving him more of our lives?"

"Truly?" Percival asked softly. "I just wanted to get out of that sad, stuffy room so that I could do this."

Then he clasped Roy's cheeks, pulled him in, their waists fitting snug against one another, and kissed him with such fervor that Roy stiffened. But as Percival deepened the kiss, the prickles of stubble above his upper lip scratching against Roy's skin, Roy smiled against Percival's mouth, powerless to resist.

How could he? *Why* would he? It was one of those kisses that, upon the sealing of the lips, made you forget the world and then, upon the parting of the lips, made you remember its countless beauties... and that you were standing before the brightest.

Once he drew back, taking a few moments to catch his breath, Roy encircled Percival's waist with his arms and kissed his forehead. "A very valid reason. In fact, I strongly endorse this reason." He traced his thumb across Percival's jaw. "But I'd still like an answer. Do you think the Governor will hold up his end of the bargain? What if we're walking into another trap? What if we're just trading the freedom of the other islands for the freedom of a couple scholars?"

"It might *seem* that way, darling," Percival said, "but one of the wonderful things about knowledge is that once it's let loose into the world, it's practically impossible to fold and tuck back away. The Orphic Basilica housed millions of ideas, and some of us have clung to these despite the years that have passed. Like those ideas, then—while we work on expanding the Law of Intervention for the Governor—we'll work on getting some others out."

"And if we can't?" Roy argued. "If we don't find a way?"

Percival shrugged. "Then at least we'll have had time to meet the other scholars, starting with Briar's surviving compatriots, out in the open and plan what to do next. I'm sure that navigating this new academic landscape will not be a solitary endeavor." He winked. "After all, it's always better to collaborate, no?"

Chuckling, Roy laid his hand on Percival's chest. "Too true. Though I suppose that, moving forward, that principle won't be *universally* applicable. Our community needs one another, now more than ever, but as for the Droves here, I think the future will be looking very different without the Old Ones around."

"How so?" Percival asked, pulling himself gently from Roy's grasp, his gaze once again shifting warily about the courtyard.

"For one thing," Roy explained, "I know the Matron. And I know that as a commander, her *sole* motivation was protecting Northgard from the Old Ones. So now that the enemy has been eliminated, it's safe to say her honor and her standing as a military leader are far too important to uphold the alliance. The Governor will have to sweeten the deal, make it easier for the Matron to comply, and what could he possibly offer her that she couldn't just take back on her own? So, for the time being, he won't have direct control of the Droves—who once bent to his every whim and mandate—and with the strictures against scholarship lifted, she'll be able to pull all the Droves back to the Iron Citadel."

"He's lost," Percival said. "Without his Blighted soldiers, he doesn't have his authority. And without his authority, he's just a bereaved grump. This deal is his only pillar of support, and even if we *do* expand the Law . . ."

"We'll still have our people back."

"Yes," Percival whispered, his voice turning glum. "If not the library."

Roy, having already started his own grieving of the library, had been mulling something all this time, though. "But is it truly gone?"

Percival regarded Roy carefully, hopeful but not entirely comprehending. "What do you mean?"

"Well, the catacombs," Roy said. "It was a necropolis, remember? And much larger than the base of the Orphic Basilica."

"So we could get in . . ."

"Underground," Roy finished. "And who knows underground better than a bunch of scholars in hiding? Maybe we'll be able to dig out enough—and *learn* enough—to build it back again."

Percival grinned. "Let's get started, then."

They ambled out of the courtyard, hand in hand. The few remnants of clouds they'd seen before entering the Governor's office had since dissipated. Tufts of light gray hung in the sky, but with the weather still turning, they were already melting into the great wide blue. A pleasant chill teased the air, though it was barely noticeable beneath the warmth of the sun, which shone bright, freed from its smothering cage of black clouds.

Roy started down the hill on which the Governor's manor stood, then passed through the opened gates ringing the expansive, snow-speckled property. The complexes, streets, and back alleys of Rasileus, all now flooded with sunlight, sprawled out before him. People emerged from communal shelters—which were ruined nearly beyond repairment by the battle between the ghosts and the undead—and blinked, gaping with varying expressions of amazement. Some civilians wandered helplessly through the lattice of streets as though in a catatonic night terror, their faces dazed and streaked with blood.

A woman was calling out for her son. She screamed and wailed and, amidst her confusion, tripped over the carcass of an Old One. As she struggled to get to her feet, leaving a bloody handprint on the soldier's chest plate, a ghost materialized before her, the crimson shade of its eyes rapidly disappearing. She accepted the proffered hand, then stared longingly at the ghost's features. "Jonny?" she whispered. "My . . . My Jonny, is that you?"

His heart swelling with hope, Roy averted his eyes from the scene, then went still. He hadn't realized that Percival had left his side until he saw him standing near the mouth of an alley, speaking and laughing with a ghost. Percival nodded at something the ghost had said, then pointed to Roy, who waved while passing Percival a questioning glance.

Owen, Percival mouthed, then went back to his conversation.

Roy folded his arms around himself, smiling.

Well, said a voice from Roy's left. *The Governor may be crooked as they come, but at least he picked out a handsome one for you. That being said, you never told me you fancied blonds, Roy.*

Even before Roy faced his sister, his eyes were spilling over with tears. "Briar?" he murmured, suddenly forgetting all about her two-faced carving, buried somewhere in the ruins of the library.

Because she was here.

Aside from her voice, whose sweet sound he could never misplace, it was reasonably difficult to discern Briar's features. He could see the roundness of her eyes, but not their brown depths. He could see the angular shape of her face, but not the skin or the blue veins running underneath. When she lifted her hands and covered these indefinable characteristics, though, as if embarrassed, the chilling details of her fate came forth: a thick length of rope pulled taut around her neck, her face littered with bruises and footprints.

Roy's eyes widened. "Briar, what did they—"

I don't wish to talk about it, Roy, Briar interjected. *I don't want to ruin these last moments with you.*

It took everything in him, every lingering trace of self-discipline, not to cry out in frustration and demand from Briar the truth of her murder, no matter how harrowing it was or how much hearing it would hurt him. But he honored her wishes, mostly because he didn't want them to part on bitter terms.

Even so, I guess we can't get out of discussing Gabriel, Briar said, her red eyes flashing with an emotion that was hard to parse through the shadows enshrouding her. *I saw him, Roy, after you and Percival freed us from purgatory. He was ripping through the Old Ones. His eyes were infernos. His screams sounded like laughter. He was a barbarian, a beast of a man, but I suppose his liberation presented him the chance to do what he did best . . . and, in some sort of twisted way, redeem himself.*

Roy was promptly caught off guard, but he couldn't find a persuasive argument to support his denial. Gabriel had always demonstrated a streak of sadism when he'd abused Roy, and so Roy found it no hard feat to picture Gabriel soaring through Northgard, cackling and gibbering like a lunatic, slipping beneath the Old Ones' armor and driving them to sheer insanity from the inside out.

I'm sorry, Briar whispered. *Perhaps I should've kept my silence.*

"No, I'm glad you told me," Roy said. "I don't think I'll ever remember him without feeling *some* fear, nor do I think I'll ever be able to disassociate him from my weakest days, but it's become a little easier to talk about him."

A touch of amusement entered Briar's voice. *Because of Percival, you mean.*

Roy rolled his eyes. "Am I that transparent?"

Maybe, Briar said. *Or maybe you're just happy.* When Roy smiled at the ground, she placed a smoky, tenebrous hand on his arm—which passed through the top layer of his skin. *No, don't do that. Don't act coy. You deserve this love. We both know you do, Roy. Don't hide what you have with him.*

"I don't know if I love him," Roy said. "I don't think we're there."

Not yet, but unlike some of us, you both still have time. Briar shooed him away. *Now, goodness, why are you still bickering with your little sister when you have a man to get back to? That's rather sad, don't you think? Go and kiss him until he's breathless and red in the face, you idiot.*

Roy laughed. "All right, all right. So long as you find Irene before you go."

Don't worry, Roy, I'm one step ahead of you, Briar said, then glided toward a tall ghost loitering on the corner of a sunlit street. She hooked her arm through the ghost's—Irene's—elbow, and they set off together for one final stroll.

Roy was still smiling and watching the two ghosts drifting around the corner and out of view, his eyes filling with tears, when Percival joined Roy after his reunion and farewell with Owen.

"It went well, I assume?" Roy asked, sniffling.

"About as well as yours, it looks like," Percival said. He kissed Roy's temple. "Apparently Owen knew Tessa and a couple of Briar's other associates. Perhaps we can start there. Are you ready?"

"Maybe a little later; there's no rush," Roy said. "I think, for right now, I just want to find a place to sit with you in the sun."

"I think I want that, too."

They did not have to look too far. For down the cobbles of every street and on the summit of every hill, there was sunlight. And for the first time in what felt like forever, that sun brought warmth.

ACKNOWLEDGMENTS

Well, where do I start?

Thank you to my agent, Thao Le, for championing this story even after that behemoth of a manuscript I sent you (230,000 words! What was I thinking?) when you first reached out to me. I could not be more grateful to have you, and the Sandra Dijkstra Literary Agency, in my corner.

Thank you to my editor, David Pomerico, who helped me steer this originally messy and unnecessarily complicated story onto the right path with his wisdom and meticulousness. Thank you also to Isabella Ogbolumani for her assistance, to Laura Galán-Wells for the sensitivity read, and to everyone working behind the scenes at Harper Voyager. I'm so happy, and still quite stunned, to be a part of this community.

Thank you to my parents and my brother, Jack, who have not once discouraged me from pursuing this dream—and it's too late to do so now. I've gone ahead and made it everyone's problem.

Thank you to my partner, J, mostly for his smile—and all right, yes, his laugh—but also for his generosity. All those late nights and early mornings that I've spent working on this book, I'm writing about love. And when I'm writing about love, I'm writing about you.

Thank you to the authors whose books initially made me want to write *Honour & Heresy*: Nick Cutter, Jean Hanff Korelitz, Donna Tartt, V. E. Schwab, Deborah Harkness, and, of course, Stephen King, who inspired the opening scene of chapter twenty-four. I'm nowhere near the level of talent to which these incredible storytellers have ascended, but they have given me hope.

I have some family and friends to thank (and there are definitely some I'll miss, but I want to keep this brief, so bear with me!), all of whom have supported me throughout this journey. To Chloe (yes, again); Jasmin; Monique; Rowan; Liz; Nicole; and my nan, cousins, aunt, and grandparents—you all have made this road a little easier to cross.

Finally, thank you to anyone who read the back of this book or has been waiting for it to come out or heard about it from a friend and thought this strange, sad story was something that you might enjoy. And if you didn't, thanks for giving it a go anyway! I have plenty of other tales to tell.

ABOUT THE AUTHOR

MAX FRANCIS is an author of queer fiction. He has a bachelor's degree in creative writing, which he studied at the Royal Melbourne Institute of Technology. He currently resides in Melbourne, Australia, where he's either hard at work on his next project or watching some absurd B-grade horror film. *Honour & Heresy* is his debut novel.